Heartstone

Heartstone

D. C. Brod

*To Michelle —
Happy Birthday +
best wishes.
D. C. Brod*

Five Star • Waterville, Maine

This novel is a work of fiction. Names, characters, places and incidents are either the product of the author's imagination, or, if real, used fictitiously.

First Edition
First Printing: June 2005

Published in 2005 in conjunction with Tekno Books and Ed Gorman.

Set in 11 pt. Plantin by Liana M. Walker.

Printed in the United States on permanent paper.

Library of Congress Cataloging-in-Publication Data

Brod, D. C.
    Heartstone / D.C. Brod.—1st ed.
      p. cm.
    ISBN 1-59414-289-0 (hc : alk. paper)
    1. Women teachers—Fiction. 2. Fathers and daughters—Fiction. 3. Quests (Expeditions)—Fiction. 4. Missing persons—Fiction. 5. Chicago (Ill.)—Fiction. 6. Archaeologists—Fiction. 7. Islands—Fiction. 8. Relics —Fiction. I. Title.
PS3552.R6148H43 2005
813'.54—dc22   2005004985

For Greg, Ali, Kenzie and James . . .
and all their possibilities
and in memory of Jane Jordan Browne

Acknowledgments

Heartfelt thanks to the many people who provided support during the writing of this book:

To Rachael Tecza and Donald Brod, who probably read every version of this novel that ever existed (without complaining or rolling their eyes) and provided invaluable feedback and suggestions.

To Tom Moriarty, gemologist, who introduced me to alexandrite and sparked the idea for this novel. (Please excuse any liberties I took with the stone, Tom.)

To readers, technical advisors and people who opened their homes to us while we were traipsing across England in search of Arthur: Maria Alderson, Miriam Baily, Michael Black, Matt Clemens, Kim and Bruce Cobban, Cecelia Downs, Jacqueline Fiedler, Vonelle "Buddy" Kostelny-Vogts, Wendi Lee, Marilyn Nelson, Joan O'Leary, Patrick Parks, Keith and Maryanne Peterson,

Michael Seidman and Mark Richard Zubro.

To John Helfers, my editor.

And to the late Jane Jordan Browne, a remarkable woman and literary agent, and to her staff at Multimedia Product Development.

Prologue

Twenty miles off Land's End, England,
1 a.m., April 4th

It took twenty minutes via helicopter to fly from any one of the Scilly Islands to Penzance. Benjamin Pike had spent the first half of this relatively short trip convinced that the man sitting next to him intended to kill him before they arrived. It had been an excruciating, regret-filled ten minutes. Regrets made all the more painful because if he could have gotten to Penzance, he'd have made them right. He'd have talked to Max, told her everything. Fearing her anger or outright rejection wasn't a good enough reason to hold back, nor was it fair to her.

In the midst of his self recriminations, he spotted the lights of Cornwall's coast, appearing like bright, tiny gems on jewelers' velvet, and hope sparked in his chest. If they planned to kill him, surely they'd have done it by now.

He glanced at Tommy. His large, round head rested

9

against the back of his seat and his arms were folded across his broad chest. It was too dark for Ben to make out his face, and he wondered if the man had fallen asleep.

By shifting, he was able to peer between the two seats in front and could make out the pilot's profile, cast in an eerie shade of green from the glow of the craft's instruments—the slash of a nose, the ubiquitous toothpick now gripped steady between his teeth. Krett seemed intent on flying the craft.

No, Ben decided, if these men had orders to kill him, he'd be sinking into the Atlantic by now, and his escorts would be on their way back to the island like a flight crew returning from a successful mission.

He ran a hand through his thick, white hair and wiped at the dampness accumulating on the back of his neck. Strange to be sweating a thousand feet above the ground in a helicopter without any doors. His face was numb with cold. He wiped his hand against his khakis, drew in a deep breath and expelled it. What if he had died without being able to explain any of this to Max? He clenched a fist and wrapped his other hand around it. He needed to call her as soon as he could get to a phone. Ask her to come here. Insist on it this time. She'd be confused at first, perhaps angry, but she had to understand how her destiny and the stone's were entwined. As was his. He refused to believe otherwise.

The helicopter bumped over some turbulence and Ben squeezed his eyes shut. He put himself back on the island, imagining what he'd say when he returned. Why had Murdoch been in such a damned hurry to get him off the island? He couldn't have known Ben's plans. Could he? Damn. He was so close. Thirty years, and it had finally come together like the pieces of a miraculous puzzle. He'd found the final piece—seen it, touched it. He could make it whole.

If only he'd gotten past Murdoch, Ben knew he could have

explained. He believed in a world where reasonable minds prevailed. There had to be a way to recover.

After he called Max, he would call Antony. Within two hours, they'd be on their way back to the island. With any luck, they'd be there by morning. Murdoch would wait until then to report Ben's alleged misdeed.

Ben sucked in a deep breath and released it slowly. He visualized the stone, imagined holding it, feeling its warmth. Its greens danced and vacillated, cloaking the flame within. *Consider your advantages,* he told himself. *Work from there.*

Beside him, Tommy shifted his bulk and dropped his hands into his lap. Ben glanced out the door. It took a moment for him to re-establish his bearings, and when he did he knew something was wrong. They were still out over the water. England was on the right. They were heading north rather than east toward Penzance. Why? What was north? . . . Wales was north. He tried to swallow, but his throat constricted. Rhys Lewis lived in Wales. They weren't taking him to Penzance. They weren't going to kill him. They were taking him to Rhys Lewis first.

Ben's thoughts spiraled toward the inevitable outcome of that encounter. Once Lewis had Ben, he'd be able to control Max. Ben couldn't let that happen.

He glanced at Tommy, who perhaps was not here to kill Ben, merely subdue him. They weren't expecting him to go quietly. Despite the man's current state of repose, Ben knew that Tommy would enthusiastically thwart any attempts he made to hijack the helicopter. Which, he realized, was what he had to do. Soon.

When he looked at Tommy again, Ben saw that his head now rested on his shoulder. He had to be asleep. A plan formed. It was a desperate plan, but there were no sane ones available. If he could get his hands on Tommy's gun, he could threaten Tommy with it, forcing Krett to take him to Penzance. The hell with Penzance. Just get him down on Cornwall soil.

Ben's heart thudded against his chest as he worked out the logistics. Tommy carried his gun in a shoulder holster beneath his left arm. Ben had seen it when the big man's jacket flopped open as he climbed into the craft. A big chrome revolver. Ben sat to Tommy's right so he'd have to lean across his body with his right hand to reach the gun. Unfortunately, Ben was left-handed, but he could play a decent game of darts with either hand, so he knew he could maneuver well enough. But it wasn't simply a matter of slipping the gun from its holster. He'd have to undo the holster snap and pull it free. The seat belt limited his range of movement. He considered releasing it, but he was literally inches from a long fall into the ocean that would kill him as surely as a bullet in the brain. If Tommy woke in the middle of this, Ben wanted a fighting chance. The steady vibration of the helicopter might help cover his movements. A drop of sweat slid between his shoulder blades and he shivered. This was insane, he told himself. Tommy was a trained killer. But he apparently had instructions not to kill Ben. Yet.

Get on with it, he told himself. If he thought about this much longer, he'd freeze up. He'd be in Rhys Lewis's living room and it would be too late. Too late for everything.

He edged around in his seat as much as the belt would allow. After looking to make sure Krett was still occupied with flying the helicopter, he gently lifted the edge of Tommy's wool coat. The smell of must and dried sweat rose in a wave and dissipated. Beneath the jacket he wore a light-colored shirt, which allowed Ben to make out the dark mass that was the holster. Holding his breath, he reached into the jacket and felt for the butt of the gun, then the holster, found its snap and, gritting his teeth together, nudged it open. It was like flicking on a switch. Grunting his surprise, Tommy jerked his head up and locked his huge hand around Ben's wrist, twisting.

It shouldn't have been much of a contest—Tommy outweighed Ben by at least fifty pounds. But his right arm was wedged between Ben and the seat, and he was fighting to hold onto Ben and get out from under him at the same time. Ben pressed his shoulder into Tommy, gaining traction by bracing one foot against the front seat; he could feel the rumble in the big man's chest as he struggled. Ben managed to snake his free hand across Tommy's belly toward the gun.

Just as he yanked the revolver from its holster, the helicopter dropped and swerved to the left. The momentum propelled Ben forward, throwing him off balance and freeing Tommy from his pin. Before Ben could recover, Tommy had one arm wrapped around his neck, the scratchy fabric pressing hard into Ben's windpipe. He grabbed for the gun, knocking it from Ben's hand. It fell between Tommy's feet, and he had to let go of Ben in order to go after it. Ben gulped air and dove first, but his seat belt held him back. He pressed the release, and when it gave, he lunged. Tommy caught him under the chin with the toe of his boot, and Ben gagged as a bolt of pain shot up his jaw. This time Tommy reached the gun first and Ben thought he heard him cackle as he picked it up. Ben seized the thick wrist with both his hands and prayed for an adrenalin rush as he tried to wrench the weapon away.

A loud report set Ben's chest on fire. He pitched backwards. Colors swam in his head and blood surged up his throat. The helicopter lurched again and then the floor fell out from under him.

Falling, he thrashed wildly, but found only air. This was wrong. He hadn't finished. There was so much to do. To witness. Then, as the universe slowed, his panic receded. He felt no pain, only release. Like letting go and feeling your muscles sigh. But still he resisted. People needed him. He hadn't finished the fight. Pikes didn't give up. *No, they don't.* Then he experienced a moment of piercing clarity and all the pieces tumbled into place. This was his time. Spreading his arms, Ben closed his eyes and submitted himself to his faith in a legend and in a daughter who would have to find the answers herself. And as the black water rushed to him, he prayed that she wouldn't come to despise him for what he'd given her.

Chapter 1

Chicago, Illinois, April 15th

As Maxine Pike unlocked and pushed open the door of her second-floor apartment, Fiona nosed past her and headed for the kitchen, where she lapped loudly at the water in her bowl.

Max slammed the door shut with her hip and tossed her jacket, along with the Great Dane's leash, onto the nearest chair. Not yet noon and already it had been a day of small scourges. Nothing disastrous, but wasn't it the little stuff that brought you down, gnawing away at you like rats' teeth? She shuddered.

Noting the blinking call button on her answering machine, Max rewound the tape and listened to her messages as she unwrapped two slices of American cheese for a sandwich. While she'd hoped to hear from Ben, she was only a little disappointed when the first message was from her office mate's daughter, Kenzie, who had actually called to talk to Fiona. Smiling, Max listened as she spread low-fat mayonnaise on wheat bread, picturing the three-year-old with her serious, blue eyes and reminded herself she'd promised Kenzie a photo of Fiona. Kenzie chatted for more than a minute, telling the dog about her trip to the dentist and her fitting for her aunt's wedding. Then Alison, Kenzie's mother, came on. "Hi, Max. Sissy and I are going to the movies tomorrow night. She wants to see a chick flick and I want to see something blown up. Why don't you come along and cast the deciding vote? Give me a call."

Max was thinking how it all depended on who was blowing things up, when the next message clicked on. It was her real estate agent, sounding chirpy as ever, informing Max that the seller had rejected her offer on his house. "I believe I warned you the offer might be too low," she added, then asked Max to call her.

"Damn," Max said without much feeling. Leaning against the counter, she ate her sandwich and listened to the kitchen clock ticking the seconds away. She could think of only two ways to recover from a miserable morning and since there was no man in her life and she wasn't in the habit of bedding strangers, she decided now was a good time to make that photo for Kenzie.

After cleaning up the dishes, she transferred her darkroom equipment from the closet in her office to the small bathroom.

The series of unpleasant events had started at the post office. She'd intended to go in and buy a roll of stamps while she mailed the three bills, but as she drove past the building she saw her department chair, Cheryl Horchow, climbing the steps. Max didn't feel like sparring with the woman while on spring break, so she pulled up to the drive-up mail slot. The moment she let the three bills slip from her hand, it hit her. Had she put stamps on those envelopes? No. Damn. It hadn't even occurred to her. *How dumb can you be?* she thought. As she sat there, stunned by her actions, the guy behind her in the SUV honked loud and long. Max's foot slipped off the clutch and her car shuddered and died. Fiona, who had been curled up on the back seat of the Honda Civic, rose like Godzilla from the sea and began baying as the guy continued to lay on the horn.

Max got the car started and pulled away from the mailbox. She knew she ought to go into the post office and throw herself at the mercy of a civil servant, but Cheryl would probably still be in there and Max wasn't going to reveal her air-headed actions to someone who thought she was marginal to begin with.

As she merged onto Halsted, she pushed up the button for the Civic's window. It rose three inches and stopped. She pushed the button again, harder, and the window emitted an urgent moan—it wanted nothing better than to go up—but didn't budge.

"Hardly a disaster," Max chided herself now, as she set the enlarger on a board spanning the sink.

"Bad things happen in threes, don't they girl?" The harlequin Great Dane regarded her briefly from the hallway, then resumed cleaning herself. Max closed the bathroom door. "By law, the rest of the day has to be charmed." Besides, it was Friday, and next week was her spring break. Plenty of time for the fates to turn.

After filling the developing trays and lining them up in the tub, she positioned the negative she wanted to print—Fiona in her chair—beneath the enlarger's lens. She supposed that one day she would give digital photography a try, but there was something about the process of developing a print that she craved. As she adjusted the shot, cropping out the edge of the couch, she felt some of the tension leave her shoulders.

The rest of the morning hadn't been awful, she told herself. Just frustrating.

Even if it hadn't been a drizzly April day, Max couldn't park her car on Chicago's north side with a window open. Might as well leave the keys in the ignition and the engine running. So, she'd driven to her local service station only to learn that Raoul, the mechanic, wasn't expected in until eleven. She and Fiona sat in the small office inhaling oil and gasoline fumes until Raoul arrived and pulled the window back up—by sheer force—and made her promise not to open it again until he could look for the real problem.

Max slid the exposed print into the developing solution and nudged it down into the tray with a pair of tongs, completely submerging the white paper.

"You'll survive," she told herself. The bills would come back, she would get the window fixed, and she wasn't all that sure she wanted to buy a house anyway.

Maybe the rejection was an opportunity to examine her ambivalence and that twinge of relief she'd experienced upon learning her offer had been turned down. She ought to want to buy a house, so what was the problem? There'd been so many reasons it seemed like a good idea—more space, an extra bathroom for a darkroom, an investment, a commitment. She should want a house. She'd worked hard to reach her five-year goal a full six months ahead of time—tenured English instructor at Coulter Community College with the means to buy a house. And now it was all she could do to remember why she worked so hard to get here. Maybe it was the commitment part that made her balk. It placed a period in her life, when she was so much fonder of commas.

Max knelt on the doubled-up throw rug, reached into the tub and rocked the tray gently from side to side. The black-and-white image began to emerge. She thought she'd captured Fiona's gentle nature with this shot of the big dog draped over the beanbag chair. It was in the eyes and in the way the late afternoon light softened the shadows.

Then the phone rang. Please be Ben. Her father would help her out of this malaise. At times he knew her better than she knew herself.

Juggling the tray with one hand, she groped for the portable phone on the toilet seat with the other.

Later, Max would recall noting the British accent as Walter Bacon introduced himself as Ben's solicitor in London.

"It's dreadfully unpleasant discussing this by telephone . . ." He continued, explaining Ben's instructions, and then, when Max said, "Go on," he began to read Ben's words.

" 'If I have not contacted you by the fifteenth of any month, you must presume that I am dead and act in accordance with my request. My heirs must be brought together at the earliest possible date to learn the details of their legacy.' "

As she listened, Max leaned her weight against the door. When her knees went wobbly, she slid to the floor, feeling the cool tile through her sweat pants. "Do you know what happened?" Her words sounded cracked and brittle. Behind her, on the other side of the door, Fiona scratched to be let in.

"I don't," Bacon said. "We've been trying to learn the circumstances and have made enquiries to that end, but I'm afraid at this time we haven't an idea." He explained how Scotland Yard had been notified, and every possible lead was being exhausted. Then he added, "Your father and I have had this arrangement for nearly three years now. He has never failed to call." He paused. "I gave him the entire day of the fifteenth. I kept hoping."

Max had so many questions, she didn't know where to start. "Why would he need a clause like that?"

"I'll answer that as completely as I can when I see you."

"He must have been involved in something dangerous. What—"

"Again, Miss Pike—"

"But you don't know that he's dead, do you?"

"We don't," he assured her, "and the truth of it is, I'll not be convinced of it until we have proof. Nonetheless, his instructions were specific and he made quite certain that I understood the importance of carrying them out." When he continued, his words sounded strained and thin. "Your father was not merely my client, he was also my friend. This seems premature to me as well, but I assure you it is precisely as he directed."

Max pushed her short, blond hair off her forehead, nearly poking out her eye with the developing tongs. She stared at them for a few seconds, trying to recall why they were in her hand. "I understand." Her response had been automatic; she was far from understanding.

Squeezing her eyes shut, she remembered Ben asking her to come to Wales last month. She should have gone. Instead, she'd asked if he could wait until spring break. Canceling classes or finding someone to sub for her just wasn't done for anything but an emergency. Even though Ben hadn't called it an emergency, she should have known. How often did he make that kind of request? This week was spring break and she hadn't talked to him since last month. What kind of daughter was she?

"There's one other thing," Bacon interrupted her self-recriminations.

She waited.

"Your father left a message that you are to contact a man

there in Chicago, before coming to London." He paused. "Ben did stress that."

"Who?"

"Elliott Schiff. He's a curator at your Field Museum. I've got a number for him."

She pushed herself up from the floor. "Let me get a pen."

Temporarily blinded by the move from safe light to daylight as she opened the bathroom door, Max stumbled over the Great Dane sprawled across the hall. Recovering, she made her way into the kitchen, Fiona's claws clicking behind her on the wooden floor.

Setting the tongs on the counter, Max took a pen from the "Carpe Diem" mug. "Go ahead," she said, and wrote the name and number on the bottom of her grocery list. "I'll call him right away."

"Good," Bacon said, then added, "but it's late Friday, so getting here by tomorrow is probably a bit difficult for you." He hesitated. "I've got to be in York on Sunday, but I could cancel if—"

"No, don't," Max said. The idea of waiting another day appealed to her. Not rushing it meant Ben had more time to get hold of her—to tell her this had all been a horrible mistake and he was sorry he'd worried her. "Monday will be fine."

"Thank you, Miss Pike." She could almost hear his sigh of relief. "Shall we say eleven on Monday morning then?"

She told him that sounded fine and wrote down the office phone number and address he gave her.

"Don't hesitate to call if you have any questions before then," he said. "If I'm not here, Amanda, my secretary, can get in touch with me."

She thanked him, suddenly anxious to get off the phone and be alone with her thoughts.

But then Bacon continued, "There is one other thing I

hope you can help me with. I have to ring your sister, and I'm afraid the number I have on file has been disconnected."

Max dug her tattered address book from the junk drawer. "She probably has a new number." Olivia always had a new phone number.

Olivia occupied most of the "P" and all of the "Q" pages. When she thought about it, Max couldn't recall the last time she'd spoken to her older sister for a reason other than a change of address. Olivia's last move had landed her in Paris.

Bacon thanked Max for the number and said, "Again, if you're not able make the connections in order to be here on Monday, give Amanda a call and we'll reschedule."

Max added the solicitor's name and number to the "B" page in her directory before disconnecting the call. Then she stood, leaning against the kitchen counter, staring at Fiona lying on the beige tiled floor. Her eyes burned and her chest felt tight.

"How am I supposed to 'presume' that you are dead, Ben? How can you even ask that of me? And wouldn't I know if you were dead?" Shouldn't it feel like someone had ripped out one of her lungs?

She looked over her shoulder at the grocery list lying on the counter and then at the phone number just below "grapes." She picked it up. Who the hell was Elliott Schiff?

Chapter 2

Jillian chewed on a thumbnail as she waited for the water to boil. Large bubbles rose in the saucepan and she set the oven timer for three minutes, then deposited a slice of wheat bread into the toaster.

She hated this waiting. Each day that passed with no news, Rhys's temper grew shorter. It was like living with a cobra.

The egg bobbed and floundered in the boiling water, as though it were fighting the inevitable. Jillian's scalp tightened. She thrust out her jaw and exhaled sharply; stray wisps of hair lifted off her damp forehead.

After she assembled his breakfast tray, she cleaned up her own lunch dishes. Long ago she'd stopped trying to match her schedule to his. He often didn't go to bed until the sun was up; then he'd sleep a few hours and ring Jillian when he wanted breakfast.

The first time Jillian Babcock saw Rhys Lewis,

standing beside the reflecting pool, hands clasped behind his back as he stared into the image of the Washington Monument, she didn't realize this tall, poised man was the one she'd spent three years and most of her savings pursuing. She'd expected someone older. When he looked up and his gaze settled on her, she felt a mild surge of electricity—a vibrant hum—which made her acutely aware of her own body: the film of perspiration on her upper lip, the chill of the slender gold chain around her neck and the press of satin against her breasts. Had she known he was her father, she might have been troubled by her reaction, but she didn't know.

Moments later, when he introduced himself, and she felt the color rise in her face, she'd been unable to look away from him. His eyes, an odd cinnamon shade, never wavered, and she had the uneasy impression that he knew exactly what her body and mind were experiencing.

At his suggestion, they'd gone for coffee. They drank theirs the same—black with sugar. He'd explained the extent of his relationship with her mother—a one-night stand that neither had pursued. After that, Jillian did most of the talking as he asked her questions. She told him everything: how she'd been raised by her grandparents, the string of jobs for which she was overqualified and undervalued. As she spoke, finger crooked tightly in the mug's handle, Rhys nodded his understanding, appearing open and sympathetic. Just as it occurred to her that their conversation was a lot like a job interview, Rhys asked if she would consider working for him as his personal assistant. Without knowing what he did for a living, she had accepted.

Since then she'd learned a great deal about what he did, but little about who he was. Rhys's confidence was hard won and every morsel he gave her was manna.

She could hear the television as she drummed her nails against the oak door. Rhys's muffled response came a moment later.

When she entered the room, Rhys was facing the forty-two-inch, high-definition screen wearing a maroon silk robe, one fist cocked at his hip while the other wielded a toothbrush. His eyes never left the television, and his only acknowledgment of Jillian's presence was a nod toward the images on the screen. A reporter stood in the parking lot of a strip mall as he told the camera how a forty-four-year-old man had gunned down three travel agents working out of a storefront office.

She half-listened as she moved Rhys's Palm Pilot off the table to make room for the tray. Then the reporter said, "Travel Merchants," and the coffee cup clattered in its saucer as she released the tray. "Was that Diver2199?"

Rhys nodded, eyes still fixed on the screen.

Her heart pounded and she could feel the rush of energy to her fingertips. Another online conquest. "That's three this month."

The reporter, a stocky Hispanic man who kept referring to his notes, was saying that the man, who died of a self-inflicted wound before the police could apprehend him, had been an agency client, although the motive for his shooting spree was not known.

"They left him stranded in Belize when the tour went bankrupt," Jillian said. The face of a middle-aged man filled the TV screen. He had thick eyebrows and a weak chin. Jillian was still surprised when they turned out to be so average-looking.

She poured coffee from a carafe and added a level teaspoon of sugar, stirred twice, and set the spoon on the saucer. Rhys's breakfast consisted of a soft-boiled egg in a blue porcelain egg cup, one slice of wheat toast with sweet butter, a large glass of grapefruit juice and coffee. It never varied.

Tucking a strand of long, blond hair behind her ear, she bent over the computer to check messages. Nothing vital. She straightened up and turned to find Rhys watching her as he scoured his teeth. One of the many things she hadn't been able to glean regarding her father was why he brushed his teeth both before and after he ate. The idea of mixing mint flavors with the tartness of grapefruit juice made her queasy. And then there was the cigar.

"What's the news from our friend?" he said.

In the moments it took her to refocus, her shoulders stiffened and her heart began to race. "Nothing yet," she answered, silently cursing Murdoch's idiots. They were the ones who had botched it with Ben Pike, yet she was the one who had to manage the situation, not to mention Rhys's anger.

Rhys removed the toothbrush from his mouth, and his eyes narrowed as he stepped closer to her. The space between them rioted with charged particles. "This is vital."

A gob of peppermint-scented foam hit her cheek. "I talked with him this morning," she said. "Nothing."

He turned his back on her and strode into the bathroom. Jillian wiped her face. Water ran as he spat vigorously into the sink, gargled, spat again and repeated the process three times. He came out of the room wiping his mouth with a hand towel.

"Dammit, Jillian." He drank down the juice in three long swallows, grimaced slightly, then exchanged the glass for his cigar. "Are you sure this man you hired knew what he was doing?"

"I am." Then she added, "His brother is a minor player in Marquez's drug initiative, currently serving time for possession and awaiting trial for smuggling."

"Sounds incompetent."

"Murdoch says he's loyal and swears by his brother's abilities. Not only can he break into places, he can also blow them up."

The doorbell rang, but Jillian held onto her sigh of relief as Rhys walked over to the corner of his room, where a twelve-inch-screen television alternated views of the five video surveillance cameras set around the house. He pushed a button twice to bring up the main entrance. David Sandstrom.

"David?" Rhys's brows drew together and the lines around his eyes softened. "What could he want?" he murmured. "Show him in." He bit off a corner of toast.

As she walked to the front of the sprawling single-story home, Jillian didn't know whether to be annoyed or relieved by Sandstrom's arrival. She should have been used to these angry surges by now. Since Ben Pike had tumbled into the ocean before Rhys could interrogate him, he'd been more volatile than usual. And Rhys liked to take his frustrations out on her. She was convenient. But each time he did, he seemed on the verge of telling her why he was so interested in that stone. She could put up with some abuse in exchange for knowledge.

As soon as Jillian opened the door, she knew there was trouble on the porch. Sandstrom was usually immaculate—hair moussed to perfection, signature French-cuffed shirts a crisp, brilliant white and his eyes clear and alert. Now, his hair was all over the place, he wore no tie and his distress practically rose off him in redolent waves. For a second, she felt a flutter of pleasure, then reminded herself that trouble for Sandstrom was trouble for all of them.

"Jillian." He nodded. "I need to see Rhys. It's important."

A lot of things about Sandstrom bothered Jillian, not least

of which was how he pronounced Rhys as "Reeze," rather than "Reece." As close as he claimed to be to her father, he ought to get his name right. She let him feel the chill in her gaze. Jillian knew she had the reputation of being Rhys's guard dog. Behind her back, some of his clients and associates called her Cerberus. It made her smile.

She held open the door for him. With anyone else coming to see Rhys without an appointment, she'd have toyed around with him a bit. But David, a promising Congressional representative, was a favorite of Rhys's. "He's got a busy day."

When she took him back to the bedroom, the shower was running and steam billowed from the bathroom. Nothing was so urgent that it couldn't be improved on by a few minutes' waiting.

"Have a seat, David." Jillian waved toward one of two Victorian chairs flanking the French doors which opened onto the garden.

"Think you could get me some coffee?" David said, as he tried to find a comfortable position in the spindly chair. "Cream, no sugar."

Jillian smiled to herself as she left to refill the carafe, thinking Sandstrom shouldn't be overly confident of his stature with Rhys. Years ago, Rhys had established a scholarship fund, designed to assist young, disadvantaged students who showed the right kind of potential. Rhys selected the recipients himself. David Sandstrom was the fund's most visible success. A bright kid raised by a mother who earned her living cleaning rooms at a motel, David got an Ivy League education, thanks to Rhys, who later helped position him for the state legislature and partially financed his successful run for Congress. Sandstrom was bright, affable and attractive. Rhys had a lot invested in him. On the other hand, Rhys was better than anyone Jillian knew at cutting his losses and moving on.

As she set a mug of steaming coffee on the table beside Sandstrom, the shower switched off. Sandstrom glanced toward the bathroom door, then up at her. She quickly averted her eyes. If the Congressman's news was as bad as his hygiene suggested, she didn't want to be caught exchanging pleasantries with him.

On the television, a reporter was interviewing the partner of a murdered police officer. The man couldn't have been much older than Jillian—twenty-six—and had trouble controlling his emotions. Stock market figures—hieroglyphics for the initiated—scrolled by in a banner across the bottom of the screen.

Rhys came out of the bathroom, naked except for the towel he was using to dry himself. It wasn't the first time Jillian had seen Rhys naked—he had a healthy body image—and she had managed to move past her embarrassment. She never ceased to be impressed with the muscle definition in his back and shoulders. Although he'd never told her his age, she assumed he was in his early sixties, but he could easily pass for a virile fifty-year-old.

He finished patting himself off and then tossed the towel on the bed, poured himself some coffee and walked over to Sandstrom.

From where Sandstrom sat, he was eye-level with Rhys's not-so-private parts. This effectively forced Sandstrom to look up into Rhys's eyes.

Rhys studied him, then sighed and said, "What happened, David?"

"I—I think I've been set up."

"What happened?" he repeated.

Sandstrom glanced at Jillian.

"She'll hear it eventually, David. Get on with it."

Jillian could have kissed him, even though he'd only said it to make David squirm.

Finally, David began: "I had a woman over."

"When?"

"Just a little while ago."

Rhys made a show of consulting the clock on his dresser. "A nooner?"

David shrugged.

"At your house?"

He swallowed. "Abby is in Minneapolis. I—"

"David—"

"Look, Rhys, I've done this before." Elbows planted on his knees, he lowered his face into his hands. "Tinley arranges it. He drives her there in his car. She's down in the back seat. He parks in the garage and she comes in through the side door." Slowly, he raised his head, looking into his hands as though he left an impression of his face there. "This has been going on for a while. It's the same girl. She's a pro."

"What's 'a while'?"

He shrugged. "I guess about a year."

"You've only been in office for fifteen months."

Sandstrom nodded.

"What happened then?" Rhys asked, his voice tight.

Sandstrom's clasped hands were pressed between his knees. "Someone rang the doorbell. I thought it was Tinley. He'd just called and told me he'd learned something about the victims' rights bill. We needed to talk. I opened the door and it's this guy with a camera. Then I hear the woman behind me. I'd told her to stay put. She's . . . wearing a skimpy robe. That's all. It's falling open. He takes a picture and, before I can grab the camera or anything, he's halfway to his car."

"And the woman?"

"Well, she acted surprised, but . . ."

"You doubt she was."

He nodded. Despite his unchecked libido, Sandstrom was no imbecile.

"How long ago?"

"I came straight here." He shrugged. "Less than an hour."

"Did you recognize this paparazzo?"

"Yes . . . no. I don't know his name, but I've seen him before. He's freelance. I got his license plate number." He recited it.

Rhys went over to the armoire, where he removed a pair of boxers and stopped at the closet to select his clothing. Then he retreated behind a Chinese silk print screen in the corner next to the armoire. While Rhys had no reservations about parading around naked in front of Jillian or an occasional guest, she had never seen him perform the act of dressing.

"And the young lady's name?" Rhys's voice came from behind the screen.

Sandstrom took a moment to focus. "Sherry. Like the drink."

"Tinley arranged this?"

He nodded, then said, "Yeah."

Both Sandstrom and Jillian watched the screen, waiting for the disembodied response. It reminded her of the Wizard of Oz.

"You don't think Tinley tipped him off?" Sandstrom said.

"How else would he know?"

"I was thinking someone Sherry knew found out."

"You said Tinley drove her there every time?"

"Yeah."

He came out from behind the screen, buttoning the cuffs of his cream-colored shirt. "Sounds to me like she was doing a little more than riding on the floor of the back seat."

31

Sandstrom's disbelief was genuine. "But Tinley's been with me since college."

"People don't have friends in Washington." Rhys shook his head and muttered, "They have allies and they have enemies. No one else is worth knowing."

He stood beside Sandstrom and waited until Sandstrom looked up at him before saying, "You can't keep doing this, David. It was that family values twaddle that got you elected. You're what this country needs. A man who understands the fragile structure of freedom. You can't keep doing things like this."

Sandstrom bowed his head. "I won't."

"Get up." Sandstrom stood and faced Rhys, who said, "I want you to go home now. Don't leave the house for the rest of the day. Don't answer the phone or the door." He waited for Sandstrom's nod. "What have you got scheduled for tonight?"

"A fundraiser. At the Hilton."

"Arrive late, leave early." Rhys placed his hand on the younger man's shoulder. "I'm going to take care of this, David, but I don't want to be called on to do this again."

"You won't," he said, lowering his eyes.

"I know I won't." Rhys patted his shoulder, then drew his hand away and glanced at Jillian. "Show him out."

When she returned, she found Rhys in his office. Without looking up from his manuscript, he said, "Give Barney Waldrop a call. I want to see him this afternoon."

Rhys was meeting with Waldrop when the call came. Jillian recognized the familiar voice before he identified himself. She listened to what he had to say, then told him to sit tight and wait for instructions.

She considered interrupting Rhys. It was that important.

But when she opened the door to her office, she heard voices in the hall, indicating that they had finished. Jillian positioned herself in the doorway to watch them pass. Barney's name was entirely out of character with his appearance. Someone named Barney should be slow with soft edges. This one had broad shoulders and pale blue eyes that weren't so much cold as they lacked any emotion at all. A crescent-shaped scar on his chin kept him from being too handsome.

He nodded at Jillian as they passed, and their eyes locked for just a moment. She was a little puzzled by her attraction. Jillian considered most men (with her father a notable exception) a means to an end. She'd never given much thought to the potential pleasure of the ride. But recently she'd been having erotic dreams—some violently erotic—and several had featured this man.

She waited for Rhys in the living room, standing in front of the beige marble fireplace. Above the mantle hung an acrylic painting of a city park on a late fall afternoon. The leaves had turned brilliant shades of red, orange and gold, and the buildings caught the sun's last strong rays in such a way that they appeared to be on fire. The viewer saw either a dazzling end to a fall day or a blazing inferno.

When Rhys came into the room, he walked past her to the fireplace and stood quietly, staring into the flames.

Jillian waited several seconds before saying, "I have some news."

Chapter 3

Whoever Elliott Schiff was, he wasn't in his office and wasn't expected back until tomorrow. Max left a message, then started to put away her developing equipment. Ten minutes later when the phone rang, she snatched it up without checking her caller ID. When she heard her real estate agent's voice, she had to swallow her disappointment before she could speak. "I got your message," she said.

"I don't mean to be pushy about this, Maxine, but I think if you come up just a little in a counter-offer, the house is yours." She named the amount, which was more than reasonable. "And I hate to see you lose this place. It's perfect for you." She sounded so sincere.

"Sorry," Max said, not feeling sorry at all. "Something has come up that I need to take care of." She didn't want to explain. "I'm going to have to take myself out of the house market . . . for a while."

"Oh—" The syllable managed to convey both surprise and curiosity.

"Family," Max said.

The agent offered a few generic words of sympathy and asked Max to call her when things returned to normal. Max hung up, doubting she'd ever talk to the woman again.

She felt like walking, but it was raining hard now. She also felt bound to her apartment, waiting for Schiff's call—he might phone in for messages—so she settled for a trip to the mailbox in the building's vestibule. On the way down, she warned herself not to put any hope in this call. But it was too late; her annoying streak of optimism had already kicked in. Maybe this guy could tell her where Ben was. For some reason he'd gone into hiding. Or he was on a dig in some remote part of the world. Elliott Schiff would explain everything.

All her mailbox produced was five catalogues and a credit card application. She tossed the catalogues into the recycling bin and held onto the credit card application to shred when she got back to her apartment. As she started up the stairs, she saw Grey coming up the walk, a brown paper grocery bag in each arm. His shoulders were hunched and his head bowed against the rain as he tried to balance one bag against the other to free a hand.

She opened the door for him when he reached the stoop, and rain splattered against her cheek as he pitched into the vestibule. Wiping his shoes on the floor mat, he turned toward her. "Max." He smiled. "Thank you."

His gray-threaded hair was soaked, and he had to keep blinking to clear his eyes.

"You need a hand there?" She reached out for one of the bags. "So you can get your mail."

"They're a bit wet," he said, but let her take one. It

smelled like soggy paper and apples.

He mopped back his hair, squeezing some of the moisture from it, then dug a set of keys out of his pocket. "How's this weather for a man who's missing London?"

His accent reminded her of Bacon, and then Ben.

"Look at this." He pulled out a couple of catalogues and some junk mail. "I haven't lived here a month and already they've found me."

As he closed and locked the mailbox, he looked at her closely. "You all right?"

"Yeah," she said. She ran into Grey Fisher occasionally at the mailboxes or while walking Fiona, but didn't know him all that well. They exchanged greetings, small talk, and once she'd seen him at a Chinese restaurant on Belmont with a raven-haired beauty. He knew how to use chopsticks and drank Tsingtao beer.

"You don't look it." He unlocked the inner door and took the bag from her while holding the door open with his foot.

The tight lines that had materialized between his brows seemed genuine. She started up the steps. "I just got some bad news. Maybe. I don't know. My dad is missing . . ." Her throat thickened. "They think he's dead. I don't know what to think."

Grey blinked a drop of water off his eyelashes. "What happened?"

"They don't know." She barely voiced the words.

"Where was he?"

"England. Last I heard from him."

Nodding as though he understood, he said, "Is there anything I can do?"

Poor guy, she thought. Stumbled into her crisis and had the bad sense to ask how she was.

"No. Thanks, though. I'm waiting for a phone call." They stopped in front of her door. "I'd better get back there."

He tilted his chin and she was struck by how—with his narrow features and bent nose—he reminded her of a bird of prey. "If you need anything, let me know. All right?" He thrust his chin out and up. "Just two floors above you."

"I will. Thanks."

Back in her apartment she shredded the credit card application, then poured herself a glass of cabernet and stretched out on her couch. Fiona was curled up in her red beanbag chair. Her jowl and eyelids twitched with some dog dream.

Max leaned her head against the cushion, closed her eyes and recalled the last time she'd seen Ben. He'd come to Chicago last fall. Just for a day. They'd gone to their favorite restaurant, Cannizzaro's, a storefront trattoria two blocks from Max's north side apartment, where they ordered a starter of fried calamari and their usual drinks—a Scotch for Max and a Beefeater martini for Ben. Dinner with her father invariably resulted in a slight hangover for Max. She considered it a small price to pay. There was no one else with whom she trusted herself to get a little drunk.

When the drinks came, they had paused in conversation as Ben savored his first sip. He was a striking man with thick, white hair tending toward shaggy and lots of character within the lines and shadows of his face. Max had always been good at reading his eyes, and that day they seemed a little sad and thoughtful.

"Next time you're in town, you ought to give me a little notice," Max said. "There's an art teacher at Coulter you should meet."

The lines at the corners of his eyes deepened just before he smiled. "You're wearing your matchmaker hat today."

"Yes, it's the one with the big, dangling bell. The beret doesn't work. Too subtle." Over the years, she'd tried to fix him up with every woman she considered worthy of him, which really wasn't a large number. "You'd like Kim. She designs jewelry. Mid-fifties. Smart. Funny." When Ben just continued to smile and drink, she added, "Ben, I can't help myself. You're a catch."

"I know," he said, struggling to keep a straight face.

She wouldn't go into the "I worry about you being lonely" routine. While this was her main reason for wanting to fix Ben up—he'd been widowed since Max was five—she was tired of hearing how his life was so full he didn't have time to be lonely. As far as she was concerned, no one was that busy. "You need two women," she said. "One in England and one over here. Really. Let's face it, half a year with you is going to be enough for any woman. I'm pretty sure Kim would be delighted with the arrangement."

Ben was chuckling as he shook his head. "Maybe next time I'm in town."

"And when will that be?"

"Next summer," he said, then deftly changed the subject by asking about her teaching.

She gave him a look that said he wasn't off the hook, but decided not to push. "Teaching's going pretty well. Love the students. Most of the students." Max smiled as she realized what she was about to say would sound familiar to Ben. "It's the department politics I can live without."

Ben raised an eyebrow. "And you're thinking about applying to a doctoral program? You think you've got politics now."

Max sipped her Scotch. As always, the first swallow made her wonder why she drank the stuff. "I've got to go somewhere. Up seems like a good direction."

"You don't want to teach the rest of your life, do you?"

"Is that such a bad way to live?" she asked, her smile feeling a little unsteady. She'd expected support.

"I teach one semester a year." He dipped his glass and shrugged. "That's probably why I'm good at it. The burnout rate is higher for those teaching full-time."

Then, perhaps sensing his daughter wasn't prepared to argue, he asked her about the department politics.

"Well, let me say that I'm glad I got tenure last year. I don't think the new chair is my biggest fan."

"Why the hell not?" Even the slightest affront to Max's character or abilities seemed to genuinely amaze Ben. That was one of the things she loved about him.

"Cheryl thinks folklore belongs in anthropology, and that 'master's thesis' and 'fairies' don't belong in the same sentence."

Ben took the spear skewering the jumbo olive from his glass, tapped it against the rim and handed it to Max, who didn't care much for martinis but liked what they did for olives. "And she's making your life miserable."

"You could say that." She chewed the olive slowly, enjoying the pungent mix of salt and gin. "If my folklore class didn't draw high enrollment, I'd be sunk." She swallowed. "But it does."

"She might take you seriously if she knew what a thoughtful, practical four-year-old you were." He looked down at his glass and smiled. "Do you remember how you laid bare the Santa myth by asking the mailman how many houses he delivered to in a day? You figured if he could do—I don't know—a few hundred houses in six hours, there was no way Santa could do a few billion in twenty-four hours." When he raised his eyes to her again, they were full.

Before she figured out what to make of her father's tears,

39

he said, "You know I always want what's best for you, Max, don't you?"

"I know."

The deep-fried aroma arrived a few seconds before the calamari did, heaped high on a plate with a bowl of marinara sauce for dipping. She hoped the food would divert the conversation. Pikes only got maudlin after several drinks. Then they never spoke of it again.

Ben inhaled deeply and released his breath with a satisfied "Ah."

Max lifted a morsel by its tentacle and tossed it on Ben's plate. "For you," she said. With squid, Max preferred not to be reminded of what she was eating. She helped herself to a few of the fried rings.

"This grad school thing. Don't do this because you're running out of options, Max." He chewed thoughtfully for a minute, then added, "You can't always fall into something first time out. Don't push it. You're very focused. Maybe a little too focused."

"What do you mean by that?"

"There are times when you need to sit still, get quiet and listen to yourself. Find out what you really want." His eyes narrowed as he studied her. "You ever do that?"

Max shrugged. "Who's got the time?" In truth she was afraid if she did what he suggested, she'd find nothing. Then what was she supposed to do?

"Make the time." His harshness startled Max. But then he smiled a little self-consciously. "I guess with age you develop perspective. Don't be so intent on one thing that you lose sight of everything else. You know, don't focus so closely on the trunk that you miss the fact that it's part of an elephant."

Max swallowed a bite of calamari. "You've been cracking open fortune cookies again, haven't you?"

He shrugged. "What good's an old man if he can't give his daughter advice?"

"You're not old."

"Some days I feel it."

Ben taught archaeology at a small New England college that was generous in the amount of time they gave him for his field work. They appreciated having a widely-published authority on their faculty. As successful as he was, Max had always thought he seemed vaguely unsatisfied in his findings, as though what he really sought eluded him.

He drained his martini and, with a gesture toward the waitress, ordered another round. When he turned back to Max he asked, "How's the photography going?"

"Okay." She blotted her fingers with a red linen napkin. "I had a photo published in the *Tribune Magazine*. Full page."

Ben nodded his approval. "Your mother would be proud."

Max cherished the few memories she had of her mother, who died when Max was five. She'd been a tall, graceful woman with soft hands and a wide smile who wore brilliant shades of blue and green and recorded family events with her camera. Max wasn't more than seven or eight when she picked up her mother's Nikkormat and started shooting her own pictures.

Ben studied her as the waitress brought their fresh drinks. When she'd left, he tapped the olive stick on the edge of his glass and said, "Just remember you have an exciting future ahead of you."

"May I borrow that crystal ball of yours?" She accepted the olive. "Maybe it starts at graduate school."

"Maybe," Ben conceded. But, the way he bobbed his eyebrows as he sipped his martini suggested he believed otherwise.

The evening had left her confused. It had also left her with a roommate, when Ben told her his new landlord didn't allow dogs over twenty pounds. "Until I find a new place," he'd said. "It shouldn't be long."

"And what are you going to do with her when you go to England?"

He shrugged and looked at something over Max's shoulder.

"You are so transparent, Ben." She had to laugh. "Here I am trying to fix you up with women and you're foisting hounds on me."

That was six months ago. It had taken only a fraction of that time for her to grow attached to Fiona. A part of her opened up to make room for the dog, reminding Max that she was too young to be set in her ways. Ben had been right about that, too.

Since then, she and Ben had kept in touch, talking at least once a month. She'd never applied to graduate school but did look into the real estate market. Then, last month he'd called and asked her to come to Wales. She should have tried. She also should have listened harder at dinner. If she had, she'd have realized he had something serious on his mind.

She drained the glass of cabernet. A glance at her watch told Max it was going on two-thirty. It had the makings of a long wait. She thought about hauling out her photo equipment again, but decided she needed something more extraneous. Grading papers ought to do the trick. She had three sets of freshman essays and a term paper for the folklore class. If she could get into a groove, she might be able to shut down the right side of her brain for a while.

An hour and a half hour later when the phone rang, she'd just corrected the spelling of Tennyson for the third time in the same essay. She cut it off mid-ring.

"Elliott Schiff," the man said. "I have a message from

Maxine Pike." His tone was brusque.

"This is she," Max said. "Thanks for calling back."

"You're Ben's daughter?"

"That's right."

"I hope nothing's happened to him." He sounded apprehensive.

"We don't know what's happened to him. That's the problem. He's missing . . . And I received a message from his solicitor that I'm supposed to call you."

The line went silent for a number of seconds, then Schiff sighed. "Wow," he said quietly.

She gave him a few more seconds, and then said, "Do you know why I'm supposed to call you?"

"Ah, yeah. Right." When he continued, it was with the brusque tone again. "I don't know if you're aware of this, but your father had an item on loan to the museum."

"I wasn't. What kind of item?" She was thinking some ancient dagger or awl.

"A stone."

"A stone?" Ben specialized in Celtic artifacts. As far as Max knew, the only stones he was interested in were ones fashioned as weapons.

"Right. He told me if you were ever to call, I was to see that you got it."

She had so many questions, she didn't know where to start. Finally, she just said, "Are you at the museum? I can be right there."

"Whoa, wait a minute," he said. "I'm thirty thousand feet over the Grand Canyon. How about we meet in the morning at the museum? Nine o'clock?" He told her how to find his office.

"I'll be there."

When she got off the phone, she poured another glass of

wine and grabbed a bag of pretzel sticks. It was still going to be a long night. She thought about calling Grey. He said to call if she needed anything. Right now she could use some company. But she didn't trust her emotions, so she forced herself to go back to the grading.

Chapter 4

When Olivia Pike got out of the cab in front of Walter Bacon's office building, she undertipped the driver, feigning ignorance of the pound system. She wasn't cheap, just short of cash. She'd rather look stupid than poor.

It was a few minutes before her ten o'clock appointment with Bacon, so she slipped into the women's room. The flight from Paris had been a short one, and it hadn't done as much damage as the sleepless night she'd had.

As she brushed some color onto her cheeks, she decided the darker hair wasn't kind to the few lines in her face. She had it colored last week—gone from honey blond to this dark brown with red highlights. Maybe it was a bit harsh. What made her angry was that she'd done it for a stupid and, ultimately, pointless reason. Sebastian had spent too long admiring that waitress at Leon with the same color hair. Olivia had been foolish to think it was the woman's hair color, rather than her youth or the way she'd been so pathetically impressed with the old lech. Olivia was also loathe to admit that she'd attached herself to a man who liked being fawned over. Then he'd gone and taken up with her—or someone like her—and Olivia had to scramble.

A scant hour before Bacon had called, Sebastian had informed Olivia he wanted her to move out by the weekend. Bastard. With Sebastian it was always a hurry. Even sex. She told him that. It felt good—for a moment—but then he told her he wanted her out the next day. Touchy, touchy.

Which was why she'd pressed for a meeting with Bacon this morning, rather than waiting until Monday when Max was supposed to be there. The solicitor had been reluctant, but Olivia had insisted and he'd relented, telling her that they couldn't proceed with Ben's bequest until Max arrived, but he would tell her what he could. Olivia agreed. Mainly, she needed to know how much she would be getting. She was too damned close to selling off her jewelry.

Since Bacon's call, she hadn't actually thought much about Ben. If he was dead, she supposed she felt sad. But it was more like losing an uncle with an interesting occupation. He was never around much. He'd breeze through town, bring presents and thrill her and Max with his adventures, then just when Olivia was getting sick of hearing it all, he'd move on again. Max never got enough and Olivia knew she was hurting now, but life was for the living and money was for the spending. Indeed, if he was dead, Ben would appreciate the fact that in his death he was able to do something good for Olivia.

She thought about having a cigarette—she hadn't had one since De Gaulle Airport—but decided she'd get to Bacon's office before lighting up. She carefully ran liner around the contours of her mouth, filled in her lips, then brushed on a coat of red. Blotting, she admired her handiwork. Walter ought to be impressed. She'd never met him, but from his voice she pictured him as being older and pudgy, with thinning hair and nervous eyes.

A sign on the office door read: "Bacon and Bradshaw, Solicitors," and Olivia wondered what Bradshaw might have to solicit. She opened the door to a large outer office with a single desk and bookshelves lining the walls.

Behind the desk, with the phone to her ear, sat, Olivia assumed, the secretary. The black nameplate on her desk read "Amanda Wright." She wore large, red-framed glasses and a green cardigan sweater buttoned up to her throat. Her hair was almost the color of Olivia's, but Olivia assumed it wasn't a professional job. Amanda was way too pale to pull off the color. She looked like a hennaed vampire.

When she smiled up at Olivia, the corners of her mouth twitched as though the gesture required effort to sustain. She said into the phone, "I've got to go now."

Olivia turned away, not interested in this woman's private conversation. And obviously it was. You didn't use that syrupy tone with a client. Olivia's first impression of Bacon's operation wasn't a good one.

"Can I help you?"

Olivia turned to see Amanda was off the phone and apparently ready to work. "Olivia Pike here to see Walter Bacon."

"Of course," she said. "Mr. Bacon should be in directly." She nodded toward a corner of the room where three chairs flanked a low table. "Won't you have a seat?"

Olivia looked over Amanda's shoulder at the office door behind her with Bacon's name on it. It was shut. She glanced at her watch—ten-oh-five—and sighed.

Amanda watched her, her hands clasped together so tightly the skin across her knuckles was stretched white.

Olivia gave her a thin smile and walked over to the grouping in the corner. She dropped her coat onto a brown leather chair and settled into the one beside it. When she looked around for an ashtray and saw none, she assumed one would appear when she lit up. She dug to the bottom of her purse for her cigarette case with the lighter wedged into it.

"Sorry, Miss Pike. There's no smoking," Amanda said, hands still folded together. Olivia noted that her red nail polish was chipped.

"I knew there was a reason I preferred the French," Olivia muttered as she let the pack drop back into her purse.

Amanda added, "I'm asthmatic," as if Olivia cared.

Olivia rummaged through her cosmetic bag for her manicure scissors, remembered she'd moved them to her suitcase because she was flying and made a mental note to transfer them back. She needed her tools and they had to be the right ones. Scowling, she removed a nail file from her cosmetic bag and smoothed the rough edge of a nail she'd caught on the seat on the plane; the ragged cuticle would have to wait.

Every now and then she'd look up at Amanda, just to let her know she was under scrutiny. The secretary fidgeted with a paper clip and seemed to be pointedly ignoring Olivia. She tapped the keys on her computer a few times, but didn't seem to have much of a purpose. Every thirty seconds or so she consulted her watch, which pleased Olivia. It was nice to know she wasn't the only one who didn't wait well.

Several minutes later, the door opened. Olivia looked up, assuming it was Bacon. When she saw the newcomer, she knew that wasn't the case. Too young, too casual and too working class. Too bad. He wasn't unappealing. His sandy-colored hair brushed the collar of his jacket, and he glanced over his shoulder towards Olivia as he approached the secretary's desk.

"Amanda," he said, sounding as though he knew her.

"Nick," she responded, her voice tight and her smile tighter.

"I've a ten o'clock with Walter."

"Yes. I-I know."

"Shame on Walter," Olivia said. "Double-booking and then not showing up. Where are the manners you people invented?"

Nick checked his watch, then pushed back the edges of his tweed jacket and sunk his hands into the pockets of his jeans.

"Mr. Bacon shouldn't be long," Amanda said to him, adding, "I'm sorry."

"It's okay." He added a smile.

Amanda's cheeks flushed pink.

Then he nodded and turned, his gaze falling solidly on Olivia. While she was used to being noticed, she had the impression that his interest wasn't merely physical.

"Why don't you have a seat, Nick," Amanda began. "Like I said, I'm sure he'll be along at any moment—"

"That's what you told *me* fifteen minutes ago," Olivia said. She wasn't going to let this guy go ahead of her, and from the way Amanda was batting her eyes at Nick, he had the inside track. Besides, she wanted a cigarette. Maybe she couldn't do anything about Walter's punctuality, but this little excuse for a receptionist wasn't going to tell her she couldn't smoke. Slinging her purse over her shoulder, Olivia stormed the desk. Amanda's eyes grew wide behind her glasses. "Listen," Olivia said, "I've been trapped in economy class, and then in a cab that smelled like the inside of a tennis shoe whose driver's knowledge of the English language was limited to 'No smoke, please.' "

As Olivia spoke, Amanda stood. Mistake. Olivia had six inches on her. She'd been restraining herself with Sebastian for the last three months and now her full-throttle bitch mode was kicking in. It felt great.

"I could've bought a Porsche for what it cost for a last-minute ticket to London, because Walter Bacon said it couldn't wait. And what am I doing? I'm waiting for Walter." She began to walk around the desk, heading toward the office behind it. "Well, I'm going to have a cigarette and I'm smoking it in his office."

Amanda threw herself between Olivia and the door, her small hand grasping the knob.

Nick was watching the scene from in front of Amanda's desk. From his frankly curious expression, he didn't look as though he was going to intervene.

"I'll tell you what," Amanda said, wetting her lips, her gaze nervously passing from Olivia, to Nick, then back to Olivia. "I've got to use the loo. You have a smoke out here. I'm sure Walter won't mind."

"I wouldn't dream of polluting your air, Amanda." She'd found her cigarette pack and pulled one out, along with her lighter. "I'll smoke in Walter's office." She looked down into Amanda's eyes. "Will you move?" Olivia realized she didn't care about the cigarette anymore. She wanted to know what was on the other side of the door. "Don't make me get ugly."

Then the phone rang and Amanda slumped against the door.

Olivia smiled, figuring it must be the boyfriend calling back. "Aren't you going to get that?"

Amanda seemed to grow an inch. Her flat little chest expanded. "Fine," she said. "Smoke where you bloody well like." She plucked her hand from the knob and stepped away from the door.

The switch was so abrupt, Olivia didn't know what to make of it at first. She watched as Amanda snatched her purse from an open drawer, thrust it under her arm and marched toward the door. "Enjoy your smoke," she said with a smirk, and added, "those things'll kill you, you know."

The little bitch, Olivia thought as the door closed behind Amanda. When she met Nick's eyes, he frowned and shrugged. The phone stopped ringing.

"Is she always like that?" she asked.

"She's a bit high-strung."

"I wonder if she's ever heard of decaf." Olivia opened Bacon's door and stepped into the office. The smell hit her first. Leather mixed with something foul. It was a long, narrow room and his desk was in the corner opposite the door, in front of a window. The blinds had been pulled, and it was several moments before Olivia's eyes adjusted to the dim light.

"Walter?"

Amanda had been wrong. Bacon was in. Sleeping? Olivia took two steps toward the desk, then jumped back, a scream caught in her throat. On the desk, the pedestal of a large Celtic cross rose out of a pool of Walter's blood. The back of his skull was caved in and a sliver of white bone protruded from his blood-matted hair. She released the scream.

The door banged against the wall and a moment later, someone was standing beside her.

"Good God." It was Nick.

Walter's eyes were wide open, vacant and yet surprised.

She heard the sound of the door closing, but couldn't look away from the body until Nick said, "What the bloody—"

He had crossed to the door and was trying to turn the knob. It didn't budge.

"Hey." Olivia felt an edgier kind of fear take over.

Nick was yanking at the door, twisting the lock which appeared to be jammed.

"Amanda!" he yelled as he pounded his fist against the door.

From the other side of the door, a small voice said, "I'm sorry, Nick. But you shouldn't of gone in there."

"Amanda?" He pounded on the door. "Amanda!"

Silence.

"Open this." He kicked the door. More silence. Then he turned to look at Olivia. Something about the way his gray eyes darkened and narrowed told her they shared the same thought.

"We need to get out of here," she said, swallowing. It wasn't just the corpse or the smell. There was something wrong in this room.

"We do," he said, took a step back and gave it a solid kick near the door knob. He did it again.

Olivia determined his foot wasn't going to do the job. She looked around for an object. All she saw was the Celtic cross. Gritting her teeth, she lifted it out of the blood—it was as heavy as it looked—and handed it to Nick. Without hesitating, he took it from her and slammed it into the door. Wood splintered and flew. He wielded it like an ax, holding onto the bloody end and using the crosspiece as the blade. It was surprisingly effective, and after four solid hacks, he had a large enough hole to maneuver his hand through and remove whatever had jammed the lock.

Nick dropped the cross and waved Olivia through the door.

Once she entered the anteroom, she started to feel silly about her nerves. She wasn't the dramatic type. Still, it was good to be out of there. As she passed Amanda's desk, the phone in Bacon's office started to ring. Dead and still taking calls. She swallowed a giggle that was more from hysteria than disrespect. Still, her first priority was to get through this so she could contact Bacon's partner and see if he could settle Ben's estate. She couldn't remember his name, but it was on the outer door. She was reaching for the door knob when the phone stopped in mid-ring. As she started to turn toward Nick, who she assumed was behind her, a flash of white light filled the room, then a deafening crack knocked her to the floor. She couldn't hear her own scream.

Chapter 5

Jillian emptied the last of the Coke into the ice-filled glass. Carbonation bubbles exploded against her wrist. She glanced at her watch, then back to her computer screen.

The conversation had turned promising when Philly422 started bitching about railroad crossings. "The ones that make you late for work because you have to sit and wait for 10 min. for a gd freight train," he wrote. Someone suggested writing the railroad. Most agreed that was a waste of time. Proposals escalated to organized protests.

She took a sip of Coke and waited for Philly422 to say something again. She'd had her eye on him for a while, ever since she'd started reading his messages that popped up in several anti-government listservs. He had a lot of hot buttons and it had taken her a while to find the one issue he invested most of his passion in. Rhys always said the first thing to look for was someone with his anger focused. When she traced

Philly422 and found a man named William Loomis living in Philadelphia who had become a truck driver after being laid off from his government job because of budget cuts, she knew he had potential.

There it was.

Philly422: "Somebody oughta blow up the gd tracks."

The group argued about that for a while. Whenever someone suggested that such tactics were too extreme, Philly started spouting about his rights being violated. He had rights; why didn't anybody care? "Who says the crap they're shipping is more important than the stuff I haul?" Rhys would love this guy. When someone mentioned that an explosion could get people killed, he responded with: "Progress comes with sacrifice."

"Are you volunteering?" SILOMAN responded.

It went on like that; eventually, Philly422 must have figured he was outnumbered because he dropped out.

Tomorrow Jillian would send him an e-mail privately, suggesting he check out a chat room more inclined toward his way of thinking. While she was at it, she had several other promising candidates to redirect. Once there, it was a matter of fanning the fire. Before long, there'd be reports of someone blowing up railroad crossings. Maybe setting fire to a hospital. Families being killed by "perfectly normal" neighbors. Jillian regularly spent five to six hours a day on the Internet, seeking out individuals with promise, inciting them. Their hit rate was good and getting better with Rhys's psychological expertise.

This Internet sniping had been a suggestion of hers—it dovetailed so perfectly with her father's larger, more ambitious plans—and once she'd convinced Rhys that she could ensure her anonymity through an encrypted address and a few other tricks, he'd been enthusiastic, supportive and maybe even proud.

She glanced at the digital clock on her computer. Four a.m. and wide-awake. She supposed that woman was gone by now. Rhys never kept them around longer than necessary.

An hour ago when she'd brought him the edited chapters of his latest book, she knocked on his bedroom door and after hearing a distinct, "Come in, Jillian," she'd walked into the room. It was all she could do not to bolt. Her father wasn't alone. A woman, wearing a tight black dress that barely covered her rear, had her face buried in Rhys's lap. Rhys, emitting a guttural moan, had the remote clutched in his hand and channel-surfed the news stations while she serviced him. As he began to buck against the woman, Jillian placed the chapter on the bedside table, turned and left. She couldn't get that sound out of her head.

Jillian knew she put up with a lot from Rhys. Sometimes she had to remind herself of how much she'd grown since she found him. He filled places in her that she hadn't known existed. Being around him was a constant adrenaline high.

She had been raised by her grandparents, who owned a convenience store in Keokuk, Iowa. They did their best to see that their granddaughter didn't meet the same fate as her mother, a skittish, high-strung woman who overdosed on alcohol and barbiturates when Jillian was ten months old without ever revealing the name of Jillian's father. Jillian went to school, attended church on Sundays and didn't give her grandparents much cause to worry.

Once she went away to college, she adapted quickly to the freedom, experimenting with drugs, religion and sex. She found drugs disappointing, religion pointless and sex a major disappointment. All that sweating, grunting and fumbling, and for what? An orgasm. She could manage that herself. The first time she had sex, she remembered looking at her lover afterwards, as he lay there grinning like an idiot, his limp penis oozing on his thigh, and she'd felt some mild disgust, but mostly curiosity. This rather repulsive act did have a purpose—it shifted the balance of power to her side and she learned how to exploit it.

When she was a sophomore, a private detective spoke to her sorority on ways to check out a man before becoming involved with him, advising them to take advantage of records that were available to those interested enough to look. She took a couple of computer classes and learned how to get around on the Internet. With some advice from the detective, she'd begun the slow process of locating her father. Her grandparents seldom spoke of her mother, so Jillian had little to start with. She'd tracked down a couple of her mother's friends—acquaintances, really—who named a string of boyfriends. Apparently her mother had been sexually promiscuous since the age of thirteen, and her chosen form of birth control appeared to be abortion. Once Jillian realized it was something of a miracle that she was even born, it was easy to convince herself that her life would have significance. When her mother's college roommate told her about the visiting professor her mother had been infatuated with, Jillian sensed she was close. (She had refused to believe her father was a drunken frat boy.) Further digging produced the name Rhys Lewis. When she learned he was a psychologist of some renown, she was afraid he'd think she was trying to take advantage of his success. But when Jillian first called to introduce herself to him, he'd acted shocked, then pleased. Since then, she had learned that nothing shocked Rhys Lewis.

She couldn't deny the fact that Rhys was the first man she'd met who didn't seem boring or trivial. From that day on, Jillian's association with her father, although strictly business, had been a flood of pure energy. She'd never felt so vital; her potential had no limits. He'd slowly assimilated her into his life, his work and his goals. While it had been only two years, the person she had been before seemed a stranger to her.

"Any further word on the stone?"

Although she hadn't known he was standing behind her, she wasn't startled, having grown accustomed to his constant proximity. He leaned against the door jamb, cigar wedged between his first and second fingers.

"Not yet," she said. "But she's got a meeting with Schiff this morning."

He walked into her office and, using the edge of a pewter ashtray she kept for his visits, knocked a half-inch of gray ash off his cigar. It lay there like a slug.

Rhys nodded. "Book yourself on a flight to Chicago this afternoon. I want you to be there."

She waited for him to elaborate, but he merely placed the edited chapters she'd given him on her desk and switched on the television, to the twenty-four-hour news cable channel he had purchased last year. On screen, a reporter was giving yet another account of Congressman Sandstrom's murder.

". . . Sandstrom left the fundraiser early and was attacked in the garage." The reporter consulted her notes. "The cause of death was a knife-inflicted wound." She went on about how officials from the President on down were decrying the act, calling for an all-out effort on the part of the D.C. police to find the killer. "We cannot allow ourselves to become victims—"

"Blah, blah, blah," Rhys finished.

Then the scene cut to Senator Jordan Fenster, gun rights advocate, who was holding forth on the steps of the Capitol building. "God knows how different this might have been if David Sandstrom had been carrying a weapon. Citizens should have the right to be as well armed as the criminals."

"Well said, Mr. Fenster," Rhys murmured. "David's death was not a total waste."

He looked up at Jillian, smiling. "I see you've got my new chapters ready." She handed them to him and he flipped through the pages. This book was about the debilitating aspects of being cheated and what an empowered person could do about it. These new chapters discussed the practicality of lawsuits.

When Rhys was finished with the book, he placed it on the table beside the laptop Jillian was using and hit the "mute" button on the remote. Then he walked behind her and began kneading her shoulders. He knew exactly which muscles to manipulate and how hard. The tension trickled from her slowly.

"Jillian, what was it that prompted you to find me?"

The question surprised her. Not only was it unexpected, but she'd told him about the man who spoke to her sorority. Rhys never forgot a conversation, so she knew he was looking for something else.

"I wanted to meet you."

"And . . ."

"Know you."

He exhaled sharply. "What else?"

She had to think. "I suppose I felt that I was owed you. That there were things I should have because of you. A person I should be."

"Go on."

"Well, I have a history with you—whether you knew me or not—and I guess I wanted to know myself better. And to see what parts of me I owe to you." She paused. "So I could honor them."

He patted her shoulder.

She waited.

"You and I aren't so different," he finally said.

She didn't know how to respond to his admission and twisted around so she could see his face, thinking she'd find a clue in his expression. "How is that?"

"I never knew my father either," he said, taking a seat on the edge of her desk.

"Really?" She wondered what she had done to earn what he was about to give her. The pulse in her throat throbbed.

"When I was growing up, the man I knew as my father had no time for me. You see, he wasn't really my father and he knew it. My mother was raped. Supposedly." He stared past her for a moment, as though focusing on those memories, then looked into her eyes as he said, "When I was seven, a cousin of mine told me that my father was a demon."

"A demon?" Horns and tail?

He nodded slowly and Jillian felt he was waiting to see if she'd look away. At the same time, she was beginning to understand why he had waited so long to share this. This meant he trusted her. She returned his nod, and he continued in a calm, almost soothing voice, "It horrified me at first." He folded one arm over his midriff and rested his elbow on it. "But gradually I realized that these strange thoughts and images I'd been having since I'd been able to think were his legacy to me. As long as I did what I was put here for—followed his dream, if you will—he wasn't going to hurt me. I was his son."

When he paused, she asked, "What kind of thoughts?"

"Oh, mainly about my family, my classmates. Doing things to them. Raping my mother, then killing her, along with my father and brother." An affirming nod. "I had many plans for my brother." As he pinched his chin between his thumb and forefinger, the edges of his mouth curved up. "Our neighborhood was big on get-togethers, you know. Everyone would be there—parents, grandparents, children. Lots of food—chicken, potatoes, mince. One big, jolly blowout." His eyes sparked, and she had an image of Rhys as a little boy—serious, bright, angelic-looking. "I'd fantasize about adding poison to their liquor and soda bottles. Wipe out every one of them. I even experimented with the neighborhood cats. You know, to see how much was required."

He looked to Jillian and she knew he wanted to be prompted. "So, what did you do?"

"Instead of being horrified by these images, I recognized that thoughts such as these must be acknowledged, embraced, and yet, at the same time they must be channeled into something constructive. So what if I slit my brother's throat while he's sleeping? The kick lasts only a short time. Enough behavior like that would eventually get me arrested, and then what would I do with my father's vision? He had plans for me. The devil doesn't do things to us. Not personally. That's what people are for." He paused. "And some people are meant to do violence, and others—a handful—are meant to orchestrate it."

"You've done all this for your father?"

"It started that way. But in order to be truly successful, one must love what he's doing." He looked past her and Jillian saw how the color of his eyes deepened. "And I do. You see, in the end I came to realize that those thoughts I had weren't really terrible. Once I realized that, I understood my purpose. Violence is a part of life. There's beauty in it. Why has the film *Bonnie and Clyde* become a classic? No one had ever filmed violence as it is. Bodies jerking in a death dance as they're riddled with bullets. Why do people slow down to view an accident? Rent videos that splice one catastrophe into the next more horrific one? Life thrives on violence and chaos. It invigorates us. Stimulates us. Arouses us." He drew

61

in a deep breath and released it in a satisfied sigh. A moment later he looked at Jillian and said, "But I never forget that he's there watching me. Judging me. Testing me."

She had almost worked up the courage to ask him how his father expressed his approval or disapproval when the phone rang. She wanted to yank the plug from the wall, but it was Rhys's private line, so she picked it up.

"Jillian, it's Simon. Let me talk to Rhys."

She handed the phone to Rhys and repeated the name.

"Yes?" he said into the receiver. Then: "Is it taken care of . . . ?" As he listened, the lines between his eyes furrowed with concentration. After a minute he glanced at Jillian, rolled his eyes heavenward. "You told me Amanda was stable." He sighed. "So what happened?" He listened for a minute, then said, "I don't care how you managed it as long as you did." He nodded once. "So, where is she now?" Now he smiled. "Good." Then, "I'll be in touch."

He replaced the phone on the receiver, stared at it a moment and said, "Stupid bitch."

"What happened?"

"That silly woman Simon recruited was supposed to call Simon after Bacon's two clients went into his office. Simon was to set off the device then. But, before they arrived, Bacon caught Amanda going through his papers. He confronted her and she bashed his brains in." He shook his head in disgust. "Frankly, I'm amazed they managed to pull it off."

"So, they're all dead?"

"They'd better be."

"Well, that's good." But it should have gone smoother and Rhys knew that. No doubt Simon did as well. According to Simon Murdoch, Amanda had been a perfect recruit. Rhys had agreed. She was highly suggestible. Walter Bacon had a number of international clients, and it had been relatively simple, with some forged documents and photos, for Simon to convince Amanda that Bacon, along with some of these clients, was smuggling drugs into England, making them available to school-aged children. Rhys understood the workings of the human mind and he knew it took little to convince a bored, uninformed person like Amanda of conspiracy and then of her own importance in averting disaster. Rhys's theory that most people were bored and uninformed was central to his vision. "Has Simon cleaned up after himself?" she asked.

But Rhys had switched on the television's sound again and turned his attention to the screen. This cable channel was the first of many he hoped to acquire, and he'd changed the format from mostly insipid talk shows to all news, featuring as much graphic footage as was available. Now it broadcast images of a fire devouring an apartment building. The reporter had one ear plugged as she tried to hear herself over the bleating sirens of fire trucks and ambulances.

Jillian knew better than to interrupt him now.

Chapter 6

"I don't understand," Olivia said to the inspector. "I'd never met the woman. Why would she want to kill me?" She touched her lower lip, which her tooth had clipped when Nick landed on her. It was a little puffy, but with some makeup it wouldn't be so bad. She supposed she should consider herself lucky to survive a bombing with no more than a cut lip. The doctor had assured her this ringing in her ears would go away soon. According to the inspector, the bomb had been placed under Bacon's desk. It would have made minced meat of Olivia and Nick if they'd been in the room.

When it did go off, Nick had thrown himself on her and a piece of wood from the door had gashed his head. They'd taken him to the hospital and her to New Scotland Yard. She hadn't seen him since and supposed she ought to make a point of thanking him. Whoever he was.

"That's what we're attempting to ascertain."

Chief Inspector Jack Riordan sat across from her, ankle on his knee, tapping a pencil against the side of the table. He was a tall, slender man, with most of his height in his legs. He wore horn-rimmed glasses and a necktie that was almost as thin as his lips.

"What do you think happened?"

"I think she planned to kill Walter Bacon with the bomb. One way or another she jumped the gun, so to speak. Killed him with the cross."

"So, why kill us?"

"It may be as simple as eliminating witnesses."

Olivia didn't think it was that simple and suspected that Riordan didn't either. "Why would she stick around after killing him? I mean, she was just sitting there on the phone when I arrived."

"Precisely," he nodded.

Olivia thought briefly about how Amanda might have enjoyed the prospect of killing her. "You know, that woman didn't impress me as the kind of person who knows much about bombs. Do you think there were others involved?"

"I'd bet on it. She was probably talking with him when you walked in. Perhaps that call at the end—the one she didn't answer—was some kind of signal." He paused. "We're checking phone records."

Olivia found all this both logical and disturbing. She swallowed hard and focused on the wire-grated window and the thin, gray clouds beyond it. "Have you found her yet?"

"Not yet."

Well, of course not, Olivia thought. She was probably halfway to Switzerland by now. She flicked ash off her cigarette. At least they let her smoke. She glanced at her watch. Almost one. She hoped her room at the Savoy hadn't been given away.

"Miss Pike?"

She looked at him.

"Again. Why were you there?"

After a sip of weak coffee, she said, "My father was his client." She explained about Ben's disappearance, his instructions and Bacon's call.

"Did you stand to inherit?"

"I think so. Something. To be honest, I have no idea what my father was worth." But she knew that their mother came from a wealthy family.

Riordan uncrossed his ankle and moved forward, bringing his arms to rest on the table. "Do you know if your father had any ties to the illegal drug trade?"

She almost laughed, remembered this was a murder investigation, and said, "No. I'm sure he didn't. Ben wasn't interested in drugs."

"Was he interested in money?"

"Not especially." Then she said, "You should ask my sister about him. They were much closer."

"Where is your sister?"

"In Chicago."

He jotted a note on a legal-sized pad. "Was she supposed to be here this morning?"

"Bacon told me she'd be in later on Monday."

"So, why did he want to see you today?"

"I asked to see him."

"What couldn't wait?"

"I was in Paris. It was no big deal."

"When did you make these arrangements?"

"Last night. Late."

Riordan frowned. "And you say Amanda wasn't surprised to see you?"

"She didn't seem to be."

There was a knock at the door and when Riordan opened it, his body blocked her view of the person on the other side. They spoke quietly, then Riordan excused himself.

Hunger seemed an inappropriate urge, given the events, but Olivia's stomach was rumbling. She dug through her purse and found a half tube of peppermint Lifesavers. Judging from the effort it took to chew one, they'd been in there a while. As she sucked on its stale sweetness, she lit another cigarette.

Riordan was gone for almost twenty minutes and when he returned, he had Nick with him. Nick had a bandage, about two inches square, on the back of his head, near the base of his skull. The image tripped a flashback of Walter's head—bloody and misshapen. An ice cube skittered down Olivia's vertebrae.

He nodded to her and sat in the chair Riordan indicated, which was next to hers.

"Do you two know each other?"

"Not before this morning," Olivia said, glancing at Nick, who didn't respond.

"Then you don't know why Nick Llewellyn was at Walter Bacon's office this morning," Riordan said.

"I don't."

"Your father never mentioned him?"

"No." She looked hard at Nick, curious now. He'd propped his elbows on the arms of the chair and stared down at his clasped hands. He was maybe a couple years younger than Olivia, and good looking in a scruffy way. He hadn't hit on her yet, even though he'd saved her life. "You knew my father?" She leaned toward him. "Don't tell me you were his lover?"

Nick's response was an abrupt laugh, followed by a shake of his head, which implied she was hopelessly wrong. "No," he said, finally turning toward her, "but my mother was married to him."

It was several moments before Olivia could respond. "That's bullshit," she said.

Nick shook his head again. "Afraid not."

"Benjamin Pike—my father—was married to your mother?"

"He was."

"You can prove it?" He nodded and she said, "How long?"

"About eighteen months."

Olivia thought about the last year and half. She probably hadn't even spoken to Ben in that long. Nothing personal. They just weren't terribly interested in each other's lives. But, Max . . . "Did my sister know?"

"I don't believe so."

Olivia hoped that was true. She couldn't wait to tell her. "Did you know about us?"

"Not until yesterday."

For the first time since this exchange began, Olivia glanced across the table. Murder investigation aside, Riordan seemed to be enjoying the hell out of this little soap opera.

"Why the secret?" Olivia asked Nick.

He shifted in his chair. "I doubt it matters—"

"I'd like to hear," she said. Riordan was watching Nick.

"It's a complicated situation. My mother's not well . . ."

"What's wrong with her?"

"That's not at issue."

Riordan said, "It could be relevant to what happened today."

"It's not." Nick shook his head. "As I said, it was a complicated relationship. But it's nothing to do with Walter Bacon's murder."

Olivia had always considered her family—Max and Ben—on the dull side. Pleasant, but definitely not "A" list people. This secret—potentially tawdry—life of Ben's intrigued her and, in an odd way, made her protective. "I agree," Olivia said. This was her family. She was not going to learn the details along with this cop sitting across from them.

Riordan looked directly at Nick and said, "Were you and your mother named in Benjamin Pike's estate?"

Nick didn't answer right away. Then he said, "He's just missing—"

"With specific instructions on how to handle his estate should he go missing. For all intents and purposes, he is dead."

Nick's jaw muscles tensed.

"Well, Mr. Llewellyn?"

"Yes, Ben made provisions for my mother."

"And you?"

"Not as far as I know."

"Did you owe Benjamin Pike money?"

He leaned forward in the chair, closing the space between himself and Riordan. "You wouldn't be asking me that if you didn't know, now would you?"

The cop didn't even blink.

"In a way," Nick said, sounding angry, defensive. "He put up some money, along with me, for a pub. You could call him a silent partner. We'd intended that eventually I'd buy him out."

"Had you begun that process yet?"

"It'd been only a year."

"If anything happened to him, would you be out of the debt?"

He barely hesitated. "Yes."

This meddling cop was starting to anger Olivia. Nick Llewellyn may be an interloper, but it was her family and none of Riordan's business. "Why are you interrogating us? We were almost killed. Why don't you do something useful, like finding Amanda?"

"We have found her," Riordan said, pulling his gaze from Nick so he could direct it at Olivia. "At about half-eleven, in her flat. Either she'd hanged herself or had some assistance. Either way, she's dead."

The interview took another twenty minutes. It was after two when Riordan walked them as far as the elevator. He told them he'd be in touch, and Olivia didn't doubt him.

Once he'd left them, Olivia turned toward Nick and said, "We've got to talk."

"I agree," he answered, pressing the "down" button.

"Miss Pike?"

She turned toward the voice. The man approaching her was in his mid-forties, with thinning blond hair and full, ruddy face.

"I'm Cliff Bradshaw, Walter Bacon's partner." He nodded at Nick. "Good to see you came through with only minor injuries."

The elevator pinged and the doors slid open. They waited for it to empty, then all three got on. Bradshaw stood across from Olivia, and she got her first good look at him. He had the kind of face that usually went with a pudgy body. But Cliff Bradshaw was fit, possibly muscular underneath his silk-blend suit.

"Dreadful business." He spent a few seconds studying her

and then said, "I was thinking perhaps I could help you. I wasn't your father's solicitor, but I was a contingent trustee, so I am somewhat familiar with his situation. I just wanted to assure you—" he broke off as though an idea suddenly struck him. "If you haven't any plans, perhaps I could answer any urgent questions you have over lunch?"

A step in the right direction. "Well, yes. I'd appreciate that."

"So would I," Nick said, although from the look on Bradshaw's face, he hadn't included him in the invitation.

"Very good," Bradshaw said without a trace of sincerity.

Chapter 7

Max had graded one set of essays and was through a quarter of the term papers. She knew she took longer than most to grade a paper, but she thought the extra time she put in—correcting all spelling and punctuation errors, writing questions in the margins, maybe making them think—paid off. Besides, she was convinced this was the only thing that had kept her sane tonight. Not to mention sober. After consuming half a bottle of wine, she'd switched to club soda. Then she'd graded until about three a.m., tried to sleep, given up at four-thirty. She tried reading, but every book she picked up either reminded her of Ben or England. Between papers, she'd watched the sky lighten. Now it was the soft gray of a mourning dove.

Her eyes felt gritty and she thought once she finished this paper, she'd try to find something to clean. She felt so damned useless.

She read a few lines, stopped and started to giggle. The student had referred to Mercury as "king of the messengers." The image of this guy with wings on his feet and a crown on his head cracked her up. She supposed her sense of humor had been compromised by the lack of sleep, but it felt good to laugh. In the next line the student noted that in this age of electronic mail, AOL was probably the messenger king. That was when it occurred to Max that she hadn't thought to check Ben's e-mail.

She pushed away from the dining room table and headed for her small office. When Ben was in town, he used her computer to check his messages. She knew his password, and while he trusted her not to go snooping around in his personal life, this was different.

When she logged onto her e-mail server, she checked her own first—nothing but spam—then went to Ben's mail. One message. It was from "Believeit" dated April twelfth. She clicked it open. One sentence: "You need me, I'll be in Penzance on the 13th. Antony." Max drummed her nails on the desk's surface, then clicked "reply" and typed: "I am Ben's daughter, Maxine Pike. Ben is missing. I'm trying to find out what happened to him. Please contact me." She signed it, added her own e-mail address and her phone number and sent it. Then she checked Ben's "out" mailbox and old messages. Nothing. Leaning back in her chair, she sighed. "I could use some help here, Ben."

She glanced at her watch and added seven hours. One p.m. in Paris. Even Olivia, keeper of strange hours, ought to be up. She punched in her number; the phone rang twice and a man answered. *"Oui?"*

"Bonjour," she said, *"Parlez-vous* English?"

"Yes."

She told him who she was and asked if Olivia was there.

He let loose a string of French words that were probably better left untranslated. Then he said, in English, "I don't know where she is and I don't care."

"Thank you," Max said, and hung up before he treated her to more French lessons. *Olivia strikes again.*

Fiona had followed Max into her office and was now watching her. "She ought to come with a warning label." If her sister wasn't in Paris, she was probably already in London. Maybe when she called Walter's office, he could tell her where she was staying.

While Max was thinking about Olivia, Fiona moved over to her chair, laid her head on Max's lap and sighed. Although Max seldom walked her before seven, she wasn't usually up this early. Funny the way dogs react to a change in their person's habits.

"Okay, girl."

The rain had stopped and the cool morning felt good. She thought how she shouldn't be such a stranger to six a.m. Fiona pulled on the leash and sniffed the air as they turned at the end of the walkway and headed north.

As they passed Max's green Civic, she reminded herself to take it in before the end of spring break to have Raoul check out that window. It was the kind of thing she might forget. Then she remembered she'd likely be in England most of next week. A lot depended on today, just a few hours from now. That was when she noticed a guy sitting in the car parked in front of hers. It wasn't all that unusual; he might have been waiting for someone. But then, as she passed his car, she saw that his head was tilted back against the headrest and his mouth was open. Probably asleep. Or passed out. He seemed quite still. She paused. Maybe dead? Normally, she wouldn't have considered crossing the parkway to the car, which was a big, tan Cutlass, but Fiona's curiosity had been aroused and she was pulling Max toward the car.

The driver's side window was open and when she got right up to the door she smelled cigarettes. He wore a Cubs cap pulled low over his forehead and a line of drool extended from the corner of his mouth. He snorted. Just as Max was backing away, Fiona rose up on her hind legs and propped her front paws on the door. That was when the man opened his eyes, saw Fiona and cried out. The strangled sound caused Fiona to go into a barking jag, and Max had her hands full trying to calm the animal. When she had her under control, she saw that the man was wiping his face and straightening his hat. He'd reddened considerably.

"I—ah—was just—" he started.

"No, never mind, I'm sorry we bothered you." She steered Fiona toward the sidewalk. "Just wanted to make sure you were okay."

He gave her an odd look and nodded, then pulled his hat down even lower and started his car.

Well, Max thought, at least he'd stopped to sleep it off.

The rest of their walk was without event and on the way back, as they approached her apartment building, the Cutlass was gone. She also saw that the light in Grey's living room was on.

Chapter 8

Bradshaw took Olivia and Nick to a pub on Victoria Street where Nick greeted the bartender by name. She told herself if Nick hadn't been along, Bradshaw would have taken her someplace decent.

Orders had to be placed at the bar and when Cliff asked what she wanted, Olivia said some kind of salad, figuring there couldn't possibly be anything here worth eating. "And a glass of chardonnay," she added.

Now she nibbled on the dry cheese and watched Nick and Cliff wolf down shepherd's pie and lasagna, respectively. They each washed it down with a pint. Olivia's wine tasted flat.

They talked as they ate. While Olivia wanted to cut straight to the inheritance part, she knew it wouldn't look good for her to bring it up, so she decided to pursue Nick's connection to their family.

"How long had your mother and my father been together?"

Nick swallowed his bite and regarded Olivia for a few seconds before saying, "Twenty-five years."

Olivia did a quick calculation, subtracting twenty-five from her own age. She came up with ten. Once she'd determined that Ben hadn't cheated on her mother, who died when Olivia was eight, she let herself ponder that quarter of a century number. "That's a long engagement."

"They weren't romantically involved that entire time. At least, I don't think so. Ben and my father had been friends since university. When my father died, Ben was at his funeral. A year or so later, he was in our lives."

When she thought about it, the idea that Ben had been carrying on with this woman for years didn't really surprise Olivia. She'd never figured Ben for the celibate type, although she tended to imagine him with a string of different women, none of them quite equaling Olivia's mother. The fact that he kept this from her and, she assumed, Max, was really the most intriguing aspect. A man taking up with the spouse of a deceased friend begged all kinds of questions, not to mention implications. But she didn't want to appear crass in front of Bradshaw by suggesting anything.

"I don't remember Ben giving me a new address," Olivia said. "How long was he living with your mother?"

Nick took a drink. His ale was a reddish amber and he held the swallow in his mouth for a moment before gulping it down. "He never gave up his flat."

"Interesting." She tried to sound thoughtful. "They never lived together?"

"Off and on," he said. "But Ben was around a lot. He was like a—" he broke off.

"You can't tell me he was like a father to you. Benjamin Pike didn't do 'father.' "

Nick laughed. "You've got that right then, haven't you?" As he set down his mug, Olivia noticed the elaborately carved silver ring on his third finger. "No, I was going to say he was more like an uncle. To me. He was a good man. Good for my mother and good to me."

Olivia couldn't let it go. "Twenty-five years together and they never lived together?"

He regarded her briefly and Olivia saw a spark of amusement in his gray eyes. "Isn't that better than living with a string of different people over a period of twenty-five years?"

"Not necessarily," she said, then moved off the subject before it got personal. "And you just learned about my sister and me? Who told you?"

He finished chewing a bite and swallowed. "My mother."

That was what really made this interesting. "Why wouldn't he want us to know about each other?"

"It wasn't a typical marriage." When he spoke, he was impaling a pea with a fork tine, and not looking at Olivia.

"Why not?"

His gaze passed over her on its way to Bradshaw, who had been observing their exchange with interest. "Have the police talked to you about Bacon's supposed involvement in drugs?" he asked Bradshaw.

Bradshaw wiped his mouth with a paper napkin. "They have. I tell myself it would be funny if they weren't so bloody serious about it. Walter would no more be involved in that sort of thing than . . . I would." He paused as though examining those last two words again. "Well, I suppose the police are keeping an open mind about me as well." He sliced off a corner of the lasagna. "What I can't understand is Amanda's involvement." Frowning, he shook his head. "All that is deeply troubling to me. Amanda had been with us for years. I can't imagine . . ."

Olivia thought about the plump little secretary who didn't seem capable of fending off a persistent telemarketer, let alone bashing in her boss's head. "Maybe Amanda was the one involved in drugs."

"I doubt it," Bradshaw said, then finished chewing the bite. "Her younger brother died of a heroin overdose. As a result, she was involved in a number of anti-drug campaigns. No, Amanda wouldn't have been party to that sort of thing."

This was getting way off-course. "Shouldn't we let the police solve this? I mean that's what they're paid to do."

"You're right," Bradshaw said. Nick just shrugged and shoveled another bite of lunch into his mouth.

Olivia broke off a piece of the unidentifiable white cheese. "So, are you familiar with my father's business?"

"To a degree," Bradshaw answered. "As I said, Walter convinced your father his estate ought to have a contingent trustee." He glanced across the table at Nick. "He has some rather unusual conditions attached, one being the fact that upon his disappearance—as opposed to his death—this trust would go into effect."

"Why would he be so worried about disappearing—as opposed to dying?" Olivia asked.

"I really can't say."

When Nick didn't offer anything, she said, "Well, I can take a guess. Ben must have been involved with people who knew how to make other people disappear."

"I suppose that has to be considered," Bradshaw allowed. "There is supposed to be a letter from your father that might explain this. I've never read it and, as far as I know, Walter didn't either."

"Well, can't we get the letter?"

"That's the problem. Ben's file is missing."

Nick's jaw was frozen in mid-chew.

"Do the cops know this?" Olivia asked.

"Yes."

"I guess that explains why they were so interested in our business with Walter Bacon."

"We'll have to see how this plays out," Bradshaw said.

Olivia wondered what else this disappearing letter was supposed to tell them. "What about Ben's estate? Were his instructions on dividing his assets in that letter, too?"

"No," Bradshaw shifted in his chair, "that is spelled out in the trust. He wanted his estate divided among the three of you." He nodded toward Nick, then Olivia. "You two and Maxine."

Olivia glanced at Nick, then said to Bradshaw, "Some of that money was my—Max's and my—mother's. She died when we were young."

"Well, that's another thing . . ." he shifted his gaze to the table, "I'm not certain how much there's going to be." Olivia waited for him to look at her, but he continued talking to his fork. "Somewhat less than there might have been, say, six months ago."

"What are you talking about?" Nick had managed to swallow his bite.

"I hesitate to say much at this point, because I haven't been thorough, but a preliminary look at his accounts would indicate he'd liquidated some of his assets recently." He crossed his arms over his chest and sighed. "Took some rather hefty penalties for early withdrawals."

Nick appeared more puzzled than shocked.

"There must be some mistake," Olivia said. "If he's smuggling drugs, shouldn't there be *more* money?"

"He wasn't smuggling drugs," Nick said, sounding firm.

"Like you'd know," Olivia snapped and turned back to Bradshaw. "Shouldn't there be more money?" she repeated.

"Arguably." Then he added, "Although drug money is usually laundered. Wouldn't make much sense to toss it in with the retirement fund, would it?" He managed a grim smile.

"You can't think there's something to these suspicions?" Nick asked.

Bradshaw sighed. "I didn't know Ben Pike well at all. I thought I knew Walter, but the police have found evidence. I keep telling myself he was set up. But by whom?"

The money had to be there. Somewhere. Ben must have reinvested those funds. A really great stock tip could make early withdrawal worth the penalty. She refused to believe Ben would leave her with nothing.

"What's being done to find out what happened to Ben?" Nick was asking as Olivia tried to refocus on the conversation.

"The police are looking into his disappearance. I expect they'll be stepping that up now. I've an independent investigator on it. Your father's last known location was here in London." He paused and canted his head. "When's the last time you saw Ben, Nick?"

"Not since February. But he called me last month and asked if I could meet him in Wales. I couldn't get away, and he said we could talk later."

"Why do you suppose he wanted a meet?"

Nick's mouth pressed into a thin line as he shook his head. "No idea."

Olivia wasn't sure she believed that, and judging from the narrow-eyed look Bradshaw was giving Nick, the lawyer didn't either. But, Bradshaw just nodded, then pushed his plate away and centered the pint of beer in front of him.

"Well, I apologize for not being better informed. This is going to take some time. Nick, you live in London, don't you?"

"Out near Kew."

Bradshaw acknowledged that with a brief nod, then turned toward Olivia. "Are you on a tight schedule?"

"I have nothing pressing at home." *Nor do I have a home or a ticket to get me there even if I did,* she added to herself. "I suppose I could stay a few days if it would help to have me here."

Bradshaw smiled. "Indeed, it would."

"There's something else." Nick took a couple more swallows of ale, draining the mug. He caught the bartender's eye and made a circular motion with his hand, indicating another round. When he looked at them again, he drew in a deep breath and released it. "Something I need to ask you both about. Ben had an item that belongs to my family. A gemstone."

Bradshaw frowned and Olivia asked, "What kind?"

"I don't know what it is. It's a good size. Thirty, forty, maybe even fifty carats." He hesitated. "I believe it's a green stone. Or red. I'm not certain."

Olivia raised her eyebrows and exchanged a look with Bradshaw. "What *do* you know?"

"Well, until Ben went missing, I didn't know for certain that it even existed." He drove his fingers through his hair and touched the bandage at the back of his neck. Then he settled his arms on the table again. "You see, it's part of my family lore, you could say. Supposedly it's been handed down from generation to generation for—I don't know—hundreds of years. But, until recently, I didn't know there was anyone living who had actually seen it."

Red or green, Olivia was thinking. Ruby or emerald? "So, who *has* seen it?"

"Ben and my mother. Something she said makes me believe that Ben had the stone."

"What did she say?"

"Well," he shifted in his seat, "that before my father died, he'd given it to Ben."

That meant it was Ben's, Olivia thought as Nick added, "For some reason he'd asked Ben to hold onto it. My mother believes it had gotten my father killed, and now Ben."

"How?" She supposed that anything made more sense than the drug theory.

"She didn't get any more specific than that, I'm afraid."

"Wouldn't she tell you?"

"No," he said simply and his look warned her not to press. Then he got up to collect the drinks at the bar.

"Sounds a bit far fetched," Bradshaw said under his breath.

As Olivia watched Nick pay the bartender and gather the drinks, she had the sense that, while Nick was probably holding back information, he was also desperate for answers.

"Don't you think?" Bradshaw prompted.

"Well, I love family lore tales," she said, turning her smile on Nick as he set their drinks in front of them. Especially when they involved dangerous, precious stones.

Bradshaw thanked him and, after Nick sat, said, "Wouldn't a stone of that kind have some kind of provenance?"

Nick shook his head. "I've looked." He regarded Bradshaw for a few moments, then said, "It's an unusual stone."

"It would seem," Bradshaw said, sounding skeptical.

"How did your father die?" Olivia asked.

"A boating accident off Holyhead," he said and added, "northwest tip of Wales."

"Are you sure it was an accident?"

"No way to tell it wasn't. He and his mate were lost at sea." After a swallow of ale, he added, "The rumor was that the stone was lost with him. Apparently that was not the case."

"What if Ben had it with him when he disappeared?"

Nick drank an inch off the new pint. "He may have. I hope he didn't."

"This gemstone." Olivia wet her mouth with a sip of wine. "We could be talking a lot of money."

"We could be."

With his arms resting on the table and his thoughtful expression, Nick seemed perfectly relaxed, as though he were having a beer with friends. The fingers of his right hand played tunes on the table.

"Now, correct me if I'm wrong, Mr. Nick Llewellyn," Olivia said, "but you're about to ask me if I should happen to run across a large red or green gem, would I please return it to you. Is that what you're about to ask?"

Nick didn't take his eyes from Olivia as he said, "It would be lovely if it were that simple, wouldn't it?"

Olivia nodded, amused. "Wouldn't it?"

"I don't expect you to hand over the stone. I'll pay you for it."

"Whatever the asking price?" Olivia raised her eyebrows.

"Get it appraised and I'll give you ten percent over its appraised value." He looked at Olivia and then at Bradshaw. "I'm willing to pay whatever is necessary."

"Why?" Olivia asked.

"As I said, it's part of my family's history." After a second's pause, he continued his appeal. "All I'm asking is that you think about it. Perhaps he said something that may give you an idea where it might be."

Olivia tapped her finger against the glass. This would be one way of recouping her losses.

"Did you tell the police any of this?" she asked.

"I didn't mention the stone."

"What if it's the reason Ben disappeared?"

Nick shook his head. "If it comes to that, I'll have another chat with Riordan. But, as I said, no one knows the bloody thing exists except my mother, Ben, me and now you two."

"We're flattered," Olivia said, thinking she'd have to call Max.

Nick drained his ale and stood. "There's my offer. Please take it seriously. Give it some thought. Ben may have said something, done something." He pulled a pen out of his shirt pocket and jotted down some words and a phone number on the coaster, then pushed it to the middle of the table. "I can be reached here."

Olivia picked it up. "The Fife and Firkin. This is the pub you and Ben owned?"

"It is."

"What if I find this stone at two a.m.?"

He nodded at the coaster. "You can reach me there."

"You live in a pub?"

"Almost. I live in a bedsit above it."

Olivia exhaled a stream of smoke toward the ceiling. "You will let us know if you find it? So we can stop looking."

"Of course." He thanked Bradshaw, bowed slightly, then turned and left.

She watched him thread his way through the crowd and out the door, then turned toward Bradshaw.

"Here's what I think, Mr. Bradshaw—"

"Cliff," he said.

"Cliff." She paused. "I don't know about this stone. I do know that my father is probably dead and I can't change that.

I won't tell you we were close, because we weren't. I respected him and I will miss him." She leaned toward Cliff. "But I need to get on with my own life. Do you understand?"

"I do."

When they left, Bradshaw got a cab for her and asked if she was free for dinner.

"Sounds nice," she said.

"Seven? Where will I find you?"

"The Savoy."

He nodded his approval.

As the cab pulled away, she hoped she had enough credit on her card to get her a room at the Savoy. But she didn't have a choice. It was all about appearances. One thing Olivia understood about money—in order to get it, you had to act like you didn't need it.

Chapter 9

Max was on the steps of the Field museum at ten to nine, along with a group of about twenty grade-schoolers and a couple of chaperones. Each wore the same bright green T-shirt with the words "Niebuhr Elementary" printed in large yellow letters across the back. One little girl—blond with a bright pink band around her ponytail—was telling anyone who'd listen that there was a dinosaur in there and it ate people.

In spite of her edgy impatience—fueled by too many cups of coffee, Max had to smile. She enjoyed visiting Sue, the t-rex on display at the museum.

But when the doors opened and she filed in behind the group of children, Max barely gave the hulking lizard a glance as she made her way downstairs to Schiff's office which was, as he'd told her, in the bowels of the building. The sign on his office door, which was open, read: "Dr. Elliott Schiff, Mineralogy Curator."

Max knocked on the door jamb. "Dr. Schiff?"

No answer.

She took a few steps into the large, cluttered room that smelled of earth and rocks. Books overflowed metal, bracketed bookshelves, and a table was covered with papers and more books. Several long display cases made of a light wood with shallow drawers were situated in two rows, one in front of the other, like an old library card catalog system. The desk was piled with books, papers, and a computer occupied one corner. One rock, a gray specimen that glittered, seemed to have a favored position on a wooden block. The walls were covered with photographs, many of them featuring a middle-aged, slightly overweight man with a graying beard and curly, thinning hair. In most of the photos he wore a multi-pocketed khaki vest and some variation of a denim shirt, with the sleeves rolled up to just below his elbows. Whether he posed alone or with others, the main focus of most of the photos was rocks.

One photograph dominated the wall. It was of a cave with huge, column-shaped rocks in gradients of pink and pewter.

"Beautiful, isn't it?"

Max turned and saw the man in the photographs crossing the room. "Fingal's cave," he said, approaching. In his right hand he carried a large envelope.

"I've never seen anything like it," she said. "It looks like a pipe organ. What kind of stone is that?"

As he looked up at the photo, his chest expanded. "Columnar basalt," he said, then added, "It's in the Hebrides."

He turned his attention to Max, transferred the envelope to his left hand and extended his right. "Elliott Schiff." Max shook it and introduced herself.

"Sorry to keep you waiting. I had to get this." He handed her the envelope. Whatever it contained was about an inch thick.

She could tell by the way his gaze lingered on the envelope that he wanted to know what was in it, but then he smiled and nodded. "Thanks for coming."

"You were a student of Ben's?" She tried to place him, but couldn't.

"Up in Wisconsin," he said. "My major was geology, so I took only a couple courses from your father, but he was a great teacher."

While she realized his use of past tense meant only that Ben was no longer his teacher, she felt a swell of sadness.

"You haven't heard from him?" Schiff asked. "Since we talked."

"No." Her eyes misted. Blinking rapidly, she said, "So, Dr. Schiff, what about this mysterious stone?"

"Elliott," he said.

He walked to the door and closed it, then gestured toward a wooden chair facing his desk. She sat and he rolled his chair around to the side of the desk, resting his arm on a book covering its edge. He took a moment to study Max; it was a rather frank look that suggested curiosity more than anything else.

Then he reached into a vest pocket and produced a large, green stone. He held onto it for a moment before handing it to her. She took it; it fit easily into her palm. Its surface was smooth, rather than faceted, and the depth of its color almost hypnotic.

"It's beautiful. What is it?"

"Alexandrite. Or something very similar. Forty-two carats." As she ran her thumb over the stone's surface, Elliott explained how he'd conducted a couple of tests on the stone, even though Ben hadn't asked him to identify it. Then he chuckled and added, "I don't think Ben cared what it was."

"Why wouldn't he?" It had grown warm in her palm, and when her fingers closed around it, she could almost feel a pulse.

"I don't know." Elliott rubbed his hands together. "He was pretty circumspect about this." With his elbow he nudged the book out of the way and propped his arm on the desk. Then he rested his chin against his fist. "If Ben were anyone other than a mentor, I'd never have kept it."

"How did he come to give it to you?"

"He was through Chicago last October." He explained how Ben had asked him to keep the stone until Max contacted him.

She had to wonder why—if she was to wind up with it—didn't he give it to her in the first place? Only one logical reason came to mind. "You were keeping it safe for him, weren't you?"

He puffed out his cheeks, then released his breath in a sigh and nodded. "Basically."

"Was it on display?"

"No."

"So, you were hiding it as well."

He shrugged as if it were no big deal. "Well, we have a larger number of stones than we have space for. At any one time, they can't all be on display."

She gave him a dubious look and he smiled, a bit sheepish, and nodded. "Truth be told, this stone's provenance is a little," he made a wobbly boat gesture with his hand, "sketchy."

"Provenance? That's the stone's pedigree, isn't it?"

"Yep. I could've gotten in a world of shit for holding onto this."

"Ben has a gift for choosing good people."

Elliott accepted the compliment with a nod.

Max held up the stone. "This is worth a lot of money, isn't it?"

He raised his eyebrows. "Oh, yes."

"But Ben didn't care about money. So, there must be something else about it that makes it precious." She looked down at it again. "What do you suppose it is?"

"That I don't know." He leaned forward, elbows on his knees. "It's a puzzle. You see, it's alexandrite, but it's polished into a cabochon, not cut. Alexandrite is always cut, faceted." He stroked his beard. "If it isn't cut, alexandrite is just another precious stone."

"What do you mean?"

He scooted back in his chair so he could open the top right desk drawer. From there he produced a pen light, which he shone on the stone. Max thought she saw the moss green deepen, but other than that, nothing.

"So?"

He snapped off the light. "Alexandrite's beauty is in its color change. It turns red or a purplish red under artificial light, but you see the color change only if the stone is cut." He nodded at the stone. "There's a reason that stone isn't cut. And I'd dearly love to know what that is."

Ben wasn't a geologist. He was an archaeologist and interested in antiquities. "But gems haven't always been cut."

"True," Elliott agreed, then said, "but the thing is, alexandrite wasn't discovered until the early twentieth century, long after stones were regularly cut." He paused. "It was found in Russia and named after Czar Alexander II."

She turned the stone over. It seemed perfectly shaped. "Just because it wasn't discovered, that doesn't mean it didn't exist."

"True again," he said, gazing down at the stone.

She felt the way she did the first time she saw an iceberg—

all the more amazing for what wasn't visible. "So, if this were discovered hundreds of years ago, it probably would have been unique. Used for something special."

"That stone is unique," Elliott said with a decisive nod.

"You're speaking as a scientist?"

He looked past her for several moments, then reached across a stack of books to pluck the glittering stone from its carved stand. After gazing at it for several more seconds, he looked up at Max and said, "I love stones. I love the way they feel . . ." he put it to his nose, ". . . smell . . ." then he put it to his ear and gave her a half smile as he whispered, "I love what they tell us."

He glanced toward the photo of Fingal's cave. "I am in awe of stones. They're amazing. Timeless. We count their ages in millions, billions of years. Can you even conceive of a billion years?" He held up the rock. "If you believe there is any kind of power within the earth, this is where it would be." He lowered it. "Some stones have more to say than others."

She understood what Ben had seen in Elliott Schiff. "What do you suppose this one is saying?" she asked.

He smiled, kind of sadly, and nodded toward Max, "I don't think it's talking to me."

Back in her car, Max considered waiting until she got home before examining the contents of the envelope, but she considered it only for a second or two, the time it took her to find a pencil, which she slipped between the glued part of the envelope and the fold and yanked up, tearing it open at the top.

She'd figured from the feel and shape that the envelope contained a book, and she wasn't disappointed when a thin volume slipped into her hand. It looked and smelled old and felt slightly oily, the way old, much-handled books did. Embossed in red on a plain green cover were the words: *Y Stori O Bedwyr.* Welsh, she thought. The title was repeated on the spine, along with the author's name: Thomas Williamson. Its publication date was 1851. The corners were frayed a bit, but otherwise it was in excellent condition. She opened to the first page. Also in Welsh. While she didn't speak the language, she did know that Bedwyr was Welsh for Bedivere, one of King Arthur's knights. The story of Bedivere. Any further study would require a translator. She thought of the stone in her purse as she flipped through the pages. If she could read this, perhaps she'd know the connection. A photo slipped from the pages and lodged next to the gear shift. She crammed her hand down between the shift and the seat and retrieved it.

The photo was of Ben and two other men. It was taken recently—she recognized the Pendleton shirt she'd sent him for Christmas. To Ben's right stood a black man, several inches taller than Ben, which made him of average height, wearing round wire-rimmed glasses and, despite the smile for the camera, a serious face. The man on Ben's left was quite tall, probably six three or four, with auburn hair and a close-trimmed beard and mustache. They looked like three friends or colleagues stopping work for a quick photo. She turned it over and read the word "Alyssum." She recognized Ben's neat, blocky print, but the only Alyssum she knew of was the flower.

She'd hoped for some answers, but all she'd gotten were more questions.

Chapter 10

Olivia watched in horror as the hotel desk clerk snipped her VISA card into two pieces. She felt the cut as if it had severed an artery. "There's been a mistake." She hoped the clerk hadn't heard that catch in her voice.

"Sorry, Madam, we haven't a choice in these matters." The gold tag on her jacket said, "Miss Stapleton," and she didn't look at all sorry.

"Of course you do," Olivia spat. "Would you have sliced up Luciano Pavarotti's card? Julia Roberts'?" She tried to think of another celebrity she'd seen since she'd been there. "Jeremy Irons'?" He was local, wasn't he?

"Have you got another card, Miss Pike?" Miss Stapleton's eyes betrayed her contempt for Olivia and her credit habits. She stood there, flaunting her scrubbed youthfulness. Olivia wanted to smack her.

She could have sworn she had made a payment last

month. Her usual minimum payment on a maximum balance. Without people like her, credit card companies would be out of business.

"Another card?" the clerk repeated. Her smile showed signs of strain.

Not likely. Her VISA card was the healthiest one in her wallet.

"Perhaps you'd like a word with our manager."

"I would." Maybe the manager was male.

Miss Stapleton picked up a phone and pushed a button, keeping her eyes fixed on Olivia until she began to talk, then she turned away so Olivia couldn't tell what was being said. A minute later, when she hung up, she turned back to Olivia. "He'll be here straightaway."

Without thanking her, Olivia stepped away from the counter and watched as Miss Stapleton cheerfully greeted the next in line, a kid who couldn't have been more than twenty-five, wearing khakis and a cotton shirt. Americans.

When the manager, Mr. Tate, finally made his appearance, he was polite—almost pleasant—but firm. And although he was more than happy to agree with Olivia that it was the fault of the credit card company, he wasn't going to extend her credit. When he offered to let her use a telephone to call the credit card company, she declined, as they both knew she would.

"I've stayed at the Savoy many times," she said.

He nodded with as much sincerity as his pointy chin would allow.

When she glanced toward the counter, Miss Stapleton was pretending to be busy with some forms, but Olivia knew she was keeping a gleeful eye on her. "Mr. Tate," she said, "is it all right if I leave my suitcase here while I get this straightened out?"

He barely hesitated. "Of course. Just leave it with the porter."

"I came in early this morning and had some business. He's got it now."

Tate nodded again, eyebrows raised, waiting.

"There's something in it I need."

"Of course." He seemed relieved that it would be that simple.

Once she was reunited with her suitcase, she dug out a change of clothing. Fortunately, there wasn't much to the little black knit dress, and it fit easily into her purse. Then she found the women's room and took a moment to pull herself together.

This would work, she told herself, touching up her lipstick. She'd call Bradshaw and tell him she'd meet him at the restaurant. She'd find a women's room where she could change. After dinner with Bradshaw, she'd have a place to stay tonight. She believed that. She had to. Her only other option—unthinkable—would be to find Ben's apartment and stay there. The place was probably dingy and smelled of old newspapers and garlic. If Ben cooked, it was usually Italian. She had an abrupt, almost painful memory of Ben making a pot of sauce on a cold winter night in Wisconsin. Max always chopped the garlic—Olivia didn't like the way it made her fingers smell—and Olivia set the table.

Brushing away the memory, she checked her cash. Fifteen pounds and change. Olivia glanced at her watch. "Shit." In London with five hours to kill and no money to spend. "Welcome to hell," she muttered.

Chapter 11

Ben's flat was just south of Victoria Street, only a short distance from New Scotland Yard and the pub where he'd lunched with Olivia Pike and Cliff Bradshaw, so Nick decided to walk there, see if he could learn anything. He didn't know if Bacon had anyone check out the place. He doubted it; Ben had only just gone missing.

Hard to figure what Ben had been up to. He felt certain, after that lunch, that neither Olivia Pike nor Cliff Bradshaw knew. And Nick's mother wasn't talking. On hearing the news of Ben's disappearance, she'd had a single outburst in which she'd blamed this stone for it all and tried to make Nick swear if he did find it, he'd throw it away. How could he promise that, when he'd only just learned of its existence? He supposed his refusal to either ignore or destroy the stone helped send her into a downspin. It didn't seem to take much anymore.

He hoped he might run across something at Ben's flat that would at least give him direction. At this point, he was stalled out and angry. But as angry as he was with Ben for keeping him in the dark, he couldn't resent him.

Ben was a larger-than-life sort of person. Interesting to be around. Supportive to a degree. "Ben didn't do father," Olivia had said. Nick chuckled to himself. In a perverse sort of way, he liked knowing that she apparently hadn't had a markedly different experience from his.

One fact had been undeniable, however. No matter how good a son Nick was to his mother, how many flowers he brought her in rough-cut bunches or how many high marks he earned, he could never make her as happy as Ben did. Her eyes shone when Ben was around and her laughter was light, girlish. Ben had literally saved her life. And if he didn't love her at first—his presence was more an act of loyalty than love—Nick believed he did come to love her. She certainly believed it. It would have been easy for Nick to resent Ben, but it would have forced him to resent his mother's happiness, and perhaps her sanity, as well.

Now that he knew there was something else linking Ben to his family—the stone—he began to realize that Ben was more than a trusted friend to Nick's father. For whatever reason, the two were bound together by this stone, which possibly had gotten one or both of them killed. Instead of being angry with Ben for never giving the stone to him, Nick wondered if perhaps he should be thanking him.

Ben rented a small, two-bedroom flat on the second floor above a shop in Strutton Ground, a short street jutting out from Victoria. Nick had been here many times before, and he recalled how the low-key bustle of the neighborhood agreed with Ben. His flat overlooked a greengrocer with fresh fruit piled in boxes outside the door. A dispensing chemist occu-

pied the ground floor of Ben's building. After collecting
Ben's mail—a letter and two bills—Nick entered through the
back and climbed the stairs. The letter was from someone
named "Terry" in Oxford. He supposed he'd wind up
opening it, as he would the bills, but figured he ought to
wrestle with his conscience some first. Opening a personal
letter would be admitting that Ben wasn't ever going to be
able to do it himself. He slipped the mail into his pocket and
dug the apartment key, on a keychain with his own, from his
pocket.

When he opened the door to Ben's flat, Nick was struck,
as always, by how little Ben accumulated. The flat might have
belonged to a monk. In the living room were a couch and a
chair in mismatched plaids, an end table and coffee table that
did match, but only because they were painted white, and in
the corner, a chess table. A Walkman and a small television
sat atop low bookshelves across from the couch. In the
kitchen he had a few pots and pans, three place settings of
dishes and a refrigerator bare except for a jar of olives, a loaf
of bread and some sliced ham that smelled long past its
prime. Nick tossed the ham into a plastic bag to dump on his
way out.

When he passed the chess table, something made him stop
and look down at it. An image from twenty years ago washed
over him and he recalled the first time he'd beaten Ben at
chess. He'd just turned twelve. He could still remember how
his hand shook as he moved the rook, placing Ben's king in
checkmate. He'd been nervous partly because he thought he
must have missed something obvious; he couldn't possibly
have beaten Ben. But he'd also been nervous because Ben
liked to win. Would he still play with Nick if Nick could beat
him? And there'd been that moment of stunned confusion as
Ben took in the chessboard, his eyes darting from one piece to

another. Then he'd pressed lips together, nodded once, looked up at Nick and, after a moment's scrutiny, smiled. "Well done," he'd said. It was a while before Nick was able to beat him again and then gradually, he began winning more often. Though they never kept track, he figured they were about evenly matched. Good chess partners weren't easy to come by.

He started to walk toward the bedroom, then turned and looked down at the chessboard again. Now he saw what was wrong. The pieces. Nick and Ben always had a game going. When they finished one, they would immediately start another to continue the next time. Even when Ben went off on some dig or back to the States to teach, they had a game going. And while he couldn't remember the precise positioning of the pieces from the last game—it had been at least two months—this was most definitely not it. Ben would never have left his queen open like that, and Nick wasn't in the habit of sacrificing a rook for a knight. It might have been as simple as Ben knocking the pieces off, but he'd have put them back in their right places or, if he couldn't recall the setting, he'd have placed them to start over. It was as though someone else—a non-chess player—had knocked the table and figured the placement of the pieces didn't matter.

Hardly grounds for bringing in the police, but it made Nick pay closer attention. When he did, he saw other signs that someone had been here: a kitchen drawer not quite closed and the contents in disarray, sugar spilled on the counter and in a closet, sheets which were neatly folded were also stuffed in at odd angles.

In the bedroom, he stopped to examine two of the photographs on top of Ben's dresser. Until a couple of days ago, he'd thought these were Ben's nieces. In one, two young girls, Maxine and Olivia, Nick assumed, were about five and eight respectively. A woman stood behind them, smiling with a directness that seemed to be aimed more at the photographer than the camera. She was tall, like Olivia, with a couple inches on Ben, and classic features. A beautiful woman. It was a summer photo, and both the girls had white-blond hair and sun-browned arms and legs. Olivia looked up at the camera with teasing eyes and a smile that might belong to a much older woman; Maxine's grin seemed forced, her jaw locked, as though she weren't comfortable posing. Olivia had her arms around her sister, with her cheek resting against Maxine's hair. Nick couldn't tell if it was a protective embrace or one designed to upstage the other, smaller girl. In the more recent photo, the sisters were grown and Olivia still had several inches on Maxine. She also still had the same come-and-get-me smile, but Maxine's had relaxed some and her eyes were lively, amused. Like Ben's. Olivia had her arm around Maxine in this photo as well. The embrace wasn't as encompassing, with her right hand curved around her sister's shoulder. He set it back on Ben's dresser and proceeded to go through the drawers, which also appeared to have been rifled.

The second, larger bedroom, lined with bookshelves, served as Ben's office. Nick took one look at the books and saw there was something wrong here as well. Ben organized them by size within subject. Somehow he knew the location of every volume. These were out of order. Small books with large ones. Thick with thin. It resembled a cityscape.

Again, he considered calling the police, then chuckled. "Yes inspector, the chess set is wrong and the books are out of order." Besides, after those questions this morning, when they'd asked him about Ben and drugs, they'd likely think if the place had been tossed, drugs had been the object. They'd been looking for something small, all right—the stone.

Nick sat at Ben's desk and went through each drawer.

Pens, paper and computer supplies filled the left-hand drawers. In the upper right drawer, he found an address book, which he flipped through, stopping on the "P" page to find Ben's daughters. Maxine in Chicago and Olivia in Paris. A number of other addresses had been crossed out for Olivia. She'd lived in some interesting places: New York, Boston, Rome. He set the book aside to take with him. The right lower file drawer had a few hanging files, but was only about half full. And there were gaps between some of the files, as though others had been removed. He saw a shard of white at the bottom of the drawer and reached in between the files and pulled out the paper—a copy of a news clipping from the *Times*. He scanned it. Something about a foundation—Caliburnus—being investigated for links to an extremist group in the western United States. Nick folded the paper and stuck it in his pocket. He sat there for a minute or two, thinking and drumming his fingers on the arm of Ben's chair. His gaze fell on a stack of books on Ben's desk and then an author's name on one of the spines: Weldon Terry. He pulled the book from the pile: *Myth and Legend in Great Britain*. The oversized hardcover had glossy pages and color photos. He turned it over and opened to the inside sleeve. A man with wispy white hair and a bow tie smiled at him from the photo. The brief bio said he lived in Oxford. On the title page, he found Terry's autograph. "To my good friend," it said.

Nick pulled the letter from his back pocket, tore it open and read it once, then again. He could feel his heart thudding against his chest as he picked up the address book, found Weldon Terry and punched in his number on Ben's phone.

Chapter 12

The first thing Max did when she got home was look up Alyssum in her world atlas. She figured it was somewhere in Britain. Where else would she find Ben? It was a tiny island in a group scattered like pebbles off England's southwest tip—straight out from Land's End. The Isles of Scilly.

She studied the photo. Was Ben telling her to go to Alyssum or to find out about these two men?

She poured herself a mug of that morning's coffee and put it in the microwave to reheat, then picked up the Bedwyr book and thumbed through it. The fact that it was an Arthurian book was no surprise. Ben had hundreds of them. If this one contained some new, groundbreaking theory, surely Ben would have shared it with her. So, maybe its contents weren't the key. Maybe it was valuable simply because it had been published a century and a half ago. She supposed a book expert could tell her. At the same time, she tried to think of

103

someone who might be able to translate the Welsh. It wasn't a language commonly offered in college curricula and she thought she'd be better off calling one of the experts on Celtic mythology that she'd accumulated over the years. Or maybe the British consulate could help her.

The microwave beeped and she removed the mug, blew the steam off and took a sip. She had to keep going. When she stopped moving forward, thoughts of Ben had a chance to gang up on her, shooting her emotions to the surface. Tears spilled and her nose ran.

She went online to book a one-way ticket to London, gulped at the price but went ahead and put herself on an early-evening flight Sunday night. She'd sleep on the plane and be ready to face Bacon—and Olivia—in the morning. In her heart she hoped she'd be seeing Ben instead.

She queued up several CDs and hit the "play" button, then went into her office and switched on her iMac. She pulled in a deep breath and told herself to stay focused. If Ben was alive, she would find him. But before she went running off to England, she needed to know a few things about where she was going and, if possible, why.

While the computer booted up, she removed the stone from her jeans pocket. She thought it ought to be somewhere safe, considered and rejected several different places, then wound up returning it to her pocket, where it nested by her hipbone.

She logged onto the Internet, was disappointed to find no mail waiting for her, then did a search on "Alyssum."

She'd barely gotten started when someone came to the door. With the music, she might not have heard it, but Fiona started barking and when she went out in the living room to check, she heard the knocking. Since anyone coming from outside would probably have rung the bell—the building's security was seldom breached—she wasn't surprised to see Grey on the other side of the peephole.

She gave her short, blond hair a quick finger-combing before opening the door to him.

He wore a brown, moleskin jacket over jeans and a beige sweater. She could see hesitation in his eyes.

"Hope I'm not bothering you."

"Not at all."

Fiona had come to the door and was happily sniffing his outstretched hand, which he then used to pet her. "Hullo, Fiona," he said, as though she were a bright toddler. The few times Max had run into Grey while walking Fiona, he always took the time to greet her.

He looked up from the dog and said, "I wondered how you were getting on?"

"Pretty well, thanks." She stood back so he could come in, hoping he would. She didn't socialize a lot. When school was in session she was around people all the time, and being alone in her apartment felt good. But being on break forced her to live with the fact that she didn't have much of a social life.

"Would you like some coffee?"

"If it's no trouble."

"None at all." She cringed slightly. "Actually, it's left over from this morning."

"Aged coffee. The best kind."

While she poured it, Grey asked if she'd heard anything about her father.

"No," she said feeling the sigh in her chest. "I saw a guy this morning who gave me something he'd been holding for Ben." The book was lying on the coffee table, so she didn't see much point in trying to keep it secret. She picked it up and handed it to him. "I don't suppose you read Welsh, do you?"

"Sorry." He ran his hand over the cover, caressing the embossed words with his fingertips. "This is a beautiful book." He turned it over and opened it carefully. "My knowledge of rare books surpasses my knowledge of Welsh, but not by much I'm afraid."

She'd left the photo on the table beside the book and Grey picked it up.

"That's Ben in the middle," she said.

He looked from the photo to Max, then back again. "I can see the resemblance."

"We're both short," she agreed.

"There's more," he said, still examining the photo. "Aside from the physical, you've got that same expression."

She looked over his shoulder and saw the slightly wry smile and the alert, curious eyes.

"Do you think?" she said, feeling that "thank you" wasn't appropriate here, although she was both flattered and moved by his observation.

"Definitely." He glanced at the back. "Alyssum," he said, and nodded.

"You know the place?"

"I've heard of it. It's in the Scillies." His eyes narrowed. "And it's known for its gardens. You can see them in the background here."

She looked closer. Blurred bunches of pink and white bordered the photo's edges.

"Supposed to be a beautiful place."

"That's what I've read," she said. "So far all I know is that it's privately owned by a guy named Arthur Penn."

Grey frowned as he nodded and handed the photo back to her. "Always wanted my own island."

"Me too. It's been on my Christmas list for years."

The microwave dinged.

"Do you take anything in your coffee?"

"Nothing."

When she returned with the steaming mug, he was studying the photos on the wall behind the couch. After examining each one, he asked her whose they were.

"Mine," she said, sitting in an oversized armchair.

"They're good." He thanked her for the coffee and moved in closer to the middle one, a garden in the late afternoon. "This could be England."

"It could," Max tucked her feet under her, "but it's Chicago." She told him about the couple she knew whose narrow, brick-enclosed garden was like no place else in the city. "You can sit back there and imagine you're anywhere." In any reality, she almost added, but stopped herself.

"Arcadia," he murmured. Then he said, "The focus appears to be the sundial, but it really isn't, is it?"

When he glanced at her for confirmation, she said, "What do you think it is?"

He turned back to the photo. "It's the butterfly perched on some ivy, isn't it?"

"That's right. With those gossamer wings, I thought it looked like a fairy."

"The lighting and such does add to the impression," he said, as though he knew exactly what she meant. "Have you ever seen one?"

He'd asked the question in such a matter-of-fact way, not taking his eyes from the picture, that Max figured he wasn't being facetious. But she didn't want to scare him off, so she just said, "Not recently."

He glanced at her, eyes narrowed slightly, then smiled and nodded his head toward the picture. "Who was it who said, 'Vision is the art of seeing things invisible'?"

"Jonathan Swift, I think," she said, though she knew it was

Swift's line and believed Grey knew that as well.

"Do you always work in black and white?"

"Usually. I like working with shadows and light."

He studied her, his brows drawn together. Then he smiled and nodded, then took a sip of coffee. "You know, I shouldn't keep you," he said. "Just wanted to see how you were getting on."

"Thanks." She stood. "That was nice of you."

"We're neighbors." He placed the mug on the kitchen counter and when he turned to leave, he shoved his hands into the pockets of his khakis. "Ah, listen, I know you've a lot on your mind, but, well, I figure you've got to eat, so I was wondering if you'd care to join me upstairs tonight for dinner?"

"I'd like that."

"I make a respectable red sauce and can cook pasta with the best of them."

"I think I'd still like to."

He smiled crookedly. "Good," he said and lowered his eyes. Fiona was standing there and he bent to pet her. "Perhaps we can continue our discussion of fairies."

Before she could respond, he gave Fiona a final pat and straightened. "You're welcome to bring your friend here."

"That's easy," she said. "Can I bring anything else?"

"Just yourself," he said. "Around seven."

After he left, she stood looking at the door, thinking this probably wasn't the time to get involved with anyone, but then when did one get to choose that sort of thing?

Then she remembered that Alison had asked her to go to a movie tonight. She called her friend, hoping for the chance to explain to Alison rather than her answering machine. Unfortunately, she wasn't home, so Max left a message saying she'd be out tonight, but would give her a call tomorrow.

Then she returned to the Internet, where she found a map of Alyssum. It was roughly the shape of a figure eight with diverse vegetation, ranging from pastureland to short, scruffy plants able to withstand rough winds. As the printer labored over the map, the phone rang. It was Olivia, calling from London. Collect. Max accepted the charges without hesitation.

"You sound almost happy to hear from me," Olivia said.

"I am," she said, a little surprised to find it was true.

"There's been a little mix-up with my credit. I'll pay you back for the call."

"Don't worry about it." She walked into the kitchen and wedged the phone between her chin and shoulder as she took a can of berry-flavored sparkling water from the refrigerator. "I should be there Monday morning." She snapped the can open.

"Don't bother."

"Why not?" She took a sip.

"Walter Bacon's dead," She said, and proceeded to tell Max what had happened in Bacon's office.

"Jesus," Max said when she'd finished.

She'd taken the soda into her living room to stand by the picture window looking out onto the courtyard. By the time Olivia had finished, she'd sunk to the floor. "Thank God that guy was there."

"Praise the Lord," Olivia said.

Noting her sister's sarcasm, Max said, "What was his name again?"

"Nick. Nick Llewellyn." A long pause. "And you're not going to believe who he is."

Max reached up and took her soda from the window sill. "Go ahead."

"Ben's stepson."

She set the can on the floor, but kept her hand on it. "Ben was married before Mom?"

"Nope," Olivia said. "He married her eighteen months ago."

She couldn't have heard right. "Ben was married?"

"Yes, he was. But, don't worry, he didn't rush into it. They'd been together for twenty-five years before that."

"No."

"Sorry, Max."

"Nick is his son?" When she felt the cold against her knuckles, she realized she'd squeezed the can so hard, the soda was spilling over.

"No," Olivia said. "He's *her* son. I'd say he's in his early thirties."

"It can't be true." This was so bizarre, so incredible, she didn't know how to feel. "Why didn't he tell me? I mean us."

Olivia sighed. "You meant 'me.' That's okay. To be honest, I thought you'd tell me you knew all along."

"No. Shit, no." Her brain was scrambling to put together an explanation that would make sense, but kept banging into walls. "Are you sure this guy's on the level?"

"Seems to be. Cliff Bradshaw is checking him out."

"Who?"

She repeated his name and said he was Bacon's partner.

"Does he know anything about what happened to Ben?"

"No, but he's hired some kind of investigator to look into his disappearance. And then—you're going to love this—" she took a dramatic pause, "the cops think Ben and Walter Bacon were involved in the drug business."

"That's bullshit."

"I knew you'd say that."

"This is crazy," Max said.

"I know," Olivia sighed. "Listen, I'm having dinner with Bradshaw tonight, so maybe I'll know something tomorrow."

"Why wouldn't Ben want us to know about his life?" Max asked, and at the same time realized that Olivia wouldn't have a clue.

"I don't know for certain, but I'm betting it's got something to do with Nick's mother. The new Mrs. Pike."

"What? What do you mean?"

"There's something weird with her. I don't know what it is yet, but I'll find out."

Beyond the confusion, Max was hurt. Why wouldn't Ben tell her? Didn't they share everything? Then she thought of the stone.

"You there, Max?"

"I'm still coming there." She wanted to meet this Nick character, not to mention the woman Ben had married. "What's Nick like?"

Olivia took a moment, as though considering the question. "I don't know. He did throw himself on top of me when the bomb went off, but he was probably just being polite. I mean, he couldn't very well save his own ass and leave mine hanging out there."

Max almost smiled. It was such an Olivia thing to say. "Tell me more."

"Well, he's tall, with sandy hair, intense eyes. He wears his hair a little long, but—"

"Olivia," Max said, "I don't care what he looks like. What's he like? Were he and Ben close?"

"I would guess they were," Olivia said after a moment. "Ben helped him finance the pub he owns, and then he said Ben asked him to come to Wales to talk about something."

"When?"

"Last month. But he couldn't make it, so he never found out what it was about."

Didn't that sound familiar, Max thought. She wondered

why he couldn't go, and if he felt as guilty about not making it as she did. Then it struck her: Ben must have planned for them to meet. So, maybe he was going to tell her about this other life of his.

"I'll know more after I talk to Bradshaw," Olivia was saying.

"When you have dinner with him, ask him about a place called Alyssum." She told Olivia what she'd learned on the Internet.

Before they hung up, Olivia said, "Do you know anything about a stone?"

"A stone?"

"Yeah, some stone Ben had. Big, green. Or red."

"What about it?"

"Nick says it belongs to his family, but Ben had it."

"What kind of stone?" Would Ben want Olivia to know about the stone?

"I don't know. He says he doesn't either. It's been in the family for a long time. He wants it back and is willing to pay for it." She paused, as though waiting. "Max, do you know anything about this?"

"I need to get over there," she said.

"Max? Have you got the stone?"

Max and Olivia weren't the closest of sisters. As children they'd never spent nights sharing secrets and giggling into their pillows. As adults they were willingly ignorant of the details of each other's lives. Olivia probably figured Max would be shocked, and Max knew that Olivia would be bored. But at the core of their relationship was a mutual respect, which had come from growing up together more or less on their own. And one of the components of that respect was that they never, ever lied to each other.

"Max?" Olivia prodded.

"Yeah," Max said, defeated. "I've got it."

"You get your ass over here," Olivia said.

She'd withdrawn the stone from her pocket, and as the light played off the greens, she thought of Alyssum and the facts about the island she'd just begun to uncover. "I'll be there Monday."

Chapter 13

Nick parked along St. Giles Street and elbowed his way into the crowd at The Eagle and Child. The popular Oxford pub attributed its odd name to a story in which an earl adopted a child that had been fostered by an eagle. Affectionately known as the Bird and Baby, the Eagle and Child was deceptively large, with small, narrow rooms strung together and winding their way to a back room with skylights and an array of plants.

When Nick had called Weldon Terry that afternoon, the old man had sounded quite upset over Ben's disappearance and, before Nick could ask for a meeting, he'd insisted that Nick drive up to Oxford that evening. Nick didn't need urging. Weldon's letter to Ben had mentioned the stone, calling it the "heartstone," and Nick was counting on some answers.

Terry had suggested this pub. "Can always use a pick-me-up," he'd said, humor softening his crisp accent.

In his photos, Terry appeared a somewhat disheveled man with his glasses slightly askew and his hair—what there was of it—in need of a comb. As Nick tried to find him in the crowded rooms, he felt a tug on his sleeve. Turning, he saw nothing but air. Another tug accompanied by the words, "Down here," lowered his gaze.

"Weldon Terry?"

He smiled. "How nice to meet you, Nick. Call me Weldon."

Weldon, looking precisely the same as in his photos—right down to the bow tie—sat in a wheelchair, his hand extended toward Nick. They shook. "Grab a drink and follow me."

"What're you drinking?" Nick asked.

"Guinness."

Nick ordered a couple of stouts, then followed Weldon back to a room off the entrance with two small octagonal tables and a dark wood-paneled fireplace. He settled into a bench as Weldon scooted up to the table.

"Thank you." Weldon accepted the pint from Nick, who noted that the one in front of him had an inch left. "Next one's my treat."

"Fair enough."

Weldon wheeled the chair back a few inches, then repositioned himself at a slight angle to the table, so he faced Nick. After pushing a thin wisp of hair off his freckled forehead, he nodded and said, "So, you're Nicholas."

"How did you know me?"

Weldon drained the one pint and pushed it aside, then wrapped his hand about the fresh one. "Ben was always showing off pictures of his children."

Nick studied the older man for a moment, trying to decide if he was being straight with him. Finally, he said, "That's

115

nice to hear. A bit difficult to believe, but nice to hear."

Weldon sat back in his chair. "And why is that?"

Shrugging, Nick said, "Ben wasn't the fatherly type."

"In ways, he was a very private, guarded man, wasn't he?" Then he added, almost offhand, "But we wouldn't be having this meeting at all were it not for those pictures."

Nick cocked his chin. "I don't follow."

As he submitted to Weldon's scrutiny, Nick detected an edge of shrewdness underlying the humor. "Over the phone, you were merely a voice stating you were Nick Llewellyn. You might have been anyone. But now that I've met you, I can see you're the same young man I saw in those pictures."

"Being careful," Nick said, nodding. He felt as though he was still being sized up.

"Always try to be," Weldon said with a sigh, as though that necessity was regrettable. Then he said, "Tell me, Nick, how's your mother doing?"

"Well enough. Considering." Usually when someone asked about Nick's mother, they didn't care to hear more than that. But Weldon was leaning forward slightly, eyebrows raised, as though waiting for Nick to continue. "I think she'll be fine." Weldon nodded and sat back.

Nick was anxious to get to the subject of Weldon's letter to Ben, but wary of broaching it head-on. He took a swallow of stout and asked, "How long did you know Ben?"

Weldon gazed up at the ceiling. "Oh, we've been friends fifteen years at least. We began a correspondence after he wrote me about one of my books. Next time he was over here, he looked me up. I did enjoy his company." He paused long enough to sample the stout. "We spent many an hour discussing the Arthurian legends. It was his passion."

"Don't I know that." Nick rubbed his thumb over a scar in the table. "I spent my youth jealous of a king who, if he ever lived, had been dead for more than a thousand years."

From Weldon's hurt look, Nick was afraid he'd insulted him by suggesting that Arthur never existed. But then Weldon said, "Ben was proud of you, Nick. Said you had the best free house in London."

"He would say that." He grinned. "He owned half of it."

"No matter." Weldon's response was immediate and Nick assumed this business arrangement was not news to him. "Ben wouldn't of said it, if it weren't so." He paused. "Always asking me down for a drink, he was. I meant to, but some things you put off because, well, there's always more time." Sighing, he shook his head.

"You're still welcome."

Weldon nodded his thanks.

Nick hesitated with his next question. "I confess I've not read much of your books, but from what I've gathered, you believe Arthur existed. Do you?"

"I do. And he did. Most historians concur. Perhaps not as a king, but certainly as a major chieftain. But that's not the Arthur you're referring to, is it? You're talking about the mythical Arthur."

"Yes. And you believe in him as well."

"I do! And you know what the beauty of it is? Who can prove me wrong?" He giggled. "Some think I'm a dotty old man, and for reasons other than Arthur, they may be right. But to believe in Arthur is to believe in myth, goodness and in possibilities. When you consider the state of the human condition today, what could be wrong with that?"

Nick had seen the same certainty in Ben, only Ben hadn't been giggly about it. "I suppose you and Ben were good for each other that way."

"Oh, yes." He gave Nick an odd look. "Why didn't you share his enthusiasm?"

"It hadn't done my father much good." Not ready to go into his family's history with the stone, Nick went on the offensive. "Actually, there's a specific part of the Arthurian legend I'm curious about. In your letter to Ben you mentioned the heartstone."

Weldon eyed him over the pint as he drank. After setting it down, he said, "Did Ben ever mention it to you?"

While Nick was tempted to tell him that Ben had spoken to him about it, he knew how easily that lie could be exposed. "He didn't."

Weldon nodded as though he'd expected that answer.

Nick realized that Weldon had the advantage in terms of knowledge, but Nick had a material advantage: a right to the stone. "The stone belonged to my family," he said.

"I know," Weldon said, as though this was not a point to be argued.

"So why is it that I'm the one who knows sod all about what's going on?"

"I wouldn't be offended, Nick—"

"I'm not offended. But it's my family."

"I know. But with your father's death, your family lost knowledge of their legend."

"That wasn't my doing." Nick's grip on the pint tightened. "And that means it doesn't belong to us anymore?" Whatever this legend was, he wasn't about to give it up.

Weldon shook his head and raised a finger. "Now, I didn't say that, Nick—"

"What *are* you saying?"

With a sigh, he lowered his hand to the table. His body sagged into the chair and when he spoke, he sounded sad. "I wish Ben were here." He shook his head slowly. "I don't know everything. What I do know would be so much better coming from him."

"He's not here." Nick tried to think of a way to draw it out of Weldon, and decided to see how far back his connection to his family went. "Did you know my father?"

He nodded. "We read together at Cambridge." After a pause, he added, "Elias was a good man. I was at his funeral. Ben and I probably met there, but neither of us recalls." A shrug. "Probably best at the time," he added and hurried on, explaining how years later when they began corresponding, Ben told Weldon the tale about Bedwyr and the heartstone, which got them both doing research. Once into the story, some of his animation returned. "Thought I'd heard them all. Caliburn—that's Welsh for Excalibur just as Bedwyr is Welsh for Bedivere . . ." He paused. "Actually, Caledfwich is the Welsh word, but it's a bit much to deal with. At any rate, Caliburn isn't often described in Arthurian literature and when it is, the hilt is usually engraved or plain, not embedded with gemstones, especially stones that change color."

"You're telling me that the heartstone came from King Arthur's sword?" Weldon had related that in such a matter-of-fact way that Nick wondered if he'd heard correctly.

"It did," Weldon said. He continued, "Several years ago I found an obscure little text written in the eighteenth century." His eyebrows bunched together as he frowned. "You said you went through Ben's books?"

"The ones in his flat."

"I'm surprised you didn't run across this one. I gave it to him as a gift one year."

"I didn't," he said, recalling the way the books in Ben's office had been shelved.

"It's titled *Y Stori O Bedwyr*."

"*Bedivere's Story*," Nick said, nodding.

The wheelchair creaked as Weldon leaned forward. "Do you speak Welsh?" He almost whispered the question, as though it were some secret, guarded language.

"Some." Nick shrugged it off, then asked, "You haven't a copy?"

"Just a photocopy." He reached into a brown leather portfolio wedged in the side of his chair and extracted a large envelope. "Wasn't the easiest thing for me to give away, but it was the tale I'd heard first from Ben, all right. Told from the point of view of Sir Bedwyr, the one-handed knight."

"One-handed?"

Weldon beamed. "Bedwyr's left hand was severed in battle. Hence, he became noted for his expertise with a spear. He was also a Welshman, which is why, in this version, the sword is Caliburn instead of Excalibur." As he talked, he drew a pile of paper from the envelope. Nick estimated there weren't more than sixty or seventy pages. "The book tells how Bedwyr served Arthur faithfully and how he came by the stone."

"How did he?"

Weldon eyed Nick as though he were evaluating the strength of his skepticism. "Think your Welsh is good enough to get you through this?"

"Probably." When his father was alive, they spoke Welsh around the house. Sometimes his dreams were in Welsh, especially as of late.

Weldon nodded as though that pleased him. "Good. Very good." He pushed the manuscript across the table. "I think you ought to read it for yourself."

Smiling, Nick said, "You're going to make me work for it."

Weldon turned serious. "You have to want this, Nick." He patted the pages. "Read the entire work. I think you'll find the ending especially interesting. Bedwyr chronicles a visit from Merlin. Myrddin in Welsh."

"Right." Nick glanced at the pages and took another drink. "What happened to Bedwyr after Arthur died?"

"Read and learn," he said. "I will tell you this—you are a descendant of Bedwyr."

It took some effort to temper Nick's first reaction, which was a clutching kind of thrill he hadn't felt since he was a kid. But then his practical side took over. To admit to Bedwyr's existence outside the pages of a book meant he had to accept Arthur as well. "No one can trace his family back that far. That's at least fifty generations. It's simply not possible."

"It is if the heartstone links them." He placed the manuscript's title page in front of Nick and tapped a stout finger on the author's name. "Is this name familiar to you at all?"

"Williamson's a common name."

"Ben traced your family's history back as far as he could. You are a descendant of this man. Thomas Williamson."

Nick shrugged. "All that means is the legend goes back as far as the eighteenth century, when one of my ancestors made up this story to go along with an odd stone."

"Nick." Weldon's tone scolded.

"Really. I mean, it's a long time since the supposed occurrence."

"Who better to describe the exploits of Bedwyr than a descendant?"

"I don't know." Nick wasn't ready to accept this, but he didn't want to hurt Weldon by saying that the story only proved that a fondness for fabrication ran in his family.

"You respected Ben, didn't you?" Weldon asked.

"Of course."

"Then how can you explain his convictions?"

"I never thought one required the other."

Weldon stared into his glass, then looked up at Nick. "Ben had the stone."

"He told you?"

Weldon shook his head. "No, but I knew. Ben was obsessed with the legend, and the stone. It was his life. The way he lived revolved around it. And he spent every moment away from you, your mother and his daughters looking for the sword. Did you think the reason Ben's archaeological digs produced little was because he didn't know what he was doing? He knew exactly what he was doing. He was looking for Caliburn. Nothing else mattered." Weldon nodded toward the manuscript. "Read this."

Nick fanned the pages filled with an old typeface as Weldon continued in a thoughtful tone. "No one ever believed the stone was lost with your father. For a time after Elias died, I think Rhys figured I had the stone."

Nick looked up. "Rhys?"

Weldon blinked, uncomprehending. "Rhys Llewellyn. Your uncle."

"My uncle?" Nick said, too stunned to manage a proper sentence.

Shifting in his wheelchair, Weldon seemed to be experiencing profound discomfort. "Good Lord, you really have been kept in the dark." His brows pulled together and he shook his head. "This can't be good," he muttered as though speaking to a third person at the table.

"For God's sake, man."

Weldon took a long swallow of his Guinness, licked a bit of foam off his upper lip and said, "All right. Your father and his brother had a relationship one might call strained. I believe the stone was at the heart of it. As the older brother, Rhys contended the stone was his birthright. For whatever reason, your grandfather didn't concur and he gave it to your father.

After your father died, Rhys insisted it was now his. I believe your mother told him she didn't have it. Said Elias must have had it when he drowned." As he spoke, he stared into the fireplace. "Elias must have had some apprehensions, and he gave the heartstone to Ben because he feared what would happen to it if he were to die suddenly."

"You think my father saw his own death?"

He turned toward Nick. "I do."

"Did Rhys ever come to know that Ben had the stone?"

"It's entirely possible, though I can't be certain because Ben never spoke of it." As he stared past Nick, he was sliding the pint back and forth on the table, creating miniature seiches of stout. "I do know that Ben had been compiling information regarding Rhys's activities—he mentioned it in a letter. Though I don't know what he'd come up with."

Nick regarded Weldon carefully. "Would Rhys kill Ben to get the stone?"

"Not if he didn't know where Ben had hidden it." He repositioned his pint on a coaster. "He couldn't afford to have the stone's whereabouts die with Ben."

"What if they did?"

Weldon shook his head. "Ben would've made some provision. He knew the threat Rhys posed. Ben was neither stupid nor foolish."

"What would Rhys do with the stone?"

"Your uncle . . ."

"What?" Nick prompted.

"Rhys is strange. Your father seldom spoke of him and I met him only briefly at your father's funeral. But if you're going to pursue him, Nick, I'd be careful. If I didn't know he was your father's brother, I'd swear . . ." he hesitated again, "well, he's evil. I believe that. I can't say how. Not that I won't, I just can't put a name to it. Be very careful about him,

Nick. I believe with all my heart that he mustn't get the heartstone."

"You believe it's that powerful?"

"If the tale is true, then the stone has been handed down through the centuries. One individual of each generation becomes the stone's caretaker. Holding onto it until . . ."

"Until what?"

"The sword surfaces."

"Right," Nick said, not bothering to hide his skepticism this time. Sitting back, Nick pondered the words. "Whether I believe the story or not, I have to find it. It never should have got away from my family."

He drained his stout and saw that the old man, who might or might not be crazy, was watching him. "I wouldn't get too attached to it, Nick." When Nick didn't respond, he added, "It may be that your family's role as the stone's custodian is finished."

"And I suppose you know what's going to happen to it."

"It must be returned to Caliburn." Weldon patted the manuscript. "Read this."

"So, what happens once the sword is intact?"

"Arthur returns."

"Right." He paused. "*King* Arthur?"

Weldon tapped a stubby finger on the manuscript and gave Nick an emphatic look.

Nick sat back against the bench with a deep sigh. He couldn't sustain his anger with Ben. He would not have wanted to die with his secret; it must have made his dying hard. "What was Ben doing . . . at the end?"

The old man looked at him, a strange glow in his eyes. Leaning over the table, he lowered his voice and said, "I believe he was on to Caliburn." He nodded once. "He already had the heartstone. What else could it have been?"

Chapter 14

Under normal circumstances, Olivia would never arrive before her date, but she didn't know Cliff Bradshaw yet. He could be the fidgety type, and she didn't want him trying to call her at the Savoy. So, she was waiting for him, under the solicitous eye of Simpson's maitre'd, and wishing she'd worn something other than black, which blended into the dark-paneled walls of this old restaurant. Not that she'd had a choice.

Still, the little black dress had fared well, considering it had spent the afternoon in her handbag. Most of the wrinkles had disappeared once she put it on and any that were left, well, it was a great dress. When Cliff Bradshaw came through the door, the look he gave her acknowledged that fact.

"Sorry I'm late," he said, kissing her cheek.

"I just got here," she said and the maitre'd', a short, balding man with lively eyes, gave her a conspiratorial smile, greeted Cliff by name, then showed them to a table.

The room was elegant, with high ceilings, dark walls, crisp white linens and the clink of glasses and silverware. The rich smell of beef and gravy made her slightly nauseous. She preferred salmon to steak and would not have eaten wild game on a bet. But she did follow Cliff's suggestion and ordered the Guinness soup as a starter.

She was attentive, asking him about where he lived, his taste in art, theater. She let him boast a little—his prized possession was an original Landseer.

"Isn't he the one who does the . . ." she paused, as though collecting her thoughts, hoping he'd finish for her because she had no idea who the guy was.

"He's a wildlife painter." He refilled her wine glass with the unspectacular Merlot he'd ordered and raved about.

"That's right," she said, nodding in agreement.

"I'm quite the outdoorsman," he said. "Enjoy hunting, fishing." He drank some wine. "What about you?"

"I fish," she said.

"What kind?"

"Trout," she said because she liked the way they tasted and thought that fly-fishing looked like a graceful sport. "My father used to take us to Colorado for the fishing." In truth, she'd spent two incredible nights at the Broadmoor in Colorado Springs with a kickboxing instructor named Rudy Chen, and that was all she knew of Colorado.

"The American West," Cliff sighed as though he'd spent his fondest years there. It was enough to send him off on a series of anecdotes centering around his travels to Montana and Wyoming. Some tales involved fishing, most didn't.

By the time they brought the cart with the beef and Yorkshire pudding for Cliff, Olivia had to keep blinking her eyes to keep them from glassing over. He dug into his entree like a starved wolf and, as Olivia picked at her salmon, she asked if he'd learned anything more about Ben.

"Yes, in fact." He gulped down his mouthful. "Just an hour ago I spoke with the investigator Walter had hired. Seems your father was last seen in Hugh Town on St. Mary's. That's in the Isles of Scilly."

"I talked to my sister today and she said Ben mentioned a place called Alyssum. That's in the same group, isn't it?"

Cliff was nodding. "Well, that's good then. I've arranged transportation to Hugh Town. Tomorrow afternoon. I'll see about getting over to Alyssum." He patted her hand. "We'll get this sorted out."

She smiled her gratitude, then brushed her fingers across the back of his hand and said, "Cliff, how long do you think it will be before Ben's estate is settled?"

He dipped a chunk of beef into a puddle of gravy. It was the first time she'd seen him without an immediate reply and she saw it as a warning.

"I'm sorry," she said. "I must sound like a terrible person. It's just that, well, my sister asked." He looked up at her and his eyes had softened. "I promised I wouldn't tell anyone, but you need to understand." She paused. "You see, she's in some financial trouble. I've offered to help, of course, but, well, Max has always seen me as the competition. She'd never take any help from me. It would be like losing." She set her fork across the plate with the salmon not half finished. "It's hard to explain. Maybe when you meet her . . ."

He raised a hand. "No need to go on. I've a cousin just like that. Resents the fact that I've made something of myself and he's teaching the classics to secondary school students."

She nodded her understanding.

"We'll get this taken care of as soon as humanly possible, Olivia."

"Thank you, Cliff."

"Curious thing about that stone, eh?" He chewed thoughtfully. "Don't suppose your sister knew anything about it."

She frowned and shook her head. "Nothing."

Cliff nodded as though he'd expected that. "Perhaps it's nothing to do with all this."

"Probably not."

After dinner, they walked outside together, toward that moment of truth. When he nuzzled behind her ear, she could smell the after-dinner brandy on his breath and she knew she had him.

But then he said, "What say we go to the Savoy? Hate to waste your room. It's just down the street. We can practically walk there."

"Oh," she said, letting him hear the disappointment.

"What?"

"Oh, nothing." She shrugged one shoulder. "It's just . . ." She bowed her head as she smiled, letting her hair fall over her right eye. "Landseer. I'd love to see his work."

Cliff smiled his approval. "Well," he said, "I suppose that's possible." He frowned. "But—"

She wrapped her hand around his arm. "It's just a room."

Chapter 15

After spending three hours hunched over her computer, Max pulled herself away from the Internet and did some stretches to relieve the tension that had claimed her shoulders. She collected the pile of paper the printer had spewed out and left her office. Fiona was in the living room, settled into the red beanbag chair, her large paws draped over its side. She looked up at Max, issued a loud, wide yawn, and returned her chin to her paws.

Max spread the papers over her dining room table, dividing them into three groups: Alyssum, Arthur Penn, and the Caliburnus Foundation. All three had potential connections to Ben, but as far as she could tell, none of them had anything to do with a stone. She got a gray legal pad and a pen from her briefcase and wrote the words "Alyssum," "Penn" and "Caliburnus" across the top. She'd start with connections to Ben.

Alyssum, one of a remote group of islands, claimed an Arthurian connection. The Scillies became islands in the final battle between King Arthur and his nephew, Mordred, when the king and his army were pushed west beyond Land's End. To prevent Mordred's reinforcements from following, Merlin summoned up an earthquake, engulfing the soldiers as the land submerged. Arthur and Mordred were the first to die on the newly created islands, which had been the land's highest peaks.

Max had never heard this particular aspect of the Arthurian legend, but almost every area in England claimed some variation of the myth. Ben would have known about it, of course. Max respected his love of the legend, the king, and was convinced her father had become the man she loved and admired because of his devotion. Beneath the "Alyssum" column she wrote: "King Arthur."

Despite Arthur Penn's reclusive reputation, Max found a photo of him in an article on the Penn family. As she'd come to suspect, he was the bearded man in the picture with Ben. As soon as she made that connection, she tried to call him. It had taken almost twenty minutes of overseas operators for her to discover that Mr. Penn had an unlisted number. No surprise. Wealthy recluses tended to be like that. She'd try to find an e-mail address.

According to the article she was looking at now, Arthur Penn's family had owned Alyssum since the 1300s. Although none of the articles she'd uncovered indicated a link between Arthur Penn and King Arthur, Max was certain there was one, because fifteen years ago Penn had established the Caliburnus Foundation. Caliburn was Welsh for Excalibur. On the pad, beneath Arthur's name she wrote: "King Arthur."

The pile of articles on the foundation portrayed it as a

well-meaning organization. Grants of varying amounts were awarded to individuals involved in projects that "elevate humanity." She found an interview with Arthur Penn, in which he talked about the foundation. "Our philosophy is based on the belief that one person can make a difference. I know that sounds trite, but that doesn't make it any less true. It must be true, else we are doomed. That's where it starts. One person. We give our grants to people with ideas that excite them. Ideas that excite us because they excite them. It doesn't have to be anything earth-shattering, such as discovering the cure for cancer or peace in our time. In fact we seek out causes that might have trouble receiving funds.

"We're not unique. Thank God for that. There are a lot of people making a difference. I just want to be one of them." Later in the article, he said, "We have the advantage of being small. We don't answer to a lot of people. Only five of us on the board assign the grants."

Several of the articles featured grant recipients and, on the surface, their projects seemed worthwhile. A woman in Nepal worked among the leper colonies. Another studied owls in Madagascar. A young man named Greg was trying to get Western European universities to organize into an international basketball league. A teacher in rural Virginia had discovered the positive effects of classical music on learning. Students in his district were now listening to Mozart during study periods. One incident the foundation didn't claim, but had been attributed to Caliburnus, involved a pilot who flew into a game preserve where men armed with automatic rifles hunted down tired, old zoo animals. According to the article, the pilot and an assistant relieved the hunters of their weapons, and transported the animals to an actual preserve. Mostly good, worthwhile causes.

One article, however, related the activities of a group in

Arizona that had received a government grant and money from several environmental organizations for some innovative energy-efficient housing. Caliburnus was one of two foundations that had backed one or more of the group's members. Five years ago, the group was linked to several bombings targeting government offices. She wondered at what point Caliburnus had given them money. Perhaps "elevating humanity" had many interpretations. If Ben was investigating this foundation and found more questionable endowments, maybe it was looking less like bad judgment and more like they were funding terrorists. Research like that could get a person killed.

As Penn had noted, there were five members of the foundation's board: Fletcher Winwood, a genetics scientist; James Nelson, president of a wildlife organization; Vonelle Fiedler, violinist and CEO of a skin care company; Wallace Harvey, head of a drug company (an asterisk followed his name); and Arthur Penn.

She followed the asterisk and found that Harvey had been on the board for less than a year, after replacing Moira Hoffman who, at age fifty-two, had died in a skiing accident in Switzerland. A news item said there had been no witnesses, and authorities believed she'd become disoriented and skied off a cliff.

Searches on each of the board members revealed that they were a diverse group, living in Europe and the United States. She noted that Fletcher Winwood lived in Winnetka, a Chicago suburb. Once she had a little more information, she'd give him a call.

The connection to Ben was sheer speculation. If he'd applied for a grant, what would it have funded? As far as she knew, Briggs College footed the bill for his digs. Maybe if they'd had a disagreement, Ben would have sought funds elsewhere. She made a note to call the college. Meanwhile, she sent an e-mail to the Caliburnus Foundation, addressed to Arthur Penn, and asked when he'd last seen Ben and if he had any idea where he was now.

She stretched out her legs beneath the table. The stone sat winking at her from beside the water glass. What was the stone's role in all this? She supposed it was possible that Ben had unearthed it in one of his digs. Maybe he'd been digging on Alyssum. If so, wouldn't it be Arthur Penn's stone? And what about this guy Olivia told her about—Nick Llewellyn? What about his family's claim to the stone? Ben couldn't have stolen it. He wouldn't do such a thing.

When she added two more columns to her list—"The Stone" and "Ben"—it was easy to see the connection. Hard to accept, perhaps, but easy to see. Except for the stone, which was an unknown factor, the one thing linking each column was King Arthur. Ben's specialty was ancient weapons. Swords, in particular. Swords, important swords, sometimes had gems in their hilts. And, to Ben, there was no more important sword than Excalibur—Caliburn. But, how could he know where the stone belonged unless he'd also found the sword?

Had the stone come from Alyssum? Then she remembered Elliott Schiff telling her alexandrite had been discovered in Russia. Was it even possible to find it on Alyssum?

She found her purse and her little notebook where she'd written his home phone number when he'd offered it. A woman answered on the first ring. After Max identified herself and asked for Elliott, the woman said, "He's not here." Her voice sounded strained.

"Can you take a message for him?"

"I'm sorry," she said and stopped.

Max gave her a few moments and then said, "I spoke with

him this morning at the museum. He gave me his home number. If this isn't—"

"No," the woman said. "This is Elliott's sister. He's been in an accident. This afternoon. He was hit by a car while crossing McFetridge."

"Oh, God. Is he all right?"

"He came out of surgery about an hour ago. Serious but stable."

"Stable," she echoed. "That's good."

The woman murmured something in agreement and, after wishing him well, Max got off the phone. She wanted to know more but, either out of fear or consideration, she couldn't bring herself to ask.

Chapter 16

The past twenty-four hours had been brutal on the people in Max's life. Ben was declared missing and presumed dead, Olivia was nearly killed by a bomb in London, Walter Bacon would have been killed if he hadn't been dead already, and Elliott Schiff was hit by a car. Four incidents that would have seemed random except for one thing: the stone in her pocket.

Max switched on the radio, tuning to the all-news station. If Elliott had been hit by some woman trying to keep her kids from fighting in the backseat, that was one thing. If it had been a hit and run, that was something else.

Taking out the stone, she sat cross-legged on the braided area rug. She wasn't sure she believed everything Elliott told her about stones and their power, but stroking its glossy surface did seem to calm her. Sort of like lying on the couch with a book in one hand and her other resting on Fiona, feeling the rise and fall of the dog's warm chest.

". . . Curator Elliott Schiff's condition . . ." Max's head snapped up. ". . . has been upgraded from critical to stable after four hours of surgery at Northwestern Hospital. Schiff was the victim of a hit and run this afternoon. Police are interviewing witnesses, but at this time . . ."

Max let herself fall back against the rug and stared up at the white ceiling, thinking if she looked away she would spin out of control. She'd known it was hit and run, even as she'd decided not to ask. Ben, Olivia, Walter Bacon and now Elliott. One dead, one possibly dead and two very lucky. To think that these occurrences had been coincidence would be foolish. Then there was Ben's marriage to a woman Max had never heard of. On one level, it was a deception that forced her to question the very basis of her relationship with Ben. At the same time, the profound trust she placed in that relationship helped her to believe that Ben had good reason for his actions. Then there was Nick Llewellyn. If his claim to the stone was legitimate, why would Ben put it in a museum? Unless he was making it safe for Nick.

As she lay on the rug, trying to make sense of it all, she heard the radio voice announce traffic and weather at six-thirty-eight. "Damn." She jumped up and pocketed the stone. In twenty minutes she was supposed to be at Grey's. It wasn't much time to get ready and walk the dog. Walk Fiona. "Damn." She heard Fiona lapping water from the toilet bowl. Walking the dog around the block had suddenly taken on a menacing aspect. Once she realized that, it angered her more than scared her. These walks had become a stress reliever; she needed them as much as the dog did. She wouldn't be spooked by this. On the other hand, she didn't need to be reckless either.

"Out, Fiona?" Fiona's collar jangled as the dog trotted over to her.

She slipped on her waterproof poncho, then got a paper lunch bag from a kitchen drawer and tore a couple paper towels off the roll. She put these into her left pocket, along with her keys. After some digging through several other drawers, she found the can of mace she'd received as part of a Christmas gift last year from a friend and put it into her right pocket. The stone remained in her jeans pocket.

By the time she pulled Fiona's leash off the kitchen hook, the dog was prancing in place by the door, wagging her tail.

"Let's go," she said, hooking the leash to Fiona's collar.

The night had turned cool and though it wasn't raining hard anymore, the wind had picked up. For a while she tried to keep her hood in place, then gave up. She'd need to spend a few minutes with the hair dryer before going up to Grey's. A car passed, tires hissing against the asphalt, and strains of "Come by My Window" faded into the night. It was quiet, but lighted apartment windows reminded her that it was early. Most people were probably involved in dinner or its cleanup.

Max and Fiona walked east to Halsted, where pedestrian traffic picked up, then they angled back west and into a small park off Sheridan Road.

After much snuffling about, Fiona found an acceptable toilet. Max waited, unfolding the paper bag, and when Fiona had finished, used the paper towels to clean up the pile and deposited it in the bag. As she scrunched up the bag's edges, Max conceded that there were times when she wished Ben had given her a poodle.

Normally, Max would have spent some time running Fiona, but they were going to be late for dinner at Grey's, so they headed home. A half block from the apartment building, Fiona's ears went up, her attention focused directly ahead. A moment later, Max heard footsteps and saw a figure walking toward them. He'd come around the corner from Grove.

Fiona's growl started as a low rumble, unbroken except when she sucked in a breath. With her ears laid back, jowls twitching, and her gentle soul buried deep, the dog made a formidable ally. Max had seen her respond like this only twice before, and both times the mailman had been involved. Max transferred the leash and bag to her left hand and slipped her right into her pocket, thumbed off the top of the mace can and wrapped her hand around it.

When the man was close enough for Max to see that he wore a police uniform, she told herself that Fiona was growling because of the uniform. Then she tried to think of the last time she'd seen a beat cop in this neighborhood. She shortened up on the leash.

He approached, slowed and came to a stop, nodding to her, his thumb hooked in his belt. He was of average height and build with a thick scar on the curve of his chin. Looked like a dog tried to chew it off. "Evening," he nodded at her. "I'm checking out some complaints about a prowler. You happen to see anything?"

"No." His partner and the squad car could be looking elsewhere.

He stared at Max for a moment, then looked down at Fiona. "That's a big dog you've got there."

"She is." Max could feel Fiona quivering against her thigh. "She's not good with strangers," she said, although it couldn't have been further from the truth.

Raindrops beaded his dark leather jacket and the bill of his hat. "A dog that size, you've got to be careful. Could hurt someone."

Fiona shifted and her low-pitched growl faltered. "She's okay."

The cop glanced toward the street as a car approached,

then turned back to Max. Even though his eyes were in the shadow of his cap, she could feel them on her. It occurred to her that, just because he was a cop, she didn't have to wait to be dismissed. She gave the leash a gentle pull and started to move away.

The cop said, "Maybe I should walk you home." Glancing around, he added, "What with that prowler and all."

Fiona retreated behind Max's legs, pulling at the leash.

She didn't want him to know where she lived, and she surely didn't want him near her door when she got there. "That's okay. I'm not going home." She squeezed the can of mace. It was probably too soon to use it.

"You shouldn't be out."

He put his fists on his hips and, in doing so, pushed back his jacket so she got a good look at the gun on his hip. Fiona's growl had become a protracted whine.

"I've got a hundred-and-twenty-pound dog. No one's going to bother me."

He stepped aside, as though waiting for her to move first. When she did, he fell into step behind her. Fiona minced along with her back hunched and her tail between her legs. Max jerked the leash, trying to get the dog to straighten up.

"Quiet night," he said, glancing up and down the street that was now empty except for parked cars.

Max saw the light in Grey's window and picked up her pace.

"Hey. Slow down." He grabbed her forearm, jerked her back a step, and didn't let go. "You've got something that belongs to me."

It would have been a good time for the mace, but she couldn't use her arm. "I don't know what you're talking about."

"I think you do." He let go of her to draw the gun, which

he pointed at Fiona's bowed head. "I am not a dog person."

Not Fiona. "It's in my apartment."

"Where in your apartment?"

"A beanbag chair." She was squeezing the can so hard she thought it would explode.

He shifted his gaze from Max to Fiona as his arm went rigid.

"Don't!" Max yanked the dog backwards.

"Why don't you show me?"

The scar on his chin had stretched, tightened, and she realized he was smiling as he took aim at Fiona who practically had her nose between Max's knees.

The noise started softly and could have been wind in the trees. But then she saw headlights and knew she was hearing tires on wet pavement. She drew the mace from her pocket, her finger on its nozzle. Before she could aim it, he grabbed her wrist and wrenched it hard. She yelped and the can clattered to the pavement. Without thinking, she swung Fiona's bag and smacked him full on the face.

As he let out a sound that was part surprise and part disgust, his grip on her faltered. Max yanked her arm free and bolted toward the street, pulling Fiona along behind her. She dodged between two parked cars. The moving car, nearly on top of her, blasted its horn, swerved and slammed on its brakes.

"What the hell!" The driver was rolling down his window. He had a high forehead and baggy eyes. "Stupid bitch. Why don't you look the hell where you're going?"

"Sorry." She glanced over her shoulder; the sidewalk was empty. Then she looked up and saw Grey's window just two buildings away.

"You're sorry! What the hell! This car is two weeks old. How sorry would you've been if I'd plowed into that goddamned Civic?" He went on.

It was her Civic, but she didn't mention it. Neither did she bother to thank him for driving down the street at this moment. She and Fiona were not hurt, the car hadn't hit anyone and the "cop" was gone. That was all that mattered. She wasn't going to stay for the lecture.

"Home, girl," Max said, and Fiona nearly dragged her back across the parkway. They didn't stop running until they were in the apartment's vestibule. She managed to unlock the inner door without fumbling, and they were through it in less time than she would have believed possible. She took the steps two at a time, without looking back, and didn't stop until she was knocking at the door to 4C.

Grey's welcoming smile faded at the sight of her. As she stood there, gasping for breath, her hair wet and her dog trembling, she realized that she was now placing Grey in danger.

"I shouldn't be here," she blurted.

He took her arm and gently pulled her into the room. "Come in and tell me about it." He shut the door behind her.

She let him take Fiona's leash, and watched as he unhooked it from her collar. The dog licked his hand and, head bowed, went straight for a corner in the living room where she curled up in a tight ball. Max was thinking that was exactly what she wanted to do when Grey said, "Why don't you give me your coat and I'll give you a drink." He helped her off with her poncho and hung it on a coat rack by the door. "You look like you could use one."

"Scotch," she said.

While he put away her poncho and got the drinks, she sat on the edge of a soft, mushroom-colored sofa. The lush strings of a guitar concerto flowed softly from a stereo speaker. Fiona was watching her, but when Max made the

141

clicking sound that usually brought her over, the dog didn't budge.

"I've never seen Fiona like that," Grey said as he handed Max a small, square glass containing an inch of amber liquid and no ice. He sat in a chair next to the sofa it matched and waited, holding his own glass. "What happened?"

"I took her for a walk. Just before we came. We ran into someone." It was impossible to explain this without telling him everything. "I don't know where to start."

After a few moments of silence, Grey said, "Does this have to do with your father's disappearance?" He was sitting forward, elbows on his knees, his eyes searching hers.

She nodded and sipped the Scotch. It had a smoky flavor and left a warm trail down her throat. "This is good," she said, and set the drink on one of two slate coasters he'd placed on the coffee table.

"When I heard that Ben was missing and presumed dead, my first reaction was no, he can't be. I'd know. But now . . ." She shook her head and tried to blink away the membrane of tears. "All this other stuff has happened." Her voice sounded ragged. "Remember how yesterday I was waiting for a phone call?"

"I remember."

"Well, his name is Elliott Schiff and he's a curator over at the Field Museum. I saw him this morning and he gave me this." She leaned back and stretched her right leg so she could dig into her pocket. Then she pulled out the stone and set it on the coffee table.

Grey didn't move, just stared at the green gem. After a moment he shifted his eyes toward Max. "Why?"

"Ben had given it to the museum on loan." She explained how that loan ended with her call to Elliott.

"That's a bit odd, isn't it?"

"Elliott said as much."

He reached for the stone, stopped and looked to Max for permission. She nodded. He picked it up between his thumb and forefinger, as though taking care not to smudge it.

"Elliott says it's alexandrite."

Grey nodded. "Whatever it is, it's beautiful." He glanced at her. "You never knew of this before?"

"Never."

He returned the stone to the coffee table. "What's this other stuff you mentioned?"

She took another, larger drink of Scotch. "Olivia, my sister, called from London today. Walter Bacon, Ben's lawyer, was killed, and Olivia and another man nearly died in a bomb explosion." She told him what had happened. "And then I tried to call Elliott Schiff just before I went out and walked Fiona tonight, and he's been in a hit and run accident."

"Is he—"

"Serious, but stable."

"And then you went for your walk?" he prompted.

She nodded. "And we ran into the man disguised as a cop—I can't believe he actually was one—who tried to take the stone. He had a gun, threatened Fiona with it."

He set his glass down and clasped his hands together. "How did you manage to get away?"

"I hit him with a bag of dog shit."

First his eyebrows shot up and then his mouth twitched a couple times, as if he were making an effort to keep a straight face.

She allowed herself a small grin. "That'll teach him to take away my mace."

When he finally let go, Max realized that her intention had been to hear him laugh. She liked the sound of it.

But he cut it short and adopted a look of concern as he

shook his head. "I'm sorry, Max. This isn't at all funny."

"That's okay."

Grey paused to pet Fiona, who had relinquished the corner and come to lie by the coffee table.

"What do you make of it?" she asked, a little surprised to find how much his thoughts on this mattered to her. She barely knew him.

He gave Fiona a final pat, looked up at her and said, "I think you should go to the police."

"I know I should."

"But?"

"There's more. I just learned that Ben had gotten married a year ago. Neither Olivia nor I knew about it. We've never met the woman. And her grown son—the one who was in the office with Olivia when the bomb went off—claims the stone has been in his family for generations." She picked up her glass, but didn't drink. "Maybe he's full of it. I don't know. But it's possible that Ben came by the stone illegally. If that's the case, Elliott Schiff would also be in trouble—"

"Elliott Schiff is already in trouble."

He had a point. She drained the glass.

Grey got up and went into the kitchen and came back with a plate of crackers and a couple spreads. "Almost forgot to be a host."

He placed it on the coffee table then poured a little more Scotch into their glasses.

"Look," he sat on the edge of his chair, facing her, "if there's a bloke running around passing himself off as a copper, they're going to want to know." He paused. "And what if he is a cop? As to your father. What if he's still alive? Wouldn't it make sense to have an international, cooperative effort to find him?"

"Of course," she said, feeling stupid for missing an obvious point.

Then it hit her in a wave. Everything. She pressed her fingers to her mouth, trying to hold back the sob welling up from her lungs. The room blurred. Before she realized he'd moved, Grey was sitting on the couch with his arm around her. She slumped against him and he stroked her hair as she cried quietly into his shoulder. This felt so good. To cry and to be held. And how strange, with all the turmoil of the past day and a half, to find that she was open to this man.

After a couple of minutes, her tears eased and she drew away, pulling down the cuff of her sweatshirt to wipe her face. She wanted to blot some of the tears off his sweater, but felt that would be too intimate.

"Sorry about that little outburst," she said.

"Glad to be of service." He left the room, then returned with a box of white tissues, which he set beside her on the couch.

Max plucked one out and blew her nose. "My grandmother never went anywhere without one of these tucked in her sleeve cuff." She laughed a little. "I just use my cuff."

When he didn't respond, she glanced at him and caught his expression before he looked away. She couldn't quite define it—maybe sad, maybe tender—but it wasn't the way you looked at a person you hardly knew.

"I guess I will go to the police," she said.

"I'm not saying you should do anything tonight, Max. Sleep on it." He seemed to hesitate, then said, "Why don't you sleep here tonight? I've a sofa bed in my office I understand is quite comfortable."

"Thanks," she said. "I may take you up on that."

Their eyes met and then shied away. A moment later,

when the timer went off, Grey got up quickly. "The pasta calls."

Max helped herself to a cracker with an olive spread. She licked a bit off the tip of her thumb, wondering how this evening would have gone if this had been a normal date. Would it even have happened? She told herself not to over-analyze it. She was here, something with basil and tomatoes was for dinner, she had a place to spend the night where she didn't have to be scared. Tomorrow she would go to the police.

Chapter 17

"I've got another job for you."

That voice. God, Earl hated the way she crept up on him. One second he was sitting in his apartment, drinking a beer and watching a rerun of "Green Acres," and the next Jillian the bitch was standing behind him. Didn't he lock that door? As he slumped lower into the couch, one of its springs poked him in the butt. He shifted his stocky frame and removed his feet from a crate that doubled as a footstool and dinner table. Without looking up at her, he said, "I thought we were finished."

She laughed. It wasn't a nice sound.

He took a couple of swallows from the can of beer, determined to not let her see him rattled.

She moved around the couch and sat on the crate, blocking his view of the TV. He figured she knew that already, so he didn't mention it. She held the remote in her

gloved hand and watched him, that little smile at the corners
of her mouth.

"Besides, I got plans for later," he said.

"I know you do. My plans."

Earl sucked on a gap between his teeth as he studied her.
With her blond hair all thick and shiny, she looked like one of
them models, though her square jaw always seemed clenched
and sometimes those broads had to smile. Earl wasn't sure
this one could pull it off. Lonny always said no woman really
looked like that without lots of help and a good cameraman.
Take one of them out from in front of the lens and there's a
big difference. But Earl had the feeling this one always looked
the same.

"Sorry." Earl shrugged, hoping to project a cool he'd
never had. "I did what you asked. You said somebody else'd
do the rest." He took a drink of beer, which tasted flat now.

"He's busy," she said. When she continued, there was a
change to her tone that Earl didn't like much. "I understand
you're good at break-ins. There's an item I want you to get for
me." She moved over to the couch and sat right next to him,
covering his hand with hers. Earl felt the jolt of cold right
through her glove and he wanted to pull away, but he didn't
dare.

"Why don't you get it yourself?" Truth was, even though
they were paying him pretty damned good, he'd rather work
for himself. He didn't like risking jail time because someone
else didn't have the balls to pull off a heist.

She crossed one leg over the other, and Earl could see the
sharp angles of her kneecap beneath the fabric that slipped
out between the edges of her trench coat. "But Earl, you're
the professional."

Earl tried to swallow. "You're gonna have to get someone
else. Like I said, I'm busy." He looked into her eyes. Big mis-

take. They sucked him in, holding him in a grasp as sure as if she'd planted her foot on his windpipe.

"Get unbusy," she said. "And then I want you to take care of someone for me."

Earl tried to swallow and failed. "Listen," he managed, "all I do anymore is break-ins. That's it."

"I think you're in a bit deep to suddenly develop a code of ethics. Don't you think, Earl?"

"I don't take care of people."

"It's that woman you've been following," she said like she hadn't heard him. "I'm doubling your fee." She reached into her purse. "My father says that anyone whose guilt can't be assuaged by money is probably too sensitive to survive in this world. Don't you think that's true, Mr. Jessup?" She pulled a pistol out of her purse and pointed it at him.

Earl felt his bowels loosen.

"I think you're a survivor," she said and handed it to him.

Earl looked away. He wouldn't take the gun. "There's some things I don't do. That's one of 'em." Earl couldn't believe he had the balls to say that to this ice queen. She wasn't arguing either. Maybe the next time he looked, she'd be gone. Out of his life. He turned. No way.

Now she held the gun in one hand and a photo in the other. It was just a mug shot, but Earl could tell from the size of the guy's head and what he could see of his shoulders that it was a mug shot of a big man. His blond hair was short and bristly and through it Earl saw a swastika tattooed an inch or so above his hairline. His eyes looked like dead things.

Earl grunted. "Who's that supposed to be?"

"This gentleman resides in the same cell block as your brother Lonny. His nickname is 'Pickax.' " She waited long enough for that to sink in. "He's been convicted of three murders. Rather grisly ones, I've been told. He's in for life without parole, so he doesn't worry about being on his best behavior."

Earl looked at her and didn't say anything.

The edges of her mouth twisted into a smile. "He owes a friend of mine a favor, who in turn owes me a favor."

Earl had never hit a woman. He'd come real close that time with LuAnn when she told him she'd been screwing that scrawny bartender at O'Brian's, but he put his fist through her stereo speaker instead. The only thing stopping him now was Lonny. He took the gun. The short-barreled .38 was cold and heavy. He hated handguns. Rifles he liked. Rifles were about hunting and shooting. Handguns were about killing.

"She'll be out for the evening," she said. "I want you to break into her apartment, look for a stone. It's green, polished, and forty carats." She showed him a drawing. "This is what forty carats looks like. It could be in a beanbag chair or somewhere else in the apartment, but I doubt it. She's probably got it on her, so you won't find it. I want you to wait for her to return. Then take it. And kill her."

Earl closed his eyes and tried to swallow. "I don't—"

"I don't care," she snapped.

"She's got a dog," he said, recalling its huge, black and white head.

"Kill the dog too," she snapped, and all Earl could think of was the witch in the Oz movie. "Kill her. And then I want you to bring the stone to me at my hotel."

"Guns make too much noise."

"Then use a knife." She leaned into him. "Or a pickax." Around clenched teeth she added, "Just kill her."

When he didn't respond, she said, "Earl. Remember. I'll be waiting."

He heard the door close when she left.

Warmth returned to his chest first, then his extremities,

like oil flowing through his veins and arteries. He let his head drop back to the couch. A few seconds later, he heard the theme song to "Green Acres," as the ending credits played.

Shit, why did Lonny have to go and get himself locked up? If Lonny were here, the ice queen wouldn't be jerking him around. Shit.

What color were those eyes anyway?

Chapter 18

They ate by candlelight at a small, round table in the dining room and Grey asked her what she'd learned about Alyssum. She told him everything she could remember, including the seemingly bizarre notion that the stone came from Excalibur.

He considered this, chewing thoughtfully, and said, "Wouldn't that be something?"

"And it would almost justify Ben's behavior. It wouldn't explain it, of course—there's a lot more to know—but I could understand his motivations."

Grey nodded, then said, "Have you considered that by keeping all this secret perhaps he was trying to protect you?"

"Too late for that now," she said. "I'm flying to London tomorrow." She sipped the cabernet. "Frustrating. That's where I've got to go to find any answers."

She realized she'd been dominating the conversation and, while Grey seemed interested, he might just be quite good at being polite. After swallowing a bite of the tomato sauce, which was spicy with olives and capers, she asked him what it was.

"I suppose you could call it my version of arrabbiata."

"It's delicious," she said. "I'm not much of a cook," she admitted. "I'm limited to things that come in boxes. Lean Cuisine. Brownie mix. Cereal." The Scotches and now the cabernet made her a little chattier than usual.

"There's really not much to cooking."

Max shook her head. "I burn stuff. Don't mean to. It just burns."

"Have you tried turning down the heat?"

"Doesn't matter. I forget about it." She curled spaghetti around her fork. "I think that's why I liked that Scotch we had before dinner. To me, charred is a flavor."

He laughed. "No one ever taught you to cook?"

"It was never a priority. My mother died when I was five. After a brief stint with a great aunt, Olivia and I were reared by Ben and a series of graduate assistants. Raised on pizza and submarine sandwiches." She paused to reflect on those years in southern Wisconsin, which were reasonably happy ones, especially when Ben was there. "We learned some interesting things, but cooking was not one of them."

"Do you remember your mother?"

"She was a beautiful woman. Olivia looks a lot like her."

"What did you inherit from her?" He cocked his chin as though trying to figure it out for himself.

"I still use her camera. Picked it up when I was eight."

"A thirty-five millimeter?"

Max nodded. "A Nikkormat. They don't make them anymore."

"That's a rather complicated camera for an eight-year-old."

"It took me a while to figure it out. But," she recalled, "I had a lot of encouragement. Olivia loved to have her picture taken. She sensed at a tender age how photogenic she was."

They each talked about their careers, comparing notes on teaching. He'd taught history in various schools in Britain, mostly public, and was now living off some investments.

"You're young to be retired," she said. "You must be a smart investor."

"I had some good advice. Got lucky."

"How do you keep busy?"

"You're not the first person to put that question to me. It's really no problem. This is Chicago, after all. Lots to do. Books to read." He smiled. "Can you imagine having all the time in the world to read all the books you've meant to read?"

"That is bliss, isn't it?"

"I believe that's the definition."

He asked her about Ben, what he was like and how he was as a father.

Max had finished her plate and helped herself to a last piece of bread.

"Ben wasn't around a lot, but he was supportive."

"In what way?" Grey split the last of the cabernet between their glasses.

She thought for a moment. "For example, that great aunt I mentioned enrolled Olivia and me in the local Catholic school." She sipped the wine. "Well, one day our teacher was telling us how St. Bernadette saw the Virgin Mary. Had conversations with her. I raised my chubby little hand and told her I'd seen a fairy in our back yard in England, although I hadn't spoken with her. Well, the nun said that was impossible. Fairies didn't exist. I said I'd seen one, and then I argued that no one could prove they'd actually seen the Virgin Mary. Or God. But we still believed in them. Well, faster than you could say 'Father, Son and Holy Ghost,' I was hauled down to the principal's office. My great aunt was called in. She was so appalled, she called my dad out of his class." She paused to remember the details. "He came running, figured I'd set fire to the cafeteria or something like that. The principal told him what I'd done, and I remember he stood there for a minute with this really perplexed look, and finally he said, 'Is that all?' "

They both laughed and Max added, "That was when Ben decided he'd be better off raising us on his own. The next year he took a job at the University of Wisconsin."

He smiled at her from across the table as he settled back into the chair. "I suppose you know what question is coming next. Did you see a fairy?"

"I did. I'm sure of it. It was as close to me as you are and about the size of a hummingbird. I don't know why it let me see it." She dabbed a breadcrumb off the tablecloth and brushed it onto the plate, letting herself feel it again—the raw joy at seeing that tiny, exquisite creature. "Actually, my mother had second sight. Became more pronounced when she was pregnant with Olivia and then with me." She smiled. "Although, to hear Olivia tell it, she was driven mad by her pregnancy."

"Your sister's a pragmatist?"

"That's a nice way of putting it."

She pictured her mother and the way the little line between her eyebrows deepened when she had a sense about something. "My mother was very intuitive. Knew the phone was going to ring before it did, when someone was going to drop by unannounced. She could tell when a friend was pregnant before her friend knew." She touched the base of her wineglass. "One day she told Ben if anything happened to her, she wanted Olivia to have her engagement ring and me to have her wedding ring. Two days later she was killed in a car accident."

"Did she see fairies?"

"Oh, yes. She left food out for them." She paused, feeling sad. "You know," she said, "as a child I never questioned any of these things. It was what I grew up with. Maybe that's why I don't see them anymore. Maybe I've lost that sense of believing without even thinking about it."

"I'll bet there are some things that bring it back. You just don't realize what's happening. You're going along, and then there's this thing or this place that's different."

"Yes," she started. "Some places. I still do find some places special. You know, where anything is possible. That garden in that photograph. There's an energy that's almost electric. You can feel it in your pores. Draw it in when you breathe. And then it's inside you. Even after you leave, you carry it with you for a while and it makes the world different. More vivid." She tried to read his expression and failed. "You know what I'm talking about, don't you?"

He leaned forward so he rested his folded forearms on the table. Still holding her gaze, he said, "I do. I believe there is more to this world than our scientists or our religions can explain. Much of it's to do with that energy you mentioned. And to discount something simply because one can't see it or touch it is to rob oneself of life's abundance. We've forgotten how to read our instinct, let alone trust it. In most of us, it has atrophied." He paused and his eyes narrowed. "What about you, Max? Do you trust your instinct?"

"I try to." Then she said, "Like with this stone. I know it isn't mine. Not in any legal way. But I feel like it belongs to me." Grey watched her intently, as though what she said wasn't foolish or outrageous. "Does this sound strange?"

"On the contrary. Stones are powerful." She thought he

was about to echo Elliott's belief, but then he said, "Almost as powerful as faith."

"What do you mean?"

"Faith doesn't have any physical properties to hang itself on. In order to merely exist, it must be powerful."

She tried to read behind his words. "What do you have faith in?"

Without hesitation, he said, "Who I am."

"And who is that?"

His eyes seemed sad and old. "We're getting off the subject."

"Are we?"

Before she could pursue it, Grey announced it was time for dessert.

It was over the chocolate torte when the subject of significant others finally came up, and it was Grey who broached the subject. Straight on.

"Are you seeing anyone?" he asked, and Max nearly sighed with relief. At last.

"Not at the moment."

"I'm surprised."

She shrugged. "Busy with school. Relationships take time."

He nodded in agreement.

Max sipped some of the strong coffee. "What about you?"

He glanced down at his plate. "Long-distance relationship. We see each other about once a month. Either I go there or she comes here."

Max felt her heart plummet three and a half stories. She could tell by the way he wasn't making eye contact that he felt awkward about it, but she refused to make it easy for him.

He spent some time gathering torte crumbs between the tines of his fork. "She was transferred to New York last year.

We're both committed to making it work. It may not, but we're giving it a shot." He finally looked up at Max.

She nodded. "And you do this by inviting women up to dinner?"

He drew away from his plate, gathering his napkin in both hands. Then he tossed it on the table. "Max, I'm sorry if this seemed like more than what it was, or is. I just thought . . ."

She waited.

"I thought with all you've been through, you could use a decent meal. I'd like to be a friend. I—"

Max held up her hand. "No, don't apologize. You never led me on. Maybe I wanted it." He hadn't touched her. Not in that way. She was a fool.

"I'm—"

"No, please," she said. "Don't. You've been a good friend. I don't want to compromise that." But she already had.

As his eyes searched her face, she clung to her composure.

"Are we all right, then?" he finally asked.

She bobbed her head up and down. "Really. I'm fine." He just wants to be friends. Fine. Boyfriends come and go, but friends can last a long time.

"Let me help you clean up these dishes."

"You don't have to—"

"I want to. I'm good at clean-up." She started collecting the dishes from the table. "This is what happens when you're invited to people's houses for dinner, but you can't return the favor because you can't cook. People love to have me over because I do the clean-up." She hurried into the kitchen with the pile of plates. "I'm an extremely popular dinner guest."

Grey wouldn't let her handle the mess by herself, but because of the kitchen's size, there wasn't much room for them both to maneuver. Max scraped plates into the garbage dis-

158

posal and loaded the dishwasher while Grey wrapped leftovers. Just as Max turned to ask him if he wanted to save the salad, Grey closed the refrigerator and turned toward her. Cramped as the area was, they wound up only inches from each other and his proximity overwhelmed her. She smelled basil and aftershave and the fibers of his sweater brushed her hand as she rose up on her toes to kiss him. If she'd thought before acting, she'd probably have backed off. But she was tired of being sorry for the things she didn't do rather than the things she did. His lips were warm and moist and after the barest second, he responded, taking her into the warmth. His arms encircled her, gathered her to him, and she felt like she'd been starving. God, she wanted to be here. The kiss deepened, along with their breathing. She ran her hands across the swell of his shoulders, folding her arms around his neck. She thought she could feel his heart thudding against her chest, but it might have been her own. Then he stopped, froze and she felt his sigh before he let her go, drawing away. He took her hands in his and his eyes looked raw with pain. "Max, I—"

She stepped away, taking her hands back, and the edge of the counter jabbed into her spine. "No," she said, determined not to let him show her any pity. She covered her mouth with her fingers. Do not fall apart. "My mistake. I'm sorry." She fumbled. "You explained. I broke the rules. I'm sorry. Look . . ." She started to back out of the kitchen. How could she have been so stupid? "I'm just going to leave now. It's best, don't you think? I'll be fine. No hard feelings. We'll talk later. I'm sorry to stick you with all those dishes, but I think I'd better go." She grabbed her poncho and as her hand found the doorknob, she prayed he hadn't bolted the damn thing. It turned. "Thank you for dinner." He either looked really sad or really sorry. She didn't want to think about which. She slipped out the door and closed it behind her.

Chapter 19

Max's hand shook so badly, she had trouble negotiating the key in the lock. It finally gave and she stepped into her apartment, slamming the door behind her. She leaned against it, letting the hard wood support her as she tipped her face up toward the ceiling so maybe her tears wouldn't spill over. "God, are you stupid." *He told you.* "Stupid. Stupid. Stupid."

The tears started—warm, salty flows that tickled her cheeks. "Oh, shit," she moaned, "I forgot Fiona." Turning, she pounded her fist against the door jamb. "Damn. Damn. Double damn." Now what? Go up and get her? Wait until tomorrow? The dog would probably rather be up there with Grey than down here with her idiot mistress. But Max wasn't keen on spending the night alone. Fiona might not be very brave, but she had a good bark. Pressing her forehead against the door, she moaned again. "I've gotta go back, I can't—"

She stepped back to open the door, and her foot landed on

something small and hard. Like a marble. Max looked down and saw two black pellets by the toe of her shoe. She looked over her shoulder and saw the deflated beanbag chair surrounded by a pool of pellets. A chill seized the base of her spine and shot its way up to her skull.

Using both hands, she twisted the doorknob, trying to be as quiet as possible. A voice behind her said, "Don't." She stopped. "Turn around." She did. A short, stocky man wearing a Cubs baseball cap and holding a handgun stood in the arched entry to her kitchen. She'd seen him before, but couldn't think of where. He wagged the gun at her. "Move away from the door."

Max let him see her hands as she stepped into the living room, her shoes barely finding traction on the pellets.

"Just give it to me," he said.

"I don't have it."

"Give it to me," he repeated between gritted teeth. His face shone with sweat, and his knuckles whitened as he gripped the gun tighter.

As Max considered her options, which seemed limited, she noticed the man's eyes widen at the same time Max felt cool air against her back.

Her first thought was that Grey had come looking for her.

"You don't hear too good, do you? She says she doesn't have it."

It wasn't Grey. The man in her kitchen paled as his jaw fell open. Max forced herself to turn around just as the man stepped into the room and shut the door behind him. He had a gun trained on the intruder.

"You sent me an e-mail," he said to Max.

Her mind drew a blank.

Then he said, " 'Believeit.' "

Of course. And he was also the man in the picture with

Ben and Arthur Penn. "Ant—"

"Say my name, I have to kill him."

The shorter man's Adam's apple bobbed up and down.

"What's your name, little man?"

"Earl," he answered with a croak.

"Okay, Earl. Put that gun down, unless you want a hole in the middle of that 'C' as in Cubs."

Earl glanced up at his cap before lowering the gun.

"On the floor. Real slow."

Max remembered where she'd seen him—asleep in his car with drool down his cheek.

Without taking his eyes off Antony, Earl crouched and set the gun on the floor. Then he stood and backed away.

"Real good, Earl. Now get the hell outta here before I decide to shoot you."

Earl hesitated, as though he couldn't believe his luck. His eyes darted from Antony to the door and back again.

"Go on," Antony wagged the gun toward the door and Earl was off like a startled possum.

Once the sound of his footsteps faded on the stairs, Antony turned toward Max. His tie was dark blue with exploding stars and galaxies. "Go get your purse and make sure you got your passport. And if you got the stone, bring that too."

When she didn't move, Antony said, "You want to find out what happened to your old man?"

"I'll get my bag."

"Hurry."

In her bedroom, Max got her rucksack from the dresser, checked to make sure her passport was in it; then she dug her camera and several rolls of film out of its bag and felt for the stone in her pocket. Follow the stone, she told herself. This is the future. Not upstairs. Not in the classroom. Here. And it starts now. When she returned to the living room, Antony was holding a jacket from her closet instead of his gun. "Here. You might need this." He tossed it to her.

"I have to stop upstairs first." She set her bag and camera on the coffee table as she slipped the jacket on. "Make arrangements for my dog."

"Sorry. Can't let you do that."

"I'll only be a minute."

"We don't have a minute." He waved his hand toward the door. "Our buddy isn't working alone."

Grey would take care of Fiona. She'd call him as soon as she could. Until then, he'd have to decide whether to be worried or angry. Then she remembered she didn't care anymore.

"Okay," Max said. "Let's go."

Chapter 20

The apartment was a single room with a bath not much larger than a closet. Yellowed wallpaper with faded fleur-de-lis covered one wall and the other three were a dingy shade of green. Cracks in the plaster ran from floor to ceiling.

The room was grim, but clean, orderly. The forks and spoons in the silverware drawer were stacked one on top of the other and the blankets on the twin-sized bed were tucked in so tightly a coin would bounce off it.

Jillian sat in the room's only chair—a plaid armchair that was quite comfortable—and watched coverage of the assassination on the small-screen television. In her lap was a bag of peanut M&Ms and she plucked a green one from the bag and ate it while watching the red-haired reporter standing in front of the Talisker Hotel on Michigan Avenue. Flashing red lights from ambulances and squad cars reflected off the rain-slick pavement, and bystanders behind the reporter waved and mugged to the camera as she told the viewers what had happened. "A conference on genetics, being held here at the Talisker, came to an abrupt and tragic end when the keynote speaker, Fletcher Winwood and his wife, Denise, were shot while returning to the hotel after a dinner with friends. A doorman by the name of," she glanced at her notes, "Stanley Johnson, was also injured." The reporter went on to say that Winwood was a leader in genetics research and widely respected because of the strong ethical voice he brought to the field. "Police believe the shots came from a building across the street. One of the upper floors. No suspects have been apprehended, but witnesses are being questioned and the police say they do have leads." The screen changed back to the newsroom where one of the anchors thanked the red-haired reporter and said, "In other news . . ."

Jillian switched the channel and found the other stations had gone to commercials. She hit the mute button. Across the street was a place called Gilligan's Tap. A red and white Budweiser sign hung above the entrance, and as she watched, a fat old woman waddled into the bar.

She heard a key being inserted into the lock. A moment later the door opened and Barney Waldrop walked into his apartment. The chair was behind the door and he didn't see her until he was pocketing his keys, and then he hesitated.

She smiled at him. "Hello, Barney." She popped a candy into her mouth.

"Jillian," he said, glancing around as though he expected to find someone with her. "What're you doing here?"

"Rhys asked me to stop by." She swallowed.

Doubt clouded his features. "Why?"

"I've got your next assignment."

He closed the door behind him. "So, he's not pissed?"

165

"No," she said. "Just a little disappointed."

He walked past her to the closet and removed his jacket, which he hung up in the small space. For almost fifteen seconds, he stood, staring into the closet. When he did turn, the move was abrupt, defensive. "I told him it was a bad situation. Too early. Too much chance of being seen."

"He understands," she said. "Someone is seeing to the stone now. We'll have it soon." She ate another candy and held the bag out to him. He came over and, without taking his eyes off hers, stuck his forefinger into the bag, fished around and pulled out a yellow one. He tossed it into his mouth and crunched down on it.

"Glad to hear that," he said and she felt his eyes taking her in, trying to read her. He nodded toward the briefcase she'd set beside the chair. "What you got in there?"

"Just some papers. I'll show you later." She nodded toward the TV. "Nice work."

"Thanks," he said, grinning a little. "They said he died at the hospital." He thrust out his lower jaw and shook his head. "Not true. He was dead on the spot."

She nodded her understanding. "They never like to admit that."

He lowered himself to the edge of the bed and unbuttoned a shirt cuff, then rolled the sleeve halfway to his elbow. "I didn't know Rhys had you delivering assignments," he said as he unbuttoned the other sleeve.

"Only when I ask him nice."

He returned her smile and placed his hands palm-down on the bed. "So, why are you still sitting over there?"

She stood and removed her trench coat, then gave him a moment to admire her in the short, black slip of a dress. With a little smile, she reached down for the bag of candy.

He started unbuttoning his shirt.

She dug a candy out and held it up to him. "Do you like red ones?"

"I do."

She placed it on the end of her tongue, then took it into her mouth as she walked toward Barney. When she stood in front of him, she brushed the spaghetti strap off her right shoulder and then her left. Barney reached for her breasts as she perched on the bed, straddling him. She let him fondle her. He groaned and she stroked his hair and kissed his forehead. With her forefinger, she traced the scar on his jaw, then lowered her mouth to his. They kissed and she slipped the candy onto his tongue. As she drew her mouth away, she pressed into his groin, feeling his erection. He groaned again, tilting his head back. His jaw shifted as he crunched down on the candy and the poison pellet it contained.

She lowered her feet to the floor and backed off him. He looked confused, then angry. Then his eyes bulged and his chest began to spasm. As he fell back onto the bed, his entire body contorted and a strangled sound escaped his throat. Jillian pulled up her dress straps as she watched, keeping her distance, until the convulsions, then his breathing and, finally, his heart stopped.

She slipped on a pair of surgical gloves. Working quickly, she proceeded to distribute the contents of the briefcase around Barney's tiny apartment.

Chapter 21

As Earl passed through the revolving door of the hotel, it was all he could do not to make a full circle and keep right on going. He'd been walking around the city for God knew how long. But the sad fact was, he had nowhere to go but here. Lonny always wanted to get out of Chicago. Live somewhere warm. Earl, on the other hand, thought he'd be happy if, for the rest of his life, he didn't go anywhere the El couldn't take him.

It wasn't that he liked Chicago so much; he just hated anything that wasn't familiar. Lonny always figured there was some better place out there. A couple of years ago, after hitting the trifecta at Sportsman's, he'd talked Earl into going to Spain with him. Said something about bulls running loose in the streets. Earl figured that was a good enough reason to stay away, but he went because Lonny wanted him to go. It had been the longest ten days of Earl's life. He couldn't understand anyone. He couldn't get a decent beer and the food gave him the shits. When they got back to Chicago, Earl nearly wept with relief. No, he couldn't survive outside Chicago. Swore he'd never leave again. Only now, because he figured the Ice Queen would eventually kill him, Earl was thinking about running. Was Milwaukee far enough?

As he stood at the door to the Ice Queen's hotel room, a drop of sweat slid down from his armpit. He couldn't bring himself to raise his hand, make a fist and smack the door. He was dead meat. This woman wouldn't appreciate a guy being upfront with the truth if the truth wasn't to her liking. Shit. Might as well stick a gun in his mouth and pull the trigger. Hell, he didn't even have a gun anymore.

Earl didn't know how long he stood there. Two minutes? An hour? He either had to knock or leave. Just as he thought he'd worked up the guts, the handle turned and the door slowly opened. Half of the Ice Queen's face appeared from behind the door.

"Bad news isn't wine," she said. "It doesn't improve with age."

Earl shifted onto his other foot. "I, uh . . ." he couldn't finish. He figured "I didn't get the stone" would be the last five words he spoke.

She stepped back from the door and held it open. Earl barely noticed the pale blue robe hanging open, or the way her dark nipples poked at the material of her gauzy nightgown. Barely. He walked past her and into the room. The bed was made, the TV off.

"It's two a.m. Where the hell have you been?"

When he turned to face her, he couldn't stop staring at her chest. Even though it might get him killed.

"What happened?"

"Well, uh . . ."

"Don't leave anything out. I'll know if you do."

He looked into her eyes and didn't doubt that for a second. "It wasn't in the beanbag chair," he said.

"I told you it probably wasn't."

"Yeah, I know. I started to look for it then."

"And?"

Earl hated bottom lines. "She came home early."

She walked toward him, stopping when she wasn't more than a foot away. He could see the tiny muscles around her eyes working and could practically feel her boring into his brain. Her jaw was like a rock. He tried to swallow, but he was all out of spit.

"You didn't kill her."

Oh, jeez. "Well, no. You said to get the stone. I didn't have it. And then, well, stuff happened."

"Stuff?" She breathed slow and deep and the sides of her nose flared.

"Like I said, she was early. So, I wasn't, you know, ready for her. But that was okay. I had the gun. I was gonna pull the trigger—almost did—when there's this black guy at the door. Raspy voice. Never seen him before. But he's got a gun."

"So did you." Her cold little eyes swept him. "Since he didn't shoot you, I assume you shot him."

"Well, um, no. Not exactly."

" 'Not exactly.' What did happen? Exactly."

Earl needed to get on the other side of this before he had a heart attack. "Well, he made me put the gun down and then he took it."

"That makes it difficult to kill her, then, doesn't it?" Her mouth was a grim line. "What happened next?"

"He told me to leave. I—I didn't have much choice." He hurried to add, "I stayed outside, though. Watched."

"And?"

"They left together."

It seemed to take a little time for that to sink in.

Finally, she said, "Let me see if I have this straight. You failed to get the stone. You failed to kill Maxine Pike. You lost your gun to some unnamed man who also took Miss Pike somewhere."

"Maybe he was gonna kill her." Earl tried to sound hopeful.

"I doubt it, Earl. Your luck doesn't run that way."

He couldn't argue.

"What happened next?"

"I went back and looked some more."

"Idiot! Did you think she'd leave the stone sitting on the *TV Guide*?"

"I guess not," he mumbled, then floundered on. "Some guy came down. Knocked. Called her name a couple times."

She breathed twice. Breathed and glared. "You're an idiot. You know that, don't you?"

Earl nodded.

She raised her hand and held her thumb and forefinger apart about a quarter inch. "I'm this close to ripping your eyebrows off and shoving them down your throat."

Earl swallowed.

She turned her hand into a fist and lowered it. "Idiot," she muttered and walked over to the window that looked out on the city. Earl didn't move. He didn't want to do anything that might set her on Lonny.

With her back to him, she said, "I want you to sit outside her apartment. She may come back. I'll meet you tomorrow afternoon. At two. Park across from the apartment building." Finally she turned to face him. "If you're not there, you'd better be wherever she is."

He nodded.

"I'll see you tomorrow, Earl." She waited until he looked

at her before adding, "Disappoint me again and your brother is dead."

She picked up the phone and punched in some numbers. Earl wasn't sure she was finished with him yet, so he waited. The Ice Queen sighed impatiently and tapped her stubby nails on the desktop as the call went through. Finally, she said, "Simon Murdoch." Then she happened to glance over her shoulder and Earl could tell, from the way her whole face tightened with disgust, that he was not supposed to be here anymore.

"What are you waiting for?"

He shrugged. "Anything else?"

"Get out of my sight." Then, into the phone, "Simon. Jillian. We've got a problem."

Earl shut the door to 817 behind him. He was alive, but being alive didn't feel so hot right now.

Chapter 22

After Jillian hung up with Simon, she removed her laptop from its case and set it on the desk, ran her hand across its smooth, dark surface, feeling for the tiny scratch where she'd dinged it against some sharp edge. Then she plugged it into the cable hookup. This marvelous concoction of memory and chips would get her mind off the current snafu, which she could do nothing about right now.

Sure enough, within minutes she'd been transported into the virtual universe where she read her e-mail, searched lists, browsed. In an odd way, this empowered her. She directed a malcontent toward an anarchist website and clicked "send." Maybe because it was so easy to manipulate so many of these people.

An hour later she lowered the lid on her laptop, stretched and decided to take a bath. Simon should be calling her back and she didn't want to give him the satisfaction of having woken her. Never mind that it was—she glanced at the digital clock on the desk—almost three a.m.

She turned on the bath water and added half of one of the little hotel bottles of bubble bath, smelled it—a heavy floral—and poured in the rest. She screwed the cap back on before tossing it in the trash.

Let Simon work at it from his end, she thought. Tonight there was nothing she could do except worry and what was the point in that? If Simon handled things, Rhys wouldn't have to know about it until it had been resolved.

But instead of imagining Rhys's anger, she found herself rerunning her encounter with Barney Waldrop. Her first murder. She felt no remorse—only a strange elation. She found herself checking the mirror to see if it showed—surely there'd be an aura or at least a glow about her—but she looked the same has she had before. But there'd been no hesitation. And not just because she was following an order. It had been so easy. No, that wasn't the word. Natural. It had been as natural as . . . dying.

Her only regret was that she hadn't had sex with him before she poisoned him. She'd never felt such raw desire—hadn't thought her body capable of it—and the strength of the emotion surprised her. Continuing to replay it in her mind as she brushed her hair, she felt herself moisten as she imagined him sliding into her, exploding just as she slipped the candy onto his tongue. How would it have felt if he'd been inside her when paralysis shut down his system? His system. She shivered.

She'd slipped off her nightgown and had one foot in the steaming water when the phone rang. Figuring it was Simon, she didn't try to hide her annoyance when she answered.

"What is it?"

"Did I wake you, dear?"

At the sound of her father's voice, she pulled her foot from the tub and grabbed one of the terry cloth robes the hotel provided. "No, I was about to take a bath." She tried to keep her voice light as she shrugged on the robe.

"I wondered how your meeting went this evening."

She wedged the phone to her shoulder as she gave the robe's belt a tug. "Without a problem."

"Good. And you? How are you holding up?"

"I feel incredible . . . like I could do anything." She stood at the window looking out toward the lake, which was indiscernible from the night sky.

"Good." He really did seem pleased.

"Well, my bath's getting—"

"And how did your other assignment go?"

She placed one hand against the window, letting the cold seep into her skin. Then she said, "Simon didn't call you?" Of course he didn't.

After several moments, Rhys said, "What's going on?"

This wasn't her fault. She had to make him see that. "It seems that one of Benjamin Pike's friends—someone Simon knows—has intercepted the girl." Before he could respond, Jillian rushed ahead, "Simon has assured me that he's handling it."

After several moments of silence, she added, "You might want to give him a call." She wasn't a bit ashamed of her deflection. Simon would have done the same to her.

"Perhaps I will," Rhys said.

Just when she thought the deflection had worked, he said, "Jillian, you do know why I asked you to deliver that message tonight, don't you?"

"Yes." He hadn't said it in so many words, but it had to do with selling assets before they became liabilities.

"The secret is in knowing when to cut them loose." After a

pause, he added, "Please know that I never hesitate."

"Of course."

"Now why don't you get yourself some rest, dear."

"I will."

"Good night," he said. "Enjoy your bath."

Chapter 23

Max poured herself another cup of coffee from the carafe, ignoring the box of fresh bagels. Her stomach churned at the thought of food.

She could feel the stone in her pocket, pressing against her hipbone. Whenever she tried to figure out where it was taking her, she had so few answers and so many questions, her brain overloaded.

The initial rush of certainty had faded, leaving crevices for doubt to sink in. With doubt came regret. She should have tried harder to talk to Grey before she left. Insisted. Antony would not have gone anywhere without her. Her action, instead of attesting to faith, showed signs of dementia. And what must Grey be thinking?

Out the window of the small jet, a thin line marked the horizon. They sped toward that slash of red. Max pressed her cheek against the cool window.

She needed to get back to the way she felt when she left the apartment with Antony. Decisive. Resolute.

As they had driven from her apartment to the airport, Antony kept checking the rear-view mirror. She'd tried to study him, catching glimpses as they passed beneath the streetlights' glare, which gave his dark skin a golden cast. He wore a wool cap and his leather jacket squeaked when he turned the wheel. Although he was thin and wiry, beneath the jacket his shoulders were broad. He looked like he might be a swimmer or a rock climber. Whatever he was, he wasn't responding to her attempts at conversation, so she listened to the radio, where a voice told her how much richer and less stressful her life would be if she drank a certain brand of green tea.

When the commercial ended, a different voice said, "This just in . . ." Antony tensed up. "Police say they have identified a suspect in the shooting at the Hotel Talisker earlier this evening where the National Conference of Genetics was being held. Keynote speaker Fletcher Winwood . . ."

Antony turned up the volume.

". . . his wife, Denise, were killed as they returned to the hotel from dinner. The doorman, Stanley Johnson, was injured. Police have declined to release further information regarding their suspect. More as it becomes available."

Antony made a fist and banged it against the steering wheel.

Fletcher Winwood. It took a moment for her to recognize the name. "He's on the Caliburnus board, isn't he?"

"Was," he amended. Then he glanced at her. "You have got the stone, haven't you?"

"Yes," she said, figuring if that was all he wanted, he'd have gotten it by now.

He nodded, as though she were confirming what he knew,

then turned up the radio even louder, discouraging further discussion.

Antony's silence wasn't reinforcing her decision to go running off with him. It wasn't until they were heading northwest on the expressway toward O'Hare that he seemed to relax.

She clicked off the radio. "When does our flight leave?"

"Whenever we get there."

She interpreted his deep sigh as one of resignation. "You chartered a flight?"

"You could say that." He glanced at a black minivan passing them on the right.

She studied his profile against the glare of passing headlights. "What happened to Ben?"

He took his time answering. "Not sure. Nothing good. He was on Alyssum. I was gonna meet him there. Next thing I know, he's gone and nobody's talking."

"But you don't know for certain that he's dead."

When he didn't respond, Max said, "Did Arthur Penn know anything?"

Frowning, he shook his head. "He only knows what Murdoch tells him."

"Who's Murdoch?"

"Simon Murdoch." His grip on the wheel tightened. "He manages Alyssum. And he's Arthur's half-brother and his lawyer."

"And why is that bad?"

He drove in silence for a minute, then said, "Maybe I oughta explain some things."

"I'd really like that."

He took his time, apparently gathering his thoughts. Then he began: "Last year Ben starts writing Arthur Penn. They hit it off. All of a sudden Arthur's got this new best friend. I got suspicious." He slowed to let a car merge in ahead of them. "I check Ben out and decide he's all right. We talk. I guess he figured he could trust me, because he tells me how Simon Murdoch's got him worried." He paused. "Now, up until then, I figured Simon was okay. He's Arthur's bastard half-brother and Arthur's done a lot for him. But Murdoch's smart and savvy. Far as I could tell, he was doing okay for Alyssum." He waited as a jet thundered overhead, then continued. "Murdoch came to Alyssum about four years ago. Right before I met Arthur. At the time, Arthur had another guy working with him. All of a sudden there's a lot of money missing and it winds up in this guy's bank account. Looks like embezzling. So, he's out and Murdoch's in."

"So, how does Ben know that Murdoch's bad news?"

"He'd been researching the foundation—Murdoch and Arthur along with it." He slowed as the traffic into O'Hare thickened. "Found a situation a few years ago where some funding 'accidentally' went to a pretty sleazy group."

"I think I read about that."

"Supposedly, that was a mistake." They passed under the sign welcoming them to O'Hare. "Arthur and the board gave them money based on some environmental stuff they were doing and on Murdoch's recommendation. Caliburnus wasn't the only foundation to make that mistake, by the way. Turns out that was just a front to hide the fact that they were building a doomsday arsenal. Arthur'd have nothing to do with them now." He glanced at Max. "What else do you know about the foundation?"

"That its aim is to 'elevate humanity.' "

"That's what Arthur aims for it to do. He's the real thing. Remember that."

"And Arthur trusts Murdoch?"

"He does."

Max chose her words carefully before speaking. "Sounds

like he's not the greatest judge of character. Should he be in charge of a foundation?"

"It's his money."

"All of it?"

"Yep. But it's more than that." After several moments, he continued, "There's something about the guy. He really believes in people. Believes they're good. Idealism like that needs protecting. Once you meet him, you'll see what I mean. There's nobody else could run the foundation. Not yet, anyway." She heard him sigh. "Look, I'm not saying he's perfect."

"Sounds like it's dangerous for him to be on that island."

"Maybe. But taking him off Alyssum . . ." he shook his head. "That ain't gonna happen."

"Why not?"

When Antony didn't respond, Max decided not to push it. "So," she said, "tell me more about this bunch of phony environmentalists."

"Arthur chalked the whole thing off as an oversight. Like I said, the group had a good cover. Arthur just figured Murdoch hadn't seen it either when he made the recommendation to the board. Well, Ben did some investigating. They're a bunch of racist idiots who think God wanted the world one color and of one mind. Turns out Murdoch knows some of these folks— Ben showed me pictures of him with their leader—but Murdoch claims he didn't know what they were into. Ben figured that Murdoch was involved with them."

"Could he prove it?"

"Hadn't yet," he said, "but he had some information he wanted to show me. Said it linked Murdoch with a guy named Rhys Lewis." They exited into the rental car return area. "We'll have to save that conversation for later."

At the airport, they were met by a man about Max's age whom Antony introduced simply as Sam. He had thinning red hair, an easy smile, and a loping gait. Max trotted to keep up with the two of them. "Yeah," Antony said, "Sam's here in case I fall asleep at the wheel."

Max grabbed his arm. "You're flying the plane?"

He stopped and when he turned around, he was smiling, apparently amused by Max's reaction. "Who did you think was gonna fly?"

"Gee, I don't know. One of those people wearing a uniform, I guess."

"Hell, no. We're taking a little one. You're our only passenger." He continued walking. "You'll like it. Or maybe not. One or the other."

It wasn't so bad. Although the ride was bumpier than in a large jet, she liked the informality of it. The main cabin, with its wooden table and comfortable chairs, reminded her of a den.

Before they left Chicago, he gave her a book. "Read this," he said, "so you got some background."

The book, *Alyssum: Isle of Beauty and Myth*, related the island's colorful history with a mingling of legend and fact. Most of this she'd learned from her Internet search, but the book detailed the Penns' claim to the island, which had been in the family for more than six hundred years. Alyssum had been a gift from the Black Prince. One of Penn's ancestors took a spear for the prince, who was so grateful he offered (through his father, King Edward III) the man's son a dukedom. The son asked for Alyssum instead. The Penn estate, the island's main residence, the "castle," had been constructed in the 1830s from the remains of the original structure built in the middle of the twelfth century.

After finishing the book, Max kept her sight fixed on the horizon, which grew brighter with every mile, as they neared England.

Chapter 24

The damp April breeze whipped through Olivia's hair as she left Cliff's carriage house in the Maida Vale area of London and headed south.

Five a.m. in Chicago and Max still wasn't home. Olivia had started calling her sister at six London time when she'd been nudged awake by one of her weird feelings. She hated those uninvited thoughts and images, but they were too creepy not to act on.

Cliff, thinking she was silly for phoning someone at that hour, tried to initiate sex again. The fact that Olivia couldn't be induced said more about her level of concern than anything else. They'd had a great night together, despite Cliff's annoying habit of asking her how she was doing every five minutes.

She pulled up the collar of her trench coat and pushed on, vaguely aware of the barges on the Grand Union Canal as she crossed it—splashes of red on the gray water. Hyde Park was more or less her destination, but this was a thinking walk rather than an arriving one. God, she thought—that was a Max observation if she'd ever heard one.

The walk took longer than she'd thought it would. She'd stopped at a shop to buy a few essentials—deodorant, a toothbrush and manicure scissors—and it was going on one p.m. when she got back to Cliff's. The house felt empty when she closed the door behind her, even though Cliff's car was in the garage beneath the house. He'd gone to meet one of the investigators he'd hired to look for Ben and said he'd be home by noon.

"Cliff," she called, aware of how her voice intruded on the silence. No answer. Either he'd gone out for a minute or he was on the phone.

She slipped out of her trench coat and hung it on a rack in the foyer, then combed her hair and applied lipstick in the brass-framed mirror that hung above a small table. As she brushed a speck of lint off her black dress, she wished Cliff would get around to asking her to stay for a while. Then she could collect her suitcase from the hotel; she was in dire need of a change of clothing. With a final swipe of her lip brush, she returned her tools to her purse and went upstairs to see if she could distract Cliff from his phone call.

She found him sitting in his brown leather chair with his back to the door, his head resting against one of the chair's wings. They hadn't done much sleeping last night, had they? Smiling to herself, she moved up behind him, running her hand along the back of the chair and then slid it down Cliff's shoulder. When she bent down to kiss him, she stopped. He wore a long-sleeved shirt with narrow blue stripes. The right cuff was buttoned and the left was rolled above his elbow. His left forearm lay on his thigh, palm up, as though he were waiting for someone to place change in it. And he wasn't actually resting against the wing, he was slumped against it, his head lolling back against his shoulder.

"Cliff?"

As she moved around the chair to face him, the toe of her shoe touched some small object on the carpet. Before she could look down to see what it was, she saw Cliff's eyes, open, seeming to stare at her—into her—but seeing nothing. His mouth hung open. Then she saw his necktie—red with the gentle swirls of gray—knotted around his biceps, one end trailing over his crotch. Stepping back, Olivia saw the syringe—silver against the beige carpet.

She pulled in her breath so fast it caught in her throat and she nearly choked on it.

Call the police, she told herself, backing away from the chair. Did they have 9-1-1 over here? Glancing at the objects on his desk—the photo of his kids, a fountain pen, a book by Tom Clancy—she whispered, "No." This man did not do drugs. As she backed out of the room, she searched for signs of violence, a struggle, but saw nothing out of the ordinary. Maybe she was wrong. Maybe he did do drugs. How well did she know him? She needed to call the cops, but could take a few minutes to think this through first. Cliff was beyond help. She, on the other hand, could use some. She had no money.

As she spun around and ran for the stairs, she told herself Cliff would want her to have any money she found. She took the stairs so fast she nearly fell down the last seven. Wait. She should make sure she had everything of hers first. Then the money. Or should she forget about her own stuff? Indecision, a relatively uncommon dilemma for Olivia, froze her in mid-step.

As she stood at the base of the stairs, one hand still

clutching the rail, some movement caught in the corner of her eye made her turn to look to her right, into the living room.

"Hello, Olivia."

The voice came from the corner darkened by shadows. Slowly, a man came toward her. Beside Olivia, the floor creaked and she spun around. Standing not two feet from her was a larger man, solid, with a pencil thin mustache, no neck and a thin ponytail. He nodded to her.

She turned back toward the other man. "Who are you?"

He walked up to her, stopped and said, "Simon Murdoch."

The name meant nothing to her. He was several inches shorter than Olivia with gold-streaked brown hair and boyish features. His accent was American with a trace of the South.

"I don't know you," she said.

"You will." When he smiled, dimples broke out on either cheek. "Why don't you sit for a minute," Murdoch said, although nothing in his tone implied she had a choice.

The big man's eyes, hard and black like ball bearings, flickered toward a chair.

"That's Tommy," Murdoch said. "He wants you to sit down, too."

Olivia swallowed against a sour taste rising in her throat and sat in the bentwood rocking chair beneath the Landseer.

Murdoch pulled an ottoman up to her and sat so he could look at her straight on. He wore a leather bomber jacket and black driving gloves. Tommy stood off to the side, hands clasped in front of him like a butler awaiting instructions.

"Olivia—"

"Why did you have to kill him?" The words fell out before she could stop them.

He ran his hand over across his mouth, pulling at his lower lip, then rested his chin on his fist. "He was sticking his nose where it didn't belong." He sounded like a man who was tired of explaining the obvious. "He wouldn't have been welcome on Alyssum. Neither would you."

Oh, God, she thought, *I'm next.*

"If I were you, I wouldn't set the cops on us. Me and Tommy here have alibis and," he patted her bare hand with his gloved one, "we don't leave any sign of ourselves behind. Understand?"

Maybe he wasn't going to kill her. "What do you want?"

"I have one very simple question."

She waited.

"Where is your sister?"

"In Chicago," she answered without hesitation.

"Not anymore."

"Then I don't know."

Murdoch continued to stare, apparently disappointed with her answer.

"I swear," she said. "I don't know."

Murdoch glanced over his shoulder at Tommy. "You believe her?"

Tommy shook his head. The movement was small and stiff.

Murdoch turned back to Olivia, annoyed. "We don't believe you."

"I tried to call her this morning. She wasn't home."

His expression remained flat as he said, "When's the last time you talked to her?"

"Yesterday."

"Did she have the stone?"

If Olivia told him Max did have the stone, that would put Max at risk. But Max was supposed to be in Chicago. Olivia was sitting next to a man who had just killed the man she'd slept with last night. In terms of imminent danger, Olivia had

Max beat. "Yes," she said and figured from the way his eyes didn't change that this wasn't news to him.

"Where do you think your sister would go?"

"I don't know."

"You don't know." Each word fell like a rock.

Murdoch pushed the ottoman so he was sitting next to Olivia. She tried to sink deeper into the chair. He took her left hand by the wrist. She tried to resist, to pull back, but her effort barely registered. Soft leather stroked the back of her fingers. Then he wrapped his hand around hers so that his thumb rested against the inside of her little finger.

"Think real careful, Olivia," Murdoch said, looking into her eyes. "You sure that little sister of yours didn't say something?"

Murdoch increased the pressure on her finger, bending it back so it was at a right angle with her hand.

"I swear." Her finger looked so thin and white.

"Look at me."

She did.

"Where's Maxine?"

"I don't know." She had to tell him something. "London. She was booking a ticket to London."

Without taking his eyes from hers or changing his expression, Murdoch slowly bent her finger back until it snapped. A bolt of white-hot pain exploded in her head. She heard a shrill scream that she didn't recognize as her own. Everything faded to gray. Next thing she knew, Murdoch had released her hand and was talking to her, his mouth inches from her ear. "There's one reason you're not upstairs lying beside old lover boy with a needle in your arm."

She couldn't bring herself to look at her finger.

"Do you know what that reason is?" His tone was sharp now.

She nodded, then saw he was waiting for her to speak. "To help you find Max."

"Very good." He smiled and nodded. "Then you understood how important it is for you to communicate with us." She nodded again and he took a business card from his shirt pocked and tossed it on her lap. "I expect I'll hear from you. Real soon." He patted her hand and said, "I'd put some ice on that if I were you."

When Olivia worked up the nerve to look at her hand, all she could think of was how odd her finger looked. Dazed, she pushed it back into place. God, she didn't even feel it. Shock, she thought. Coiled up on the chair, her head bowed to her knees, Olivia rocked herself. Only when she remembered there was a dead man upstairs, did she move.

Chapter 25

They landed at Heathrow in a drizzle. The descent had been rough and Max was glad to get her feet on the ground, even though it was wet. After they passed through customs, Sam wished them luck and went to take the tube into London.

Antony's plan was for them to fly a smaller plane to a private landing strip in Cornwall and then drive the rest of the way to Penzance. "They'll be looking for us to fly into Penzance or Land's End."

He steered Max through a large waiting area filled with molded plastic seats and surrounded by shops. He tossed his flight bag onto a chair and motioned for Max to sit next to it. "You stay here. I'll be right back."

She must have dozed off, because the next thing she knew he was sitting on the other side of his bag, scowling at his cellular phone. She smelled grease and beef and her mouth began to water. She'd fallen asleep draped over Antony's flight bag, and as she pushed herself up, she rubbed at the zipper imprint on her cheek.

"Can't get hold of the guy," he said. Then he slipped his phone into his jacket pocket and pulled out a wad of cash, which he handed to her. "Hold onto this." She thumbed through it and counted roughly three hundred pounds.

"What's this for?"

"In case we get separated. Don't use your credit cards. They're too easy to trace." Before she could question him, he handed her a foil-wrapped burger. "Here."

As she devoured the burger, Antony kept looking around the area, almost as if he were expecting to find someone in particular, and as soon as she finished, he stood and picked up his bag. "We need to move," he said. "Too many people around here."

"Who or what are you looking for?" she asked as she followed him through the concourse.

"Don't know for sure. Murdoch I know. But they've got recruits."

" 'They?' You are going to tell me about this, aren't you?"

"Soon."

He steered her into a bar and had her sit at a small, round table in the corner with her back to the entrance. After he bought two Cokes, he sat in the chair across from her.

In a corner above the bar, a closed-caption television was tuned to CNN. As Max glanced up at it, she did a double-take when she saw the camera panning across the front of the Hotel Talisker, just a few miles from her apartment. The picture switched to a photo of Fletcher Winwood and his wife and then to a shot of the suspect, a Barney Waldrop, who was found in his hotel room, an apparent suicide. Newspaper articles and tracts on the evils of genetic engineering were found in his apartment. When Max saw Waldrop's face, with that crescent-shaped scar on his chin, "Oh, my God," slipped out of her.

"What?" she heard Antony say.

"I've seen him before." As she told him about the episode with the cop outside her apartment, Max wasn't sure what kind of reaction the story would draw from Antony. More questions, perhaps. Curiosity. She hadn't expected to see the flare of anger in his eyes and she drew back into the seat.

"First," he said, pointing a finger at her for emphasis, "I don't want to hear about you doing stupid stuff like that. Coulda gotten yourself killed. And second—"

"Wait," Max grabbed his finger. "You know, Antony, I'm touched by your concern for my safety. You've gone to a lot of trouble to bring me over here. You're watching me like a mama Rottweiler watches its pup. But you barely know me. Explain." She tossed his hand back at him.

"Do you think that assassination," he jerked his thumb toward the TV, "and what happened to you aren't related?"

"Well, of course they are." She was tired, confused and he was talking to her like she was stupid. "It was the same guy."

Frustrated, Antony shook his head, and when he continued, his tone was gentler. "That's not what I'm saying." He studied her, apparently weighing his thoughts. Finally, he said, "You've got to understand there are people in this world set on making it unlivable for everybody but themselves. And a lot of their activities are in the States."

"Activities?"

He pushed his glass out of the way and folded his arms on the table. "How old are you?"

The question was unexpected, and she didn't answer right away. But then Antony nodded and said, "Work with me."

"Okay. I'm thirty-two."

"In your lifetime, how has society changed? In a bad way."

"We're more violent," she said, after giving it some thought. While she supposed there might be other trends worth arguing, that was the first thing that came to her mind.

Antony nodded. "How do you see it?"

"Terrorism. Riots, road rage, random shootings." Then she added, "Fifteen years ago I didn't have to be afraid to go to school or accidentally cut someone off on the expressway."

"Why? Why are we more violent?"

She sipped the Coke, barely noting how the ice had melted and it tasted watered-down. "There are all kinds of explanations and I suppose they all have some validity. We're afraid of things we don't understand—"

"It's always been that way. What recently has changed things? What do they blame violence on?"

"Everything from TV and video games to single parent families to the loss of spirituality. Stress."

Nodding as though satisfied, he folded his hands together and said, "Good points. But what if there were also a deliberate effort to push people toward this kind of behavior?"

"A conspiracy?"

He nodded. "It'd be easy," he said. "Think about it. All you have to do is infiltrate some social group—special interest, a gang, a classroom, whatever—with one person who doesn't give a rat's ass about whatever that group's purpose really is, and is there only to push the group outside the frame of rational thinking." He gestured toward the television above the bar. "And he knows he's not going to be wanting for coverage."

The news show was now reporting a suicide bomber.

"And think about it. How do you protect yourself from some nut who stands on an overpass and drops chunks of concrete on passing cars? Some sniper who shoots people putting gas in their cars? Some guy who's seen one too many

193

trees cut down and just can't take it anymore?"

"You're saying that every act of madness—civil disobedience gone amok—is caused by some group?"

"Of course not. I'm just saying it's not all that random. And it's like a virus, you know? Once it starts, it builds on its own, gets fed by an occasional manufactured incident, and before you know it, the land of the free and the home of the brave is the land of the paranoid run by the psychos."

"And then what?"

"Disorder and chaos. Things get bad enough, folks'll start trading their freedoms and rights for security. Look at how the terrorist attacks changed us. Once things start spinning out of order, there's no stopping them. America becomes a country waiting for someone to step in and set things right."

Studying him, she considered his theory. His gaze didn't waver and Max had no doubt that he sincerely believed all this. And while she wasn't prepared to embrace it, neither could she dismiss it. The same guy who had threatened her and Fiona had killed two people at a convention. If this guy wasn't insane—and she believed that he wasn't—then there had to be some connection between the two incidents. Antony's explanation was all that she had right now, but there were some big pieces missing. "How could this person stop the chaos once it's spun out of control?"

"There are all kinds of ways to profit from chaos and fear if you know where it's coming from. Stock markets, security systems, firearms. Making way to put your own people in power is just one of them. Scared people are easy to predict and control." He paused. "And what if it's for its own sake?"

"Violence for the sake of violence?"

"Why not? People create art for it's own sake. To some people violence is just another art form. What if there's somebody out there, somebody with a lot of influence and a lot of people doing his bidding—some guy who thinks he's Picasso?"

"Who is this guy?"

"That guy I mentioned before. Name's Rhys Lewis."

"Who is he?"

"A self-help guru who's just getting into broadcast." He glanced at the TV. "He's also puts a lot of his money into scholarships for disadvantaged kids."

"Sounds like a monster."

Antony gave her a pointed look. "Yeah, well once you understand that those scholarships are a form of recruitment, he's not looking so benign."

"What about that guy who killed Fletcher Winwood in Chicago last night? The one who tried to get the stone from me. Was he one of Lewis's recruits?"

"Yep. That was Barney Waldrop."

She nodded at the TV above the bar. "They're saying he killed himself. Why?"

"Bet he had some help. He'd served his purpose. One reason that Rhys has gone all these years without attracting any attention is because he knows when to cut folks loose. Permanently."

"And that hasn't happened with Murdoch yet?"

"Not Murdoch. Lewis has got a few people he trusts—or still needs. He won't be done with Murdoch until he gets Alyssum." He paused then added, "Murdoch's smart. He might figure out a way to keep himself useful."

"Okay, I'm not sure I buy all this, but let's say I do. Where do I fit in?" She held up her hand to stop him before he said anything. "Better yet, where does the stone fit in?"

"Okay. First, Murdoch and Lewis want the foundation. And Alyssum. There's a lot of money in the foundation. And like I said, there's something about Alyssum. An energy. I'm the last guy to buy into this New Age crap, but you've got to be there to know what I'm saying."

He retrieved his drink and took a sip before continuing. "They've already started to move in. Caliburnus's board of directors is made up of only five people. Arthur and four others. Last year one of them died in a skiing accident."

Max nodded. "I read about that. What was her name? Moira—"

"Hoffman. Moira was replaced by Wallace Harvey, a friend of Murdoch's. Murdoch talked Arthur into that one. He seems okay on the outside, but he thinks like Murdoch."

"Can you prove it?"

"He got one of Rhys's scholarships." He jerked his thumb toward the TV screen. "And now Murdoch'll have a say in who replaces Winwood. That'll put two on the board. They're moving slow because they wanna do it clean." He paused. "And I'm betting it's Rhys Lewis who Murdoch tries to sell as the next board member."

"And because he's a philanthropist he'll be considered."

Antony nodded.

"If all they want is the foundation, why don't they kill Arthur Penn?"

"Murdoch doesn't stand to inherit much. He'll still manage Alyssum and all, but the foundation is in a kind of trust, which he can't touch."

"Does Arthur have any children?"

"Not yet." Then he said, "I think Rhys wants Arthur alive. For the time being."

"Why?"

"I'm not sure." He paused. "But I think they're getting ready to make a move."

"What makes you say that?"

"The way everything's coming together all of a sudden. Murdoch had been talking about bringing Lewis out to meet Arthur. Now that Winwood's dead, I know why."

"Why does Rhys need Alyssum?"

"In a way it's irrelevant and in a way it's everything."

Max waited.

"Rhys is gonna go on doing what he does, no matter what. He feeds off it. He needs the kick. He feeds off of violent images. He's an addict. With the foundation's money, he's got more resources." He paused, seemed reflective. "He likes to corrupt—the foundation, its people."

"You mean Arthur?"

Antony regarded her for a moment, and then said, "I doubt he could do that. It's like they're opposites, you know? I saw Lewis at one of his seminars." He snorted. "All these losers paying this guy to tell them how to not let people walk all over them. Teaching them to be 'smart victims,' Lewis calls it. He tells them it's all about getting what's coming to you. Getting the kick. Arthur sees it as giving whatever you can. Making things better."

He'd been looking past her, toward the entrance, as he said this, and now he got out of his chair and grabbed his jacket.

"Come on. We're going."

"What's wrong?" Max glanced over her shoulder and saw no one watching them, just travelers on their way to other countries. But then Antony took her out of the bar and guided her upstream, so to speak. People heading in the opposite direction pushed against them, moving quickly as though they were about to miss a flight. One man, wearing a tan overcoat and pulling a small suitcase on wheels, kept looking over his shoulder and ramming into people as he barged ahead.

"Where you got the stone?" Antony asked.

"In my jeans pocket."

"Which side?"

"Right."

He linked his left arm with her right arm, pulling her close. "Whatever happens, don't let go of me."

Before she could ask what was going on, a woman screamed and a second later someone cried, "Bomb!" More screams and the orderly stream of travelers became a stampede. Antony swung her around as the flood caught up with them, carrying them along. Max clung to Antony, who was trying to steer her toward the edge of the crowd. Bodies pushed against her, and it was all she could do to keep on her feet. A woman, her face twisted with fear, screamed words in a language Max couldn't understand as she tried to claw her way past everyone, nearly knocking over a young boy wearing a black beret. Instinctively, Max started to reach for him, to keep him from falling. Antony yelled, "Don't!" in her ear just as someone grabbed her left arm, nearly yanking it out of its socket. Antony countered, pulling so hard in the opposite direction he lifted Max off her feet. That momentum was enough for her to wrench her arm back, and she slammed her foot down for all she was worth. It crunched into someone's instep and a woman howled. Antony steered her forward and to the right and then they stumbled into a narrow corridor. Barely breaking stride, he pushed her through a door and into a room with tiled floor and walls. Urinals lined the walls. They appeared to be alone. Outside, she could hear the panic of humanity fleeing the bomb. If it had gone off, she hadn't heard it. She felt in her pocket for the stone, relaxing slightly when she found it.

"Shouldn't we get the hell out of here? There's a bomb somewhere."

"I don't think so," Antony said calmly, finally releasing her. He rubbed his hands against his face, as though drawing the tension out. Finally, he looked at her and said, "See how easy it is to get normal people thinking like a mob?"

They waited for the panic to diminish. After several minutes, Antony cracked the door to look out. Standing behind him, peering over his shoulder, Max saw that the mob had thinned and security had arrived. "Let's go," he said, taking her arm again as he led her out the door.

"Antony, what's the stone got to do with all this?"

"No time for that now."

She had the impression that he was afraid she'd balk when she learned the stone's purpose. In light of the world conspiracy he'd just described, that notion was disconcerting. She'd never been, and wasn't now, afraid of the stone; but for the first time it occurred to her that maybe she should be.

Chapter 26

The smell of his aunt's Welsh cakes filled the small kitchen. As Nick sat across from his mother, he saw how she was wasting away. It hurt—almost a physical pain—to know he was powerless to draw her out of her depression. After Nick's father died, it had taken Ben. Who would come after Ben?

Carrie Llewellyn was a small woman, and her thick hair, the color of moonlight, at times seemed to overwhelm her. Today she wore it loose so it came down to the middle of her back. She held the teacup between her palms as though drawing warmth from it. The veins on the backs of her hands were like green rivers flowing beneath sheets of ice.

She wasn't an easy person to love, and yet two of the men Nick admired most—his father and Ben—had loved her. She'd always been brittle, although it wasn't until Nick's father's death that she'd sunk into her first major depression. Nothing that Nick could do made a difference. Then Ben came along and gave her new life. He'd been there for them ever since, even as Carrie's bouts with depression became more frequent and extended. Finally he'd married her so she could benefit from his insurance should anything happen to him. Nick never doubted that Ben loved his mother, but believed that Ben's devotion had initially been prompted by his loyalty to Nick's father. In a way, that made Ben even more admirable to Nick, and he marveled at the bond that must have existed between these two men. Without Ben, Carrie might have wound up in a government-run institution, and Nick would have been fostered out. It was that devotion that kept Nick from resenting Ben for never telling him about the stone, forcing him to go to his mother and extract it from her one painful truth at a time.

Too keyed up to eat, Nick picked up a cake and broke it in two, setting the larger half in front of his mother. After a moment, she set her cup down, tore off a small corner, placed it in her mouth and began to chew slowly.

Nick raked his hand through his hair. This would take time. News of Ben's disappearance had her on the brink again.

"I met Ben's daughter, Olivia," he said. "She's quite beautiful." He smiled. "And bitchy. And tall. Must take after her mother." Nothing. "At any rate, she knows what she wants. If she comes upon the stone, I expect she will find the highest quote, then extract an extra ten percent."

At his mention of the stone, Carrie's eyes met his, then looked away. She tore off another piece of the small cake, but didn't eat it. When Nick told her of Ben's disappearance, Carrie had wailed, "It's the stone, that bloody stone." Then she'd crumpled and huddled up in the corner of the couch, crying softly, inconsolably. Nick had given her one of her pills and called his mother's sister to see if Carrie could stay with her for a few days. She'd barely spoken since, refusing to respond to Nick's questions about the stone. Initially, he understood it was her depression that had her wrapped so tightly that nothing from the outside could penetrate. But Nick recognized the symptoms and stages of his mother's illness, and now he believed it was at least partly her stubborn nature that kept her from talking.

He leaned toward her, across the table. "I need to know more." He paused. "Prior to Ben's disappearance, I didn't know for certain that the stone existed. It's more than a family heirloom, isn't it?" When she wouldn't respond or meet his gaze, he continued, "Let me tell you what I learned from a friend of Ben's. It's called the heartstone. According to legend, the stone came from the hilt of—"

"I know the story," she snapped. "And I don't give a damn what it's called, it's trouble."

Nick breathed deeply. "Then you can tell me about my Uncle Rhys."

Carrie turned to him, eyes wide. She wrapped one hand around the other and rested her forehead on the fist.

"Mum," he leaned forward, arms on the table, "all I know is that he was older than father and thought he should have the stone. I need more than that."

She raised her head and, from the defiant look in her eyes, he knew he was in for a fight. "You need to know nothing."

"He came to the house once, didn't he?" As Nick watched, his mother's gaze darted toward him then returned to rest on her clasped hands.

Nick ran his thumb over his lower lip a couple of times, trying to coax the memory to the surface. "It might have been the night of father's service. He was a nice-looking man, well dressed, seemed quite pleasant, but I believe he upset you." When she didn't respond, he continued, "He made a bit of a fuss over me. But now that I look back on it, he was really threatening me, wasn't he? You scuttled me off to my room and I didn't hear what was said."

Carrie was watching him now, slowly shaking her head.

"It was him, wasn't it? He'd come here for the stone."

Nick held his silence. Several minutes passed. Finally, with a deep sigh, his mother focused her attention out the window and said, "He had lovely brown eyes. Odd shade." She paused and Nick could hear her breathing.

"Did he ask about the stone?"

"Not at first." Her brows knitted up as she recalled her brother-in-law. "We talked." She looked down at her hands and Nick thought her face reddened slightly. "He was so easy to talk to. I felt sorry for him. How it must have been for him. In that family." She cocked her head and smiled slightly, as though puzzled by her own behavior. "I became a bit angry with Elias, you know? They must have been cruel to Rhys." She turned her eyes on Nick. "I'd never thought about it before."

"He did ask you about the stone, didn't he?"

"Yes." She paused. "I'd forgotten about it. I told him Elias always carried it. It was probably still with him."

"He believed you?"

"Not at first. You had come downstairs. As you recall, he made a fuss over you. He . . . put his hands on your shoulders, you know, close to your neck." She struggled with her words. "You . . . your neck was so small . . . those big hands of his. He wanted me to see that. He said the stone wouldn't stay lost. It would come back to you. Wouldn't stay lost. You were so small . . . with these big eyes. You were frightened."

"Where is he now?"

"I don't know," she answered quickly.

She stared out the window, chin tilted up, mouth set. Nick

crossed his arms over his chest. "Well," he kept his tone reflective, non-threatening, "how many Rhys Llewellyns can there be in the U.K.? Probably Wales. Common name, but there are ways of narrowing the lot."

She shrugged as though it didn't matter.

"He probably has a telephone, driving license."

Finally she said, "You wouldn't do that, would you?"

"If I have to."

"After I asked you not to?" Her shoulders sagged.

"I wouldn't be pressing you if I didn't believe he has something to do with all this. It isn't simply a case of morbid curiosity."

She sighed and looked down at the table. "You're right, of course. I just thought . . . hoped."

"Where does he live?" He kept his voice soft.

"The States. Last I heard. And he's got a place in Beddgelert."

"What did he do to earn his black sheep status?"

"He's evil."

Weldon had used the same word. "What makes him evil?"

She stared into her teacup for a long time. When she finally looked up at Nick, her eyes betrayed her fear. "This doesn't go beyond us, Nick."

He nodded, hoping he could keep his word.

With a resigned sigh, her shoulders slumped. "There's no easy way to tell this . . ." Gradually, her eyes came to focus on Nick and he saw she wasn't stalling anymore. Then, in her broken way, she told him about how Nick's grandmother, Elen, had been raped. After several weeks in shock, during which time she spoke to no one, she began talking again and it was as though the last weeks hadn't happened. She'd no recollection of the rape. Apparently the violation had been such that she couldn't live with the memory of it, and Elen convinced herself that it had never occurred. "They said she seemed herself again." Carrie ran her finger over a small chip in the cup's rim. Then she pushed the cup away and clasped her hands. "When she told your grandfather she was pregnant, he knew the child wasn't his. But he never told her. That would have destroyed her. Ioan tried to accept Rhys—he knew the child was blameless—but it was difficult for him. Elen doted on him. Barely a year later, Elias was born." Then she added, "Your grandfather never intended for Rhys to have the stone. He wasn't his son."

She stopped and Nick, thinking she was finished, asked, "How does that make Rhys evil?"

"It doesn't." Nick poured them both more tea and Carrie added cream to each cup. "When Rhys was twelve, he killed Elen."

"He killed his own mother? My grandmother?"

She nodded.

"I thought she died in an accident," Nick said. "A fall."

"So everyone thought. Your father . . . he saw the whole thing." She squeezed her eyes shut as though recalling the images Elias described. When she continued, her wording was deliberate. "The staircase was off the foyer. Elias had just come into the house. Elen was a few feet from the stairwell with Rhys facing her. Elias said it was like watching someone in a trance." Carrie seemed to be waiting for a sign from Nick that he was going to follow this no matter how bizarre it turned. He nodded, and she continued. "Elen was backing up toward the top of the stairs. Elias called out to his mother . . . she didn't seem to hear. Rhys stepped closer to Elen, who retreated another foot. She was at the head of the stairs, and before Elias could . . . do anything . . . she took that last step and fell to her death. Broke her neck. Elias said Rhys walked down the stairs, as cool as can be, stepped over his

mother's body, and said to your father, 'I never touched her.'
And that was it. Rhys never spoke of it again."

Nick had so many questions, he hardly knew where to
begin. "Why? Why did he kill her?"

She shook her head. "Elias was never certain, although he
said that shortly before it happened, there had been a change
in the relationship between Elen and Rhys. Elias said she
seemed almost frightened of him."

"Why?"

"Elias suspected it had to do with Rhys's father. He said
Rhys sometimes talked about having much to thank his father
for. Elias didn't understand what he meant—he believed they
were full brothers—and he asked Ioan, who took him into his
confidence."

"So, Rhys knew who his father was."

Carrie didn't respond.

"Who was he?" Nick persisted.

Staring into her tea, Carrie sighed and shook her head.
When she looked up at Nick, she forced a brittle smile. "It's
ridiculous, really. I feel silly even telling you."

"It isn't your story. You're just repeating it."

"Rhys believed his father was a demon who took on the
form of a man to lie with his mother." She fidgeted with the
teacup.

"An incubus?"

She gave Nick an odd look. "What do you know of such
things?"

Shrugging, he said, "I'm not a scholar or anything. Seems
to me I read somewhere that Merlin was the product of such a
relationship."

"Wizards." Carrie snorted. "It's silly. The Welsh are su-
perstitious that way, aren't they?"

"I suppose." Nick could tell she didn't want him to take

this seriously, and he certainly didn't want her to stop talking, so he moved the conversation back to safer ground. "What happened to Rhys after Grandmother died?"

"He stayed with the family until he went to university. No one saw him again after that."

She looked up at Nick, eyes narrowed slightly. "The story is outlandish." She laid her hand on the table. "But it is as real to them as this table is to us. That is all that matters."

"Where was Rhys all this time?"

"As far as we knew, he stayed in the States." She twisted a strand of silver hair that fell against her neck. "Your father had been careful in selecting the stone's guardian. He and Ben were friends, but Ben lived in the States. They didn't see much of each other. A lot of people were at Elias's memorial service and Ben just blended in, I suppose." She paused. "A year after your father died, Ben came round and told me he had the stone. I told him to keep it."

"Is that when you and Ben started seeing one another?"

She nodded and Nick could see the memories in the way her eyes softened.

"How did Rhys find out Ben had the stone?"

She bridged her fingers across her forehead, closed her eyes and took a deep breath. "I'm afraid that was my fault." After a few moments, she continued. "About six months ago, Ben and I were watching the telly one evening and it was after that incident in the States where a man went mad after being cut off by another driver, followed the driver to a parking lot, and shot him and two people who tried to help. Then he shot himself. They interviewed a psychologist about road rage, as they call it, and I wasn't certain, but I thought it was Rhys. His last name is Lewis now. I told Ben and he began to investigate him. He learned Rhys has a home near Washington D.C. and one in Wales." She sipped her tea and gave the cup an odd look, as though surprised to find they had been talking long enough for it to go cold. "I think Rhys must have learned of Ben's interest in him." Looking up at Nick, she asked, "Do you think Rhys has the stone now?"

Nick pushed his hand through his hair. "Probably not." Although he wasn't sure how he knew that.

He stared at the table's surface, allowing the red checks in the placemats to blur. Then he turned to his mother. "Will you explain something to me?"

She didn't respond.

He forced himself to take a calming breath. He was angry, but she was fragile. "If Rhys is so dangerous, why didn't you tell me about him before?"

"I thought if you didn't know about Rhys or the stone, neither could hurt you." Her eyes shone with tears. "I know that was stupid. But I was afraid I'd lose you as well."

"I know, Mum." He sighed. "I know."

His cell phone rang, and Nick unclipped it from his belt and noted the number from the pub in the display before answering. Frowning, he pressed the button. Leslie never called unless it was important.

"What's up, Les?"

"There's someone here at the pub asking for you."

"Who?"

"Says her name is Olivia Pike."

"I'll be right there."

Before he left, Nick sat with his mother for a few minutes, asking if she needed anything. "You and Aunt Helen ought to go to the cinema."

She shrugged—a good sign. Often his suggestions were met with no response at all.

But then, as he was leaving, Carrie took hold of Nick's arm. "You know why Ben is dead, don't you? Because he had the stone. Promise me one thing. If you get it, give it to Rhys. Before anyone else dies."

He let her read the answer in his eyes. She shook her head as she let go of him. "Fools. I married into a family of fools."

Chapter 27

At five-thirty a.m., some guy left his apartment to walk that monster of a dog. Earl figured it had to be the Pike woman's dog. Couldn't be two like that in the same building. Maybe that was the guy who came down to her apartment last night. He slumped down in his car. If that guy was walking the dog, then maybe Pike was gone for a while. He lit a cigarette and tossed the match out the window. Then he tried to figure out what the Ice Queen would do if he had to tell her he never saw that little woman go near her apartment. Probably bite his head off.

Two cigarettes later, the guy and the dog returned; Earl still hadn't figured out his likely fate.

He wished he'd brought a radio. He'd driven here straight from his meeting with the Ice Queen. Hadn't slept all night. He could barely keep his eyes open. And, Jeez, this was dull. Although he liked to consider himself of average intelligence—Lonny used to tell Earl he was as smart as the next guy, depending on who the next guy was—Earl had never found much amusement in his own company. He supposed he was happiest when he was in the Army. Not much time to think, mostly people telling him what to do. For Earl, that had been blowing things up. He'd been pretty good at it, too. But he'd seen more than one guy accidentally blow himself up and figured it was just a matter of time before he did the same thing. So, once he got out, he learned how to break into houses from Dickie Snyder. Earl didn't know if Dickie was still alive, but figured if he was, Dickie wouldn't have much to show him anymore. Earl had never been caught, which was more than Dickie could say.

About fifteen minutes later, the man left the building again. This time Earl was thinking maybe he should follow him. The way he dug his keys out of his pocket, it looked like he was going to his car. Earl slid down in his seat as the guy started to cross the street and stayed hunkered down, listening for a car door to shut. Then a shadow blocked the sun. Earl looked up and saw the guy looking down at him. Oh, shit.

He reached for his keys in the ignition, but the guy had the door open and Earl's collar in his fist before he could turn them. He pulled Earl's face to his own.

"All right," he said, his voice a harsh whisper. "Who are you and why are you watching me?"

Where was a cop when you needed one?

His grip tightened. "Tell me."

Earl looked into the dark eyes and nodded. He had nothing to bargain with.

"Who are you?"

"Jessup. Earl Jessup."

"Why are you watching me?"

"I'm not." Tighter. "Watching for a woman."

"Her name?"

"Pike."

"Why?"

"Bein' paid."

"By whom?"

"Name's Jillian something."

"Jillian what?"

"Don't know." Earl felt like he was breathing through a straw. "I swear."

"What does she look like?"

"Skinny. Blond. Icy."

"What does she want?"

Earl barely hesitated. "Some stone." He could tell from the way the guy's grip relented a little that he'd answered right.

"Now," the man said, his voice real calm, "this is a very important question." He squeezed a little tighter, paused and said, "Where is Max?"

Earl sensed this guy wasn't going to like his answer. He pulled in as much air as he could and said, "Don't know. She went with some black guy." Everything looked gray. "I swear. I don't know where he took her."

After a long second or two, Earl's throat opened up. The man reached past him and yanked the keys from the ignition. Then he grabbed Earl's arm. "Get out."

Earl tried to move, but couldn't. *Christ,* he thought, *I'm frozen here.* Then he remembered his seat belt and unbuckled it. The guy hauled him out of his car and around the back to the trunk, which he opened using Earl's keys.

"Get in."

He looked around for a witness. Six a.m. on a Sunday wasn't exactly high-traffic time for this area. Where the hell were those cops? The joggers? He glanced into the trunk, which reeked of spilled beer. "You're not sticking me in there."

"Make enough noise, someone will hear you."

Even though this guy had no more in the way of weapons than Earl had, Earl knew he didn't have a choice. He never had a choice. Shit. He climbed into the trunk and with a loud clang, everything went black. Too bad he never gave much thought to breaking out of places.

Chapter 28

"She's in your office," Leslie told Nick.

Something in the way she spoke made him stop. "What's wrong?"

"The lady's all strung up."

" 'Strung up'?"

"Distracted. You say something and it's a minute before she responds. I'm no psychiatrist, but I'd be careful with her." She paused and tucked a pint under the Courage spigot. "I gave her a dram of whisky. Wasn't sure that was the proper thing to do, but she needed a stiffener. Put it down in one swallow, she did. She's on her second. Asked if she wanted anything to eat, but she didn't. I feel sorry for her." She looked up at him from beneath thick, dark bangs and gave him one of her easy grins. "I usually don't feel sorry for her type, if you know what I mean."

"Thanks, Les."

When Nick opened the door to his office, he saw what Leslie meant. This was not the stunning, brash Olivia Pike he'd met the other day. He'd seen these eyes in news footage of refugees—both haunted and numb. He did recognize the cigarette; its ash was almost an inch long. Then he noticed her little finger.

"What happened to your finger?" He closed the door behind him.

She looked at the purple, swollen digit as though it were a distraction. "I fell." She didn't bother to sound convincing.

He pulled a chair up to his own desk, straddling the seat.

"Do you want to sit here?" She flicked the ash into the wastebasket.

"Not right now."

He emptied an ashtray full of paper clips onto the desk and pushed it toward her. "We should have someone take a look at that finger."

She took a drag off her cigarette. "That's the least of my problems right now."

"Right." Nick placed his forearms on the chair's back and folded his hands together. "What is your most urgent problem?"

She stared at the wall without answering.

"Why did you want to see me?"

Finally, she turned to him. "I thought you might have some idea just what in the fuck is going on."

"Meaning?"

"You know what I mean." Her eyes were full and when she blinked, a tear slipped out. She brushed it away with her thumb. "I can't get hold of my sister."

"Is she still in Chicago?"

"I have no idea." She inhaled on the cigarette. Her lipstick left a red mark on the filter. "Like I said, I can't get hold of her."

Nick wasn't sure why he felt the stab of concern over Olivia's sister, whom he'd never met. Then he realized Olivia was asking him something. "Pardon?"

"Pay attention," she snapped. "Have you heard of a place called Alyssum?"

"It's in the Scillies. Why?"

"Max found a picture of Ben. Taken on Alyssum. He was with two other guys. One of them was . . ." She pressed her fingers to her forehead. "Penn. That's right. Arthur Penn."

"Arthur Penn," Nick repeated. The name wasn't familiar.

Olivia sighed and took a drink. "Cliff Bradshaw was supposed to fly there tomorrow."

"Bradshaw knew him?"

"Knew of him. He's rich and publicity shy. Runs some kind of foundation." She pulled in a deep breath and turned toward Nick. "This is about that stupid stone, isn't it?"

Nick shifted in his chair as he studied Olivia. "Did your sister know about the stone?"

When she looked away, he knew he'd guessed right. "She's got it, hasn't she?"

"She did have it. God knows anymore." She stubbed out the cigarette. "What is it about that stone, anyway? And don't tell me it's a family heirloom. People are getting killed."

"Who?"

She released her breath with a sigh. "Cliff."

"How?"

"Drug overdose. I found him in his office. There was a syringe on the floor."

"You certain he didn't inject himself?"

"I'd bet on it." She paused and drew in a shaky breath. "This guy was there. Simon Murdoch. He probably did it." She glanced toward Nick, who shook his head. "And there was some other guy who was big, but didn't have much to say. They're looking for Max."

"Is that what happened to your finger?"

She didn't answer for a minute. Just stared past Nick. Then she swallowed and said, "I think Simon Murdoch enjoys hurting people." She reached into her purse and tossed a business card on the desk. "I'm supposed to call him if I find Max." Her lips pressed into a grim line. "Then he left."

Nick took the card. It had Murdoch's name and phone number and nothing more. He slipped it into his pocket. "Did you call the police?"

She shook her head and sniffed. "I left. I don't know why. I panicked, I guess. They'll probably think I killed him." She dug into her cigarette pack. "I was with him last night."

"Your leaving the scene wasn't a point in your favor, I'll grant you." He paused. "But first they have to prove that it was murder."

Her swollen finger, with its bright red nail, looked as if it belonged on another hand, attached to another person. "Are you telling me everything?" He felt certain that she wasn't.

"All you need to know." She lit her cigarette and drew on it, squinting her right eye as she blew a stream of smoke up toward the ceiling. "It's your turn. Tell me about the stone."

He barely hesitated. "It's called the heartstone and is believed to be a stone that came from the hilt of Caliburn." Then he added, "That's Welsh for Excalibur."

When her expression didn't change, he said, "That's the sword that belonged to—"

"I know what it is, for Christ's sake. Do you think you Brits are the only ones with a liberal arts education?"

Nick shrugged.

"Are you serious?"

"Quite."

"For Christ's sake, Nick. That's a goddamned fairytale."

Defending this tale came easier to him than believing it. "To some."

"Does that make it worth killing people over?"

"Apparently." He shifted in his chair. "It's also the implications."

"What implications?"

"The return of the stone to the sword supposedly portends the return of King Arthur."

She gaped at him. "You can't tell me you believe this . . . crap."

He shoved an open hand through his hair. "Someone believes it enough to kill for it."

"Who?"

"Rhys Llewellyn. Lewis as he's known in the States. My uncle."

"Your uncle?"

He nodded. "He's the family's nasty secret."

"What are you going to do?"

"I'm going to find him."

He finally saw a flicker of defiance in her eyes. "I'm going with you."

"Why?"

She picked up the whisky and swirled the liquid so it left a coating on the side of the glass. He thought she was going to drain it, but instead she set it down on the desk and flapped her wounded hand in a hopeless gesture. "Because I haven't got anywhere else to go right now."

Chapter 29

They were held up at Heathrow for several hours while the police brought in the sniffer dogs and the bomb scare was checked out. Antony had been right; there was no bomb. Max tried to convince herself that the panic had nothing to do with the stone. But she couldn't dismiss the woman screaming in a foreign language who, while fleeing from the threat of being blown up, had attempted to wrest her away from Antony.

Antony dozed for about an hour, slumped down in a chair, and while Max wanted more answers from him, she realized he needed the sleep. As she sat on the hard chair, considering all that had happened in the last few days, she had the sensation of being watched. She looked around; people were standing and sitting in every available space. Finally, she saw him—a boy of about thirteen or fourteen, wearing a black beret and staring at her. Swallowing down a surge of fear, she poked her elbow into Antony's arm, and he woke with a start.

But before she could point the boy out, he'd slipped into the crowd.

To apologize for waking him, she got them both some coffee. He'd taken about two sips when his phone went off.

"Yeah . . . Bruce. Went fine. Thanks . . . That's okay . . . Listen, you got anything small available? . . . Heathrow . . . Yeah, sure." He glanced at Max and said, "He's checking."

"Who is Bruce and what is he checking?"

Antony grinned. "He's the guy who loaned me the jet to fly you over here."

"So, now you need something smaller to fly us to Cornwall."

"You got it."

"Why didn't you ask him for the smaller plane earlier?"

"I like to plan as I go. The fewer people know what I'm up to, the happier I am."

"Don't you trust him?"

"More than most." He turned his attention back to the phone. "Yeah . . . Great. No problem . . . Thanks."

He stood and pocketed the phone. "Let's go. We're driving up to Luton. He's got a plane for us there."

Luton was only about forty miles north of Heathrow, but they had traffic to contend with and the ride took almost ninety minutes. Along the way, Antony told her about Bruce Langford. "He's a friend of Arthur's. Arthur's got a lot of grateful friends."

"Why's that?"

"He's got a way of making people want to do things. Good things. Hard to explain, but when you meet him you'll see what I mean." He paused. "Bruce, the guy who owns the jet and the plane, is one of the foundation's grant recipients. He used the money to establish a division of his company that flies people to places they need to get to real bad but don't have the money. He doesn't charge. Say you got a kid who needs emergency surgery. Something like that. Also been known to smuggle good people out of bad places. I've done some flying for him. There's about nine or ten owners of small fleets involved. At any time, there's at least one plane or jet available. Bruce got it all organized. He knows how to make rich people feel guilty."

"Have you decided where we're flying to yet?"

"Yeah, I think I'll give Peter Thorpe a call. He's got a private strip outside of Helston."

"Is he one of Arthur's recruits?" she asked, not liking the way the word was interchangeable with Rhys's people.

"Yeah." He took a drink from a can of Coke and fit it back into the holder. "A new one. Don't know him myself, but I figure he'll let us fly into his airstrip." He paused. "That's the way these folks are."

"Nice man."

"I hope so."

"You sound dubious."

"I was born dubious," he replied.

"This doesn't surprise me."

The corners of his mouth twitched, like he was suppressing a smile.

"How did Arthur recruit you?"

He drove for a ways before saying, "A woman I was real close to received one of the grants. She'd set up a small hospital in Rwanda. Rebels came in one day and trashed the clinic, killed her and two of the staff. There were only three. Arthur got there about the same time I did, a couple days after it all happened." He paused and added as an aside, "That was back when Arthur left Alyssum. Hardly does anymore. Well, there was one nurse trying to keep a score of really sick people alive. All I wanted to do was bring my friend home. Far as I was concerned, the rest of 'em could go to hell." They were stopped at a light and he turned his head toward Max, looking into her eyes, and even though the intimacy seemed uncomfortable for him, he held onto her gaze as he continued. "Arthur talked me into flying out some people who were in really bad shape. Mostly little ones. He did it without making me feel guilty. Never offered me a penny. Just took me around, showed me what Thea had done—with so little—and what she'd wanted to do." He swallowed and looked away. "I wound up staying and helping out for more than a year while they got another grant and rebuilt the clinic. After that I came to work for him." Behind them, a horn blared. Antony scowled into the rear-view mirror as he pressed the gas. They drove a couple blocks before Antony said, "I'm no do-gooder, Max. I toss a few bucks in the Salvation Army buckets around Christmas time, and that's about it. But I think a person who knows himself knows when something's right to do." He glanced at her. "That's all."

"That's a lot."

Antony shrugged.

Once they finally got in the air, the flight over southern England took a little more than an hour. Although the sky was overcast, they'd left the rain behind in London.

The plane, a small Cessna, seated only four people and the imposed closeness added to Max's tension. She tried to follow their route on a map Antony had given her and was able to pick out the river Tamar and the flat, granite plateau of Bodmin Moor. It didn't seem to take any time before they began following the path of 394, a dual carriageway that went through Helston.

"Antony . . ." He sighed before she could continue.

"What?" she asked, defensive.

"Every time you start a sentence with my name, I know it's gonna be a hard answer."

"I'll make it a true or false." She smiled. "Antony, you didn't come clear across the ocean to bring me to Alyssum just to help me find Ben. It's because I have the stone, isn't?"

"That's right."

"Well, why didn't you just take the stone from me?"

He shot her a look that seemed both disappointed and shocked. "I don't do stuff like that."

"I've been around this stone long enough to know that the usual rules of engagement don't apply."

He grunted.

"What do you need me for?"

He didn't answer right away and Max was afraid he'd decided he'd told her enough. But then he said, "Ben was supposed to tell you all this."

"What?"

Another long pause, and Max prompted him with, "Was he going to tell me when he asked me to come to Wales?"

Antony glanced at her, but didn't respond.

"Why Beddgelert?"

"Rhys has got a home there. Ben was watching him." He sighed and continued. "He wanted you to meet Nick. Explain what was going on."

"I knew I should've gone," she said.

"Don't beat yourself up," Antony said. "Ben wasn't sure that was the thing to do."

"Why not?"

"Oh, he trusted you all right. He just . . ."

"What?"

"He knew he had a lot to ask of you."

"All he had to do was ask."

"I never thought he should tell you anyway. The way I see it, if a thing's supposed to happen, it'll happen."

"What's supposed to happen?"

She wasn't expecting an answer from him, so when he said, "Langford's place is right near here," she was disappointed but not surprised. She'd get it out of him later. He studied the terrain, looking out the small window on his side, and finally said, "See this little road under us?"

"You're going to tell me," she said, determined to get an answer.

"Once we get the car," he said, "but for now make sure you see that road."

It looked like a beige ribbon twined around a wooded area which they were passing over now. "I see it."

"It's just beyond these woods here."

As promised, the dark green trees gave way to a grass airstrip, which was probably the length of two football fields and about as wide as one.

"This is it?" They didn't seem to be descending.

"We're coming in from the other way so we'll have the wind against us." He gave her a quick grin. "It'll help us stop."

"I'm all for that."

They passed over a hangar, big enough for perhaps two small planes. Northwest of the hangar sat a large, two-story brick house with a stone patio. The garage was set off so that it faced the side of the house and there were two cars in the paved driveway. Access to the airstrip was a gravel road that branched off the main road and cut between the house and the hangar, clipping off the southeast corner of the yard before it came to a stop at the airstrip.

Antony banked the plane, bringing it around slowly, then began the descent. Fields and hedges sped by in a blur as the ground came up. Max grabbed the edges of the seat. The plane bounced once, twice, three times as the wheels touched down, and they sped down the strip toward the trees. When they were about twenty feet from the woods, Antony turned the Cessna and taxied back toward the hangar, bringing it to a stop just off the runway with its nose angled toward the building.

Max didn't see a soul around, but Antony didn't seem to be looking for anyone. "Thorpe said just to leave it here," he told her and she climbed out, relieved to be finished with airplanes for a while.

As they cut across the lawn, Antony nodded toward the maroon car in the driveway. "Thorpe said to take the Peugeot."

"This guy is really generous."

He just grunted.

Max climbed in on the passenger side as Antony opened the driver's door. "Shit," he said, adding a scowl. "He was supposed to leave the keys in the car."

Nothing dangled from the ignition but when Max flipped down the visor, a set of keys dropped to the leather seat.

"Shit," he said again without much emotion. "I was supposed to leave the keys in the plane." He tossed her his flight bag.

"Put them under the visor," Max suggested.

Antony was grinning as he turned toward the plane.

Max rolled down a window and breathed in the fresh air. After all the noise and commotion at Heathrow, the quiet here seemed almost eerie.

Just then she heard the crunch of gravel and saw a car appear on the other side of the house and speed down the access road toward the airstrip.

Having placed the keys, Antony had just dropped to the

ground and he unzipped his jacket as he looked in the direction of the car. The small, dark sedan swung around, spraying gravel as it lurched to a stop. Max's first instinct was to see if he needed help, then decided for a lot of reasons that wasn't a good idea. From the Peugeot, she had an unblocked view of the airstrip, but it was at least a hundred feet away and she couldn't see well. Then she remembered her camera with its telephoto zoom. While she wouldn't be able to make out details, it would be an improvement. She held it up to her right eye, focused and waited.

Judging from the way Antony's shoulders had slumped and he glanced up at the sky, Max guessed that he wasn't happy to see the car's occupants. A big man got out of the driver's side, came around to the passenger door and opened it.

The younger man who got out was smaller and wore a brown tweed sports jacket. As he stood, he drew his jacket back and slipped his hands into the pockets of his khakis. Antony, arms crossed over his chest, looked down at the younger man. While she could see them talking, she couldn't hear their words. The big guy stood off to the side, hands folded, at the ready. Max snapped a photo. After about a minute, Antony unfolded his arms and planted his fists on his hips for a second, then gestured widely with one arm, as though taking in the entire area. The younger man paced a short line back and forth in front of Antony, head down. Then he stopped and must have issued some signal because the big man walked over to the Cessna and opened the passenger door, then disappeared inside it. Less than a minute later, he climbed out. Through the lens of her camera, Max could see the shrug he delivered to the younger man as he waved his hands in a "what can I do?" gesture. Now, the younger guy was angry. He raised his voice as he continued to pace. His movements were jerky, no longer fluid, and he kept his hands in his pockets as though he didn't trust them out on their own. Antony appeared to be watching, waiting. A couple times he ran his hand over his smooth head, but otherwise he kept his arms folded across his chest. At no time did he look toward her and the car.

Finally, the younger man stopped pacing, yelled a final word or two at Antony and literally kicked the ground, sending a tuft of grass flying. Max pressed the shutter release. He walked back toward their car. She snapped again as he glanced over his shoulder at Antony who had dropped his arms to his side. He opened the passenger door and, just as he was about to climb into the car, he pulled a small gun from his pocket, turned and shot Antony in the chest. Max had pressed her finger to the shutter release before she realized what was happening. She lowered the camera as though her naked eye might give her a different picture. But Antony still lay on the ground. She wanted to cry out, felt she should, but was mute. Frozen in place.

As she sat, numb, her mind fighting to connect thoughts, she realized the man who had shot Antony was staring right at her. Defiantly, she pressed the shutter release again. Then she dropped the camera to the floor and told herself to move. As she climbed over the gearshift, she kept her eyes on the two men who were now getting into their car.

Damn. Everything in this car was backwards. She couldn't make her left hand turn the key the right way. And the clutch. Damn. Where the hell was it?

The engine screeched as she tried to find reverse. The sedan was moving toward her, cutting across the lawn. Then she heard a gunshot, followed by another, and four more. She thought they were firing at her, but then the sedan slumped to one side and then the other. After several more feet it was moving like a dog rubbing its butt across a carpet. That was when Max saw Antony, still lying on the ground, but with a gun in his hand. He was alive. As she watched, the younger man got out of the car, looked at the flattened rear tires, then toward Antony.

Max fumbled around for first gear. She could run the guy down. But then she heard another gunshot, looked up and saw the man shoot Antony in the chest four more times.

"You bastard." Max found reverse and floored the accelerator.

Chapter 30

Earl slept for a while, curled up in the trunk of his own car. He felt like a turkey falling asleep on Thanksgiving. In the oven. He'd lost track of time and couldn't read his watch in the dark. Still daylight, judging from the crack in the floorboard. He banged on the trunk's lid with his foot, as he'd done every ten minutes he'd been awake. "HEY! ANYBODY! HELP!" God, he wanted to get out of here before the Ice Queen showed up. He'd rather explain how he got here to a cop than to her. "HELP! ANYBODY! HELP!"

He fought to stay awake, but the warmth and darkness acted like a sleeping pill. He dozed.

The next thing he knew, blazing light blinded him. He squinted, unable to see past it and unable to remember what was going on.

"What the hell are you doing in here?" He recognized the flinty voice and everything came back to him in a whoosh.

Adjusting his baseball cap so the visor partially blocked the light, he could make out the familiar, bony figure, square jaw and then her harsh little mouth. "I asked you a question," it said.

"Well, I, um . . ." He pushed himself off the floor of the trunk, his joints aching. "This guy," he nodded at the apartment building across the street, "he made me. Don't know how." He stumbled through his explanation.

When he finished, she said, "And he overpowered you with what?"

"He's stronger than he looks." Earl wanted to add that he was more than he seemed, but then she'd want to know what he meant and Earl didn't know how to explain.

"What's this man's name?"

Earl shrugged. He hadn't thought to ask. She stared at him for a long five or ten seconds, then looked past him, toward the apartment building. "Your brother's as good as dead."

From the start, Earl knew it would come to this. When it did, he had hoped he'd have the balls to tell her to go screw herself. Her cell phone rang before he had time to work up the nerve.

"What?" she snapped into the phone.

Earl climbed out of the trunk and slammed it shut, then leaned his butt against it. Whoever was on the phone had caused a total attitude change in the Ice Queen. She'd tensed up and her eyes had widened so Earl could see the whites surrounding the blue.

"I thought that Simon . . . ?" She listened for a while. "I see. Then what about the . . ." Earl zoned out then, preferring the silence in his head, rousing himself when he heard her say, "I'll be flying back to London first chance I get."

He nearly peed with relief.

The Ice Queen continued, "I'll call you when I land."

After disconnecting, she stared off past Earl again, like she was figuring something out. One of the many things Earl hated about all this was how half the time he felt like a punching bag and the other half he felt invisible.

Without looking at him, she said, "I understand you know how to blow things up."

He considered denying it, but knew that was pointless. "Yeah."

"Good." She dropped her cell phone into her purse. "Pack your suitcase. We're going to England."

Earl wanted to climb back into the trunk.

Chapter 31

Nick played the melody of an old Welsh folk song about a blind harpist, fingering the keys with his right hand as he hummed softly. After the first few measures, his left hand began to fill in with the bass keys. He stopped humming and concentrated on his fingering until his hands remembered. Then he let his mind drift off. His memories of Wales were dim, like images from dreams that had once been deep-rooted, but had faded away so that only their edges remained vivid.

He'd never lost the language, though. When they moved to England, they had spoken Welsh at home. That stopped after his father died, when his mother practically forbade its use. While this had puzzled Nick, at the time he thought perhaps it reminded her too much of his father. Now, he realized it was more than that. She'd been afraid of anything that linked them with Nick's uncle. If she'd had her way, she'd have rubbed the country off the map.

He should've gone to Wales last month, when Ben had asked. But there'd been the pub and Leslie's son had been down with the flu. Ben had said it could wait. But Nick had to wonder if things would be different now had he gone. Like twenty-seven years ago when Nick's father had asked if he wanted to go sailing. He'd passed—one of the kids down the road had new ponies to ride. To this day, Nick believed that Elias and his friend wouldn't have gone out so far had Nick been on board. Then there was his mother: he'd gladly ceded his responsibility to Ben. The spiked ridges in the pattern of his life were places where he'd declined, couldn't be bothered. Let another person down, sometimes fatally.

He stopped playing mid-chord. Tomorrow he'd go home. As he sat on the bench, the chords still thrumming in his fingers, he looked down at the ring on his right hand. It had been his father's. Beneath the carved dragon was its inscription "*Marchog Amddiffynnydd*," Welsh for "Knight Protector." And didn't that have an ironic touch to it?

A pleasantly drunk voice urged him to keep going. "Do the one about the cockle woman," he added.

"Another time, Danny." Nick left the bench and returned to the bar, where he pulled a bitter for himself.

Leslie had offered to put Olivia up for the night, and for that he was relieved. He'd have his fill of her soon enough. As he scanned the room, looking to see if any of the half-dozen or so customers needed a refill, Weldon Terry popped into his head. *Don't be daft,* Nick told himself.

If Terry had been the one to tell Nick that Rhys was some sort of supernatural being, he'd have written it off. But his mother, the woman who steadfastly refused to acknowledge God, had planted this idea in his head and now he couldn't shake it. So far, he'd resisted the urge to ring Weldon. Not because he thought the old man would tell Nick he was being foolish, but because Weldon might convince him it was all true. He took a gulp of bitter, swished it around and swallowed. Then again, perhaps Weldon could explain how a human got mistaken for a half-demon. Nick moved down to the end of the bar, looked around to make certain no one was within earshot, picked up the phone and punched in Weldon's number.

Weldon seemed pleased to hear from Nick. "Did you read the book?"

"This afternoon."

"What did you think?"

"It . . . it's interesting."

"Do you understand why the stone is no longer in your custody?"

"I said I read it. I didn't say I agreed with every word." He wasn't going to let this old man talk him into anything.

"Fair enough."

Nick pushed on to the reason for the call. "When we spoke the other day, you said my uncle was evil. How did you mean that? I mean," he rushed ahead before he could stop himself, "was his evil a genetic thing?" That sounded all wrong. "Wait, that's not what I mean . . ."

"Take your time," Weldon said, "I'm listening."

"Well," Nick began again. "This will sound absurd, but when I spoke with my mum about Rhys, she told me a few things. Rhys wasn't my grandfather's child. He was the product of a rape. That much is fact. But then my mum said the story goes that the rapist was an incubus." He managed a weak chuckle.

"I knew it!" Weldon's excitement practically gushed through the phone line. "No one had ever told me, but I suspected."

"Well, assuming this isn't simply legend—"

"Nick," he said, "you can stop qualifying. I know you're reluctant to accept this. Look at it this way. If I'm right, then you're forewarned. If I'm not . . . if Rhys is simply a foul, evil mortal, then all you've done is added a bit of folklore to your cocktail party repertoire." He continued before Nick could respond. "Now, you asked my opinion. I cannot honestly say whether he's the real thing or not, though I wouldn't be surprised if he were. An incubus is a demon who takes the form of a human to sleep with a mortal woman. The product of that union is a wizard." He paused, as though sorting his knowledge. "Actually, there are two sorts of wizards: mortals who learn the craft of magic and those who are, shall we say, born to it. We won't concern ourselves with the former."

Nick leaned against the bar. "Supposedly Merlin was fathered in the same manner. Why is one good and the other not?"

"Excellent question with, I believe, a simple answer. Merlin's mother was a nun. Also, he was baptized. I would guess that Rhys wasn't. And, I think you'll find that Merlin isn't without his . . . shall we say . . . puckish tendencies."

"You're talking about Merlin in the present tense. Even if he did exist during Arthur's time, he wouldn't be around today. Would he?"

"Never underestimate the power of the spirit."

Rather than engage in a metaphysical discussion, Nick asked, "What sort of powers would a wizard have?"

"Illusory abilities, hypnotic powers, powers over animals, plants." Then he added, "Merlin had some predictive powers."

"Can a wizard change the future?"

"That's one of those paradoxes. You see, even if you're able to see the future, who knows what events occurred to bring it about? If you try to tamper with the present because you believe it will alter the future, how can you know what you're doing wasn't intended to happen?"

Nick wasn't certain, but he thought that made sense.

"Are you going to find Rhys?" Weldon asked.

"That's my plan."

"Be very careful."

"Any advice?"

He didn't answer immediately, apparently giving the question some consideration. Finally, he said, "Don't let him charm you. I know you think that's not a worry, but he may be able to make you do things you'd not otherwise do. Also, the Rhys I recall was distinguished-looking and an elegant dresser. I suspect he's on the vain side. I'm not certain how that may help you, but there it is."

"Well, thanks."

"If you need to talk to me, I'll be here."

Nick thanked him again and hung up, wondering just when in the conversation he stopped thinking all this was silly.

Chapter 32

After a night visited by one unsettling dream after another, none of which she could remember, Max ate a light breakfast and headed toward the steamer office at the corner of Quay Street and Wharf Road.

When she'd fled from Helston yesterday, she'd driven with the assumption that the man who had killed Antony knew she'd head for Alyssum, and Penzance was the first logical departure point. For that reason, Max had considered driving all the way to Land's End, but by the time she reached Penzance, her nerves were spent.

The drive hadn't taken long and was a straight shot on 394 of only about forty miles, but it was forty miles of reliving the moments surrounding Antony's murder. She'd parked near the docks, telling the lot's proprietor that she'd be gone overnight. Then she'd learned she was too late to catch a steamer to the Scillies, so she'd found an inexpensive bed and breakfast for the night.

Now, if she concentrated on Antony's objective—getting her to Alyssum—she could still put one foot in front of the other.

At first she'd wondered if he was paranoid. Now he was dead. So was Ben. One reason she'd never accepted Ben's death was that she'd never allowed herself to imagine the circumstances of it. Having him gone forever was hard enough, but facing the fact that his death had probably been violent was nearly unbearable. With an effort, she diverted some of that grief into anger, resolving that she would take this stone to Alyssum, and she would not die in the process.

Any way she approached Alyssum had its risks. But Max figured the steamer to St. Mary's would be crowded and probably had some form of security.

The man at the office counter was tall and slender with a head that seemed too large and round for his neck. He reminded Max of a jack-o'-lantern. After paying for the one-way ticket, she still had two hundred and thirty-two pounds left.

"Any luggage?" he asked.

"No, I'm just spending the day."

"St. Mary's is lovely."

She noted his flat, west country accent. "Actually, I'm going to Alyssum. How do I get there from St. Mary's?"

"There'll be a launch to meet up with the steamer. Five quid." Then his face clouded over and his hand froze as it was handing her the ticket. "I'm afraid the gardens are closed today."

"Oh. Well, I'm sure I'll enjoy St. Mary's."

"That you will." His relief showed in his smile. "The *Scillonian* leaves in about an hour. They'll be boarding any time now. Enjoy the day."

She walked the few blocks to the pier and the steamer. The gulls' sad cries mingled with the sound of water slapping against the side of a boat, and the sea smell triggered a distant memory. She was walking on a beach with her parents and Olivia, linked together hand to hand—Ben, Max, Olivia and their mother, Suzanne. The waves splashed their bare ankles, and the sand squishing between her toes made Max feel so alive. Maybe she could do this.

As she neared the line of passengers boarding the *Scillonian*, she noticed a large man wearing a dark gray suit. He stood out among the casually dressed tourists and the steamer's uniformed staff. Did he look familiar or just out of place? Then she saw his thick neck and thin ponytail. Damn. Deciding she'd never get past him, she started back up the pier.

Now what? She needed to hire a boat, but couldn't go down to the harbor because that was probably where they'd be looking for her. Her best bet might be one of these pubs along the waterfront. Where else would a boatman hang out?

She tried the door to the first pub she passed. Locked. Of course. Pubs didn't open until eleven and it was barely nine-thirty. She spent the time running from one shop to the next, picking up a map of Alyssum and a penlight and a phone card. During that time she decided she wouldn't go directly to Alyssum. She'd find a way to get to Bryher, the island closest to Alyssum, and from there see if she could rent a boat. She wasn't much of a sailor, but the islands were so close together—less than a quarter mile—she could practically swim the distance.

At one minute past eleven, she tried the door to The Ferryman. Small and dimly lit, the pub smelled like an ashtray. Wooden stools lined up against the bar resembled careless soldiers. Two were occupied. On one sat a heavily-bearded man with a prominent Adam's apple. He stared into the mirror behind the bar as he slowly blew a stream of smoke into the air. Another man, farther down the bar, reminded Max of the pirates that had made the town famous. His hair was wild and dark beyond the receding hairline. One eye squinted at her and the other, wide open, stared.

A double row of small tables made up the rest of the pub's seating. Max saw only one female customer, and she had a series of tattoos down the side of her arm. Apparently The Ferryman did not cater to the tourist trade.

The bartender had been watching Max from the far end, and now she walked toward her. The woman was in her thirties, with bright red hair cut into severe bangs and coming down just below her ears on the sides. She wore a silver stud in one nostril.

"I wonder if you could help me," Max said as the woman stopped in front of her, only the scarred, wooden bar separating them. "I'm trying to get out to Bryher. Do you know of a boat I might be able to hire?"

The woman rested her arms on the edge of the bar. "Why don't you take the *Scillonian* like the rest of the tourists?"

"I missed it. I don't want to wait until tomorrow."

Leaning against her folded arms so that her breasts bulged beneath her black tank top, the bartender cocked her chin and said, "Doubt that you'll find anyone here, but you might—"

"I can take you."

Both Max and the bartender looked to see who had spoken. The bartender tossed her head back and laughed—an odd staccato sound.

Standing, the pirate wasn't much taller than Max. He wore a knit cap and his stomach spilled over his belt like a sack of grain.

"Roy, you're not fit to cross the street."

She was probably right. The scruffy beard barely covered cheeks flushed by wind and booze. He wobbled on his feet. What time of the day did Roy have to start drinking to achieve this state of intoxication by eleven a.m.? How sober did one have to be to pilot a boat? The bartender wasn't laughing anymore.

"You're half again as wet as you look if you take him up, dearie. He'll spark out before you're a mile out." Then she added, "If you're lucky."

Grinning, Roy didn't offer an argument. Max counted one missing tooth and two brown ones. "How much?" she asked.

"What's your offer?"

"I can give you a hundred pounds."

He snorted. "Barely pay for petrol." But he didn't turn away.

Max crossed her arms over her chest. "How much does your trouble cost?"

He smirked in reply.

She turned toward the people at the tables. All were watching her. "Is there anyone in here with a boat who's willing to take me to Bryher who doesn't think it's funny to dick around with the price?" Her challenge met with indifferent silence.

Finally, Roy said, "Five hundred pounds."

"Two hundred."

"Four hundred."

"All I've got is two hundred." At once, she felt smart for holding back thirty-two pounds and stupid for telling everyone in the pub that she was carrying that much cash.

Roy stared. Max didn't want to think about what might be going on inside his head. Finally, he smiled to himself and said, "Two hundred it is then."

Max wanted to be alone on a boat with this guy about as bad as she wanted to use the toilet here. But she didn't have a choice in either matter.

Roy rubbed his palms on the seat of his pants. "Let's go."

"I have to make a phone call first."

The bartender nodded toward the back. "Past the loo."

After stopping in the loo, Max used the phone card she'd just purchased to call Grey. After two rings, his answering machine clicked on. Damn. "Grey, it's Max. You're not going to believe it, but I'm in England. I'm sorry I left like I did. That was rude. I'm going to Alyssum. I hope you give me a chance to explain. Everything. If Fiona's any trouble, please put her in a kennel. I'm so sorry to dump on you like this." She hesitated, thinking she had so much more to say, but so little facility for the language at the moment. "I'll call again when I can. Bye."

When she returned to the bar, she found Roy passed out on one of the tables. So much for her ride.

"It's for the best, you know." The bartender slipped a pint under a spigot. "It wouldn't have ended well."

With a resigned sigh, Max hoisted herself up onto a barstool. "I'll have one of those."

When the bartender served her, she asked Max what was so special about Bryher.

It was the question Max had hoped for. She sipped the beer, set it down, looked into the woman's harsh eyes and said, "It's where my fiancé is honeymooning with my maid of honor."

The woman's jaw dropped. "Go on," she said, leaning on the bar.

Max nodded.

"You don't want the rotter back, then, do you?"

"She can have him." Max smiled and took another sip. "I

just booked a room in the same B&B. So I can be near them."

"What're you going to do then?" She'd lowered her voice to a conspiratorial level.

"I'm going to give them a preview of hell," Max said.

Apparently the barmaid was practiced at this sort of thing. Before long Max had a virtual arsenal of ammunition for payback. When the woman, whose name was Alice, treated Max to another beer, Max figured she'd won an ally. "There's a bloke comes in here most days," she said. "He might be able to help you. Hang around a bit."

Max drank slowly.

About an hour later, Alice was pouring a stout. She kept her eyes on the steady stream of ale and said, "At the table in the corner farthest from the door is that bloke I mentioned." She motioned toward the table with a wag of her little red head.

At the indicated table sat a slim man with a bony face and narrow, close set eyes. "Who is he?" Max asked.

The woman removed the pint from under the spigot and handed it to Max. "He takes people to the islands. He might be a bit out of your price range, but it wouldn't hurt to buy him a beer. Never know."

When Max hesitated, she said, "There're a lot of guys who'll tell you they'll take you anywhere, but this is how he makes a living."

"Thanks." Max paid for the ale and took it to the corner table. Expressionless, the man chewed on a toothpick as he watched her make her way over. She set the pint on the table. "I'd like to talk to you about getting to Bryher."

He glanced at the pint. "I talk for free."

"That's a bribe. I'm hoping you'll take me there for two hundred pounds. Today."

He frowned slightly, then removed the toothpick from

his mouth and took the pint. After a couple swallows he lowered the glass and nodded at the chair across from him. Max sat.

"What's in Bryher?"

"Personal business," she said.

He returned the toothpick to the corner of his mouth, where it bobbed up and down a couple times as he studied her. His eyes were a washed-out shade of gray.

"What do you usually charge?" she asked.

"One person. In a hurry. I could get five hundred to fly someone to Bryher. Easy."

"Fly? I thought you had a boat."

He glanced toward the bar. "Lady Alice didn't say it was a helicopter?"

"She didn't say what it was. I assumed." A helicopter would naturally be more expensive. She sighed. "All I've got is two hundred. Plus change and that's it." She didn't know how much a boat from Bryher to Alyssum would cost her and figured thirty pounds wasn't going to make or break this deal.

"How you planning to get back from Bryher?"

"I have no idea."

"I won't do it for free, you know."

"I wouldn't dream of asking."

"It'll have to be tonight."

"That's fine."

The toothpick bobbed a few more times. "All right. Two hundred."

Max really wanted to trust him. "Why are you doing this? For two hundred pounds."

He frowned. "Way I see it you're making a bigger investment than most of my fares. To them, five hundred is a fancy dinner. With you it's your net worth."

"You're right," she sighed and nodded. "Thanks."

"Be at the heliport at seven. It's at Eastern Green, 'bout a half mile east of town."

"I'll find it." She rose from the chair, hooking her bag over her shoulder. "By the way, what's your name?"

He flicked his toothpick to the floor and extended his hand to her. "Krett," he said. "John Krett."

Chapter 33

Nick got on the M1 at its start in northwest London. The rain had picked up and he needed the wipers, which screeched against the window in opposition to John Coltrane's saxophone. They'd likely run into worse weather before they made Wales. No, the rain wasn't the source of Nick's discomfort. He glanced at Olivia.

Her left hand rested on her lap, the little finger splinted with a thin, wooden stick. Leslie, who had taken Olivia in like one of her stray cats, fancied herself something of a healer. She'd also given Olivia a change of clothing. The pants were short and baggy and the linen jacket a bit large on her, and Nick doubted Olivia would choose to wear a T-shirt that read "University of Spirituality," but she still managed to look amazing.

"How's the finger?"

"Great," she said without much enthusiasm. "Last night

she put a 'healing potion' on it. I smelled like rancid pesto."

Nick was encouraged by her sarcasm. The long ride would be made even longer by a monosyllabic passenger.

"What did you say your uncle's name was?" she asked.

"Rhys. Rhys Lewis." He turned the tape down a bit.

"What's he going to tell us?"

"My guess is, since we're both after the same thing, he won't be forthcoming. Perhaps the most we can hope for is a confrontation." He could feel her watching him.

"You're from Wales?"

"Snowdonia. That's in the north of Wales."

"How long since you've been back?"

He rubbed the back of his neck and touched the bandage. The three stitches were starting to itch. "We moved to London when I was young. Haven't been there since."

"You're kidding? It's practically in your back yard."

"My mother didn't care much for Wales."

They rode in silence for several miles. She seemed so composed. Hardly like a woman whose lover had just been murdered.

"Bradshaw must have had them worried," Nick said.

Olivia blinked and turned toward him. "I suppose."

"Did any names come up other than Arthur Penn?"

"Not that I recall."

"You two didn't discuss business much then, did you?"

"What's that supposed to mean?"

He shrugged. "Just that. This is all about Ben and what he was doing. Seems likely that you might have chatted about such things."

"All I know is that he was going to Alyssum." She began digging in her purse.

"Did Max tell you about the stone over the telephone?"

"How else would she have told me?"

"You were at Bradshaw's?"

Olivia stopped digging. "I suppose you think his phone was tapped."

"Or Max's. How else would they have known where the stone was?"

"How do you know they did?"

"Just a feeling."

While he let the silence ride, Nick could feel her watching him. When he glanced at her, she resumed her digging. A moment later, she pulled out a cigarette.

"Such a fuss over a rock," she said.

"Sorry," Nick said. "No smoking."

Her eyes widened as she turned to Nick, cigarette poised at her red lips.

"Bad enough having to put up with it at the pub," he muttered.

"I thought everyone over here smoked." She dropped the cigarette back into her purse. "My luck. Getting stuck with Mister Clean Lung."

"Your father understood the stone's importance."

"Don't tell me you believe this Arthurian crap."

"The stone's story is intriguing."

"What is its story?"

"You want to hear it?"

"It's a long way to Wales."

Indeed. "Actually, the ending is a variation on Malory's. When Arthur was dying after being mortally wounded by his nephew, Mordred, he asked Bedwyr to take Caliburn and throw it back into the lake from whence it came."

"Why?" She found a stick of spearmint gum in her purse and popped it into her mouth.

"In those days it was customary to throw the weapons of a vanquished warrior into a lake or pond. Arthur got the sword from the Lady of the Lake, and Bedwyr was returning it to the same lake." He paused to pick up the thread. "Well, Bedwyr can't bring himself to throw away such a magnificent weapon which, among other things, he believes will make him whole again."

"Whole again? Dare I ask what was missing?"

"His hand. He lost it in battle and compensated by becoming skilled with the spear. So, he lies to Arthur, saying he threw it back when actually he hid it. The king doesn't believe him. Bedwyr goes back and still can't do it. He lies again, and again Arthur doesn't believe him. The third time he does the deed, and an arm rises out of the lake and takes the sword. When he describes to Arthur what he'd seen, Arthur believes him."

Nick passed a lorry on the right and moved back into the left lane behind a van, settling into a steady speed. "The Williamson version has a different twist. In it, Caliburn has three large gemstones embedded in the hilt. It is late in the afternoon when Bedwyr comes to the lake. He tries to throw Caliburn into the water, but can't bring himself to do it. It's a magnificent weapon—again, he believes it will bring him power and make him whole. He hides the sword and when he returns to Arthur, Arthur asks him what he saw. He tells him he saw the still waters and a great white swan cutting a vee across the lake. Arthur accuses him of lying and orders him to go back and complete the task. Once again, he can't bring himself to do it. He'd convinced himself that to commit Caliburn's fate to the bottom of a muddy lake would be wrong. So, once again he hides it and tells Arthur he saw only the still waters and the swan."

Olivia snorted softly. "Bedwyr wasn't a quick study, was he?"

"It's part of the legend, Olivia. Bear with me."

"I'll try."

"Thank you. Arthur accuses him of lying again. He's near death and convinced his faithful knight isn't going to carry out his final wish. Bedwyr returns to the lake and, as he's sitting there with the sword, trying to summon up whatever it will take him to complete the task, the middle stone—the one that changes from green to red—falls into his hand."

"Damned convenient."

"He tries to put it back into the cavity, but it won't stay. He keeps it. This time he throws the sword into the lake and sees a hand rise out of the water, catch the sword, brandish it three times and disappear beneath the water. He tells Arthur what he saw and the king believes him. Arthur asks him if he saw the swan and Bedwyr says it was too late in the evening for swans. Arthur seems satisfied. He can die at peace now."

"Arthur didn't have a clue that his faithful knight swiped the stone?"

"I expect he did, but understood it was meant to be. There was further use for the stone."

"What was the significance of the swan?"

"Perhaps she was the lady in the lake."

"What lady?"

"Nimuë. The nymph who gave Arthur the sword."

"Right. A nymph." Olivia removed the wad of gum from her mouth, wrapped it in foil and deposited it in the clean ashtray. When she spoke again, Nick was a little surprised to find she hadn't moved past Bedwyr's tale. "You know, it's a nice story and I'm sure Max would love it, but I'm sorry. Human nature hasn't changed all that much in fifteen hundred years. If some knight got greedy enough to take the stone to begin with, then I'll bet one of his descendants was greedy enough to see what he could get for it."

Nick glanced at her. "How did you come by your cynical nature? Couldn't have been Ben."

"Very little of my personality has anything to do with Ben. One has to be present in order to be a bad influence." She tucked a strand of hair behind her ear. "Besides, I'm not cynical. Practical yes, cynical no."

"Of course not. Taking up with Bradshaw—a man you barely know—is a sterling example of practical behavior."

"It is when you don't have the money for a hotel."

"Ah. Now I see. Which of London's budget hotels turned you turned away?"

She muttered a couple words as she turned to look out the window and Nick said, "Sorry, I didn't catch that."

Chapter 34

Even though a cool mist coated the countryside, Earl felt slimy with his own sweat. He figured he probably smelled; he knew his mouth tasted like he'd been eating canned dog food. He'd rather be in bed in his dingy apartment above One Stop Liquor Mart than anywhere else right now. Why did he keep that damned passport? It wasn't like he ever wanted to use it again. But he'd kept it and here he was, sitting in the back seat of this puny car a couple of hours west of London. According to all the signs they'd followed, they were near Oxford. Might as well be Timbuktu.

He had thought the Ice Queen was bad. She damned near melted next to her old man. Jeez. Earl kept his eyes fixed out the window. Every time he looked up and into the rear-view mirror, the old brown eyes under the upside-down vee eyebrows locked onto his. Rhys Lewis—what a piece of work.

Earl figured he must look as lousy as he felt. Otherwise

he'd never have convinced them he wasn't in any shape to assemble a bomb. It was the truth, but Earl had found that didn't count for much with these people. But the plane ride had left him in a weird kind of jittery stupor, and they must have seen it. But if the old man hadn't had someone else to call on, Earl wondered if they'd have made him do it. It wasn't much consolation knowing that, although he hadn't made the bomb, a bunch of innocent people having a good time in a pub were still going to die. But what could he do? He'd be dead before he got to the cops.

Earl closed his eyes and tried to call up a pleasant memory. The Cubs-Cards double header at Wrigley Field the year before Lonny got sent up. Baking in the bleachers. Then the car lurched to a stop and the ivy-covered walls blurred and snapped.

"Come along, Mr. Jessup."

Reluctantly, Earl opened his eyes. They were parked in front of a little brown house with shutters, window boxes and flowers blooming along the walk. Rhys Lewis held the car door open for him. Apparently the Ice Queen was sitting this one out. Earl didn't see where he had a choice. He squared his cap and climbed out of the car. Lewis put his arm around Earl's shoulders as they walked up to the house.

"You're important to us, Earl."

Earl grunted and kept looking down at the grass sprouting up through the cracks in the walk, which had been modified so there were no steps, only a concrete ramp up to the stoop.

Lewis patted him on the back before releasing him. "Just remember who hired you." He waited until Earl looked up at him. "Loyalty and success bring rewards. Failure can be unfortunate." Earl nodded and turned toward the door, painfully aware of the eight or ten inches Lewis had on him. "Say something, Earl. Let me know we speak the same language."

"I understand," he managed.

Earl heard what sounded like classical music coming from inside the house—kind of a nice, light tune—then he realized Lewis was staring at him. Earl glanced up and Lewis raised one pointy eyebrow. Confused and a little annoyed, Earl turned back toward the door. Oh. The bell. He pressed his finger to it and a double chime sounded inside. Maybe the big guy was scared he'd break one of those yellow nails of his.

After almost a minute, the doorknob turned and the door swung open to an old guy in a wheelchair. Violin music poured out the door. The man had thin gray hair and wore a faded blue sweater over a white shirt and a striped bow tie at his collar. Smiling, like he wasn't expecting guests, but was okay with it anyway, the guy looked first at Earl and then at Lewis. When he got an eyeful of Lewis, the wheelchair slid back a couple inches.

"Good day, Mr. Terry." Lewis said the words like he had tipped his hat along with them.

Terry's bow tie bobbed up and down as he swallowed. He set his lips and said, "Do I know you?" His voice sounded about as tight as one of those violins.

"My name is Rhys Lewis." He nodded. "May I come in?"

Terry folded and unfolded his hands a couple of times and seemed to be trying to come up with a reason to slam the door in their faces. Finally, he said, "I believe it would be best if you tell me why you're here first."

"I just want a few words."

"About what?"

"What do you say we drop the pretense, Mr. Terry? Maybe we've never met, but we each know exactly who the other is."

Terry regarded Lewis with a cold expression. "All right," he said. "But I still want to know why you're here."

254

Lewis flattened his tie against his chest, the tips of his fingers disappearing behind his jacket lapel. "You've been counseling Nick Llewellyn, haven't you?"

"I don't see where that's any of your business."

"Oh, but it is." Lewis put one hand on the wheelchair's arm and pushed it out of his way. Terry tried to stop the backward motion by grabbing the wheels, but he was too slow.

Once Lewis was in the living room, Earl stepped into the house and shut the door. Terry glanced at him and a wave of shame passed over Earl. He'd been on the receiving end of bullying too often. Being on this side felt even worse.

Terry grabbed the wheels of his chair and rolled himself right up to Lewis. Earl had to hand it to the little guy. He might be crippled, but he wasn't going to let anybody roll over him. Which was, Earl noted, more than he could say about himself.

Meanwhile, Lewis was eyeing the place like maybe he'd make an offer. It was small, with a fireplace in the middle of the long wall surrounded by a stereo system and rows and rows of record albums. Family photos lined the fireplace mantel. In one of them, taken not too long ago Earl guessed because Terry looked about the same, Terry stood next to a plump, gray-haired woman with a big smile. Lewis spent some time examining that photo and then returned it to the mantel. "This must be your late wife." He adjusted another photo of her, a full-face shot taken when she was younger and thinner. "Lovely woman. What was her name? Lydia?"

Lewis looked down at Terry who glared back at him without answering.

Turning his back on the photos, Lewis said, "What did you tell Nick about me?"

"The truth." The old man worked the muscles in his jaw like he was chewing something in the back of his mouth.

"I suppose you know the truth." Lewis crossed the room to a table in front of a bay window. Books were spread out over the table, some open, some stacked on others. A fifth of whisky and a half-full glass made Earl's mouth water. Lewis picked up one of the books. "*Spawn of Immortals,*" he read out loud and checked out the spine. "Here's your truth." He opened the book and began to page through it. "You think I'm half-demon, don't you?"

"It's what you believe, isn't it?" Terry answered.

"And what you want to believe." Lewis waved the book over the table. "Demons, witches, vampires. Your life must be lacking. So empty that you're actually hoping that they do exist. Just to make things interesting." Turning back toward Weldon, he added, "I'm your last, best hope, aren't I?"

Terry wrapped his scrawny little hands together. "It's a hobby, nothing more."

"A hobby?" Lewis reared back his head in mock surprise. "You devote more time to your hobby than most people do to their profession. It borders on obsession. What do you charge for a speaking engagement, anyway?"

"Demonology is merely one aspect of mythology."

"I see," Lewis nodded. "So, you put the devil right up there with Zeus and God, don't you?"

"I don't put him 'up there' at all."

Lewis smiled, apparently amused. "You know, talk like that can get you a reputation, Weldon." The old man winced when Lewis used his first name. "Most people probably think you're a little crazy."

"The opinions of others could not concern me less," Terry said, and Earl believed him.

"Of course they don't." Lewis didn't sound convinced. "What do you and Nick talk about?"

Terry raised his chin. "I'll not reveal the content of our

conversation. Suffice to say that Nick is a bright young man more inclined toward his father's ways than his uncle's."

Again, Earl noticed how carefully Terry spoke his words, and it occurred to him that Terry must have just put that dent in the fifth.

"Have you told anyone else what you think about me?"

"Don't flatter yourself," Terry said. "I've better things to do with my time than hound the likes of you."

Earl didn't think he sounded convincing, but Lewis said, "I'm glad to hear that. I make a good living as a psychologist. People find it easy to bare their souls to me. They might have second thoughts if they suspected I was in league with the devil." He paused, then added, "Ruining one's reputation—one's livelihood—could get you sued."

Terry raised a scraggly eyebrow. "Just bringing suit would ruin your reputation."

"Good point."

Terry was looking a little uneasy as Rhys consulted the book again. Holding it open in his left palm, he paged through it. While he read, Terry wheeled to the right side of the fireplace where the stereo occupied most of a low shelf above a row of cabinets.

Lewis tapped a page of the book with a nail. "Do you think this artist's rendition—bat wings, scales and horns—is accurate?" He looked up and didn't seem surprised to find that Terry had moved.

"I doubt it," Terry said, raising his sagging chin.

"It wouldn't terrify you?"

"No." Then he added, "I think the notion of a devil who looks like the rest of us is infinitely more frightening than that one in that book."

Lewis showed the book to Earl. "Would you be terrified?"

The thing looked like a cross between a human and a

dragon and, yeah, if it were standing here in the room with him, he'd be pretty damned scared. He shrugged.

"Never mind." Lewis returned to Terry, taking a long second to note the gun on the stereo shelf, within Terry's reach. Earl saw the open cabinet and figured that was where he'd gotten it. Lewis didn't mention it, though, just flicked an eyebrow like he found it kind of amusing. Then he looked down at Terry. "Weldon here understands terror. Don't you, Weldon? As you said, it's not the monster that terrifies. It's the familiar." He continued to flip through the book, only now he seemed to be looking for something.

Terry glanced nervously at Earl, who dropped his gaze to the wooden floor. Up until now, Terry had seemed to be holding his own. Earl didn't know where this was going, but he didn't want to watch.

"Ah, here we are," Rhys stopped. "Conjuring." His finger ran down the center of the page as he scanned it. When he'd finished, he snorted an amused chuckle and snapped the book shut.

"I'll tell you how to summon up the devil. It's easy. You don't need black candles, mindless chanting, and a slaughtered goat." He walked over to where Terry sat and bent at his waist so he was at eye level with the crippled man. "All you need is the courage to look inside yourself." With the edge of the book, he tapped Terry on the chest. "He's in here. And here." He tapped his own chest then waved his hand toward Earl. "He's even inside Mr. Jessup."

Earl imagined a lump of ice in his chest.

"You just have to know where to look."

"That may be what you'd like to think, Rhys, but it's just not so. He may be inside you, but he's not within everyone."

"You're sure of that?"

"I know what I'm talking about."

That seemed to amuse Lewis, who smiled in a way Earl's third-grade teacher used to smile at him; even though he was dumber than dirt, she liked him anyway.

"This is your life, isn't it Weldon?" Rhys said, waving the book at him. "That's quite sad."

When Terry didn't respond, Rhys said, "When was it that you last had a real life?" He paused, smiled slightly. "Or, should I say 'a wife'? When did you last have a *wife?*"

Earl could practically hear Terry's teeth grinding together.

"Her name was Lydia, wasn't it?"

"Leave her out of this, Rhys."

"She was the love of your life, wasn't she?"

Terry didn't speak.

"What was it that happened to her?"

Lewis watched Terry, his expression concerned. "Weldon," he said, "you're not looking well." He reached in front of Terry and switched off the stereo, lopping off a violin in mid-scream. "There, that's better. Loud music makes it difficult for us to visit, don't you think?"

Cold fingers stroked Earl's spine as he watched Lewis crouch next to Terry and pat his knee. Terry cringed and drew back, his right hand hovering over the gun. "How long has it been?" Lewis's voice was the same, but his tone sounded different, almost soothing.

Terry rested his hand on the gun. Then he looked down at it, although Earl thought it more likely that he needed to look *away* from Lewis. Terry breathed deep a few times, but that didn't keep him from tensing up so bad he started to shake.

Terry took the gun and wheeled his chair back a couple feet, leaving Lewis's hand suspended in air. "Get away from me."

Lewis clasped his hands at his chest. "You don't really

mean that. Do you?" He started walking toward Terry. Real slow. "Let me see, Weldon, when was the last time you and Lydia were together?" Terry shook his head as he pointed the gun at Lewis, holding it with both his hands. Lewis didn't seem to notice it as he said, "Of course. It was your niece's wedding, wasn't it? A perfect summer day. And she was a lovely bride, wasn't she?" He stood in front of Terry now and a chair blocked the old man from moving back any farther. "She wore her mother's—your late sister's—dress. And, according to tradition—"

Terry held up the gun, his hand shaking. "You can't tell me what I already know. You can't make it any worse than it already is."

Lewis glanced over his shoulder at Earl. "Do you know this story, Earl?"

Earl couldn't move. He wished Terry would pull the trigger but wondered if that would stop Lewis.

"You're the only one here who doesn't know it. Maybe what we need is an objective opinion. I often tell my patients how important it is to gain some objectivity."

Terry adjusted his grip on the gun, but it still shook.

"Weldon had a little too much to drink." Lewis glanced at the bottle on the table. "I see you still enjoy the spirits, Weldon." Then he knelt in front of the old man, so he looked straight down the gun's barrel, and placed his hands on Terry's legs. "They had a lovely time." His fingers started kneading the skinny, lifeless thighs. "But Weldon here insisted on driving home."

Earl wanted to turn away, but he couldn't. He felt like he was watching a lion stalk one of those tiny-hoofed antelopes.

"I'll bet she told you to slow down, Weldon. After a few drinks you think your little Vauxhall is a Porsche, don't you?

When you saw that curve coming up, I'll bet you thought you could make it."

Terry started chanting something that sounded, to Earl, like a mouthful of alphabet soup. The words came from the back of his throat. The whole time, he seemed to be staring into Lewis's eyes. Earl didn't know how he could stand it.

"The car must have made a horrible sound when it tore through the fence and into that tree. A big old oak tree. Metal and glass and then . . . nothing." Although Terry kept chanting, Earl didn't have any trouble hearing Lewis. "Do you remember the last time you saw your Lydia?"

Terry's voice got softer, and he stumbled over the sounds. Tears slid into the creases on his face.

Earl wanted to tell Lewis to stop, but he couldn't. He couldn't speak, he couldn't close his eyes and he couldn't block out that voice.

"You were still sitting up, all buckled in; maybe you still had your hand on the dashboard where you braced for the collision. Was it still there?" Terry didn't answer. "But there was definitely something wrong with Lydia. Your beautiful wife." Terry had stopped chanting, his finger frozen on the gun's trigger. He couldn't pull it and he couldn't let go. Sweat rolled off his shiny forehead and mixed with his tears. "Then you looked down at your crushed legs and saw her head in your lap. Where the tree limb had deposited it."

Earl nearly doubled over. He saw the old lady's head as sure as it had been dropped in his own lap. And he saw hate and rage in Terry's eyes, but Lewis's voice was real gentle as he said, "You killed her, didn't you?"

"It . . . was . . . an accident." A strand of saliva stretched between his lips.

"It takes an evil man to kill the love of his life." Lewis put his hands on either side of the gun and took it from Terry, easy as if it'd been handed it over. He stood and set the gun in Terry's lap, then patted the old man on the shoulder. "Who's the devil, Weldon?"

As Lewis backed away, he glanced at Earl and, with a jerk of his chin, gestured toward the door. Earl took one more look at the old man with the gun in his lap, felt he should do something, but didn't know what to do or how to do it. So, he opened the door and Lewis walked past him. Earl followed, closing the door behind him. His legs felt like jelly and he had to concentrate on each step. He'd gotten to the end of the curved walk where some pink petunias overflowed onto the concrete when he heard the gunshot. He put his hands over his ears and then felt a hand on his shoulder. He shuddered and jerked his head up.

"You'd be smart to follow instructions. Your brother isn't the only one at risk, you know."

Earl knew that his soul was also at risk, and though he'd never given much thought to its welfare, he knew that hanging out with Rhys Lewis and the Ice Queen would be like dipping it in acid. But he also knew he didn't have one-tenth the backbone it would take to stand up to either of them. Never had. Never would. He didn't want to think about what they'd tell him to do next.

Chapter 35

Croeso-i-Cymru. Welcome to Wales. The rain was barely a mist by the time they entered Wales on Route 5 east of Llangollen. Nick had almost forgotten the gentle rise of the hills and the way the mist veiled the land, muting its colors.

"Ever been to the States?"

Nick glanced at Olivia and saw that she had sliced off a chunk of the cheddar Leslie had sent with them. She handed it to him. "Once. About eight or nine years ago. I met a woman from Minneapolis who was at university in London. Went to visit her." He chuckled. "Excellent time of year to be in Minneapolis—January. Never knew it could get so cold."

"Her, or the weather?"

"As it turned out, it was London she'd been in love with." He took a bite of cheese. "Those things do have a way of wearing off once you change the setting."

"So I've heard," she mused.

The sharp cheese made his jaw ache. He swallowed. "So, you've never been rejected by a lover who's lost interest?"

"Not because of the setting."

As they rode through the hills, he began to feel the draw of the land, as though recalling a forgotten but vivid dream.

"You ought to pay close attention," he said. "Some say this is Arthur's country."

"I thought that was southern England."

"Everyone lays claim to the man."

"You British take your legends seriously, don't you?"

"Some do. Some don't. Some try to make money out of them."

"Which group do you fall into?"

"Don't know." He gave it a few seconds. "Not the latter."

"I don't see how you could have been around Ben for long without being brainwashed."

"I was bloody-minded. Determined to be more difficult to win over than my mother."

"So, you never bought into it?"

"I learned to respect myth, but didn't share Ben's passion."

She smiled. "He always did have trouble finding the line between reality and fiction."

"Sometimes it's not so obvious."

Olivia offered Nick another slice of cheese. He shook his head.

"Your father took all this quite seriously," he said. "I think that's why he fancied Britain. We are steeped in legend and myth. You're a country with so many diverse groups, and you're a comparatively young country. Aside from your native Americans, which most of you aren't, you have no single source for your myths and legends. They get watered down. Sometimes you try to rationalize them."

"What's wrong with that?"

"Nothing's wrong with it. Not really." He continued, a little surprised by his own thoughts, "Ben never tried to explain the myths away. He believed there were certain aspects to life that were best experienced rather than examined. He was that way with some people," Nick said, thinking of his mother, "and with legend."

"Ben was naïve."

"I wouldn't call it that. Idealistic, perhaps, but not naïve." He paused. "Makes for damned interesting entertainment."

"Give me a break. It's all kid's stuff. Fairytales."

"Kid's stuff, you say? Hardly. Well, perhaps the watered-down versions are fairly tame, but the more, shall we say, sophisticated, versions rival soap operas."

"I don't watch soap operas."

"I know. You prefer to live them." He felt her glare and kept his eyes on the road as he suppressed a smile.

"I'll bet you're just dying to tell me one of these tales."

He shrugged.

"All right. Let's hear one."

"Are you certain?" he asked. "Hate to bore you."

"I'm certain."

"Let me think of a suitably titillating one for you." He paused. "Ah, yes. I've got it. Has to do with Arthur's conception."

"Don't make me beg."

"I wouldn't dream of it," he said and began, "Uther Pendragon fancied the wife of one of his dukes, the Duke of Tintagel. Tintagel's on the north coast of Cornwall. There are ruins there now, supposedly built on the original ruins. At any rate, the duke and the king had been snapping at each other for some time. In a gesture that was probably interpreted by the duke as conciliatory, but was actually part of Uther's designs to get the fair Igraine into bed, Uther invited the duke and his wife over for a meal. When Igraine made it clear that she wasn't interested after Uther made it clear that he was, well, that was enough to escalate the war. Now Uther was a man with a mission. He couldn't get this woman out of his head. Mad for her. He told Merlin as much. Merlin agreed to help him on the condition that any fruits of the union be handed over to him. Uther was so filled with lust he said, 'Fine. Whatever it takes.' On the eve of a major battle when the duke was at one castle and Igraine at another—Tintagel—Merlin cast a spell on Uther so that he looked exactly like the duke. Uther went to Tintagel, and Igraine, thinking her husband was lucky to get furlough, took him into her bed. Arthur was conceived."

"Wait a minute," Olivia interrupted. "You're telling me that Igraine thought Uther was her husband?"

"That's why he needed a wizard."

"Hmph. I think she knew exactly what she was doing."

"Perhaps you ought to write your own interpretation."

"Go on."

"As fate would have it, Igraine's husband was killed that night, effectively ending the war. Distances being what they were, Igraine realized that the man who climbed into bed with her couldn't have been her husband. She married Uther."

"Cut. You're telling me that Igraine, whose rejection of Uther's advances was enough to start a war, is now willing to marry the guy?"

"What's the widow of a duke to do?"

She smiled. "Go on."

"Once Igraine learned she was pregnant, she was, naturally, a bit apprehensive. She confided in Uther, who told her not to worry; it was he who came to her that night in the mist."

"And she said . . . ?"

"Well, naturally, she was relieved."

Olivia nodded slowly. "I think I would have liked Igraine."

"I suspect you two would have gotten on famously." He continued, "Eight months later, Arthur was born. True to his word—and because one doesn't frig about with a wizard— Uther handed the babe over to Merlin."

"How did Igraine take that?"

"I imagine she was devastated. But she had to survive. She had other children. Realistically, she'd no choice."

After a moment, Olivia said, "All that's rather sick, isn't it?"

"I knew you'd enjoy it."

Chapter 36

It had been a cool night in Penzance, but it was downright cold several hundred feet above the town, and getting colder as they headed out over the Atlantic in the small helicopter. A door would have provided some protection from the wind, but Krett explained that many of his clients hired him for aerial photography and preferred the unobstructed view. Max pulled up the collar of her jacket and drew the seat belt tighter, thinking she wished her goal were as simple as some good pictures.

The full moon, well into the night sky, washed the landscape in white light. She hadn't figured out yet how, once she got to Alyssum, she'd find Arthur Penn. She couldn't march up to his residence and ask to see him. She'd be all right if Arthur answered the door, but when he lived in a castle, what were the odds? Too many people wanted to make sure she never got there.

She'd spent the afternoon researching Alyssum and studying the map she'd purchased. The island was almost two miles long and, at its widest, three-quarters of a mile, shaped roughly like a figure eight. The northern, smaller part was rocky and windswept with barren heath and the remains of an ancient castle on its tip. The southern section, which comprised the largest area, was farmland and the setting for the gardens and Arthur's home. East of the gardens by about an eighth of a mile were some relatively steep cliffs and several small coves. Beaches lined Alyssum's southern shore. When she closed her eyes, Max could picture the main road circling the island's perimeter and inroads leading to the gardens and the castle.

Alyssum's landing quay was at the island's narrowest point. Max planned to arrive at a less conspicuous spot—one of the small bays—find her way to the castle and wait for Arthur to make an appearance alone. Here, she admitted, the plan went beyond her control. Given the hour of her arrival, she might have to spend the night in the gardens. As if all this wasn't bleak enough, a storm was predicted before midnight.

The flight took less than thirty minutes. As the helicopter began to descend, Max tried to identify the other islands while they were still high enough for perspective. In the light of the full moon, she thought she could make out Alyssum's irregular figure eight shape. She tapped Krett on the arm and when he turned to her, pointed at the larger island. "Alyssum?" she shouted above the wind.

He nodded. They passed over her final destination and the narrow strait of water. Max could see lights on Bryher where a few homes and shops were clustered, but they stayed south of the populated area. Krett flew with his head out the door, apparently looking for the landing area. As they descended, she saw a small campfire near the island's shore. She sat up, trying to see below. And she could make out a man standing beside the fire, hands on his hips.

"Keep your head down when you get out," Krett shouted.

As it touched down, the helicopter jolted and settled at an angle on the rocky ground beneath it. But she was here and could see lights from the town not too far off. She yelled "thank you", released her shoulder harness, crouched and ran from under the blades.

As she straightened, she caught her shoe on a rock and would have gone down had someone not grabbed her arm. When she recovered enough to thank him, she turned and found herself face-to-face with the man who had killed Antony.

"Nice to finally meet you, Miss Pike." Dimples creased both of his cheeks and his grip on her tightened. "I'm Simon Murdoch."

"You bastard."

Behind her, she heard a shoe scuffing stone. She spun around and saw the pilot standing back a few feet.

"And you've met John Krett." Murdoch waited until she turned back to him before finishing. "He works for me."

As he led her toward the fire, she tried to yank her arm from his grip, but he was stronger than he looked. "Two ways we can do this, Maxine," Murdoch said, jerking her around so she faced him. He released her and she still felt the imprint of his fingers. "There's the easy way and the hard way. The easy way is you hand over the stone. The hard way is we take it off you. Either way, I'm going to get it." Shadows filled the hollows in his face and hid his eyes. "What's it gonna be?"

"You killed Antony in cold blood, you bastard."

He sighed as though his patience was being tried, then reached for her rucksack. She backed up. With a wave of his hand, he gestured toward Krett, who seized her around the waist with both arms. Murdoch grabbed for her rucksack and Max kicked out, hard. She wasn't aiming for his crotch, not really, but that was where the toe of her trainer connected. Murdoch doubled over with a loud grunt, grabbing his balls. Struggling against Krett, Max tried to kick him as well—anywhere—but he maneuvered out of her way.

Next thing she knew, Murdoch had recovered with a vengeance, smacking her face twice, first one side and then the other. She tasted blood and her cheeks burned. With one hand, he grasped her neck and squeezed as he used the other to peel the rucksack off her shoulder.

Once he had it, he released her and backed off, retreating to the other side of the fire. Krett adjusted his hold, pinning her arms behind her back. Murdoch crouched on the ground and opened her bag, first pulling out her camera, which he held near the fire so he could read the settings, then put it aside.

He dumped the bag's contents on the ground and sifted through the pile beside the fire, then slid his hand into each inner and outer compartment. When he finished, he tossed the empty bag, then stood and walked around the fire so he faced her. Krett yanked her shoulders back.

Murdoch stepped right up to her so she couldn't blast him in the balls again. "I know you've got it." His jaw was so tight his mouth barely moved. "I will search every inch, every cavity, of your body, Miss Pike. I think you know that. So, why don't you just hand it over?"

Her shoulders felt like they were going to pop out of their sockets.

"Well?"

She hadn't come all this way, at the expense of so many, to hand the stone over to this bastard. She sucked up a mixture of blood and saliva and spat it at him. His expression didn't change as he wiped his chin and began to search her.

He started at her neck and worked his way down. He went about it methodically, groping her chest with the same rough expedience with which he dug through the pockets of her jacket. When he found the hard lump in her jeans pocket, he stopped and looked up at her, and she saw cold triumph register in his eyes. She tried to kick out at him but he slammed his foot down on her instep, grinding it into the soil. Then he thrust his hand into her pocket and plucked out the stone.

He stepped toward the fire and crouched beside it. "So, here's what all the fuss is about." He held it up to the flame, then took it back into his fist and pocketed it.

Max tried to swallow, but her throat felt like it was coated with sand. A light breeze brushed her forehead, drying some of the dampness. In order to recover the stone, she had to get out of this alive, but didn't think Murdoch was going to let that happen.

He stood. "Mr. Krett here'll take care of you."

Holding onto one of her arms, Krett began to lead her toward the helicopter. Max dug her heels into the gravel. With a forceful yank, Krett pulled her down on her knees and started dragging. She regained her footing, stumbling along behind him.

When they reached the helicopter, Krett handed her off to Murdoch while he went around to the other side and climbed into the pilot's seat. He'd left the engine idling, and now he revved it up, preparing to lift off.

"Why don't you ask Krett here what happened to your old man?" Murdoch yelled the words into her ear.

She glanced at Krett, who nodded like he'd just been introduced, and Murdoch shoved her into the passenger seat. "Dumped him over the Atlantic with a bullet in his belly." He stepped back, clearing the blades. Cupping his hands around his mouth he hollered, "Give him my best." Krett shifted his toothpick from one side of his mouth to the other as the helicopter lifted off.

Process that later, Max told herself. She watched Murdoch walk back toward the fire, staring at something in his hand. As far as he was concerned, she was dead.

The helicopter gained altitude as they moved across the narrow strait, toward Alyssum. The island was close. Max looked down into the black water. She guessed they weren't more than thirty feet above the water. Maybe less. How deep was it? Did it matter?

With a darting move, she kicked out at Krett, aiming for his knee, then swung her other foot out the opening. As she groped for a hold on its frame, Krett snatched her arm and tried to haul her back in. The helicopter lurched and she kicked at him again, smacking an instrument that caused the lurching to escalate to bucking. When Krett released her, she grasped the frame and pushed herself off the seat and out of the helicopter. The rush of air hit her and the sensation of freefall was so unexpected, for a fraction of a second she didn't realize what was happening.

When she hit the water, she threw her arms and legs out to the side, attempting to slow the plunge. The cold knocked the breath from her lungs as she sank. Kicking, she began to rise, her chest on fire. She battled the urge to inhale. Then she broke the surface, gulped air and immediately sank again. God, it was cold. When she rose again, she managed to stay on the surface by kicking and using her arms. She sucked in air by the lungful, but couldn't get enough. *Calm down. Don't hyperventilate. You're almost there.* She tried to get her bearings by doing a three-hundred-sixty-degree turn.

When she did, she saw the helicopter spinning awkwardly. Krett had maneuvered it farther away from the islands, out over the open sea, but it was losing altitude. As Max watched, it keeled over onto its side and crashed into the water. An explosion sent a fireball into the air, lighting the sky with an orange glow, and then the night was still except for the sound of Max's hands sculling the water.

She looked back at Bryher and then turned toward Alyssum, which appeared closer, but she couldn't judge the distance. Her breathing had eased some and, as she rolled onto her back, she told herself she could swim a quarter of a mile without a problem. It probably wasn't that far. Millions of stars speckled the heavens. As she backstroked, one shot past the others on its way toward oblivion.

After a few minutes, her muscles ached and it became increasingly difficult to raise her arms. It was hard to coordinate her kicking. Maybe the island was getting closer and maybe it wasn't. She swam harder. From what she recalled of her first aid training, she had about ten minutes to get out of this cold water before she started having serious problems. Her body was strung tight and shivered convulsively. The smaller you are, the faster it gets to you.

"Ben." It seemed odd to be calling the name of her dead father rather than God, who might be in more of a position to help her. But she felt Ben's presence. And he was urging her to keep going. She was not going to die here.

After another minute, she rolled over on her stomach and the toe of her shoe jammed into the rocky bottom. The dark shoreline was only a few yards away. On shaky legs, she stood up in water not much past her waist and stumbled ashore.

The night air's warmth was as welcome as it was unexpected. She wanted to lie down and rest, but pushed herself up off the ground before she could seriously consider it. She had to get to the road. She had to find Arthur Penn.

A quick survey of the beach told her it wouldn't take her

around the island. It was enclosed by a slope that was mostly rocks with a few sparse bushes. She'd have to go up and over to get to the road. The rise wasn't steep. She told herself if she were dry and on vacation, she might climb it for fun. Even cold, wet and scared, she knew she could get up there. The moon's light provided some assistance as Max began her assault on Alyssum.

Chapter 37

"Beddgelert," Olivia read off the map. "You said *bedd* meant grave or tomb. What does *gelert* mean?"

According to the instructions Nick had gotten at the pub several kilometers back, it was only another kilometer to his uncle's house. Pressure behind his eyes augured one of his rare, but usually brutal headaches. And now Olivia was acting the attentive tourist. It was an unlikely role for her, and Nick figured she must be trying to distract him, which meant his nerves were showing.

"Gelert was a dog," he said.

"A dog? What did a dog do to get a town named after it?"

"It died."

"Oh. Well, I'm in the mood for a sad story." She folded up the map. "The others were so uplifting."

"Aren't you tiring of my stories?"

She gave him a pointed stare with a cocked jaw for emphasis. "Just tell me about the damned dog."

Nick sighed. "If you insist." He steered the car around a curve on the narrow road. The stone walls on either side gave the impression of driving through a small canyon and the fog made it even more so. "Prince Llewellyn—no relation—came home from hunting one day and found his dog, Gelert, standing by his small son's empty bed. The dog was bloody and there was blood all over the place. Believing that Gelert had killed his son, the prince slew the dog. Then, a few moments later he heard his son's cries. He went outside and found his son—scared but otherwise fine—next to the body of the wolf that Gelert had killed. Overcome by remorse and grief, the prince buried Gelert in grand fashion. But he was so distraught by what he'd done that he never laughed again."

Olivia said, "Is that story true?"

"What do you think?"

"It sounds like some pub owner whose business was off the main road wanted to attract patrons. Easy enough to invent a story, put a few rocks on the ground and call it a dog's grave."

Nick figured the entrance to his uncle's place should be coming up on the right.

"Do you believe it?"

"I don't know." He glanced at her. "Believing is hard, isn't it?"

"How do you mean that?"

"Easier to write things off. Less trouble." The entrance, surrounded by a vine-covered stone arch, emerged in the fog.

He turned into the drive, saw the big house twenty feet ahead and stopped. He'd imagined his uncle living in Childe Roland's dark tower. This wasn't it. From their position, he could see only a portion of the manor home, but behind its green-shuttered windows, the warm, golden light suggested comfort rather than despair.

"I thought he was the bad seed," Olivia said.

"I didn't say it paid poorly."

Abruptly, Nick shifted into gear and proceeded. As they pulled up to the door, he saw how the drive curved past the house in a semicircle, joining the road again. An array of flowers and bushes lined the curve. He shifted the car into neutral and yanked up the hand brake.

"Showtime," Olivia muttered.

As Nick rang the bell, he glanced at Olivia, envying her calm. "Remember what we agreed on?"

"I know. I'm supposed to behave and follow your lead."

That wasn't how he'd put it.

They waited almost a full minute and, just as a surge of relief tempered Nick's disappointment, the door was opened by a tall, distinguished-looking man. Nick swallowed hard. "Rhys Lewis?"

"Yes? I am Doctor Rhys Lewis."

This was not what Nick had expected. Evil incarnate didn't have an engaging smile, nor did he wear a faded rust-colored cardigan over a tan polo neck. Even the eyes were wrong—warm brown behind a pair of bifocals.

Nick tried to find something of his father in the man's countenance or carriage, and saw nothing to link them.

"I'm Nick Llewellyn," he extended his hand, "your nephew."

Rhys barely hesitated before taking it. "Yes, of course." His grip was firm and dry. "You have your grandmother's eyes."

No one had ever made that observation.

Rhys studied him, his expression bemused. Finally, as Nick extracted his hand from his uncle's grasp, Rhys arched an eyebrow and shook his head, saying, "Forgive me for staring, Nick, but I wasn't aware that hell had frozen over."

His bewilderment seemed so genuine that Nick had to chuckle. He nodded toward Olivia. "This is Olivia Pike."

Rhys turned to her and bowed, his smile ingratiating. "Delighted." He kissed the back of Olivia's hand, then let it drop.

"Let's not stand out here," he said. "Come on in where it's comfortable." Nick detected the barest trace of a Welsh accent in his words—maybe it was the slight voiceless quality he gave to his l's. But only a trace. "This is quite an occasion. Occasions call for sherry. Don't you agree?"

Being invited in for a glass of sherry was not a scenario Nick had imagined.

Rhys must have noted Nick's hesitation, because he grinned broadly and moved aside, waving them past him. "I know. You're wondering how I manage to comb my hair so it covers up the horns."

Nick heard Olivia laugh and felt her hand at his back. They stepped past his uncle and into a vaulted entry with a huge, oval braided rug and white walls set off by dark trim. A wooden chandelier, resembling a wagon wheel, hung from the ceiling.

"Did you drive up from London?"

"Yes, in fact, I did."

"All this way," Rhys mused. "Must have been a long day."

"Not bad," Nick said, wondering how he'd guessed London.

Along the way, Olivia commented on the house.

"It is lovely, isn't it?" Rhys said. "My practice has done well for me."

Olivia stopped to examine a huge oak buffet, showcasing a collection of pewter plates and serving dishes. She picked up a platter and ran her hand over its surface. When she turned it over to examine the underside, Nick saw the initials "RHL" were etched into the plate. "I thought this looked like Hugh Monahan's work," she said, obviously impressed.

Rhys was practically beaming as he came up to her. "I had him do a set for me." Olivia exchanged the platter for a creamer, which was also labeled with Rhys's initials. "He has no peer." He cocked his chin and said, "I have a collection of his candlesticks in the parlor."

Olivia and Rhys chatted as Nick followed, unsure of his instincts. He tried to distract himself from his headache by observing his uncle. Rhys walked with an energy that took a few years off his age, which, if Nick had calculated correctly, was about sixty. His initial impression of this man was at war with what his mother and Weldon had led him to expect. And if Rhys was uncomfortable with the unexpected visit, then he was doing an excellent job of hiding it. Nick warned himself to stay guarded.

The wooden floors gleamed and Nick could almost hear the echo of their footsteps. Somewhere, a clock ticked loudly, but he never saw it. They followed Rhys down a hall and passed through the dining area which opened out into a drawing room with overstuffed, high-backed furniture. While the pieces appeared rustic, the look seemed manufactured. The wooden dining room table was scarred and pitted, but polished, and there were no stains from steaming mugs of coffee or spilled wine.

"When you moved in here," Olivia was asking Rhys, "did this place need a lot of refurbishing?"

As Nick gazed up at the high, molded ceilings, Rhys explained, "Actually, no. It isn't as old as it looks. I had it built to resemble a home I visited in Provence, which was more than a century old. I instructed the builder to spare none of the conveniences." There was that playful grin again. "Proving that I can have my cake and eat it too."

"It would seem that way," Nick agreed as he walked over to a large stone fireplace where the flames snapped and danced. Its warmth helped alleviate the chill brought on by the incessant drizzle. He turned his back to it. Olivia gazed out the floor-to ceiling windows that covered one entire wall.

Wedged into the corner of the room was a small, glass-topped drinks table. Bottles clinked as Rhys moved them about, selecting a decanter filled with amber liquor.

"When the weather cooperates, you can see Mount Snowdon from here. When it doesn't, you're lucky if you can see my neighbor's sheep."

Nick joined Olivia at the windows. He thought he saw shapes moving in the mist, but it might have been a trick of the eye.

"I hoped one day we would meet, but I sensed you would have to take the initiative," Rhys said, and Nick turned as his uncle approached them with two delicate crystal vessels filled with sherry. He handed one to Nick and the other to Olivia.

When he gave Olivia her drink, he commented on her finger. "That looks rather painful. What happened?"

"Rock-climbing accident," she said.

Rhys raised a skeptical eyebrow, but didn't argue. He then returned to the bar where he lifted the third glass in a toast. "To initiative."

Nick hesitated, then took a sip. Olivia followed suit.

After they'd drunk, Rhys gestured for them to sit. Nick hesitated, but Olivia promptly settled into a straight-backed upholstered chair and Nick, figuring his uncle had a height advantage on his side anyway, finally did the same.

Their chairs were separated by an oak end table situated on the edge of an oval rug with a floral design. A porcelain figurine of a Greco-Roman-type hero faring badly against a serpent occupied the center of the table. Across from them, a divan faced the chairs. Only a small coffee table separated them, so the grouping was rather intimate.

"You mentioned your practice," Nick said, resting his elbows on the chair's narrow wooden arms. "What is your work?"

Rhys had seated himself at one end of the divan. "I'm a psychologist. I've got a practice in Virginia where it's almost as beautiful as it is here. I've worked in a number of cities in the States, however, and some of my clients travel hundreds of miles to see me." He had a matter-of-fact way of talking, so none of this sounded like boasting. "Air travel has really changed the way we consider distances, hasn't it?"

"I suppose it has," Nick responded. Then he asked, "Why did you relocate to the States?"

"I went to university there," Rhys said, and added, "got to like the country. More diverse than here."

"This is just your vacation home?" Nick asked.

"More than that. There's often a primal connection to one's true home. If you allow it to, it has restorative powers." He filled his chest with air. "A man needs to be in touch with his roots, don't you agree?"

"I suppose." Nick had only a vague awareness of his distant past. At times, his childhood memories seemed to belong to newsreel footage from another life.

"Of course," Rhys began, "not everyone has a sense of his past. That's a real pity, I think." He regarded Nick, who observed that his uncle's eyes weren't so warm after all.

Before Nick could think of something to say, something to let his uncle know that Nick was, indeed, a part of his family's past and future, Rhys had turned toward Olivia.

"Are you Benjamin Pike's daughter?"

"I am."

"We'd met only recently. I was sorry to hear about his disappearance."

When Olivia didn't respond, Rhys continued, "We had occasion to . . . talk of things."

"Things?" Olivia asked. "What kind of things?"

Instead of answering her, Rhys said, "How is your sister?"

Her eyes narrowed. "How do you know my sister?"

"Ben mentioned her."

"She's fine," Olivia said, sounding wary.

"And, Nicholas, where is your mother living?"

He'd squeezed his eyes shut against the pressure in his skull that had spread and deepened. Opening them slowly, he focused on his uncle, blinked, and said, "London."

"And that's where you are as well." It wasn't a question.

"I've a pub there."

Rhys crossed his ankle over a knee and settled deeper into the divan. "Of course. The Fife and Firkin, I believe it's called."

"You know of it?"

He nodded. "Been there once or twice." He reached into a humidor and extracted a cigar. "Decent place, as I recall."

"I don't remember seeing you."

Rhys clipped off the end of the cigar. "Must have been your day off."

"How do you know about the pub?"

"Just because I estranged myself from my family doesn't mean I lost all interest in you people." He paused, then added, "I've never lost sight of you."

"How is it you know Ben?"

"Mutual interests." Then he added, "I understand he and your mother were married."

"That's true."

"Must be devastating for her. Having the two men in your

life disappear without a trace."

"Yes, well, she'll manage."

"As I recall, she was quite a desirable woman."

Nick smiled politely. "She was my mother."

"Of course," he said, then added, "I imagine you were a tremendous support to her after your father disappeared. Lucky to have you."

Nick shifted, pushing himself back in the chair.

As Rhys went to light the cigar, he stopped. "My manners. Would you care for one?" He raised the cigar and Nick shook his head. "I suppose, customs being what they are today, I should offer it to the lady as well."

"No thank you," Olivia said, "but do you mind if I have a cigarette?"

"Not at all."

She cast Nick a triumphant look as Rhys set a crystal ashtray on the table and lit her cigarette.

"We all have our vices, don't we?" Rhys winked at Olivia, then settled back onto the divan, where he lit his cigar and drew on it, tilting back his chin as he savored the taste.

Watching his uncle, Nick had a sense he was observing an actor in a set, on a stage, and Nick was sitting way back in the cheap seats. He felt oddly displaced.

When Rhys turned his eyes on Nick, his slight smile made Nick think his uncle had read his thoughts. Rhys exhaled in a satisfied sigh and, as the smoke wafted across the table, a wave of nausea swept over Nick. He swallowed and after a moment it passed. His head throbbed.

Rhys shook his head apologetically. "I'm sorry. I just can't tell you how tickled I am you stopped by. I have no idea why you're here, I'm just so pleased that you are." His expression sobered and, when he continued, his manner and tone were confidential. "You know, it all got rather unpleasant. I never wanted that. Your father and I never got along, but, especially with these years behind me, I believe I understood the situation better than he did." He quickly added, "Not that Elias can be blamed. No. As I said, hindsight has given me perspective and I can understand his feelings and motives. Your father never had the luxury of perspective; he died so young. Back then I was just plain angry. Couldn't tell me anything. That's why I left when I did."

To his surprise, Nick found it took little effort to put himself in his uncle's place. His choices had been limited.

Rhys settled back into the couch, and puffed on the cigar. "I'm curious about something. Were you raised on horror stories featuring your Uncle Rhys? Did your parents send you scurrying off to bed with the threat 'Or your Uncle Rhys is going to get you'?"

"Actually, until two days ago I didn't know you existed."

From the way his brows drew together in a troubled pause, Rhys seemed confused and maybe a little insulted. That felt good to Nick. But then he smiled and nodded as if this made perfect sense. "Of course. The Llewellyns have practice at rewriting family history." He cocked his head, examining his cigar as though it were this new perspective. "But, honestly, I would've thought it difficult to keep me a secret for that long."

"The Llewellyns," Nick said, "can be very tight-lipped when they set their minds to it." When Nick examined this surge of anger, he realized he'd directed it at his own family for keeping him in the dark all these years. "What were they afraid of, do you suppose?"

Beside him, Olivia cleared her throat as she tapped an ash off her cigarette, and he felt her watching him with an intensity that seemed out of character.

"The Llewellyns," Rhys said, "have always been defensive in the face of adversity."

"I suppose," Nick said, drawing away from Olivia's scrutiny. His mother never talked to him about the past, but she must have confided in someone. He remembered more than once walking into a room and feeling the abrupt abeyance of conversation hanging heavy in the air. There was one day—must have been at least twenty-five years ago and how was this memory suddenly so distinct?—he had asked her a simple question. Something about his father. She turned on him, her hair wild, the little lines around her mouth so deep they looked like stitches. Her words hurt him. What was it she'd said? Christ, that was it. She'd hissed the words: "Do you know what happens to little boys who stick their noses where they don't belong? They get their little peckers cut off, that's what." Christ. How could he have forgotten? Why had it come to him now? Like it had happened yesterday. The pain behind his eyes intensified and a cloud of cigarette smoke drifted under his nose.

Rhys's voice filtered through the fog. ". . . I'd like to believe if I had a son, I'd have trusted him more. I hope Ben was a better father to you."

Nick drained the glass of sherry. In less time than he thought physically possible, Rhys had refilled his glass. Olivia spoke, but he couldn't make out her words. Nick raised the glass to his mouth, then stopped as another image filled his head. His mother was making love with a man in the bed she shared with Nick's father. They moaned and writhed, and Nick couldn't see her partner's face, only a pair of white buttocks with his mother's legs wrapped around them. He knew it wasn't his father—Elias stood at the door, his eyes slashes of fury, his fists at his side. Nick's mother called out Ben's name. Nick pressed his fingers to his eyes.

"So," Rhys was saying, "did raging curiosity bring you here today, or something more specific?"

These memories could not have happened. He recalled Weldon's warning about Rhys. It felt like the man had burrowed into Nick's mind like a tick into flesh. This notion, which came as suddenly as the images of his mother, made a great deal of sense to Nick, but he was powerless to embrace it. He took a gulp of sherry into his mouth and it tasted like blood. His throat muscles seized.

Rhys drew on the cigar, exhaled slowly, and as the smoke dispersed, he nodded. Nick's throat opened and he swallowed; the taste of blood was gone.

Something jabbed his ankle. He looked up to see Olivia practically crossing her eyes at him as she snubbed out her cigarette.

"Well, actually, I am . . . ah . . ." Nick set the glass on the table and told himself the bastard couldn't mess with his head if he didn't let him in. Just answer the question. Only, now he couldn't recall what it was.

"I imagine there are certain specifics you're curious about. Things you weren't comfortable asking your mother." Rhys had notched his cigar in an ashtray. Now he folded his hands over his stomach and waited.

"Yes, actually . . . I, er . . ." Nick pulled at his collar and felt the heat rising off his throat. The knot of anger—aimed at his family—had grown larger and he couldn't repress the sense of resentment. "I can't imagine the truth ever being that wretched. Not worth the lie. Unless, of course, I was intentionally deceived. What was it like for you?"

Rhys nodded his approval. "Well, let's see." He looked up at the ceiling. "Your father was Ioan's fair-haired boy. He excelled in his studies, sports, and was respectful of his elders. In short, he did everything the eldest son was supposed to do.

Unfortunately, he was not the eldest. I was. I didn't follow the conventions. Still don't. I do, however, accept my responsibilities." His gaze settled on Nick who couldn't find his own voice.

Beside him, Olivia said, "Was your unconventional behavior prompted by the fact that Ioan wasn't your father?"

Rhys didn't turn away from Nick. "Of course," he said, as though the point was obvious. "For one thing, your grandfather couldn't stand being in the same room as me, much less calling me his son. There was, however, an advantage. You know how a blind person's other senses can be extraordinarily developed. His sense of smell and hearing may be so much more acute than that of the sighted person. One compensates. I was deprived of many things because your grandfather refused to acknowledge me. At first, it hurt me. Then it made me angry. I channeled that anger into a passion to succeed." He paused. "Also, I've learned I've much to thank my natural father for."

"For example?" asked Olivia.

He smiled at her. "I have extraordinary people skills."

Olivia sipped the sherry as she sat forward in the chair, glanced at Nick, then said to Rhys, "Too bad you can't thank the man in person."

"Who says I haven't?"

"You've met?"

Rhys smiled. "Let's just say we are aware of each other."

"Who is he?"

"I doubt you'd know him." He paused and cocked his head, re-examining Olivia. "Although, I could be wrong."

He turned toward Nick. "Tell me—"

"Come on," Olivia wheedled. "Give us a hint. I know a lot of people."

As Olivia attempted to engage his uncle in banter, Nick

288

shifted in his chair, bracing his elbows on his knees, and forced himself to look at the rug and away from those eyes that seemed to have paled in color so they were almost golden. He concentrated on the red rose blossoming on the rug, its edges lined in black. Blocking out all but the flower, Nick felt a little of his clarity returning. Even his headache had abated slightly.

Rhys cleared his throat. "Getting back to responsibilities. I consider the heartstone my responsibility." He paused. "That is what our visit is about, isn't it?"

"Yes." Nick ventured a glance at Rhys, whose expression remained open and inquiring.

Rhys leaned forward, also resting his elbows on his knees. "You and I are alike, you know."

Nick shook his head.

"We each believe the stone should be ours." He waited. "You because your father had it and I because it should never have gone to your father."

"But it did."

A small shrug. "It's never too late to correct a mistake."

"It was no mistake."

"It was," Rhys said. "But you're in a position to rectify that error."

"The heartstone doesn't belong to you or to me. It belongs in the sword. Without it, the sword is merely an artifact; without the sword, the heartstone is merely a stone."

"Well rehearsed." The lines radiating from Rhys's eyes deepened with amusement. "And what will happen then?"

"Arthur's return." Nick paused. "And the way I see it, either you want to stop that from happening or you want to corrupt the outcome."

" 'Corrupt.' Interesting way of phrasing it."

"Do you think I could have another sherry?" Olivia asked.

"Just how are the Llewellyns supposed to figure into the equation?" Rhys continued as though she hadn't spoken.

"I believe it's been in my family all these years for a reason."

Rhys leaned back in the couch and shook his head. He reminded Nick of a teacher disgusted and disappointed with his pupil. "The Llewellyns. So self-important." The intense disdain set Nick back. "I presume you know the story." Without giving Nick time to confirm or deny, he continued, "Then you know Bedwyr for what he actually was: a thief. A common thief who betrayed his king. And his friend. For you or any of your family to presume that you've any right to that stone is arrogant, and to presume you are instrumental in its future is beneath contempt." He nailed Nick with his glare as he spoke. "Bedwyr stole the heartstone. It will take someone of considerably more character to set it right."

"I suppose you believe that person is you." Nick's anger was like a pendulum, first swinging one way and then the other. He tried to focus it on his uncle and, at the same time, keep it in check, sensing Rhys could draw on it. His headache had shrunk to a small, acutely painful knot behind his left eye. He'd begun to think of it as a living thing. "And you aren't even a descendant."

Nodding as though he'd been waiting for that, Rhys said, "It's no coincidence that I'm a bastard. The descendants of Bedwyr finally have some character in their blood. Part of the responsibility in possessing the stone is knowing when to relinquish it." He paused. "And whom to relinquish it to. You Llewellyns don't even know how to let go."

"We know what's right."

"You are correct about one thing," Rhys continued. "Something remarkable is about to happen. But you and your family will have nothing to do with it."

"Bedwyr wasn't a thief. What he did was out of love for his king."

Rhys laughed. "Think about it, Nicholas. Who passed down your story from generation to generation? Do you really believe Bedwyr would have cast himself badly?"

"What Bedwyr did, he did for Arthur."

"He stole *from* Arthur."

"Thievery pales in comparison to murder. And you were your mother's favorite."

Rhys drew in a deep breath and released it with a sigh. "Oh, I can imagine how that story has been embellished over the years."

"I know. You never touched her."

"My mother and I had a special relationship. Your father was jealous. I loved her. I had no reason to want her dead." He studied Nick. "Your father wasn't accustomed to being denied anything. Especially the love of his mother." He reached into his pocket and withdrew a watch attached to a silver chain. When he snapped it open, Nick could make out the imprint of a serpent on the cover; its green eyes stared at him. Rhys gazed at the contents of the watch, his expression almost tender. "She was beautiful," he said, holding the watch out to Nick. "Have you ever seen her picture?"

Before Nick could respond, Rhys took his hand and placed the watch in it.

Although Nick had seen a few pictures of his grandmother, he'd never seen her so beautiful. Forever young. In the full-face photo, she gazed at him with eyes that were both haunting and penetrating.

"What did I tell you?" Rhys said, his voice soft, almost gentle. "Your eyes."

They were. Then he looked into his uncle's eyes and saw his grandmother and himself.

He sensed movement beside him, but didn't realize that Olivia had gotten up from her chair until she snatched the watch from his hand, snapped it shut and handed it to Rhys.

She looked down at Nick and said, "Let's go."

Barely glancing at her, Rhys said to Nick, "Ben had planned to give me the heartstone. Did you know that?"

"I don't believe that."

As Rhys slipped the watch into his pocket, a link in the chain glinted with the fire's reflection. "He asked you to come to Wales last month. Didn't he?"

"So?"

"Do you know why?"

"I'm not certain, but—"

"He wanted to explain about the stone. He knew it was mine, but also knew you wouldn't hear it from me."

"He was right," Nick said.

Resting his arm on one of the cushions, he focused exclusively on Nick. "The greatest mission a child can have is to carry out his father's, but it's important to recognize when that mission was misguided to begin with. You're in a position, Nick, to rectify that. We both know you were no more meant to have the heartstone than this woman you brought with you. I know it. Ben knew it. You see, Nick, you have made a serious error. You are convinced the stone is yours. You believe you are its appointed guardian. Just like all the Llewellyns. When what you actually are is a descendant of a thief. A traitor."

"And what does that make you? Aside from a bastard?"

"Well," Olivia said, "I think it's time to go, don't you, Nick?"

Rhys stood and walked over to Nick, his movements deliberate. The knot behind Nick's eye tightened.

He heard Rhys say, "Olivia, would you be a dear and give

my nephew and me a few minutes alone?"

Nick didn't hear her answer; his universe was his uncle's voice, and his words sang of the truth. "You can't win, Nick. You just can't. You haven't got the skills. For God's sake, you own a pub. You're not cut out for this. You're going to let someone down again, sure as we're sitting here. Perhaps you already have. There's no shame in following your own path, especially when it's best for everyone involved. You aren't up to this, Nick."

The knot burned like molten lead. Nick squinted with the pain, unable to turn away. "It may already be too late for Olivia's sister. You'll let her down just as Bedwyr let his king down, just as you let your father down. Your mother. Ben."

Then Olivia was pulling his arm. "Let's get the hell out of here, Nick." She virtually hauled him out of the chair. Rhys stood there, looking as harmless as he had ages ago when he opened the door to them.

"Let's *go*, Nick." Olivia squeezed his arm, digging in her nails.

"Perhaps you ought to do as she says."

Nick couldn't break free of his uncle's eyes. His heart went cold and the blood in his veins turned to slush.

He heard Olivia say, "We'll show ourselves out," and then she was dragging Nick along behind her. Once they were out of the drawing room, Nick tried to manage on his own, but Olivia wouldn't let go of him.

His uncle called after them, "Remember what I said, Nick."

She opened the door and shoved him outside. He welcomed the cool, damp air.

The door slammed behind them and Olivia wrapped her hands around his upper arm. "Do I need to slap you or something?"

"No," Nick assured her, "I'm all right."

"Sure, you are." She opened the passenger door, shoved him in. "I'll drive."

"You've never driven over here."

"I'll drive as far as the nearest pub," she said.

"Fair enough." Exhausted, he slumped back into the seat and closed his eyes.

"I'll tell you one thing." Olivia ground the gears before finding first. As they drove around the curve and out onto the narrow road, she continued, "Believing isn't just hard. It's a fucking threat to your sanity."

Nick unclipped his cell phone and punched in his mother's speed dial number.

Olivia sprayed gravel as she swung the Fiat out of the driveway and onto the road.

"Stay on the left," Nick said as he counted the rings; he could almost hear them echo in the empty house.

Chapter 38

Maybe that climb was what she'd needed—something physical to accomplish—because by the time Max crawled up onto the road, her energy and a small amount of optimism had returned. She paused to fill her lungs with air that smelled of moss, blue-green ocean and moist earth, then looked out toward Bryher. A small boat with a searchlight approached the area where Krett had gone down, and two other boats were following.

She thought about Krett, the man who killed her father, the man who tried to kill her, the man who she killed. Her lack of remorse for her part was both absolute and unsettling, as was the knowledge that although Ben died by Krett's hand, it was not by Krett's decision. That man was still alive. She tried to move past these thoughts in order to concentrate on what she needed to do. This was now as much for herself as for Ben.

She knew the castle was on the southern end of Alyssum, so she headed that way, following an asphalt path that was barely wide enough for a small car. That was when she recalled reading that there were no cars on Alyssum. At least no one had that advantage on her.

As she walked, she attempted to evaluate her situation. Unless Murdoch saw her jump out of the helicopter, he'd assume she'd gone down with Krett. That bought her a little time. At the most, she had the night to find Arthur. Once she found him, she'd also have found a haven. She had to believe that. If she didn't, she might as well turn right and walk back into the ocean.

She could hear its rhythms and see its infinite darkness beyond the shore. Inland, the heath gradually gave way to farmland and fenced-in pasture. In the distance, dark shapes moved and she heard the bleat of a calf. The night sounds crackled with intensity. A bat flew overhead; insects chirped.

Out of the corner of her eye, light flashed. When she looked out over the water, she saw a bank of clouds obliterating stars as it moved east toward Alyssum. Moments later thunder rumbled in the distance and a shard of lightning descended from the clouds. She picked up her pace.

At some point she needed to turn inland, and hoped her recollection of the map would help her determine which of several roads to take. The road to the castle passed a small lake, but she wouldn't be able to see that lake from the island's perimeter.

She'd walked about a half mile when she came to the second road leading inland. As she hesitated, trying to decide if this was the way to go, she heard what sounded like the blare of a trumpet—a lean, single note. She waited. Again, the note. Turning, she made her way toward the sound.

Foliage and the scent of lilacs bordered her path. After

about a hundred feet, a dirt path split off from the main one. Max peered down it, squinting into the darkness. She saw the lake's edge and the branches of a willow tree brushing its surface. As she approached the water, a white shape glided by. It had barely passed from her sight when it turned and swam by again. The trumpeter swan practically glowed under the moon's light, and the black behind its beak stood out like a bandit's mask. Straightening its incredible neck, it raised its head and emitted the haunting sound again. It glided toward the middle of the lake and dove beneath the surface. Max waited. One minute. Two. Logic insisted that it had surfaced out of her sight. She stepped closer to the water.

Behind her, farther up the path, a branch snapped. As she spun around, a man's voice said, "Who is that?"

At the head of the path a man sat astride a dark horse. His voice, his size, the cloak he wore were not Simon Murdoch. Nor would Murdoch be asking who she was. This had to be Arthur Penn. An unseen command moved the horse a few steps closer to Max. The rider remained motionless, one hand holding the reins, the other resting on his thigh. "I know everyone on this island," he said, "and I don't know you."

"Are you Arthur Penn?"

The horse sidestepped so it could reach a leafy branch which it began to nibble.

"I am," Arthur said. "And you are . . . ?"

Relief choked her up. She couldn't speak.

"And you are . . . ?" Arthur repeated.

She found her voice. "My name is Maxine Pike. I'm Ben's daughter."

The horse swung its head, lurched back a step and turned so it stood across the path. For a moment, Arthur just stared down at Max, then he dismounted and, holding the reins in one hand, stepped up to her, as though to get a closer look.

Max had to tilt her head back to look up at him. "Of course you are," he said.

Max could feel him tensing up. When he spoke again, his words were clipped and bitter. "How dare you come to Alyssum? Your father didn't have the courage to show his face, so he sent his daughter." As he shook his head, his shoulders sagged and his voice softened. "I don't know why, after all this, but I expected more of Benjamin Pike."

A gust of wind blew damp hair against her cheek. It stung like sleet. She swallowed. "I don't know what you're talking about."

"Don't insult me." The acid made her cringe. "I opened my home to your father. I trusted him. I—I—How does he repay me? He attempts to steal the one thing that means more to me than . . . than Alyssum. Have you come to apologize or to finish what he started?"

"No." She shook her head. "Neither."

"That's it," he said as though she hadn't spoken. "You're here to succeed where your father failed."

"He wouldn't steal—"

"What did he tell you? That he left one of his artifacts here? That he—"

"He didn't tell me anything."

"—was, in fact, robbed himself? That I stole from him? Is that what he told—"

"He didn't—"

"I would dearly love to hear how he—"

"Would you let me finish a sentence?"

He stopped, and as he looked at her, his expression changed. He touched her sleeve. "You're wet."

"I know." She hadn't come here to be yelled at.

He hesitated, then unfastened his cape and draped it over her shoulders. She pulled the warm, heavy garment close around her and looked up at him again. The moonlight was being swallowed up by clouds and she could barely see the man standing less than a foot from her.

She took a few moments to gather her wits, then said, "I have come a long way to talk to you, Mr. Penn. People have died so that I could be here. I jumped out of a helicopter without a parachute and I swam to Alyssum so I could be here. I'm not sure why I'm here, but I know it has to do with a stone." He seemed to lean into her slightly, tensing at the same time. "Before I left Chicago, I sent you an e-mail to the address on your website. Maybe you never saw it. It said I was trying to find Ben. I thought you were his friend. I don't know what you believe he did, but I can promise you this: Ben would not betray a friend's trust. And he is not a thief. He can't prove that because he can't speak for himself anymore. He's dead."

The wind had picked up, heavy with the smell of rain. Lightning flashed, illuminating the scene in an eerie wash of white. Arthur stood, looking down at her.

He dropped his hand to his side. "Ben is dead?" He sounded more shocked than angry.

"He is." She paused and waited for the thunder to dissipate before saying, "All I'm asking for is a chance to talk."

"How did Ben die?"

"He was killed. Murdered. By a man named John Krett who—"

"Krett?" Arthur glanced over his shoulder toward the north end of the island. "John Krett's helicopter just crashed off Bryher."

"I know. That's the one I jumped out of."

Moments passed before he said, "Why would he kill Ben? He barely knew him."

"Because Simon Murdoch asked him to."

"Simon?" Now he sounded confused. "What's Simon got to do with this?"

She wished she could see his face. "I'm not sure, but he wants me dead as well."

A drop of rain splashed on her forehead. Arthur glanced up at the sky as though noticing the storm for the first time.

"I'm sorry," he said, reining his horse around. "Decency shouldn't be a casualty here." He gestured for her to climb up. "We can continue this discussion when you're dry."

She clutched the saddle, got her foot in the stirrup and then Arthur boosted her the rest of the way. The horse shifted beneath her, adjusting to her weight.

"Scoot up toward the front," he said.

Gripping the pommel, Max pulled herself up a few inches, then held onto a clump of mane.

Arthur swung himself easily into the saddle behind Max. He put an arm around her and sat back far enough so she didn't have to straddle the pommel.

The rain made plopping sounds as it hit the branches on either side of them. The horse's ears twitched and it shook its head. The wind tunneled up under the cape and she shivered as the chill penetrated. "We're not far," Arthur said, giving the horse a nudge. It took off, breaking into a lope.

By the time they came out of the bush-lined path, the sky had let loose. Rain poured. The castle was a quarter mile down the road, surrounded by a stone wall. A flash of lightning silhouetted the turrets against the sky and her first impression was of its immensity. Gas lights illuminated the courtyard and a number of windows on the castle's lower floors were lit up. Max wondered how many people lived there and presumed Murdoch was one of them.

Rivers of rain streamed down her neck. Beneath her, the horse's gait was smooth, and Arthur's hold on her firm. She felt herself relax, the tension loosening its grip and she realized this was the first time in days she'd felt secure. Once she recognized the odd sensation, she told herself it was premature. At best, she was entering the eye of the storm.

When they turned into the courtyard, Max said to Arthur, "I'd appreciate it if you didn't tell Murdoch I'm here."

"You'll come to no harm in my home."

She didn't argue, but her shoulders began to tighten again. While she believed Arthur's sincerity, she knew Murdoch would do whatever he could to make sure she really died this time.

Less than an hour later, Max was sitting in the parlor in a tan suede chair. A fire burned in a large, stone fireplace as the storm beat against the windows. She was warm, dry and clean, having been supplied with a change of clothing and given a room with a shower. Things seemed possible. Arthur wasn't won over, but he was receptive. He would listen to what she had to say and that was the most she could hope for at this point.

When they'd entered the castle, Max was surprised not to see any servants. The huge place seemed empty. Arthur explained that only a quarter of the castle's living space was used, and he was able to maintain the home with a staff of three—a maid, a butler and a cook. Another man ran the stables and tended a few cows, and three kept the gardens in shape. "You won't find anyone around today or tomorrow," he'd told her. "Mondays and Tuesdays the island is closed to tourists. I give the staff the time off."

With both of them dripping water, Arthur showed her to a room on the third floor which had a wardrobe filled with clothing in various sizes. "We get our share of unexpected, unprepared guests." Then he'd returned the horse to the stable and apparently seen to the animal's comfort before his own. His hair was still damp and looked darker than in the photo—more brown than red. She also noticed a few strands of gray and realized he was older than she'd thought at first. Early forties, probably.

Now he sat across from her, a glass coffee table separating them, and stroked his close-cropped beard as he listened to her. He'd assembled a tray of sandwiches and tea. She wolfed down half a sandwich before she began telling Arthur what had happened since the call from Walter Bacon. When she told him about Elliot Schiff giving her the stone, he stopped her.

"What did it look like?"

She felt an odd thrill in his asking. "It's the deepest and purest green. By deep I don't just mean hue. The stone has— I don't know—resonance, depth. You look at it and it's like you're inside a green ocean."

He nodded as though that made perfect sense, and she continued. When she got to the part where Antony showed up at her door, Arthur edged forward on the couch.

"Antony Montague?" He smiled as though recalling an old college buddy.

She nodded, hating what she was about to tell him.

He went on: "I haven't seen him for several months. What's he to do with any of this?" The mention of Antony seemed to have engaged him, given him someone he knew to fit into Max's story.

"He and Ben had been investigating Simon Murdoch and a man named Rhys Lewis. They—Antony and Ben—believed the aim of these men was to take over the foundation."

Arthur sat back, crossing his arms over his chest. His brows drew together. "I'd like to hear that from Antony."

After a moment, she said, "You can't."

He leaned toward her, slowly.

"He's dead."

Arthur stared into her eyes and Max couldn't tell whether his held accusation or were merely searching for corroboration. Then he slumped back and tilted his head toward the molded ceiling. "What happened?"

She told him how Antony had taken her all the way to Cornwall and how Murdoch and this thug had arrived there before they could get away. He didn't interrupt, nor did he look at her, as she described what she'd seen from the car. When she finished, she watched Arthur's chest rise and fall three times. His throat constricted and he lowered his head.

"You must be mistaken."

She shook her head.

"How close were you?"

"More than a hundred feet away, but—"

"That's not very close."

"I had a camera."

His eyes narrowed as she tried to explain how it was. "I wanted to see what was going on, so I used my camera. I watched through a telephoto lens. I took photos."

His look was a mixture of incredulity and disgust. "You took pictures of Simon killing Antony? What kind of pleasure did that give you?"

"You don't understand." She crept forward. "It was weird. I was too far away to see much without the lens. And once I'm looking through the lens, well . . ." she added weakly, "pressing the shutter release is . . . like breathing."

Arthur pushed himself up from the chair and walked toward the windows. Lightning flashed and the interior lights flickered. With his back to her, he said, "You're telling me you have photographs of all this?"

"I did until Simon took my camera."

He turned toward her, nodding as though he'd expected something like that. "I see."

She was losing him.

"When did he conveniently take your camera?"

"I hired someone to take me to Bryher." She hesitated. Words seemed so inadequate. "I went there first because they were looking for me, and I didn't want to come straight here. The pilot was John Krett."

"Coincidence?"

"He delivered me to Simon Murdoch." She explained how Murdoch took the stone and her camera. "He told me that Krett had shot Ben and pushed him out of his helicopter over the Atlantic. He had the same in mind for me."

Arthur kept shaking his head. "That's absurd. Simon has worked for me for the last five years. I trust him implicitly. He's no murderer."

He'd responded so quickly, he couldn't have considered the possibility that Max was telling the truth.

"Why would I jump out of a helicopter if my life weren't in danger?"

"But you weren't the one who died."

"I was fighting for my life."

"You come here and slander my friend and closest advisor and expect me to believe you." He crossed his arms over his chest. "Why shouldn't I just send you on your way?"

"Because I'm telling you the truth." Even as the words left her mouth, she knew how crazy it all must sound to him. "Look," she said, "you can check some of the facts. Walter Bacon is dead. Even if you don't believe Ben was killed, it's on record that he's missing. And Elliot Schiff did give me the stone. He's recovering at Northwestern Hospital in Chicago if you'd care to—"

"How do you know the solicitor's death had to do with

Ben?" He paused. "And there are many reasons for a man to go missing. As for this Elliot Schiff. You've had plenty of time to line up all your players. Anyone could tell me he gave you the stone. For all I know, Schiff is your accomplice and the two of you are planning on selling the—" he stopped himself.

"What is it that Ben tried to steal?"

"Don't come the innocent with me, Miss Pike."

"I *am* innocent. How do you know he tried to steal anything? Did you catch him in the act?"

"No, I didn't. Simon did." Arthur glanced down at the carpet, and Max could practically see the wall between them. It was a thick one.

Max heard a boom of thunder and saw a flash of lightning in the west.

Without looking at her, Arthur said, "I'll show you to your room. Please stay there until morning. Simon will be back then. We can't have this discussion without him."

She stood. "When you see Simon, tell him I'd like my camera back." She waited until he looked up at her. "It belonged to my mother."

Chapter 39

"Just because she's not home doesn't mean something's happened to her."

Olivia had been reminding Nick of this for the past several hours, as he tried, every fifteen minutes, to raise his mother on the phone. At the same time, she was fighting her own nagging feelings about Max's safety, wincing as she revisited her encounter with Simon Murdoch. Olivia told herself that she hadn't been specific about Max's destination, and she wasn't even sure Max was going to London anymore. Not after Olivia told her not to bother. Knowing Max, that wouldn't have mattered. Pikes were stubborn.

She glanced at Nick, relieved to be able to dwell on someone else's worries. He'd probably called every obscure relation, acquaintance and neighbor of his mother's to see if she'd stopped by for coffee. He'd even asked one of those neighbors to check out the house, which she had. No one home.

In between calls, Nick had been ominously silent. He'd drawn into himself and Olivia wasn't used to working so hard to get a man to open up to her. Even a troubled one. When they did talk, Rhys Lewis was the topic of conversation and they didn't agree on much regarding Nick's uncle.

"You don't believe any of that crap he fed you. Do you?"

He shifted on his seat. "I don't know."

"I think he put something in your drink."

"What?"

"I don't know. He's a shrink. He's probably got all kinds of mind-altering crap." She craved a cigarette like never before. "Add that to the fact that he's a therapist and you've got someone who knows how to screw you up but good."

She glanced toward him and saw he was watching her. "Admit it. You still feel woozy."

Turning back toward the road, she added, "You looked like you were watching a horror movie neither your uncle or I could see." She paused. "Well, I couldn't see it. Your uncle probably produced the damned thing."

"What did you think of him?" Nick asked.

"Impressive, I guess. He keeps himself fit. Kind of sensual." She quickly added, "You probably wouldn't have noticed that. But trust me. Your uncle doesn't sleep alone unless he feels like it."

When Nick didn't respond, she repeated her earlier question. "You didn't believe that crap he was feeding you, did you?"

"I don't know. Maybe he's right."

"It's crap, Nick! You believe that and you're doing exactly what he wants you to do."

He sighed. God, he was making her nervous. She didn't like feeling nervous around Nick. Up until now he seemed so solid. "Does what he said matter?" she asked.

"Of course it matters."

"No. Really. He messed with your mind. But you got out of there alive and now he's out of your head. Forget about him."

While Olivia did admit that the guy was weird, and had an uncanny way of holding your attention, she wasn't anywhere near believing that he'd been fathered by a demon. (More likely, it was a drunken Welshman who Nick's grandmother met at the local pub.) Rhys reminded her more of one of those TV evangelists who were always making the blind see, the lame walk and the weird flourish.

"I think he's not going to mess with your head any more than you let him. Your problem is that you feel responsible for everyone in the world. So, when something happens to one of them—as it will, I mean, everybody dies—you think you could have stopped it. Do you think you're God?"

"Of course not," he muttered. "It's just that—"

"And now you're letting your uncle make you think you're a failure and he's a demon." She paused for a breath. "Demons just don't exist."

He'd countered her with: "How would you know about such things?" She felt him watching her. "You don't believe in anything you can't assault with one or more of your senses. I doubt that you believe in molecules."

For some reason that hurt and she stopped responding to him.

Now, as he prepared to try his mother again, he said, "We're going to pick up the M4 soon. That'll take us across The Severn." Was this guy just a little too concerned about that woman?

"How much farther?"

"About six kil—Mother!"

Olivia sighed.

"Where have you been? I've been ringing you for the last three hours. . . . You went to the cinema? . . . Well, I know you didn't want me going. . . . Yes, now I know what it feels like. . . . All right, then. . . . Yes, everything went fine," he lied. "Well, he is, as you said, strange."

As Olivia listened, she tried to think of someone she could fuss over like that. No one came to mind. Not in the present or the past. Max came the closest, and yet she demanded some distance. Olivia glanced at Nick, listened to him tell his mother to stay with her sister, then promise her he'd be careful, and found herself envying him a little. After a few minutes, he disconnected the call with a jab to the button.

"She's all right?" Olivia asked.

"Fine."

"The cinema." She couldn't keep the smile out of her voice. "Probably something with Mel Gibson."

"Michael Caine," he said, then added, "she's got a thing for him." She felt him watching her. "You and my mother might actually get along."

"I'll have to meet her."

"Let me try Weldon one more time."

Olivia hoped the old man didn't get Nick all riled up about demons again.

"This is Nick Llewellyn," he said after asking for Weldon. "A friend."

He didn't speak for several seconds and Olivia assumed that Weldon was being called to the phone. But then he said, "Oh, God. . . . What happened?"

Something bad from the sound of it. She saw an exit for a rest stop and took it.

"I can't believe that," Nick said, his voice shaky. "I saw him the other day. . . . Yes, of course. I'm terribly sorry. Yes, please." His hand dropped heavily into his lap, as though the tiny cell phone had turned to lead.

Olivia pulled into a space in the car park, and turned toward him. "Nick?"

When he brought his eyes to focus on hers, their pain and anger startled her. "Weldon Terry is dead." He stopped and it was several more seconds before he continued. "That was his landlady. He shot himself." He paused again. "No note, no reason. He just shot himself."

"God, Nick. I'm sorry." She didn't know what else to say.

He shook his head and shifted his gaze from Olivia. "It was no suicide."

"Your uncle?" she asked, knowing this was what Nick would be thinking.

"Why not?"

"Did he know you talked to Weldon? How could he know you even knew him, Nick?"

"Simple enough to have me followed."

She wanted to tell him he was being paranoid, but that wasn't so easy anymore.

"For an uncle who has estranged himself from my family, he knew a lot about me."

"But, why? Weldon wasn't a threat to Rhys, was he?"

"I'm afraid Rhys might have been making a point. If he can get to Weldon Terry, renowned specialist in the supernatural, he can get to anyone. Your family. Mine." He looked into the side mirror, then turned away as though his own image disturbed him. "I never should have involved him."

"This isn't your fault, Nick." She shifted into reverse. "We've got to get to Penzance."

"Olivia," he said and something about the flatness in his tone made her stop. "I think your sister would be better off if we—I—stayed out of this."

"Don't talk like that."

"If I hadn't contacted Weldon, he'd be alive. I know that. I won't leave a wake of dead people because of some stone my family is obsessed with."

"Would you stop feeling sorry for yourself?"

He turned on her. "Who are you to talk? Of course you wouldn't know what it's like to feel responsible for another person. You've never been responsible for anyone but yourself and then just barely. So, forgive me if I don't find your exhortations convincing."

Olivia squeezed the gearshift knob. "I care about Max," she said.

Nick didn't respond.

"And we need to find her."

"You don't need me."

As a rule, weak men embarrassed Olivia. So why was she determined to see this one through his crisis of confidence? She slugged his arm. "Get over it! Listen, if you think I've spent the whole day with you because your Welsh charm is so irresistible, then think again. You're about as charming as a hangover. I'm here because I need to find my sister. You're here because you say you need to find some damned rock, although I suspect there's more to it."

"I don't know if—"

"Shut up. Let me finish. I'm not good at doing this kind of thing. I need you. At least I thought I did. I knew you weren't James Bond, but I didn't think you were Barney Fife either." She glared at him, daring him to argue. When he didn't, she continued. "Now, either stop whining or get out of this car and start thumbing your way back to London—or maybe you could call your mother to come pick you up."

"That's not—"

"This car is going to Penzance."
He returned the cell phone to his belt.
"Charming as a hangover," he muttered.
"Not quite," she said.

Chapter 40

Outside, the storm howled as it battered the windows, but Max barely heard it as she stood in front of the fireplace, staring glumly into the flames. She'd gotten her chance with Arthur and she'd blown it. "I need another." She had to convince him she hadn't come to Alyssum to steal from him, and she had to do it before Murdoch returned. "Think, Max. I know you can figure this out."

While she knew her father was no thief, there was one thing that would tempt him. Arthur must believe he'd found Excalibur. She'd suspected King Arthur's sword was involved even before leaving Chicago. The foundation was named Caliburnus. Ben would have given anything for that sword. Maybe his life. But, steal it? "No way." Murdoch must have told Arthur that Ben tried to steal the sword and sent Ben off in the middle of the night to his death.

Someone rapped softly at the door.

She didn't dare hope. "Who is it?"

"Arthur."

When she opened the door, he hesitated, peering around as though expecting to find another person with Max. "I thought I heard you speaking to someone."

"I talk to myself."

"I see. Yes, I do that as well."

His left hand was behind his back as though he were hiding something from her.

She waited. He wet his lips and said, "What kind of camera was that?"

"A Nikkormat."

"Is this it?" He brought his arm around from behind his back and in his hand was Max's camera.

Her throat tightened as she reached out for it, turning it over to see that it no longer contained any film. No surprise there. "This is it," she sighed. Holding it with the lens in her palm and her other hand supporting the body, its cold, solid weight made everything seem possible again. "It was my mother's. She died when I was a child." She looked up at Arthur. "Where did you find it?"

He sighed. "In Simon's office."

"The film is gone."

"I'll ask him about it."

"Come on in." She walked back into the room. Arthur followed.

"Yes, well, you understand I can't condemn Simon for everything you've accused him of because of a camera." He nodded at it. "But I will speak to him. I looked for that e-mail you mentioned, but didn't find it. Simon screens those for us." He shrugged and made an effort to smile. "We've been quite busy lately. Things get overlooked."

"Sure," she said, sensing she'd pushed hard enough; Arthur would have to go the rest of the way on his own.

"I found your camera after Simon left for the mainland. He told me that the stone was coming here tomorrow." He walked to the fireplace and pulled back the screen. "It's being brought by a man named Rhys Lewis and his daughter."

"Rhys Lewis is a dangerous man."

"So you say." He placed a small log on the fire, then turned toward her. "According to Simon, the stone has been in this man's family for generations."

"Can he prove it?"

"We'll know tomorrow."

The tight lines in his forehead softened. "I once had a friend . . ." he hesitated. "A teacher, actually, and a friend. He told me that a person who learned how to listen to the truth of his own heart has found the keys to wisdom. Though it is useless to him unless he also learns to trust. I try to do that."

"Is any corner of your mind open to the possibility that I'm telling you the truth?"

"My loyalty is not easily won. Once won, it is not easily lost." He looked into her eyes. "I mean, that's the whole point then, isn't it?"

She nodded.

"Forgive me, but I don't trust easily anymore. This friend—teacher, really—helped me establish the foundation. Worked with me here for a time. He was embezzling money." He shook his head. "It wasn't the money, you understand. I've plenty. But I'd have trusted him with my life. I don't believe he was a bad person, he couldn't have been. But I couldn't trust him anymore. Since then, it's not been easy."

Then he looked her square on and said, "Why are you here?"

Max chose her words carefully. "I'm not entirely certain.

Yet, I know I should be here." When he didn't argue, she went the rest of the way. "That thing you say Ben tried to steal. It's Excalibur, isn't it?"

His features darkened and he slipped his hands into the pockets of his slacks. "Then you did know."

"Not because Ben told me. He didn't. But I know what my father's passion was. You named your foundation Caliburnus. It wasn't a huge leap."

Pressing his lips together, he nodded. She noticed the lines around his eyes which belied his youthful movements. "I suppose not." He shifted, as though unsure of his place.

She had to keep him talking. "How did you come up with the idea for the foundation?"

"It was that friend I mentioned. He had some wonderful ideas, I can't deny him that. A lesson learned is a lesson learned. When I was at school, we'd talk a great deal." Arthur walked to the window, unhooked the latch and pulled it open. The sound of rain filled the black night. " 'Arthur,' he said to me, 'this world has many dark times ahead of it. Some things unimaginable to those living now.' " He spoke quietly, but with conviction. " 'Every effort must be made to elevate humanity wherever possible, or we are all doomed.' If not for him, I'd never have thought of the foundation." He approached Max as he spoke. "You see, my family's fortune is immense, but it came by some rather disreputable means. Then, we've affixed ourselves to this tiny island where we feed off our own wealth and isolation. If you can't see the harm you're doing, what's to stop you?"

He waved her to the window with him. "What do you see out there?"

"The rain. The dark." Beyond the room's light, the rain disappeared into blackness.

"Exactly. We never saw past the tip of our island. The

ends of our noses." He inhaled the rain-rich air and released his breath slowly. "When the fortune came to me, I divested myself of all outside interests and invested the money so that interest alone was enough to create a goodly number of grants annually. Of course, I've kept enough to live on, keep the place and its staff going, but all the other money is invested in humanity. There is so much need out there." He stared into the storm and when he spoke, his voice was an urgent whisper. "Now, look out again."

Max was afraid she'd see only the black. The fire cast Arthur's shadow against one wall—impossibly tall and lean—dwarfing the room's contents. She looked out the window. The dark. No sound except for the rain. Then a flash of lightning illuminated the sky and in the seconds before the thunder responded, when the lightning's impression was still seared into her vision like a green canvas, a slash of red bisected the canvas. "The stone," she whispered into the thunder. "It's the stone."

Out of the corner of her eye, Arthur's shadow nodded. "Come," he said. "I want to show you Caliburn."

Chapter 41

Max followed Arthur down long, paneled hallways toward the rear of the estate. She felt like a waif in the slacks with rolled up cuffs and a sweater that came almost to her mid thigh.

The halls smelled of wood and polish, and the rooms they passed were filled with heavy antique furniture and oil paintings of severe-looking people and horses. One room was devoted to a collection of ancient swords, which were displayed on three of the walls. Ben must have loved this place. At the same time, she thought of how strange it would be to live here, among the antiquity. How long would it take to learn all its sounds?

They came to a narrow, curving stairway beside the kitchen, which smelled of bread and nutmeg. No more than one person at a time could ascend the steps. Arthur waved his hand upwards. "Now, we climb."

When Max looked up, she couldn't see beyond the first bend. As soon as she started the climb, she realized her legs hadn't recovered from her earlier ordeal. "How many steps?"

"I've never counted."

"I don't believe you."

"All right. Seventy-two." She heard the smile in his voice. "But they're shallow steps."

One hand braced against each rough stone wall, Max continued to climb. Candle-like fixtures protruding from the walls provided dim lighting.

"The room up here looks like a chapel, though I doubt it was ever used as such," Arthur said. "My grandfather had it built. He had a real need to be alone from time to time."

"I'd think it would be hard to be anything but alone here."

"He was more sociable than most Penns. Notorious parties. All the bedrooms would be filled. Some guests had to sleep on the grounds. Wherever they'd pass out. Until my father came along, the Penns had a rather unsavory reputation. In league with smugglers, pirates and assorted thieves. As I mentioned earlier, the origin of the Penn fortune is nefarious."

"What made your father change?"

"I'm not certain. My grandmother was a good person who raised my father mostly on her own. Perhaps it also had to do with my grandfather's unfortunate ending, which involved the lift he was having installed up here. He had a bit too much to drink at one of these affairs, came up here to get away and turned left when he should've turned right. The lift was never finished, but the shaft is still there." He paused. "It's been boarded up."

"Why wasn't the elevator finished?"

"It's considered a bit of a curse, actually. Haunted, perhaps. A workman disappeared for a time during its construction. Quite strange. He reappeared without an explanation and left the island without a word to his family and was never heard from again."

By the time they reached the tower, Max was gasping for breath, while Arthur's breathing seemed normal. She decided he must be used to the climb. A sconce on either side of a heavy, wooden door lit the small area with a sickly, yellow aura. To the left was the elevator shaft. It had been covered with plywood, nailed over it in a haphazard manner without any attempt to blend in with the surrounding floor.

Arthur grasped the door handle, which was ornate, black iron. The door swung open without a sound, revealing only darkness beyond it. Then he retrieved two candles and a book of matches from a wooden box outside the door, lit both candles and wedged one into an old-fashioned, brass candleholder. He held onto the other. The flames illuminated a small room with a domed ceiling. Four wooden benches filled most of the area, the walls of which, like the stairwell, were stone with three lancet windows cut into them. Arthur gently took her arm and turned her so she faced the east wall. The floor creaked beneath her. It took a moment before her eyes adjusted to the candle's subtle lighting and she could make out the object dominating the wall. She moved closer, then turned and reached for the candle. Arthur handed it to her.

She held the flame up to the sword, which hung perpendicular to the floor, as though invisible hands prepared to plunge it into the hard wood. The double-edged blade, about three feet in length, was dulled and tarnished with age and the hilt trimmed in some kind of polished black stone. The crossbar angled downward slightly, and curved in at the ends. Two stones were embedded in the hilt—a red stone at the top and a green one on the bottom. Between the two was a cavity of the same size.

Until that moment, Max had been dubious of Arthur's claim of finding Caliburn. How could he know? But then everything came together. The sword and the stone she'd possessed only hours ago were the keys and the answer so close she could feel the breath of its whisper. As she stared, the space between the lightning and the thunder grew longer and longer. The sword glowed white hot as though reflecting the absorbed heat of the candle. This was the real thing; Ben had known that.

She imagined his thrill at seeing the sword, and the pain of knowing they'd never share this nearly leveled her. When she trusted her voice, she said, "It's incredible."

"Yes." He'd moved beside her. "Caliburn."

Retreating a step, she sat on one of the benches and said to Arthur, "Ben didn't try to steal your sword. He would have wanted it, but he wouldn't have stolen it."

Arthur lowered himself onto the bench beside her.

"He had too much respect for legend," she continued. "He knew it wasn't his."

"It's not mine either."

He didn't take his eyes from the sword. "Tell me. Did you see the stone's color change?"

"No."

"It changes from green to red, depending on the light. Like a streak of fire. Of course, it must be two colors." He looked down into her eyes. "You see, it combines the other two. The upper stone is a ruby, which stands for invulnerability, protection against wounds in battle. The lower stone, an emerald, embodies wisdom. The middle stone—the heartstone—is both green and red, depending on the light. It binds the two. Tempers invulnerability with wisdom. Each one is powerful in and of itself. But together . . ." his voice drifted off, but he brought it back with renewed intensity, "together they give Caliburn its power. The power to heal. Not the cut on a man's brow, but the wounds inside him. And the scars of the world."

Nothing he said surprised her. "Who took the stone from the sword?"

"Arthur's knight, Bedwyr," he said. "Handed down from one generation to the next."

So, Nick was Bedwyr's descendant. Of course. She looked up at Arthur. "Do you honestly believe Ben tried to steal this?"

He sighed. "I do know that Ben lied to me."

"How?"

"He contacted me under false pretenses, claiming to be interested in the foundation when actually he'd been seeking Caliburn most of his adult life. He came to believe it was on one of these islands. Having exhausted his search on the others, he set his sights on Alyssum."

"How do you know this?"

"Simon looked into his background and learned that he'd applied for permits to dig on the other islands and that he'd made discreet enquiries about Alyssum and the possibility of doing some excavating." He paused. "I saw copies of these requests."

As he finished, he watched Max as though waiting for her denial. "But by the time Ben arrived on Alyssum, you'd already found Caliburn," she said.

"Only just. Though I suppose I've your father to thank. On the other hand," he hesitated, "I believe it was meant to be found. I pass that pool nearly every day of my life. Dream by it. Stare into its waters. I've memorized it. Then, last month, your father sent me a copy of a book which describes King Arthur's final battle on these islands. Not long after I read it, I was standing by the pond. I looked down and saw it." He shook his head as though it were still difficult for him to believe. "It was late afternoon and I'd been riding. I led Tavish down to the lake for water. Any other day I might not have noticed the glint of silver, but the last threads of daylight hit the water just so. As I stared, an object appeared to be rising from the bottom. I blinked and it was back on the bottom—a narrow band of fire."

Max closed her eyes. She could see it. "Is that the lake with the trumpeter swan?"

"Yes. Why?"

She shook her head. "Go on."

"I waded out toward that light and reached into the water. I touched cold steel—then I knew it was a sword. I found the hilt, grasped it and pulled Caliburn from the water." He extended his arm in front of him, holding the invisible weapon at arm's length. Max found herself looking with him, taking in its size and splendor. Then he dropped his hand and smiled as though he knew she saw it too. "It was magnificent," he said. "Despite its tarnish, that was obvious. From the moment I held it, I knew it would be easier to cut off my arm than to give it up. I found it. I was meant to find it."

"I know what you mean," she said, thinking that was exactly how she felt about the stone. "There's a connection."

Arthur said, "Sometimes I come up here, sit and look at it, and I wonder why it's come to me." His voice softened to a whisper. "Sometimes I wish it hadn't."

"Why?" Though she thought she knew exactly what he meant.

He shook his head. Max waited, but he didn't continue.

Lightning illuminated the chapel.

"The heartstone," Max began, "what will happen once it's reunited with the sword?"

"I will be nearer to the . . . conclusion of these events."

"Aren't endings also beginnings?"

"Yes." They sat together, gazing up at the sword as the storm retreated into the east and the candle burned low. "But those often belong to someone else."

Chapter 42

When they climbed down from the chapel, Arthur led Max up another set of stairs and down a long hall to a large room at its end. One curved corner indicated it was built into a turret, and there were windows on two sides. In the room's center sat a desk with a computer, and behind it a low table with a printer and copier. Beside the table was a set of curtained French doors. Stacks of folders, papers and books covered the table and several file cabinets.

Max approached a map of the world that took up a large part of one wall, stretching from floor to ceiling.

"Each of those drawing pins represents one of our grant recipients," Arthur said.

Max examined it and saw that, while a few places in Western Europe and the U.S. were skewered, most pins protruded from areas not known for their tourist industry.

On the wall opposite the map, a fire crackled in a massive,

stone fireplace. A burgundy leather couch faced the fire. Arthur took down two pewter goblets from the mantel, filled one with red wine from a stoneware carafe. He paused, carafe tipped over the second goblet. "Sorry. I didn't ask. I can get you coffee or something else, if you'd prefer."

"I'd like wine."

"Claret?"

"Sounds good."

"I've never cared much for white wine, but I seem to exist on reds." He handed her a goblet.

Three small oil paintings hung above the fireplace; Max assumed they were Alyssum. One depicted the rocky coast. Another might have been a close-up of the same setting, revealing caves among the rocky outcroppings. A bank of angry storm clouds dramatized a purple-toned heath in the third.

"My mother . . . she painted those."

When Max looked over her shoulder, she saw Arthur gazing up at the paintings. Standing there, holding the wine goblet, he seemed so composed. It occurred to her that while she'd seen him struggle for words, his movements were never without grace.

"They're lovely," she said, taking a drink of wine, which tasted faintly of spices. "Alyssum is really three different islands, isn't it? The vegetation is so diverse."

"Therein lies her charm." He moved closer to Max and the paintings, squinting as though trying to bring them into focus. "Alyssum's land has changed since then." With his goblet, he gestured toward the one with the roiling clouds. "These last few years have been drier than our norm—the northern heath seems to be encroaching on the castle." He released a sigh. "But that's part of the beauty of Alyssum. It's always changing."

"You've lived your entire life here?"

"With the exception of my schooling."

"Do you ever get the desire to leave?"

"Not really. It's difficult to describe. I . . . and my family before me—most of us—feel an affinity with Alyssum. We aren't so much residents as we are part of the whole." He shook his head. "Sounds preposterous. If you were here longer, you might sense some of what I'm saying."

"I've done some reading on the Caliburnus Foundation." She settled into the couch, sinking into the soft leather. "You fund some amazing people."

"We do," he agreed, sitting on the edge of his desk, his long legs stretched out before him. "I'm proud of them all."

She folded one leg under her, shifting so she could face Arthur. "I read about a couple of your people who raided one of those places that lets hunters pay to kill old zoo animals. The article said they took away the guns and liberated the animals."

His grin was sly. "That's one we don't lay claim to. Not publicly at any rate." He tipped his goblet as though toasting and took a drink.

"But it was Bruce Langford's group, wasn't it?"

He nodded, still smiling.

"Was Antony the pilot?"

"Why, yes—" He stopped and the smile faded.

"I'm sorry," she said, wanting to offer something.

He didn't respond immediately, and in those seconds, Max could see the sadness etched into the lines defining his eyes. When he focused on her, his brows where drawn together. "You said Simon was there, at the airstrip. How could he have known?"

"According to Antony, the only person who knew where we were landing was the guy who owned the strip. Antony said he was new to Bruce Langford's group."

"What was his name, do you know?"

Max had already worked this out. "Peter Thorpe."

"Peter?" He sounded both surprised and dubious.

"Peter." Then she said, "Antony died to get me here."

Arthur's eyes narrowed. "Why was he so intent?"

"Because he wanted me to bring the heartstone."

Arthur stood slowly, as though suddenly stricken with age, walked over to the fireplace and set his wine on the mantel. Then he crouched before the flames, staring into them for a moment before he added one log and then another. "My loyalty to Simon must be difficult for you to understand. In a way, he represents the best that the foundation can do." Still crouching, he twisted on the balls of his feet and turned toward Max. "When I was eight, my mother left my father and me. We never saw her again. My father never spoke her name again. Years later, when he died, I found a number of letters she'd written to me. He'd never let me see them. In them she told me she'd left because she couldn't bear Alyssum's solitude. Isolation. The letters were sent from the U.S. Various cities. They'd stopped after five years." He brushed his hands against his pants and stood, taking his wine from the mantel. When he did, he glanced at the paintings above the fireplace.

Max understood why trusting another person was hard for Arthur. While she had also grown up without her mother, she'd never doubted her love.

"Several years after my father died, Simon came to me. His mother," he paused, "our mother, died years ago—five years after she left Alyssum. She had Simon out of wedlock. He was only three when she died. He showed me some letters, documents. You know, I really wanted to believe I had a blood relation. A half-brother. However, I was cautious. We had DNA tests done. They proved we are related."

"What was Simon's background?"

"He'd had a rough time of it. He'd been a bit of a drifter. Occasionally got himself into trouble. Nothing outrageous. Then he straightened himself out, put himself through school with the assistance of some scholarships. Quite a success story. When he came to me, he didn't ask for anything. He simply wanted to meet me. It took some convincing to get him to stay here."

Arthur sat on the couch next to Max. "I've never been much of a family person." He turned to her and lifted a shoulder in an apologetic shrug. "I suppose I saw Simon as an opportunity to make amends for that. I mean, here I am, trying to make a difference in the world, trying to touch people, but I'm doing it with money. I never had to become involved with them personally. We correspond, of course, but that's safe. I never had to touch anyone."

"I think I know what you mean."

He nodded. "It was important that I make a difference for this young man, my only living relation." Looking past her, he sighed, as though confronting a sad memory. When he met her eyes again, his had lost some of their animation. "It took time, but eventually we earned each other's trust. There's that word again." He paused. "All Simon needed was someone to believe in him. He's quite bright. I gave him responsibilities and once he saw he was capable, he began to come round. Grew more confident. Gradually I gave him more to do. Now he maintains the operations of the island and the foundation. The legal aspects. I manage the recipients and the accounting."

"Will Simon inherit everything?"

Nodding as though he saw the intent of her question, Arthur said, "My will leaves everything in a trust so the foundation will continue. If I have offspring, he—or she—will be head of the board of directors and will inherit Alyssum, of course. If I have no children—and I hope that's not the case—the board will control the foundation as a whole and Alyssum as a part of it. Simon will have a voice on the board and will be able to stay on and maintain Alyssum as long as he likes." Then he added, "You see, he doesn't stand to gain much more than what he already has."

"Who appoints the members of the board?"

"The board itself."

Turning toward Max, he propped his elbow on the back of the couch and rested his head against his fist. He seemed to hesitate a moment, then said, "You told me you'd read up on the foundation. What do you think?"

She looked directly into his eyes and said, "These grant recipients. They're your knights, aren't they?"

Smiling slowly, he nodded and said, "I suppose they are."

"And you're King Arthur."

The smile turned sad and he sighed deeply before answering. "No. It's just a name given me by a father who loved Tennyson."

"Are you sure you're not?"

He spoke carefully. "I've tried to emulate him. I won't deny that."

She tucked her legs beside her. "What would King Arthur do in the twenty-first century? Can't very well launch an army from Alyssum, could he? I mean, why? Just think about it. Arthur's knights went out into the land and performed chivalrous deeds. So, how does one do that anymore? And these days a person is limited by his or her resources. Even if someone wanted to . . ." she waved her hand toward the map, "study owls in Madagascar, she needs the money to live and conduct her research. You established the Caliburnus Foundation. If that's not Arthurian, then I don't know what is."

He blinked and cocked his chin, regarding her for a moment.

She smiled. "Trust me."

He moved his hand so it almost touched her cheek, then took it back.

She wanted to kiss him and thought he wanted her to, but then she remembered her last spontaneous kiss. Still, it was strange the way she felt at ease here. As though they'd sat together before on this couch, in front of this fireplace, with thunder rumbling in the distance. The way he balanced the stem of the pewter goblet on his knee, thoughtfully rubbing his thumb back and forth across its base—this gesture seemed so familiar. But she was here because of the stone, and she warned herself not to lose track of that.

Arthur took his arm off the back of the couch and adjusted his position.

"This man Simon is bringing," Max said. "Rhys Lewis. He's a dangerous man."

"So you've said." He frowned and nodded. "Perhaps it doesn't make a difference."

"Of course it does."

"The heartstone knows where it belongs. Whoever has it is meant to have it."

"Do you really believe that?"

"I do."

"You can't tell me the heartstone was meant to be possessed by someone who had a man killed in order to get it."

He raised the goblet to his mouth. "It's not over yet," he said and took a drink.

"If Rhys brings the stone, will he put it back in the sword?"

Arthur lifted an eyebrow. She wondered what she'd said that amused him. "I hope not. I expect that's why he's bringing his daughter."

"She'll put it in the sword?"

"I believe that's the plan."

"Then what happens?"

He shrugged as though it were obvious. "I'll marry her."

"Because she placed the heartstone?"

He nodded again.

"Why?"

"You asked me how I knew I wasn't Arthur. I know because he hasn't been born. Not yet." He regarded her for a few moments before saying, "He won't be conceived until the heartstone is returned to Caliburn; his mother will be the woman who does that."

She searched his eyes. "Oh." It was all she could say.

His shoulders twitched as though he found that funny in a sad sort of way. Then he stared into his goblet for several moments before turning his gaze up toward Max.

She wasn't shocked by what she'd just learned. She'd held the stone, felt its power. It was the catalyst. The woman who placed that stone in Caliburn would bear Arthur. She hadn't given any thought to filling that sort of role, but if it was supposed to be her, how could she turn her back on this? Why would she want to? She believed she could love this man. Already she admired him. He was kind and decent. Antony's devotion and Ben's instincts had not been misplaced. Arthur wasn't Grey, but he was possible.

She touched his arm, and said, "I'm the one who's supposed to have it."

It was one-thirty a.m. when Arthur walked Max back to her room. As they stood at the door, Arthur looked down at her as though he wanted to say something else. But then he shifted his shoulders and averted his eyes.

"When will Simon be back?" she asked.

"I imagine he'll come here with the others. In the late morning."

"Would you not tell him I'm alive?"

"I haven't yet." Then he frowned.

"Let me surprise him," she said. "You can judge from the way he reacts."

His eyes searched hers. Finally he nodded and said, "All right."

When Max stepped into the room, the fire still blazed and she figured there must be at least one servant working today. She closed the door, then turned and froze. Shadows obscured the chair in the corner, but the pair of feet, crossed at the ankles, were stretched out far enough to be visible in the fire's glow. As she reached behind her for the doorknob, a faint click switched on a lamp, illuminating the corner.

"Hello, Max." He pulled his legs in and rose from the chair.

Although she knew the face, seconds passed before reality overcame disbelief, and she accepted the fact that Grey Fisher was on Alyssum, in Arthur's castle, standing in the corner of her bedroom.

Chapter 43

"Grey?"

He wore a pale sweater over a dark shirt and held some small object he kept transferring from one hand to the other. As she approached, he cocked his head and a lock of gray-streaked hair dipped into his right eyebrow.

A hundred questions grappled for a voice. The dim light had washed much of the color from the room, and she had the sensation of existing inside a photograph. When she was close enough to see into his eyes and found a little apprehension there, she stopped, pushed up the sleeves of her heavy sweater and said, "Who are you?"

He nodded once. "Arthur and I go back a ways. I was his teacher. Actually, my name is Greyson Weir. I helped Arthur establish the foundation."

"You were his teacher?"

He nodded again. "And I worked for him here on

Alyssum. We had a parting of ways when he was led to believe I'd embezzled a large amount of money. I didn't, but I couldn't prove it. I'm here because he needs my help." He paused. "He doesn't realize it yet, but he will."

"Arthur doesn't know you're here."

"Not yet." He glanced at the ceramic egg in his hand, then set it on the table and tented it with his fingers. "You're the only one who knows I'm here."

Her brain had shut down. A moment ago she'd been overwhelmed with questions. Now, she couldn't remember one of them. Beside her, the fire crackled and its flames threw long, wavering shadows against the walls. Its heat touched the fine hairs on her arm.

"We need to talk," he said.

"Damn right." She'd been deceived. Right now she didn't know to what extent or why, but she felt she ought to be angry or at least more demanding of answers, but all she could think to ask was: "Where's Fiona?"

"I put her up with a friend. She's fine." His shoulders eased slightly.

"Good. Thank you." Then she said, "Did you know Ben?"

"I did. He and I—"

Her anger flared like a struck match. "Why didn't you tell me?"

"I couldn't. You—"

"Did you know he was killed?"

"I feared that." The muscles in his jaw tightened. "What happened?"

"He was shot, then pushed out of a helicopter into the ocean."

Grey sighed deeply and shook his head. "I'm so sorry, Max."

"Did you know Antony?"

She caught the quick tuck of his brow. "Yes. . . . Is he all right?"

"No," she said, feeling it like a knot in her throat. "He's dead, too. Murdoch shot him. Six times."

He closed his eyes and bowed his head. After a moment, when he looked up at Max again, the shadows in his face had deepened. She could see the pain in his eyes and wanted to do something to take it away, but the questions were coming back to her now. "How did you know Ben?"

He stepped away from the table, moving closer to the fire and Max. "Your father began investigating the Caliburnus Foundation almost a year ago. It was after he received a book that described the stone's history and its destiny—the book you showed me. The setting sent him looking into Alyssum and the foundation."

"Then you met him last year?"

"I learned of his investigation and contacted him last summer." He turned to look into the fire and Max noticed a small scar—a thin, half-inch line—stood out white against the dark stubble on his jaw. "We talked about the stone, the foundation and Arthur."

"This Arthur or the next one?"

His gaze found her again. "Both."

The wavering light reflected in his eyes made them impossible to read.

"Why didn't you tell me you knew Ben?"

"I couldn't," he started. This time she'd let him finish. "It wasn't for me to tell. Ben was going to explain all this, but he never had the chance."

She felt the emptiness in her chest. God, why hadn't she gone to Wales? At the same time, she was angry with Ben. How could he have assumed this of her? "Arthur showed me Caliburn. I know what placing the stone means."

He looked away, toward the window, then back again, and opened his mouth as though to speak. Before he could, Max said, "Ben set me up."

"No. He didn't." Grey shook his head, adamant. "Ben wanted this for you, yes, he did. But he'd never have pushed you. You would have to have wanted it as much as he did. He believed you would."

"What about you?" Her voice sounded raspy. "Do you want this for me?"

He tilted his head and looked at her for a long time before saying, "My feelings aren't at issue here."

"That's not what I asked."

"I want what's best for you, Max. I do that as your father's friend and as your friend." He drew in a deep breath and released it. "Will I ever wonder about what might have been? Of course I will. But the fact is, we'd never have met had it not been for this."

"You don't know that." She turned away from him. He was right, but she didn't want him to see what that did to her. "Possibilities are hard to let go of, aren't they?" He didn't respond, and when she looked over her shoulder, he was watching her and nodding.

Grey came up behind her, and she imagined his hands touching her shoulders, melting her stiff muscles. But, he didn't, and she'd known that he wouldn't.

She felt he was waiting for her to move on, but she didn't know where to go yet. She focused on a carving of an elephant on the fireplace mantel. It was made of marble, and its narrow, dark eye seemed to be watching her.

It was all coming together at once. No wonder Ben hadn't encouraged grad school.

"Max," he said, "right now we need to focus on the situation at hand. Dealing with Simon Murdoch and, more importantly, Rhys Lewis. Have you met either?"

"Just Murdoch."

Then she turned around and said, "Your living two floors above me was no coincidence."

He sighed. "That's right. Your father was worried. I received an e-mail from him. He told me he was concerned for your safety. That's when I moved to Chicago."

"Just like that?"

He shrugged. "It seemed the only thing to do."

"Where were you? What were you doing?"

"In upstate New York, teaching at a private school."

"You quit your job?"

He nodded.

Ben had trusted Max with the stone and Grey with Max. Before she could examine the depth of Ben's trust in each of them, Grey was talking again.

"There was some confusion. I assumed he'd given you the stone—he'd spoken of doing that the last time we'd met in London."

"He didn't."

"I realized that. Eventually." He shifted and pushed his hand through his hair, then hooked it around the back of his neck. "I wasn't sure what to do at that point. No one could reach Ben, I feared the worst. All I could do was watch you and see what you did."

She took the fireplace poker and jabbed at the logs. Sparks flew. "Damn, why didn't I go to Wales?" Another jab. "You know, everyone ought to get one thing they can do over again. It's not fair." God, how different things might be now.

"Max," Grey spoke quietly. "How did he ask?"

She returned the poker to its stand as she thought. "He called. Said I should come up to Wales, there was something he wanted to talk about."

"And when you said you couldn't . . ."

She recalled sitting in the upholstered chair, her bare feet up on the coffee table, ankles crossed. She'd painted her toenails red that morning, something she hadn't done since she was a teenager. "He asked me when spring break was. I told him. He said we'd talk then. He never called." She bowed her head and pressed her fingers to her mouth. It hurt to breathe. "He was probably dead."

Grey put his hand on her shoulder and gave it a gentle squeeze. "Don't you think if he'd really needed for you to come right then, he'd have pushed harder?" She looked up and he almost smiled. "I hadn't known Ben for very long, but when he wanted something, he had a way of getting it."

"No kidding." She pushed a strand of hair from her cheek and realized, when her hand came away damp, that she was crying. How hard would he have pushed her?

"Things are happening quickly now," Grey said. "You know that two members of the foundation have been killed by Lewis. One has already been replaced by one of Lewis's people. The other will be—possibly by Rhys himself. The remaining two members' lives are in jeopardy. As is Arthur's."

"God, you sound like Antony."

He raised his eyebrows, challenging her. "Think about it, Max. You've seen Murdoch in action; you've seen some of the things Rhys is involved in. Rhys is close to getting his hands on the foundation. It will be used to fund precisely the opposite of what it was intended for."

"If you're able to prove all this stuff—or at least some of it—why can't you convince Arthur that Murdoch is involved?"

"That's what Ben was trying to do." He thrust his hands into his pockets as though he needed to contain them. "He spent a long time building a relationship with Arthur."

"Why is Arthur so . . . dense about Murdoch?"

"One of the things that makes Arthur exceptional is this basic goodness in him. Surely you've seen that. He believes in Simon Murdoch the way a teacher believes in a student he has helped become a remarkable individual. The only bond that can be closer is that of a parent to a child. Add to that Arthur's basic nature and the fact that he feels some guilt—guilt which Simon has exploited. It would take a devastating force to sever that bond. And that's one of the reasons you're so important, Max. You've been here for less than a day and you've got him doubting Murdoch for the first time."

"What? Were you listening in on us?"

"No. You told me." He regarded her with a touch of impatience as she tried to figure out what he was talking about. Then he said, "He showed you Caliburn."

"Oh." Grey was right. For whatever reason, Arthur did trust her.

"This is deadly serious, Max." He'd come up beside her now, as if he were about to whisper secrets into her ear. "You can bet that what Ben uncovered was barely the surface. Rhys doesn't have a lot of money at his disposal. He's wealthy, all right, but his aim is to create a vast network of agents to infiltrate radical groups and identify their most volatile members—the ones who can be incited to violence. Often they're the ones incapable of seeing past their own agenda. Once embedded, there's no telling what kind of havoc these individuals can spawn. Terrorism, racial and class wars, assassinations. And then he wants a media conglomerate to spread his influence to the far reaches. That takes more money than he's got. With the foundation's money and the influence of Alyssum, he'll be well on his way."

"Okay," she said, "I understand the threat. The danger. And if my . . . participation . . . in this . . . arrangement . . .

would guarantee that none of it will happen, then I'd be crazy—not to mention catastrophically selfish—not to want it." She clasped her hands together to keep them from shaking. "But there are no guarantees. I don't expect them and I'm not asking for them. But I think I am entitled to my anger—in fact I need it right now—and I also need a few minutes where all I'm thinking about is me."

Grey waited.

"I just don't like the way this has been orchestrated. And God do I feel like a whiner for saying that." She distanced herself, retreating to the chair in the corner. "I can't look at this from any direction without going crazy. There's Ben setting me up for this. You and Antony plotting with him." Grey pulled up another chair and sat in front of her so their knees almost touched.

She lowered her face into her hands and tried to quiet some of the voices in her head so she could concentrate. Just a short time ago, as she'd been sitting with Arthur, she'd made her decision. It had come to her even before she'd realized it. And once she'd recognized her choice, she'd been relieved and a little elated to find it had come so easily. But now, learning that this had all been arranged, forced her to reexamine her decision under a harsh new light. She dropped her hands to her lap and looked up at Grey. "But it's still a marriage—or an arrangement—of convenience. Arthur deserves better than an arrangement."

"You think he doesn't want this?"

"I don't know . . . I think maybe he does. But he's got a right to know how it all came about."

"Arthur's a bright man. I'm sure he understands that arrangements are taking place." He leaned toward her again, his elbows on his knees and his hands folded under his chin. "Knowing that you chose this without being a part of the machinations—that would make all the difference to him."

Which was exactly what she'd done. She met Grey's eyes and let him see that.

"This isn't forced, Max." The pain she'd seen in his eyes had been replaced by excitement. "Think about it. Ask yourself what it took to bring you here. I'm not just talking about the people involved. I'm talking about the odds of your being here at all. What a miracle this is." In what seemed an unconscious move, he took both her hands between his, enveloping them. "Ben had to meet Nick's father, who just happened to be a descendent of Bedwyr. Nick's father had to trust Ben more than any other person in the universe when he gave him that stone. Not just to keep the stone, but to do right by it." She started to pull her hands away, but he held onto them. "That stone had been in his family for more than a millennium. Ben had to have a daughter like you—one who shares his passion." He paused. "There's something much larger at work here."

She gave him a nod, then drew her hands away. While she found herself believing what he'd just said, she wondered if this larger plan had its own contingencies. "There's still a problem," she said. "I haven't got the stone anymore."

"What happened?" He sounded more concerned than alarmed.

"Murdoch took it off me."

As she related the events, he listened without interrupting, nodding each time she tried to explain the reasoning behind her choices, and when she'd finished, all he said was, "It's all right. You'll get it back."

She was about to ask him how, but then she realized it was all up to her. So she just nodded.

Grey braced his hands against his knees and pushed himself up from the chair. "We'll talk tomorrow. I'll be at the lake in the morning." Looking down at her, he added, "You try to get some sleep."

"Yeah, sure," she whispered and the words felt raw in her throat.

The door clicked shut behind him. Max leaned back in the chair and blinked until the tears dried up and her vision cleared. Her gaze rested on the ceramic egg. She picked it up and ran her thumb over the curved, smooth surface.

Chapter 44

Jillian looked out the window of the dining room onto Chapel Street. Their table abutted the window, and it was almost as though they were sitting outside. The picturesque old street wound down from Market House to Penzance's harbor, and the sidewalks were thick with people out enjoying the bright April morning.

Things weren't going as smoothly as planned, and she hoped that wasn't an omen. They should be on their way to Alyssum by now. But, because of last night's storm, Rhys hadn't been able to leave Wales until early this morning. And then Murdoch had to scramble to replace his pilot, so they'd have a way to get there. And now this new complication: Greyson Weir.

She glanced at her watch: Nine-fifteen. Rhys should be along any time. She was too nervous to eat, but didn't want Murdoch to notice, so she forced herself. With the tip of her knife, she dug a small portion of marmalade out of the ceramic pot and spread it on the triangle of dry toast.

Murdoch held the photo of Weir. The fact that he hadn't snorted it off as a minor detail to be handled spoke volumes. This man made Murdoch nervous. "You're telling me," he slowly raised his eyes to her, "that this guy has been living upstairs from Maxine Pike and we didn't know it until," he glanced at his watch, "five minutes ago."

"I don't make a point of looking for dead men." She leveled her gaze at him. "If you were concerned about him showing up, you should have told me. I'd never seen the man before. Remember, Greyson Weir left Alyssum before I joined the 'team.' " She pressed down on the word and Murdoch almost winced. "I thought he was dead."

"So did we. Supposedly he drowned off the coast of Maine."

"Did he have help?"

Murdoch pocketed the photo. "It looked like he'd managed it on his own. There were witnesses, a death certificate. The works."

"Apparently we're not the only ones with connections."

When he shrugged, Jillian knew he was preparing to make light of it. She wondered if he'd do that when he confronted Rhys.

"It'll work out. No way he's getting on the island." He began shoveling greasy eggs and black pudding into his mouth.

"We do know that he flew into Heathrow. Probably out of New York."

"After that?" he asked, his mouth still full.

"He rented a car."

"Long as we know he's out there, we'll be ready for him."

Jillian hoped he was right.

"Where's Jessup?" he asked.

"He's on St. Mary's," she said and glanced at her watch. "We've lined up a boat to take him from there to Alyssum. He should be leaving within the hour."

"You sure he won't take an unscheduled detour? Back to the States?"

Jillian smiled as she set the knife across the top of her plate; these questions had all been anticipated. "Without a doubt."

He drained his glass of milk, licked his lips and said, "I still don't like it."

He never liked her ideas. Especially the really good ones. "How were you going to explain Arthur's death?" She watched him try to shrug it off. "He shot himself?"

"We'd have worked it out."

"Admit it, Simon. Earl is perfect. He's a small-time crook with demolitions experience who was strongly encouraged to leave the Army. Plus he's practically invisible. When it's over, his neighbors won't even be able to say he was quiet and kept to himself. His neighbors will be surprised to know he existed."

Murdoch waited while the hostess refilled his milk glass and moved on to clear off another table. "So, what if he can't go through with it?"

"Don't you see? That's why this is perfect. If he does kill Arthur, then it's taken care of. If he doesn't, someone else will. Earl will take the blame."

Murdoch grunted—the closest he'd come to voicing his approval of one of her ideas. "Why's he doing it? What's his set-up?"

She'd anticipated this as well. "I've planted enough newspaper clippings and magazine articles in Earl's apartment to convince even the most skeptical authority that Earl Jessup had an obsession with Arthur Penn and the foundation."

"Why the obsession?"

She dabbed at a crumb on the white tablecloth and scraped it onto the plate. "Because Arthur rejected his pathetic request for money to pay for his brother's defense."

Murdoch forked a chunk of black pudding. "Sounds far-fetched."

"It's not without precedent," she countered. "Your brother once paid for the defense of an indigent man he thought had been wrongly convicted of murder."

As he chewed, she continued, "Besides, it's not as though Jessup will be around to answer any questions." When Murdoch didn't respond, she said, "I assume you've arranged things on your end."

He swallowed. "No problem."

God, he was smug. Time to bring him down a notch. "Rhys is concerned, you know. He'd have preferred that you recovered Maxine Pike's body."

He shrugged. "She crashed and burned in the ocean. May take a while. May never find it." Then he smirked. "Like they say, it's a big ocean. Convenient that way."

"You found Krett." She bit off a corner of toast and chewed it. "Find her."

Murdoch stared out the window with that little half-smile that so annoyed Jillian. He glanced at her plate. "That all you're eating? A piece of toast? You've gotta keep your strength up."

"Don't worry about me."

He helped himself to another slice from the rack. "I'm not."

She pushed away her plate and replaced it with the coffee cup and saucer. "You're just lucky you recovered the stone. Rhys was not happy when Ben Pike died before his time."

Murdoch salted his mushrooms. "Who knew the guy would put up a fight?"

"I guess that's something else you didn't anticipate."

"Speaking of anticipation, does your little friend know why he's getting an all-expense paid trip to Alyssum?"

"Of course not," Jillian said, determined she wasn't going to let Murdoch put her on the defensive now. "Earl is the nervous type. No sense getting him worked up yet or giving him time to think."

"I still say he's gonna jump ship somewhere between here and Alyssum."

"He won't." She sipped the strong coffee and returned the cup to its saucer. "It's as simple as placing one fear against another. He knows he'll be asked to do something unpleasant, but he's terrified of my father and me. He'll do it." She gave him a brittle smile. "He's so devoted to this convict brother of his that he'd agree to assassinate the President to keep your friend from sticking a shiv in him."

"If you say so." Murdoch didn't sound at all convinced.

She added sugar to her coffee and stirred. "How many have you got coming to Alyssum with us?"

"Two."

"Will that be enough?" Jillian had visions of being set on by Greyson Weir and Maxine Pike.

"That plus the one in place on Alyssum."

"That's a nasty bunch of people you hang out with, Simon."

He shrugged. "You want something ugly done, you don't go to the Salvation Army for volunteers. You need ugly people."

"In that case, I'm surprised you didn't do it yourself." Jillian basked in her cleverness for a moment, then remembered that she didn't care what Murdoch thought of her.

He nodded as he chewed and swallowed. "I don't want you to misunderstand this and think I give a shit, but why do you hate me? We're on the same side, you know."

With barely a hesitation, she said, "You're in this for the money."

"You think so?" He'd voiced it more as a challenge than a question.

"What else would there be for you?" Then she leaned over the table so she could see his eyes. "Sorry, Simon, but you don't impress me as one of Rhys's misguided zealots."

To her dismay, he held her gaze as he answered. "You'd be right. I'm not."

"So, what is it? Do you believe in the legend and what it foretells?"

"Sure. Why not?"

His casual certainty took her off guard.

"There sure as hell is something going on." His gaze shifted toward the window, then after a few moments returned to her. "If that stone fits into the sword—well, that's gotta be more than coincidence."

She looked down at her plate as she wondered what it was like to be that certain.

"You don't, do you?" he said.

"Don't what?" Although she knew what he meant.

Apparently he knew that as well, because he chuckled and said, "You'd better become a believer, sister. Because you're the one who's going to need the conviction."

She raised her chin and held his gaze, trying to exude irritation rather than let him see her confusion.

He leaned toward her, and she had to fight the urge to draw back. He lowered his voice to barely above a whisper. "Let me ask you something."

Jillian didn't respond or move.

Murdoch continued, "What do you think is going to happen once you're in line to pop out the next king of the world?"

Her insides recoiled. And while she knew what he was asking, Murdoch was the last person she wanted to discuss it with. But to back off now would be to roll over and offer him her belly. Stalling for time, she said, "What do you mean?"

A smile flicked the corner of his mouth. "Well, just putting the stone in the sword isn't going to knock you up. Have you thought about who the lucky guy might be?"

"Whoever Rhys chooses." She knew his original idea had been to wed her to Arthur Penn, thereby ensuring Rhys's claim to Alyssum. But Penn's friendship with Benjamin Pike had necessitated an early demise for each of them. So now Jillian had to trust her father to find a worthy mate for her. He'd probably have to be expendable as well. Rhys wouldn't want anyone laying claim to the child.

As Simon backed off, his cheek bulged where his tongue sought out stray food particles. Then he chuckled as though he'd found something ironic in it and took a drink of coffee, swishing it around in his mouth twice before swallowing. "I think he's already chosen," he said and turned his attention away from her, toward the window. But before he turned, she saw the gleeful spark in his eyes.

Her chest went cold. Rhys would not do that to her. She managed a grim smile that she hoped didn't show the effort it took. "And wouldn't that fulfill every rape fantasy you've ever had, Simon?"

At first she thought his startled look was directed at her, but then he did a double-take and froze, staring out the window.

Jillian turned in time to see the back of a tall, dark-haired woman who was walking by.

"Shit." Murdoch slammed his cup into its saucer as he jumped out of his chair. "The sister," he said, and Jillian immediately understood.

"Bring her back here," she called after him as he charged out the door. She watched out the window as Murdoch raced after the Pike woman, disappearing from her view. Then she sat back and poured more coffee into her cup, added sugar and stirred. She didn't know what to make of this woman. When Murdoch made a point, he didn't usually have to repeat himself.

A young couple entered the dining room and sat at a corner table. Too bad. Until now, they had the room to themselves. Murdoch wouldn't be able to get physical with that woman in public.

In less than a minute, Murdoch passed the window, holding Pike by her left elbow. The dark-haired creature had an inch or so on Murdoch, and Jillian thought how that must bother him.

She heard them enter the room, but didn't turn around, waiting until they came up to the table. The woman yanked her arm from Murdoch's grip and said, "Who's this?"

Jillian took another sip of coffee. "Why don't you invite her to sit down, Simon?"

Murdoch put her across from Jillian and then took the place between them. As he sat, he reached between his legs, grabbed the chair seat and pulled it in a few inches. Then he rested his arms on the table's edge, smiled at each of them and said, "Don't believe you two have met. Olivia Pike, this is Jillian Babcock. Jillian, Olivia."

As Olivia lit a cigarette, Jillian noted the splinted little finger.

"Do you mind?" Jillian waved her hand in front of her to fend off the smoke that hadn't made it across the table yet.

Olivia snapped the lighter shut and tossed it into her purse. Then she blew a stream of smoke toward Jillian. "Do I mind what?"

Jillian bit the inside of her lower lip.

"And just who the hell is Jillian Babcock?" Olivia asked.

Raising her chin slightly, Jillian said, "Rhys Lewis is my father."

"Oh." It was a reaction more than a response. Rhys's name had that effect on people.

Murdoch leaned toward Olivia. "You of all people should know it's not smart to annoy any of us."

Olivia turned toward Murdoch, slowly, as though his threat had rolled off her. "Really? What are you going to do? Break another finger?" She raised her voice. "Right here. In front of that nice young couple?"

Murdoch covered her wounded hand with his. Her wince was barely perceptible. "Not if you pay attention."

Olivia tapped an ash off her cigarette, using Murdoch's plate as an ashtray.

Murdoch said, "I want you to go and tell Mr. Llewellyn that Penzance is the end of the line for you two." He lowered his voice even more, and Jillian could barely hear him as he leaned closer to Olivia. "If either of you sets foot on Alyssum, you're both dead." He seemed to be waiting for Olivia's response, but she kept smoking and had her head turned toward the window. He applied a little pressure to her hand and she blinked and turned toward him, her eyes flat and cool.

"You don't have any reason to go there anymore." He drew out a pause, apparently enjoying Olivia's undivided attention. "Your little sister is dead and we have the stone."

The only change in Olivia's expression was a slight narrowing of her eyes. "You're lying," she said.

Murdoch shook his head. Slowly. " 'Fraid not." He released Olivia's hand and she used it to slap him hard, broken finger and all.

Jillian saw the shock register, along with the red mark the splint left on his cheek. He grabbed Olivia's wrist. Jillian thought he was going to hit her back, but then he checked himself.

He lowered her hand to the table and released it. "When she got off her flight at Heathrow, we were waiting for her."

Jillian wasn't certain, but she thought Olivia had paled. Her eyes kept flitting about, looking first at Jillian, then Murdoch, then out the window. She looked like a cornered animal, and Jillian half-expected the woman to either bolt or attack.

Murdoch regarded her briefly and whispered, "Go home, Olivia."

She leveled her gaze at him and said, "Bastard."

He smiled. "Funny. That's the word your little sister used. Come to think of it, it was one of her very last words."

Interesting the way some people dealt with shocking news, Jillian thought. From Olivia's expression, she might have heard a bad weather report. Her injured hand lay on the table, with its sad little splint. Jillian looked from the purple finger up to Olivia's face, which was beautiful in a dramatic way.

Olivia pushed back her chair and collected her purse from the window ledge. Then she walked around the table to where Jillian sat, looked down at her and said, "You may have the stone. But at least I don't have to put up with this little prick." She ground out her cigarette in a mushroom cap, turned and left.

For a moment Jillian thought Murdoch was going to take off after Olivia. He sat, practically coiled in the chair, as Olivia passed by the window, her hair bouncing against her shoulders, walking as though she had somewhere to go. But then he picked up his glass of milk and chugged the remains in three gulps. When he set the empty glass on the table, his eyes had that dangerous look and he was almost smiling.

"You really think that threat of yours will keep her off Alyssum?"

He shrugged as though it didn't matter. "I got things covered."

Rather than ask what he was talking about, Jillian bit off a corner of toast.

"Well," Murdoch rose from the table. "This little prick is going to get ready to go to Alyssum." He bent down and planted a kiss on Jillian's cheek before she could turn away. "I suggest you do the same."

"Lovely," Rhys breathed, turning the gem over in his hand. He stroked it with his thumb, gently, as though he were holding a baby bird.

Murdoch stood off to the side, looking pleased with himself and letting Rhys have his moment.

Jillian couldn't quite make sense of her own emotions. Disappointed? Maybe a little. It was smaller than she'd expected. And a dull shade of green. Smaller and rather ordinary. Like it had fallen out of a piece of costume jewelry.

Then Rhys was holding it out to her. Offering it to her. Just before she took it, she glanced at Murdoch. He winked at her and she felt her stomach spasm. But she took it—what else could she do?—and was surprised by its weight. "It's heavier than it looks," she said because she was afraid Rhys would see through a disingenuous observation.

"Leave us for a moment, will you, Simon?"

Jillian heard the door click shut behind him, leaving her alone with Rhys in the small room that looked out over

Penzance's rooftops toward the ocean.

Rhys's brown leather suitcase sat beside the nightstand, where he'd set it when he arrived only minutes ago.

Jillian watched him now, noticing a buoyancy in the way he held himself. And while she'd expected him to be elated— and clearly he was—she hadn't expected that elation to be overshadowed by relief. But it was as though this huge burden he'd been carrying around for half a century had sprouted wings and taken flight.

"What is it, dear?" He sat beside her on the bed. "I thought you'd be pleased." He cocked his chin and narrowed his eyes, as though seeing something in her expression he couldn't quite identify.

"Oh, I am," she responded quickly and held up the stone. "This is amazing." It was also amazing how easy it was to lie when the pressure was on.

"Well, then what is it?" He placed his hand on her shoulder. "You can talk to me."

While she wasn't naïve enough to buy that, she also recognized that if she was going to voice her misgivings, there would be no other chance. And she had to speak up. While she'd bedded some disgusting men as a means to an end, which was what she'd be doing for Rhys, she'd never done it with someone who held her in such obvious contempt as Simon Murdoch.

Smiling, she turned toward him. "I am so honored that you've chosen me. You know that."

Rhys's nod was almost imperceptible.

"But we've never talked about who I'll be . . . mating with, in order to bring this full circle." She hurried on before she could stop herself. "And while the act itself is so inconsequential that I feel petty even bringing this up, well, I've got the impression that it's to be Simon. And if that's what it must be, then I will . . . of course, I will comply. But I wanted you to know that while I've always gone out of my way to be pleasant to Simon, he, in turn, has exhibited nothing but contempt for me." She paused for a breath. "I just thought you'd want to know this."

Rhys didn't speak for several long moments, which was about how long it took Jillian to recognize the tight little lines that appeared between his brows as lines of puzzlement.

Finally, he said, "You think it's Simon?"

Relief flowed warm in her veins. "It's not?"

"No," he smiled, "it's not."

He put his arm around her shoulder, drawing her to him and tilting her head back. "I wouldn't do that to you." Then he kissed her on the mouth.

Chapter 45

Impenetrable dark surrounded him, pierced by a pair of narrow, red eyes. Nick held onto the stone, pressing it into his fist. The ground beneath his bare feet burned like white sand. Razor-sharp teeth nipped his calf and, when he jerked his leg away, blood trickled down to his ankle. He screamed and it was without voice; he struck out but found only air. His hand opened and the stone fell; it was like dropping a glowing coal. Everything stopped—the pain, the heat and the fear.

Then the hammering started. He blinked his eyes and saw a door. Gradually, he realized he was awake in a strange room with someone pounding on that door.

He lay still, the sweat-damp sheets twisted around his legs, staring at the brass knob.

The pounding persisted and someone called his name. Olivia. Slowly, he sat up, kicked off the sheets and dropped his feet over the side of the bed. Only a dream. He reached for his jeans draped across the chair. It wasn't real. He bent over to step into his jeans and ran his fingers over the unbroken skin of his calf. Wasn't real.

By the time he'd pulled on his jeans, he remembered he was in a bed and breakfast in Penzance. Judging from the mid-morning sun, Olivia had neglected to wake him as she'd promised. He picked up his watch and saw the time. "Dammit, Olivia," he muttered.

But when he opened the door, prepared to be angry, he saw her face all wrenched with anxiety and stopped himself.

"Max is dead." As she pressed her fingers to her mouth, her eyes and nose scrunched together.

"She can't be," he said, feeling certain without knowing why. "Why should you think that?"

Olivia pushed her way past him. "We've got to get to Alyssum. Now."

"That was the plan." Nick closed the door and stopped to zip and button his jeans. "We'd be halfway there by now if you'd . . ." Olivia wasn't listening. She'd moved across the room to the window and peeled back the curtain so she could look out on Chapel Street.

"No, not the steamer," she said. "It's too slow."

"It's also gone." He pushed damp hair off his forehead.

"We need to fly there." She fidgeted with a button on her jacket. When she said, "I'm afraid it's too late," she sounded small and frightened.

At the same time it occurred to him that she looked incredibly beautiful. That troubled him a bit, since he'd always considered himself the sort of man who found a woman's strength, rather than her vulnerability, attractive.

As he stared, Olivia walked up to him, put one hand on his shoulder and shook it. "Wake up, Nick." Nodding, he disengaged himself from her and went into the tiny bathroom that occupied the corner across from the bed. He splashed cold water on his face and neck and looked in the mirror, half expecting to see someone else's eyes looking back at him. He released his breath and walked back into the room, drying his face with a hand towel. "Why do you think your sister is dead?"

"He told me." Her legs folded beneath her and she landed, cross-legged, on the floor.

Nick sat beside Olivia and put his arm around her. That felt awkward, but he left it there. She buried her face in his shoulder, and her tears were warm on his skin. He rested his chin on her head and smelled the smoke in her hair. "Who told you?"

"Simon Murdoch told me." With her face still buried in Nick's shoulder, she held up her hand with the splinted finger. "This is Simon Murdoch."

Before he could ask specifics, she went on.

"Don't you see? I told them she was going to London. They were waiting for her at Heathrow."

"You told them she was going to London?"

He felt her head nod.

"All you said was 'London'?"

She sniffed. "Yeah."

"Well that's ridiculous."

Olivia raised her head. "What's ridiculous?"

"Of course she was going to London. Where else would she go?"

"But, I told him—"

"Of course they were looking for her at Heathrow. They'd have been fools not to. He told you that to make you feel . . ." he regarded her smeared makeup and runny nose, ". . . this way."

"But she's still dead. Even if it isn't my fault." She shook her head and buried her face in her hands. "He says they've got the stone now. But, I mean, who gives a shit anymore?"

"Why should you believe anything Murdoch tells you?" He patted her shoulder and pushed himself up from the floor. The shirt he'd worn yesterday hung on the back of a wooden chair. He pulled it on, fumbling to button it. Olivia was staring at him. "Where was Murdoch?" he asked, a bit too loudly.

"Some B&B down the street." She pushed back a clump of hair with her fingers and wiped her nose with the back of her hand. "He was there with a blond bitch who says she's Rhys's daughter. Jillian."

"He's got a daughter?"

That stopped him. For the first time Nick had to consider the possibility that Max wasn't alive. If Rhys's daughter were to figure into the end . . . Nick didn't want to take that where it led.

With her palm, Olivia wiped the corners of her eyes, regarded the black smear on her hand, then wiped it on the carpet.

Nick tossed his belongings into his bag. "Just Murdoch saying Max is dead doesn't mean she is. Of course he'd tell you that, so we'd have no reason to go to Alyssum." He glanced at Olivia to see if she was buying any of it. She nodded. "They may not even have the stone."

"I think they do." She blotted her nose with a tissue. "They seemed smug. Both Murdoch and Jillian. I think they've got it."

"All right. Let's say they do—"

"And he also said if we show up on Alyssum, we're dead."

"I don't care for that man's mouth."

"Neither do I."

Nick put on a clean pair of socks and his trainers. "I think we'd best find the fastest way to Alyssum."

"She can't be dead, Nick."

"She's not."

Olivia buried her face in her hands again and, though her voice was muffled, he heard her say, "If she's gone, nobody cares where I am."

Chapter 46

Max had never seen Alyssum in the daylight, so she had to wonder if it always glistened or if last night's rain had intensified the colors. A row of tall, leafy bushes with bright pink blossoms lined one side of the path. She brushed her hand across their velvety petals as she passed. Birds chittered and a peacock strolled by, pecking at the ground. The cool morning breeze ruffled her damp hair, making her scalp tingle. It would have been easy to get lost in the island's rhythms if it weren't for the threat presented by Rhys and Murdoch.

She knew they had not arrived on the island yet. It would feel different if they were here.

The lake covered more area than she'd imagined last night in the dark: maybe an acre, with its own small island near the east edge. The swan glided back and forth between the island and the shore, its neck almost erect, just a slight crook where it joined the body.

She didn't see Grey, so she started to skirt the lake. It was cooler here, out in the open, and she drew the edges of the cardigan sweater over her chest and crossed her arms. Just beneath the pond's surface, a school of tiny silver fish darted in precision, like a single entity. A larger fish, long and narrow, cut toward the pond's center like a moving shard of light. Max wondered in what part of the lake Arthur had found Caliburn.

When she looked up, Grey stood not ten feet away, squinting into the bright morning sun as he watched her. He seemed tired. Older. The dark stubble on his face made him appear gaunt.

"Where'd you sleep last night?" she asked, noting he wore a gray sweatshirt and faded jeans.

"Lots of places to hide in that castle." With an apologetic smile, he added, "I'm a bit grungy. Wouldn't have done to run the shower. The plumbing tends to be noisy in these old places."

He studied her, his expression unreadable, then wagged his head toward a small table set off from the lake, between two willow trees that had blocked her view as she approached the area. "We can sit here. Should anyone come this way, we'll spot him first."

"Do you know where Arthur is?"

"This time of day, with the staff gone, he's probably cleaning the stables."

"That doesn't surprise me a bit."

The wrought iron table was the size of a café table, with a chair on either side. Grey dropped heavily into one of them. He rested his elbows on the arms of the chair. "You're all right with everything?"

"I am," she said, sitting across from him. "I do have some more questions."

He nodded.

"Why are you here?"

His eyebrows lifted slightly, as though she'd asked a surprising question.

"Is it that guy mucking out the stalls?"

"Partly," he smiled, then took his time answering. "Mainly it's faith in the people I've seen here. I'm an incredibly flawed man. But I see a person like Arthur and I believe things are possible again. It also has to do with how this all came together, here, on this island." He paused. "But, I wasn't certain until I saw you."

"I was Ben's daughter. You saw what you wanted to see."

He shook his head. "I didn't know you were Ben's daughter. Not at first."

She waited.

"The first time I saw you was early last month. The week before I moved into your building. I was out running along the lake. You were sitting near the seawall; Fiona was sitting next to you." He glanced off into the distance, as though focusing. "Come to think of it, that's what caught my attention—your dog was taller than you." He turned back to her. "You were hugging your knees to your chest, looking out across the water. It was one of those blustery, gray Chicago afternoons when the sky blends with the water. You had this little smile, just the edges, sort of a cat's smile, and I wanted to ask what you were seeing. But you seemed so intent that I knew I shouldn't disturb you."

She saw amusement in the way his eyes crinkled, but she also saw some sadness and, although it took her a moment to recognize it, affection.

She had to look away. "That's one of my favorite places."

"You used to believe in fairies," he said softly. And when she turned, prepared to correct him, he added, "When did you stop?"

It put her off-guard. "It gets hard," she finally answered,

blinking her eyes as Grey blurred. "Life is so crammed with reality, it crowds out the fairies. You have to be really open to seeing them." She swallowed. "And I guess I'm now one of those people who has to see a thing before I believe in it."

"No, you're not."

It occurred to her that while she did believe what he'd told her, the absoluteness of his belief made her wary of her own, more recent acknowledgment of her fate. "You seem so certain, so confident about this. Don't you ever have doubts?"

"Of course. Faith comes with doubt. It must, else it would make fanatics of us."

She stared off toward the lake, where the swan plucked at its wing feathers. In so many ways, this felt right.

He stood abruptly, pushing back his chair. "You need to see the other side of the island."

As they walked, they shared what they knew about the foundation, and Rhys and Murdoch's plans to take it over.

She asked him about Nick and his part in all this. "He's a descendant of Bedwyr, isn't he?" she said.

"He is. I've never met him, but Ben held him in high regard. He'd intended for you two to meet before all this."

In Wales, she thought as Grey continued, "Nick's family has served the heartstone—and Arthur—well. Now, on his own, he must come to realize that his role has changed. It is no longer the stone that he is guarding."

"Will he see that?"

"I think so."

"Will he be here?"

"I'm sure of it."

At first it seemed like they were just wandering through the gardens, but then Grey would take her arm as they came to an intersection and steer her one way or another, and finally she determined they were heading north. Grey stopped to bend down and pluck a cluster of tiny white flowers from a patch growing just off the path. He smelled it, then held it out to Max.

"Alyssum," he said.

She breathed in the lightly sweet fragrance. The cluster, not much more than an inch in diameter, contained maybe twenty blossoms, each with four petals and a yellow center.

As they continued walking, Max absorbed Alyssum's mixture of flowers, grass and ocean. The day was so bright and clear that she imagined she was looking at the island through an extraordinary lens filter. This had to be as near to perfect as a world could get. And yet, Arthur's mother hadn't been able to live here. How difficult had it been for her to leave Alyssum? Her child? Was her sanity at stake? Would a place like this punish you for leaving?

They'd come out of the gardens and were heading toward the barren side of the island. The wind picked up, and Max felt the chill air grip her spine. Grey turned a full circle while walking, as though expecting to find someone following them.

"What's wrong?" She looked, too, and saw only the brown earth and the ocean.

"This is disturbing." He stopped. "It's changed."

She had felt uneasy, but chalked it off to this barren area's contrast to the rest of Alyssum. Now she waited for Grey to continue.

He looked down at the earth. "There used to be a large patch of purple alyssum where I'm standing." He lifted his gaze toward the island's northern shore. "And there isn't even a heath here anymore. A heath has life. Scrubby, determined life. Even that's gone. This is nothing. It's dead."

"Arthur said it's been a dry few years."

Grey shook his head, "It's not the weather." He slipped

his hands into the pockets of his jeans and hunched his shoulders. "Beneath us is a system of caves."

They continued walking. Despite last night's rains, the ground beneath her was dry, as though the moisture had been sucked from it.

He continued. "One thing that makes Rhys such an imposing force is the fact that he honestly believes he has a right to this island. As much as the Penns, perhaps more."

"Why?"

"Do you know the story of how these islands were created?"

"Merlin's earthquake?"

"Right. Well, when he conjured that earthquake," he pointed eastward, in the direction of the mainland, "he inadvertently trapped a demon beneath the island. According to legend, that's how the caves were created. An angry demon boring his way through rock to occupy the centuries." He glanced at Max. "You won't find this in the guidebooks."

Max looked down at the earth, which had taken on a gray cast. A demon?

"The construction of that elevator shaft released him."

Her shoes scuffed along the ground, which was so uneven she had to look where she set her feet. She wondered how far into the beyond she'd let him take her, then reminded herself that she once believed in fairies. Was it so difficult to believe something occupied another part of the spectrum?

They walked a few steps in silence and then she asked, "What happened when this demon left the cave?"

"He wanted to get back at Merlin and when he couldn't find him, he decided he'd follow the stone. That's where Bedwyr's story gets twisted into this." He glanced at Max. "The heartstone was a gift from King Arthur's mother."

She recalled the story of Arthur's conception and birth.

"But Igraine never saw the sword, did she?"

"No," he agreed. "When she gave Arthur to Merlin to raise, she also gave Merlin the stone and told him it was given to her by Margawse, the mother aspect of the triple goddess."

Max nodded. "Elaine is the virgin and Morgan Le Fay the crone."

"That's right," he said. "And this demon apparently decided it was fitting to get back at the mother." They walked mostly on rock now, as though the earth had hardened to stone. "He impregnated a woman who had married into the stone's family—Nick's grandmother—and she gave birth to Rhys."

"And Rhys believes that demon is his father," Max said.

"That's right. Therefore he believes that the cave and Alyssum are his."

"What about you? Do you believe that story?"

"I don't know." He paused in thoughtful silence. "I believe in many things that most people consider mythology at best or ludicrous at worst. Mainly I know that the world is infinite. Infinitely wonderful. Infinitely dreadful. At this moment the probabilities are such that any number of realities might evolve."

She waited a few moments for him to continue. When he didn't, she asked, "Can you see what these realities are?"

"Not exactly," he said. Again, she waited.

He shifted his stance and looked at her carefully. She had the impression he was measuring her. "I see some things. As near as I can figure, time swirls around us, not unlike a river. Mostly I see what's going on around me, along with everyone else, but occasionally I get a glimpse of the past or the future. I'm not psychic, but it's more than a suggestion; it's an image." He looked off towards the sea, then at Max. He smiled. "I don't know what allows one to see into another dimension. Someday science will undoubtedly discover a reason, but I imagine we'll be long past caring."

She returned the smile. "What do you see? In the future?"

"I can't answer that. Once I tell you what I see, that could alter it. It must unfold of its own accord."

"Nice deflection."

He gave her an odd look. "I think you could see more than you do, if you'd let yourself. You told me your mother was a sensitive. Both you and your sister may have inherited it."

"I don't think I have. And Olivia?" She had to laugh. "If Olivia ever had a prescient thought, she'd beat it to death with a stick."

"You might be surprised," Grey said. "It wouldn't necessarily be the ability to predict events or read crystal balls with any accuracy. Maybe just a strong connection to another person."

The sound came from far off, but Max recognized the staccato beat of the helicopter's blades before she saw it way off in the east.

"That's probably too early for them to arrive," Grey said, and as he spoke, it angled toward Bryher. "But it reminds me that we should save the metaphysical discussion for another time."

But he seemed distracted by the horizon, as though searching for the first sign of a coming storm.

"How does Rhys know about Alyssum?" she asked.

He turned toward her, still squinting. "Either from Simon Murdoch or . . ."

"His father," she finished for him.

He nodded. "And surely you can see the danger of allowing Rhys to occupy this island."

"He would corrupt the island."

"He would destroy the island." He kicked at the

ground. "What do you feel here?"

She looked down, forcing herself to stay in the moment. "Death."

Grey nodded. "The Caliburnus Foundation would not be as successful as it is, would not draw the kind of devotion it does, if it were managed from, say, London or Chicago. But, like all power, it can be directed toward good or evil. Evil can draw devotion as well. While the demon was trapped down there, generation after generation of Penns were accomplices to pirates, smugglers and assorted thieves. Wealthy, yes, but corrupt. I don't think it likely that that was coincidence. Arthur's father was almost as decent a man as Arthur is. But this part of the island has changed since I was last here." Grey shook his head. "It's got to have to do with what's underneath us."

Again, he looked toward the horizon. "There is no limit to Rhys's imagination or his capacity for evil. He could sit back on his foul little piece of land and watch the world feed on itself."

Max jumped ahead of Grey. "By marrying his daughter to Arthur, Rhys plans to get the island and the foundation." She thought of the more immediate threat. "He'll have to kill Arthur eventually."

"I doubt that Rhys has any intention of letting Arthur live until 'eventually'—there'd be too much left to chance."

After considering that, Max asked, "Then how is he going to lay claim to the island, if his daughter doesn't marry into it?"

"Easy if his son is running it."

She stopped. "Simon Murdoch is Rhys's son?"

"I'd bet on it."

It made sense. "Did Rhys go looking for Arthur's mother after she left Alyssum?"

"If I were Rhys Lewis, that's what I'd have done."

She glanced at him, not really surprised to find it easy for Grey to crawl into Rhys's mind.

"So, if he plans to kill Arthur, who is he planning to pair up with his daughter?" She kept walking, heading back toward the castle now, feeling instinctively that was where she needed to be. "I mean, if Jillian, Rhys and Murdoch are all related . . ."

"Don't attempt to measure Rhys on any normal scale of morality. Imagine the power he feels he would give the child."

As Max was attempting to put herself in Jillian's place, Grey continued. "Of course," he said, "if his daughter doesn't place the stone, he's quite willing to impregnate any woman who does."

Her entire body clenched. "That bastard touches me I'll—" She couldn't finish, because then she'd have to imagine the act. "I can't let him get near me."

"You aren't in this alone, Max."

She wanted more assurance than that. "Can you see what's going to happen here?"

"Some."

"Can you avert a disaster?"

"That I don't know."

"Have you been down in the caves?"

"Not yet."

"I'll go with you."

"No." Grey shook his head for emphasis. "You've got to—"

"Get the stone back," she finished for him.

"Not that either."

"Of course I do."

"No," he said, sounding as if it weren't worthy of discussion.

"Why aren't you worried about this? They have it."

"Because this is what I believe—it's not something I see in a vision, but it's an image in my heart. Max, until you set that stone in the sword, it is yours. Murdoch may have it in his pocket right now. He may pass it to Rhys, who will hand it to his daughter. But no one but you can return it to Caliburn. You must believe that."

"Then I have to get it back."

"That's too dangerous, Max. You are not expendable. Everyone else is." He stopped and waited until she looked at him and nodded her agreement. "Remember how I said there are a lot of places to hide in that castle? Well, I want you to find one of them. And I want you to hide. When it's safe for you, I'll find you."

They continued walking. The castle seemed to soak up the strong morning light.

"I still think I should get it back," she said quietly.

"Absolutely not."

We'll see about that, Max thought. She'd lost the stone. And she was a Pike. Pikes cleaned up their own messes.

Chapter 47

"And *that's* why you think Max is alive?"

Nick had just told her how Bedwyr's story ended with Merlin's prediction that the woman who returned the stone to Caliburn would become Arthur's mother. And since Max was the one who'd been given the stone, she was the one to return it to the sword. Actually, Nick saw a number of reasons why it couldn't be Olivia, but he'd opted to go with the practical choice so as not to offend her. While he hadn't expected Olivia to embrace his theory, he'd hoped for something other than blatant incredulity, as displayed in her wide-eyed delivery. He shifted on the boat's hard, narrow bench and clasped his hands in front of him. With a small shrug, he said, "It's in the story. Merlin said—"

"I don't give a fuck what Merlin said." Olivia stood and flapped her arms once. "Merlin doesn't—didn't exist."

Nick glanced toward the cabin on the small boat. Even

with its noisy motor, Olivia had projected loud enough to gain their pilot's attention. But he just bobbed his eyebrows and went back to steering. They'd taken a helicopter to St. Mary's, lucking out when a tourist charter had a couple of cancellations. The trip to Alyssum in this shoddy fishing boat, although a shorter distance, cost nearly as much. It was cold, and the wind made his eyes water and his nose run. He didn't need any of Olivia's attitude.

"Olivia, wait—"

"No, you wait. Anyone turns my sister into a—a womb for hire has got to answer to me first." She shoved her hands into the pockets of her jacket. "I kind of enjoyed your little stories on the drive up to Wales. But I knew that's what they were. Stories. Fiction. When did you start believing them?"

"There is something about my uncle. Drugs or not, Weldon was right. He is evil. I felt it coming off him. It's a pure evil. I have to allow myself to believe there is something good to counter that evil. I need this. And that good could very well be a modern-day Arthur. And if I've got a part in it, well, it's not something I care to regret for my lack of conviction."

He held her gaze as her eyes searched his. Finally she said, "Well, I don't believe any of it. It's ridiculous."

Nick stood and Olivia kept level with him. "I don't care a pin what you believe and what you don't believe," he said. "The universe doesn't revolve around you and your small-minded opinions."

" 'Small-minded'? I'll show you—" Just then the pilot adjusted the boat's steering. Nick had to sway with the boat to maintain his balance, while Olivia seemed unaffected by the boat's motion. They were heading toward a group of islands.

He couldn't decide if he was angry with Olivia or disappointed. "What makes you think your sister is being forced into something she doesn't want to do?"

"Max wouldn't have to be forced. That's what scares me. She believes in fairies, for Christ's sake."

"And you're so convinced she's wrong?"

"Well, of course she's wrong." A shock of dark hair fell over her face, curtaining off her right eye. "I never cared, because up until this point it hasn't done her any harm. Except make her a little weird."

"Why are you so convinced she'll come to harm?"

"Because I know." Her shoulders lifted and tensed, and she breathed deeply a couple of times. "This whole insane thing is going to leave a wake of damage a mile long."

At first Nick was surprised and a little touched by Olivia's concern for her sister. But then he saw how her mouth twitched at the corner, the way it did when she was annoyed. "I should've known." He smiled and nodded. "Should have known."

"What?" She turned to him, her brows drawn together.

"You're not concerned for Max. No. You're jealous of her."

"Don't be stupid." She dismissed him with a wag of her head.

"You can't imagine anyone passing you over for Max. It's never happened before. And you can't bear the idea of Max being the one to mother a returning king."

"Nick." She locked her gaze onto his. "Listen to what you're saying. Do you honestly think I want to be a mother?"

"Well, frankly, no." He chuckled, almost enjoying himself. "But you wouldn't want anyone else doing it either." He nodded again, mentally taking it a step further. "So it's not so much that you think this is all a nonsense. On the contrary. It's just that it isn't about you."

Nick could tell by the way Olivia had raised her chin and

cocked her jaw that she wasn't going to let him continue his line of reasoning.

"You know," she said, drawing out the pause. "I understand Max falling for all this. But I thought you were sensible."

Well, he'd made his point and would return to it later.

"I am," he responded.

"Sounds to me like you're brainwashed."

"You'd think the Pope is brainwashed."

"He probably is."

"Brainwashing involves force. Faith is about choice."

"But it should be based on more than wishful thinking."

Nick studied Olivia, her perfect features reddened by the sea air, and saw that her nose was dripping a little. "What do you believe in?" he asked her.

Without hesitation she said, "Me. I believe in me."

"What happens when you disappoint yourself?"

"I never do."

"Low expectations," Nick muttered as he turned his back on her and watched as they closed in on Alyssum.

Chapter 48

Jillian watched Rhys cross the heliport, his chest thrust out and his shoulders thrown back as he took in Alyssum for the first time. He reminded her of a vanquished king reclaiming his realm. Which was, to her mind, exactly what he was.

She followed Rhys and Simon, as Simon led them down a path that divided a wide expanse of lawn, then wrapped around the castle. Behind her were Simon's assistants: Tommy, with no neck and the blankest expression she'd seen since she played with dolls, and Red Sanchez, who was bald and did not appear to be Hispanic. She tried not to think about them plodding in silence behind her.

If she concentrated on placing one foot in front of the other, she could get through this, she told herself. She could get through everything Rhys had asked her to do. And once she came out on the other side, she would more valuable to him than that damned stone.

When they reached the castle gate, both Tommy and Sanchez split off from the group and headed toward the garden. The rest of them entered a courtyard shaded by a huge oak and entered the castle through an ornate, wooden door.

From what Jillian could see of Alyssum, the island was small and without much to offer except plants, birds and a few buildings. But the castle itself was impressive—huge rooms with high ceilings and wooden beams. Murdoch took them to a long, narrow room with two arched doorways, then went to find Arthur. One wall was lined with windows which looked out onto a grove of small trees and another, narrower path which led, according to Murdoch, into the garden where Earl would kill Arthur that afternoon when he went on his daily walk.

Despite the medieval setting, the room's furnishings were contemporary—gray leather couches and matching chairs with simple, clean lines, a glass coffee table, an impressionist painting—Pissarro, perhaps—above the fireplace.

Rhys surprised her by putting his arm around her shoulders and giving her a small squeeze. Before Jillian could respond, Murdoch returned with Arthur. Rhys released her to extend his hand toward the man he was about to depose.

While Simon did the introductions, Jillian took the time to recover from her preconceptions about Arthur Penn. Although she'd seen his photograph, she'd misread that smile as an oafish one and imagined Arthur was a simple-minded rube who wasn't able to maintain eye contact with the opposite sex.

In reality, he was tall with watchful, intelligent eyes. He seemed relaxed in a cream-colored sweater vest over a white shirt and brown slacks, and as he crossed the room, his movements were graceful without being feminine.

He welcomed them to Alyssum, bowing slightly as he reached for her hand. For a second she thought he was going to kiss the back of it, and then was a little disappointed when he just shook it. "What do you think of Alyssum, so far?"

"Lovely," Jillian said, adding, "lots of sun." Then she cursed herself for not rehearsing a better line.

"It has that, indeed," Arthur said. "We've more sunny days than the mainland has." He chuckled. "That's a dubious boast, isn't it?"

Hands in his pockets, he took a step back and said to Rhys, "Simon believes you'd be a valuable member of our board. I'm looking forward to discussing your vision for Caliburnus."

Rhys bowed slightly. "I am honored to be considered, although I deeply regret the tragedy that brought about the need to find a new member."

"Fletcher was not only a brilliant mind, but also a good friend," Arthur said.

Rhys sighed and shook his head. "World's gone mad."

"It would appear that way," he responded, giving Rhys a cautious look. But then his manner softened and Jillian decided she'd imagined it.

"But determining my ability to fill the space on your board pales in comparison to the main reason we've come here today." He turned toward Jillian. "I believe my daughter has something you've been looking for."

Jillian patted the small shoulder bag pinned beneath her arm. She imagined she could feel the lump, small and hard like a tumor.

But before she could open her purse, Arthur held his hands up, as though fending off a pushy saleswoman. "As long as I've waited," he began, "now that it's here, I feel we shouldn't rush it. I'd like to chat a bit, if you don't mind."

Jillian tightened her grip on the purse strap.

Rhys frowned and shrugged as though it didn't matter to him. Then he smiled. "If you can wait, I suppose we can too."

"I'd be most interested in hearing how you came to possess the stone. Learning its story."

"I'd be happy to tell you what I can," Rhys said, and Jillian was actually looking forward to hearing what he'd concocted.

"Why don't you all make yourselves comfortable," Arthur said. "Can I get you some coffee or tea?" In response to Jillian's raised eyebrows, he added, "The help is off today."

"Coffee, then," she said, wondering if there really was as much money here as Simon had led them to believe.

"Simon, will you give me a hand?" Arthur asked and, from the look on Simon's face—the flash of concern—Jillian surmised that this wasn't in the plan.

"Let me help," she said, stepping forward. "Simon has a tendency to drop things." She smiled in Simon's direction.

"Doesn't feel right putting a guest to work," Arthur said.

"I insist."

He hesitated, then waited at the doorway for her.

As she followed him, Arthur told her about each of the rooms they passed and the story behind most of the paintings. By the time they got to the kitchen, Jillian was numb with the details of his family.

"And here's the kitchen," he said rather loudly as they entered a room that couldn't be construed as anything but a kitchen. Like the room she'd just come from, it was modern-looking, with stainless steel appliances, granite countertops and a large island in the center. Arthur quickly began assembling the coffeemaker.

"I didn't ask," he said, opening one of the cupboards. "Would your father prefer tea?"

"He likes coffee. Black with sugar."

"I know it's grounds for deportation in England, but I've never been much of a tea drinker," he said. "Got attached to coffee when I spent a year in Boston at university." Then he started to tell her about his studies.

Jillian almost smiled. Now she understood what his hesitation had been about before and what his babbling was about now. He was nervous. She moved closer to him as he began another search of the cupboards.

"Can't find the carafe," he muttered. "I think sometimes Hannah hides things on me, just to remind me that I really do need her."

"Can I help?"

"No. Thanks. It's just a matter of finding something to put the coffee in. Perhaps I'll forgo that step and simply put the bloody pot on the tray."

"I'm sure that will be fine."

"I suppose," he responded, sounding preoccupied. He set four pairs of cups and saucers on a silver tray, positioning them in a semicircle around the sugar and cream.

Jillian leaned against the island, which was black with white and red specks, and crossed her arms over her chest. "What do you think about all this?"

He looked up from the tray. "It's all rather fantastic, don't you agree?"

"How do you mean fantastic?"

"Both wonderful and fantastic. A bit of each, I suppose."

"I thought you believed in this legend."

"Oh, I do." He walked past her and opened the refrigerator.

"When I put the stone into Caliburn, eventually I'll—you and I—will have a son who will change the world. You believe that, don't you?"

"It could be a daughter."

When she hesitated, Arthur continued, "I mean, why not? We're not in the dark ages anymore."

"So, you do believe?"

"I believe that the woman who places the heartstone in Caliburn will fulfill a great destiny."

As she pondered the fact that he hadn't used her name—or his own—in this pronouncement, he was watching her with some curiosity.

"Do you want to be a mother?" he asked.

"Doesn't every woman?"

"I shouldn't think so." He filled the creamer from a glass bottle. "That would make every woman frightfully like-minded, wouldn't it?"

"I've always wanted children," Jillian said, wondering if her ambivalence toward children was that obvious and, at the same time, why it was suddenly so important for this man to want her. It really didn't matter.

He seemed thoughtful as he poured coffee into each of the cups. But before he could respond, Murdoch came loping into the kitchen, red-faced and breathing hard.

"Arthur!" He looked like he'd had a bad joke played on him. "Did you move it?"

"Caliburn?" Confusion settled into Arthur's eyes. "No, why?"

Murdoch stopped, mopping his hair off his forehead. "Well, it's not there. It's not on the chapel wall."

"Not a—" Hot coffee splashed his hand as he slammed down the pot. He didn't even wince and was out of the room with Murdoch at his heels before Jillian could say a word.

Chapter 49

As the boat puttered to a stop, Olivia turned toward the shore, a good fifty feet away. "How are we supposed to get there?"

"We swim," Nick said. "Or wade. The water's not deep here."

"Tell me you're joking."

While Nick knew that Olivia was as anxious to get to Alyssum as he was, he also knew that she wouldn't care to get wet or dirty on the way. Therefore, he'd let her assume they'd be dropped at some convenient, but unattended pier. What Nick hadn't anticipated was enjoying what he'd have to do.

He thanked the fisherman, a ruddy-faced man with a large belly. Then, he grabbed Olivia's wrist, ducked under her arm, bent at the waist and pulled her down on his back, pinning her legs with his other arm. As Olivia pounded on him with her fist, Nick stepped to the side of the boat and heaved her overboard, then jumped in after her.

Olivia came up sputtering. "You bastard. This purse cost three hundred dollars."

"That's ridiculous." The cold water jolted him to the bones.

Olivia looked up at the boat, which would be difficult to climb back into, then toward the rocky slope they'd have to scale before finding solid ground. "Shit." She pulled her purse strap over her head so it crossed her chest, cast Nick a baleful look and started dog paddling her way to land.

As he followed her, he considered what they were walking—swimming—into. If Murdoch had been truthful with Olivia, then Max was dead and Rhys had the stone and Nick was too late to help anyone. Perhaps it was best not to think.

They had to swim only a few meters before finding the rocky bottom. Once Olivia had her feet under her, she surged ahead, moving as fast as the chest-high water would allow.

She reached the rocks ahead of Nick and began climbing out. It wasn't a sheer rise; boulder-sized rocks made the ascent more of a strategic climb—finding the best path with surest footholds. "You're real funny, Llewellyn." She continued her griping, but Nick tuned her out as he surveyed the area. To the east, he saw a narrow gravel path that probably extended to the west as well. But all he could see directly above them was a tall, full plant which appeared to be growing out of the boulders, and the bright, blue sky behind it. To the west, where the water crashed against the rocks, it was more treacherous. This ascent above them was their best approach. He started to climb.

"Olivia, when you get near the top, stay down." She didn't indicate that she heard him.

Cursing, Nick tried to speed up, but his wet shoe slipped

on a rock and he slid back, smacking his knee on a craggy protrusion. A spike of pain shot up his thigh; he flexed his leg a couple of times and continued the climb. She'd nearly made it to the top now; her agility surprised Nick. Broken finger and all. "Wait for me." She kept climbing.

Fine. Let her get that beautiful head of hers shot off. "Olivia!" He had almost caught up with her when he heard a loud crack and saw bits of rock scatter. Olivia screamed and Nick lunged for her ankle, pulling her down to him. Her weight knocked him off balance and he compensated by throwing himself onto a large boulder jutting out from the slope. It stopped their fall, but when Olivia crashed down on top of him, she knocked the breath from him.

She scrambled off him, grabbing onto the rocks for support.

"Who's shooting at us?" She sounded amazed.

Once Nick was able to draw in some air, he said, "Does it matter?" and pushed himself up onto his elbows. While he'd been prepared for trouble, he hadn't really expected it. He looked up and saw a large, thick-necked man peering down at them from the top of the ridge. The man raised a rifle, taking aim again. Nick sprang up and pressed himself against the rocks beside Olivia. A bullet hit the spot where he'd been lying.

"Oh, God, Nick," Olivia whimpered. "What do we do now?"

Good question. Another bullet ricocheted off a rock near his shoulder. "We go back down," he said. "Try to make our way west." No other choice. Another shot and a piece of stone grazed his knuckles. "Down," he repeated.

She started to edge her way toward the water, clinging close to the rocks and using them for shelter. As Nick began his descent, he heard a crack and then felt a searing pain across his right temple. Instinctively, he jumped, hoping he'd hit water, and not a bone-crunching rock.

He landed mostly in the water, with one flailing arm hitting something soft—Olivia—and taking her underwater with him. When they surfaced, Nick ignored Olivia's cursing as he herded her toward the rocks, using his body to shield her as best he could.

Olivia twisted around so she could swear at him face to face. "This is fucking perfect, Nick, I'm—oh my God, what happened to you?"

He felt the side of his head and his fingers came away bloody. It stung, but he figured if it had been more than a graze, it would feel considerably worse. Still, Olivia looked horrified. "You don't see a hole there or anything, do you?" he asked.

She touched it and he winced. Her expression eased. "Looks like a crease. Maybe it was just a piece of stone." Scowling, she squinted up toward the road.

Bullets strafed the water and Nick crowded them closer to the rocks. "What's your plan?" she asked.

"We opt for cover rather than access." He began pushing her toward the west. "Try to climb on the lowest rocks, so the water doesn't pull you under." The next incoming wave slammed them against a stone, and they scrambled for a hold on the slippery surface.

The water grew rougher and each wave immersed them, then tried to suck them back into the ocean. They moved slowly. The shoreline jutted out into the sea again, and as they came around the small point, a wave submerged them both, Nick lost his footing and slid into the water. The next wave bashed him against the rocks. He couldn't tell which way was up; all he saw was bright foam and blurs of gray. Then Olivia had hold of his arm and was pulling him up.

Once his hand found a tentative grip, he was able to hoist himself the rest of the way. He gulped in air and water and started coughing and sputtering. Olivia helped him onto the rocks and then kept pushing him. "Just a little farther. I think I see another way to get to the road." They climbed up for a few feet, then rested on a large boulder.

"Thanks," he said, then coughed and spat seawater back into the ocean.

"Yeah," she said, still catching her breath. She looked over her shoulder and up at the road. "You think it's still too soon to go up there?"

From their position, they couldn't see the top of the ridge. "The going isn't bad right now. Why don't we see how much farther west we can go?"

Olivia gathered her hair to one side and squeezed water from it. "We're never going to get on this fucking island."

Nick squinted up at the sun, which was on its way down but a long way from the horizon. "We could wait until dark."

"My ass'll be ice before then. Let's keep going." She started climbing, keeping low and testing each rock before putting her weight on it. They'd rounded the point and were heading inland again.

"Look at this," Olivia said, coming to a stop. He crawled next to her and saw where she was pointing.

Up about five feet was an opening between two rocks. At first glance it looked like a shadow, but there was nothing to create a shadow. Nick crawled ahead, using outcroppings to pull himself up to a small ledge.

Olivia came up behind him. "Is it a cave?"

"Would appear to be." He saw nothing but black inside. When he glanced over his shoulder toward the sea, he realized at this angle, it would have been difficult to spot from the water. "Wouldn't be surprised," he said. "For years these islands were used by smugglers. Caves made convenient places to store the booty."

Peering over his shoulder, she said, "What do you think is in there?"

"Bats, spiders."

"Bats get tangled in your hair."

He glanced at her. "I think that inclination is exaggerated." Then he added, "Didn't you know that bats are our friends now?"

"I don't need any more friends. You go first."

He crawled in on his hands and knees, and couldn't see well enough to make out what he'd entered. As he inhaled the smells of mold and dying things, an image from this morning's dream exploded in his head. "Olivia, your lighter wouldn't by chance be waterproof, would it?" He was surrounded in darkness with razor teeth gnawing away at him.

"We'll find out," she said.

Chapter 50

Walking beneath the flowering trees that arched over the path into the garden, Earl felt small and mean. In his windbreaker pocket he carried the Beretta. Its grip made his hand sweat. He hated it.

He knew he wasn't the brightest bulb on the tree, but he was a couple of watts smarter than the Ice Queen figured. She told him that Arthur Penn sat in his garden at this time every single day. She'd said his job was simple—he was to find Penn and kill him. She also said it was the last thing she'd ask him to do. What she didn't say, but what he knew, was: "and take the rap for it while you're at it." And that boat waiting for him. Right. Earl figured the odds of him getting back to Chicago made a bet on a Cubs/Sox World Series sound like a sure thing. He was dead, no way around it. But maybe if he offed this guy—whom he'd never met, how hard could that be?—there'd be no reason for them to kill Lonny.

He walked along paths cluttered with pink and white petals and stopped to examine a high stone wall coated with thick, green plants. Some had blushes of pink and red; in others, flowers sprouted up. A few of them looked like they'd grow into man-eating plants like he'd seen in sci-fi movies.

Then he heard someone say, "Beautiful, isn't it?"

Heart pounding, Earl spun around and saw Arthur Penn sitting on a green bench. Shit. "It's okay," he managed.

"It's been a warm spring," Arthur said. "Brought out the color early." He sat with one arm resting on the back of the bench, his legs crossed. For some reason he could pull it off without looking like a fag.

Earl glanced up at the sky and thought he'd never seen it this shade of blue—maybe in a movie. "Nice day," he said.

Then Arthur nodded at the space beside him on the bench. "Why don't you join me?"

For a second, Earl thought how it would be kind of nice to sit and look at these flowers. Then he remembered why he'd come here. He squeezed the gun's grip. *Shoot him now,* he told himself. *Don't think about it.*

But then Arthur said, "It's about now that a charming little goldcrest comes to feed. He's something to see."

Okay, he'd shoot him after the bird showed up. That'd work. While he was watching the bird. Wouldn't know what hit him. There's the little bird; bang he's dead. Lots worse ways to go. Having convinced himself, Earl sat on the bench, leaving plenty of space between him and Arthur.

Penn smiled easily. "He should be along in ten minutes or so."

Panic fluttered in Earl's gut. That was a long time to keep a conversation going. Maybe he should do it right now.

"Rare birds aren't unusual on Alyssum. They get blown off-course."

390

Earl knew how that felt.

"I think they rather fancy it here. Decide a change in destination isn't necessarily a bad thing."

Earl felt the sweat on his scalp and the back of his neck. Gave him a chill when the breeze hit.

"My name's Arthur Penn, by the way."

"Earl Jessup."

Arthur nodded, then turned to him with this puzzled look. "Today is Tuesday, isn't it?"

"Uh, I think so." Earl had no idea anymore.

"The gardens aren't open to the public on Tuesdays."

Earl figured since they were his gardens, he would know. He squeezed the gun grip so tight he thought it'd pop. "Uh, I came over from next door—Bryher—a buddy of mine lives there. Sorry if—"

"No, no, that's quite all right. I was just curious." He squinted up into the sky.

Neither spoke for several minutes, and then Arthur crossed his arms over his chest and started bobbing his foot. "I'm the one who shouldn't be here," he said.

Earl turned to see if he was actually talking to him and, since they were alone, he supposed he had to be. "How come?"

"I should be looking for something."

"Where'd you lose it?"

Arthur's foot stopped bobbing as he turned toward Earl, looking like he didn't quite get the question.

"You know where you saw it last?" Earl persisted. "That's what I try to do. Figure where I saw it last."

Arthur nodded as though that made sense. "Yes, well, this was stolen. I should be looking for the person who took it." For a couple of seconds he seemed to be thinking that over. Then he said, "I've lost the person."

Earl mouthed an "oh" and nodded. "Yeah, that's tough."
One time Lonny stole Earl's good hunting knife. Lonny
didn't admit to it, but Earl knew. In the end he didn't care
about the knife, but felt he'd lost part of his brother.

"What're you gonna do?" Earl asked.

"Wait. Hope I'm wrong."

"Maybe whoever took it'll get tired of it." That's what had
happened with Lonny. He gave it to Earl for his birthday one
year and Earl had to pretend he'd never seen it before. "It
happens."

After he said that, Arthur was watching him with an expression Earl couldn't read. Earl felt he needed to explain, as
fast as he could. "I didn't take it . . . that thing I was talking
about. . . . It was my brother."

"I didn't think you had," Arthur said, and then there was a
slight rustling sound and they both looked toward the bushes.

"Ah, there it is," Arthur said, leaning forward.

Earl had mixed feelings about the bird's arrival. But he
looked and saw that it was tiny with an orange stripe on its
head.

As they watched it nibble some seeds, Arthur squinted up
at the sky. "There's a falcon that knows where this fellow
eats. More than once he's almost made a meal of our little
friend."

Earl grunted. "I'd say the goldcrest is a slow learner." He
slipped his finger in front of the gun's trigger. Just point and
shoot.

"I don't think that's it." Arthur paused. "He's aware of the
danger."

"Why does he come back?" Maybe he didn't even have to
take the gun out of his pocket. Earl tried to twist around so
that he could point the gun at Arthur. No good. His jacket
was too tight. Shit. God, he hated this. He knew there'd be a

second, between the time he pulled the gun out and shot Arthur, that Arthur would see the gun and Earl had the feeling he'd look more disappointed than scared. Earl was tired of disappointing people.

"I'm not certain," Arthur said. "Perhaps he's got a sense of destiny."

Earl couldn't believe Arthur was still going on about the bird. "He's also got other places to eat," Earl said, glancing toward the little creature.

"Good point."

The bird cocked its head as though it heard something. About time you moved your little ass, buddy. Earl stood and pulled the gun from his pocket. As he pointed it at Arthur, his hand shook. He should've done this when Arthur was looking at the bird. Now he was watching Earl with this weird expression. It wasn't disappointment. Or fear. Concern?

"Sorry," Earl muttered, "I gotta do this."

"You also have other places to eat, Earl."

"I don't know what you're talking about," Earl said, but he did. He really did get it this time. "I don't do this, they kill my brother." No harm telling him.

"Where is your brother?"

"Stateville," Earl said and then added, "prison," so Arthur wouldn't think Lonny was in college.

Penn crossed his arms over his chest and his mouth curved into a tight frown. It was like he was giving this some thought. Earl had presented him with a problem and this guy was working on it.

Earl couldn't get his hand to stop shaking, nor could he get his finger to pull the trigger. Out of the corner of his eye, he saw a flutter of brown feathers and then the branch bobbed as the little bird took off. Seconds later a large shadow glided overhead. Earl willed his hand to stay still.

Shit. That bird had the brains to get the hell out before it was too late.

Arthur nodded. "There are worse things than dying, aren't there?"

Shit. Earl figured he was good as dead. Lonny too. But Penn was right. He lowered his head to his chest and dropped the gun to his side like it suddenly weighed twenty pounds. Two seconds later a shot went off.

At first Earl thought he'd shot himself. He heard movement in the bushes behind him and turned to see a thin guy with graying hair standing less than ten feet away, holding a rifle at his side. Earl had a flashback of a trunk lid closing on him. "Aw, shit," he said, feeling like he should put the gun to his own head. Right now. The big black void had to be better than life as a gutless dupe.

But then Arthur was on his feet, looking like he'd seen a ghost. "Grey?" he said, approaching the newcomer, who apparently wasn't a stranger to him. Although, from Arthur's expression, he wasn't exactly welcome either. "What on earth—"

Arthur must have seen the body at the same time Earl did. It lay at the base of a lilac bush, half in and half out, on the other side of the clearing. Judging from the broken branches and the smattering of blossoms on his back, he'd been hiding in there.

All three of them approached. Earl saw the gun, an automatic rifle equipped with a sight, next to the guy's hand. Grey kicked it away before squatting down to examine the body. He'd been a wiry bald man, wearing a camouflage jacket. Looked like a deer hunter.

Earl and Arthur watched as Grey flipped the guy over, revealing a bullet hole dead center in his chest. "Which of us was he aiming at, do you suppose?" Arthur asked.

"My guess would be Earl," Grey said, pushing himself up off the ground. "When he realized that Earl wasn't going to shoot you, he planned to shoot him. Then he'd have used Earl's gun to kill you, Arthur."

Arthur turned to Earl. "You were hired by Simon, weren't you?"

"I-I been working for Jillian."

Arthur nodded. "Same thing."

With a sigh, he looked down at the body and when he first began talking, Earl thought he was addressing the dead man. But he wasn't.

"I spent a good part of last night attempting to convince myself that the obvious wasn't true. Isn't it amazing how hard we'll work at maintaining our own reality? When no system of mathematics allowed me to add up the facts any differently, once I acknowledged the facts—Simon's friendship with Thorpe and Rhys, the camera, Antony's death—everything fell into place so easily, I saw all these things in the past for what they were. I . . . have been . . . a fool." He shook his head and a grim smile curved his mouth. "And I continue to be a fool. Wanting to trust someone can be a dangerous thing." Arthur stopped and stared off toward the rock wall. "However, Caliburn is gone now and it would appear that I am still a fool."

"No you're not," Grey said.

"Simon wasn't the only person I shouldn't have trusted."

"You didn't misplace your trust. Not in Benjamin Pike or his daughter." When Arthur looked at him, he added, "She didn't take Caliburn."

Grey turned and crouched beside the bushes, reaching for something on the ground beneath them. When he stood, he held a huge sword by its hilt and offered it to Arthur.

"*You* had it." Arthur closed his eyes for second, almost like he was praying.

"I moved it," Grey corrected. "There are too many people trying to rush things."

Arthur took the sword and changed his grip by tossing it up and catching it. When he did this, Earl noticed the two stones in the hilt and the blank in the middle. Finally he understood all the fuss about the stone.

Then Arthur said to Grey, "How can I make this right, my friend?"

Grey said, "Help us win here today."

After a couple seconds, Arthur nodded, then switched the sword to his left hand so he and Grey could shake on it.

Earl couldn't remember if he and his brother had ever done that. Lonny was always slapping him on the back.

"Earl?" It was Arthur. "We could use your help."

Stunned, Earl searched the man's eyes for the laughter he had to be holding back. It had to be there, just under the surface. He'd say "sure," and both Arthur and Grey would bust out into fits of laughter. After all, Earl had nearly killed Arthur. And even if they weren't going to kill him, they might as well have a good laugh at his expense. He couldn't blame them. But Arthur didn't look like a man about to bust a gut.

"Why?" was all he could think to say.

"I have a good feeling about you."

Earl emitted a nervous chuckle. "That's gotta be a first."

"Well, let's assume it won't be the last."

Earl glanced at Grey, who nodded; then he reached out for the other man's hand. The solid grip of his handshake triggered a warm rush of emotions as the ice encasing him began to thaw.

Chapter 51

Fortunately, Olivia's lighter was waterproof and its flame, adjusted to high, allowed Nick to investigate the crevice he'd entered. Once he'd crawled in a few feet, there was enough area to stand, although he kept his head ducked to avoid the ceiling. He'd chided Olivia about the bats, but didn't fancy having to wrestle one out of his own hair. He had only a foot or so on either side, but straight ahead all he could see was black.

"Let's see what's back here," he said.

"Why don't we just sit and wait a while?" Olivia hadn't left her perch outside the cave. "The shooter's going to think he hit us or we drowned. He'll leave. Eventually."

The passage narrowed as he moved forward. He paused, staring into the inky blackness ahead of him.

"Nick?"

"I'm going in a ways." The surrounding darkness still reminded him of bad dreams, but his curiosity won out.

"Nick, I want a cigarette."

"Don't tell me your case is waterproof." The lighter wasn't doing much good, illuminating the area just in front of him, but he couldn't have seen anything without it.

"Nick—"

"Quiet!" He'd come about ten feet down the passage when he heard something. "Come here."

A few seconds later, Olivia was there, grumbling. She wrapped her hand around his arm.

"Listen," he said. The humming sound came from deep in the cave.

"Machinery?" Olivia whispered.

"Sounds like it."

He took her hand and led the way with the lighter thrust in front of them. The passage made several turns, and Nick had the impression there was a design to it, something other than nature had constructed it. But he saw no signs of life, human or otherwise. When the toe of his shoe kicked something that wasn't a loose stone, he crouched down and picked up a piece of rotting wood. Could've been from a crate and likely had washed in from the sea. He tossed it.

At only one point did the tunnel fork. At first they took the right passage, but after several yards, it became apparent that the tunnel was narrowing, so they doubled back and tried the other way. They began to descend at a fairly steep angle, but the passage also widened.

"Hey," Olivia stopped. "There's something on the wall. Move my lighter over here."

When he did, they saw a crude torch jammed into a crack in the wall.

"You said smugglers might have used these caves?"

"That was years ago," Nick said.

"Or maybe the smugglers are still here."

The thought had crossed Nick's mind, only he imagined it was something other than rum being smuggled.

As they continued, the air felt heavy and, despite Nick's wet clothing, he was warm. The thrum had gotten louder. "We must be hearing a generator of some kind."

She dug her nails into his arm. "I don't know what's going on, but I'm sure I won't like it."

"Let's go see."

Dirt and small rocks crunched beneath their feet, making silence impossible. Sensing they were close to something, Nick shook himself free of Olivia and crept forward, stopping when he saw a man who appeared to be looking directly at him. Nick backed up, snapping the lighter shut. Darkness rushed in.

"What?" Olivia whispered.

"Someone's out there." As he spoke, he began to realize what he'd actually seen. The man had been looking right at Nick, but apparently hadn't seen him. Like Nick, he'd been in a crouch. Nick flicked the lighter again. Another light appeared, but this time he knew what he was seeing. "I'll be damned."

Olivia came up beside him, joining his image in the mirror. He reached out and ran his hand over the smooth, cold surface. It wasn't glass, it was something harder; but their reflection was sharp, even in the poor lighting. A quick inspection with the lighter revealed that the passage was completely blocked by this mirror.

"I look like hell," Olivia said.

Then, sounding a bit relieved, she added, "I guess this is the end of the line."

"Maybe not."

At waist-level, he'd discovered a handle recessed into the

mirror. He slipped his hand around it and glanced at Olivia.

She shrugged. "You go first."

The door opened to a room about twenty meters square and filled with machines—computers, printers, an elaborate-looking copier—cluttered tables and a couple of desks piled with books and manuals. Nick didn't see any humans, so he ventured farther into the space, examining its contents. In one corner, a generator chugged away. From the high ceiling hung crude lights, naked bulbs with metal shades. The cave's floor had been leveled with plywood. A CD player and a television occupied a table beside two computers—one desktop and a laptop. The desktop computer's display frame had cartoon decals on it—Mickey Mouse, Road Runner, and Goofy—which contrasted obscenely with what was on the screen, where images morphed from one nightmarish photograph to another: an oil tanker ablaze, a mob rioting outside a school, a lynching and the one that made Nick swallow and turn away: a man in the process of slitting a woman's throat open.

"Delightful," Olivia said under her breath, also turning away. She moved toward one of the walls, touching the smooth surface, which wasn't as reflective as the outer walls, more like a polished metal.

"Why mirrors?" she asked.

Beside a telephone, Nick saw a manual on computer viruses. He picked it up and thumbed through it, then noticed the notepad that had been beneath it. Printed on it in a blocky backhand was a column of words such as "Savage," "Virtual Assault," and one with a check next to it: "Jonah's Life." He replaced the book and saw that Olivia was waiting for an answer, or at least a response from him.

"I imagine these walls are to keep the damp, salt air from these machines," he said.

"Why mirrors?" she repeated.

"No idea."

Beside the computer running the graphic images lay an open bag of potato crisps, its contents spilling onto the wood grain table. The bag shifted, as if it were alive. Nick moved closer and saw a long, thin gray tail protruding from the bag.

"Gross," Olivia whispered.

As he inspected the room, Nick saw there was only one other door, which he hoped was somehow connected to the castle.

"What the hell is this?" Olivia had stopped by a machine set in one corner behind a large drawing table.

"Looks like a copier."

"I know that." She shot him a threatening look. "I'm talking about this stuff." She plucked a sheet of paper off the table. "It looks like they're trying to print money."

Nick went over to the table, where Olivia handed him the sheet on which was printed a remarkably realistic image of a twenty-pound note. He ran his thumb over the paper, and it had the feel of money. Apparently it wasn't a perfect image, because certain letters were marked with a red pen with notes off to the side: "too dark," "thready," and so on.

"There's at least a dozen of these." She picked up another sheet and then another. All had red markings on them.

Nick traded the note for a sheet of paper that looked like some sort of certificate. "They're doing treasury notes, too," he said after examining it.

"Who is?"

"Good question." He bent over the computer and touched a key to activate the screen. A website called "Downward Spiral" came up. Scrolling down, Nick saw that it gave an accounting of society's disintegration: demonstrations turned violent, drug trafficking, emphasizing the growing rift among classes. It went on. In addition to abuses against society, the website suggested laws to be enacted in order to "stem the tide." The ones Nick scanned had to do with limiting the number of people who could assemble at any one time, making it illegal to criticize law officers, laws placing homeless people in what amounted to detention camps.

"This is uplifting." When Olivia didn't respond, Nick glanced over his shoulder and saw she'd logged onto the notebook computer and brought up a calendar.

"What's today's date?" Olivia asked.

He had to think. "The nineteenth."

"Look at this," she said. "I click on the date and get a list of—I don't know—events, I guess by state."

Nick wheeled his chair over toward her, frankly surprised that she knew how to work a computer.

"I know," she said, reading his mind, "I had a friend who was a stockbroker. For my birthday he gave me a hundred shares of a drug company to play with." With the tip of her nail, she tapped the return key. "Don't ask."

She pushed the chair back so he could get closer to the screen. "It looks like someone's trying to cause trouble." A series of events were listed and each was assigned a number and an "action." Olivia ran her nail across the screen following one entry. "Here's a protest against a landfill in Streamville, Missouri, number 005463, action: blow up dumpster in councilman's front yard."

"Hardly dire," he said, wondering at the purpose.

"It gets better." Olivia pointed at the screen. Other activities, each with a number not in any apparent order, included a drive-by shooting of a "random" victim in St. Louis, and tear gas and smoke bombs in a college where the faculty was striking in Lowell, Missouri. Beside the latter entry was an asterisk with a reference farther down noting, "film crew available—4:30 p.m."

"Terrorism?" Olivia said.

"To what end? Terrorism implies there's some reason—twisted though it may be. This seems like it's designed with chaos as an end."

Olivia paused to glance around the room. "Why here? Why under the ground on a tiny island?"

"Good question," Nick said. "Check out tomorrow's date."

Four more actions were planned. "So, they're not just reporting the news, they're creating it."

Olivia returned to the menu, found a European link and clicked on it. Nick went back to the on-line newsletter, still not sure what to make of it all. Just as he was thinking they should move on, he realized Olivia had asked him a question.

"What?" When he turned toward her, her eyes seemed to have darkened.

"What's the name of your pub?"

"The Fife and Firkin," he said, twisting the laptop so he could read it.

Fear and anger lodged in his throat as he read how a bomb was to be ignited in his pub that evening. A film crew on scene to interview a shop owner across the street would be there to record the worst of it. "This is Rhys," Nick said, tapping the screen with his finger. "I don't know how he got down in this cave, or why, but this is my uncle."

He looked around and spotted a telephone on the table near the copier. Just as he reached for it, it rang. He looked at Olivia, she looked at him. He listened for footsteps but heard nothing but the ringing. Once, twice, and then in the middle of the third ring it stopped.

"Uh oh," Olivia said into the ominous silence. "I think somebody's home."

Chapter 52

Max's right leg was starting to cramp. When she'd positioned herself beneath this small table in the room housing Arthur's sword collection, she thought she'd found the perfect spot for hiding and observing. She had guessed correctly that Arthur would bring his guests to the parlor he had shown her to last night, and the sword room was next to it. An oversized table-cloth provided adequate cover and, while she couldn't hear conversations through the wall, she could hear Murdoch, Rhys and Jillian talking as they walked down the hall.

She knew this wasn't what Grey meant when he told her to hide. But Rhys was on Alyssum, he had the stone and she was going to stay as close to him as she could, until an opportunity presented itself to get it back. It would happen. It had to.

Not long ago she'd heard the commotion about the sword. She assumed—hoped—that Grey had taken it. Her deduction had been a matter of eliminating the others. She didn't take it, she didn't think Arthur had hidden it, and since Murdoch's job was to see it set with the stone, it made no sense for him to take it. So it had to be Grey. He had the motive—they needed a complication. If Rhys had the stone, then that complication would have to be the sword.

She stretched out her leg, letting her foot touch the hem of the tablecloth. Arthur hadn't told Murdoch she was here. If he had, Arthur would be looking for her, calling her name. So, he still trusted her, despite that fact that he probably thought she took the sword.

The jeans she'd found to wear weren't the greatest fit. They were snug and, sitting here in this corner under a table draped by a red and gold damask cloth, it was hard not to dwell on it.

A single set of footsteps was coming down the hall now, slowing near the door to the sword room. Max pulled her knees to her chest, and a moment later someone entered the room. The steps were fairly heavy and Max assumed this wasn't Jillian. Judging from the slow, deliberate moves, she guessed this person was inspecting the sword collection.

After a few minutes, she heard Murdoch call out Rhys's name.

"I'm in here," he answered, and Max could see the shadow of his leg as he brushed by the tablecloth.

More footsteps—carrying a lighter weight from the sound of them—came down the hall and into the sword room and stopped. A few moments later, Murdoch said, "It's quite a collection, isn't it?"

"If I were to hide a sword, this is where I'd put it. In plain sight."

"But it's not here."

"You're sure?"

"I checked. It's none of these." Then he added, "You think Arthur took it?"

"Who else?" Rhys said. "We didn't take it. You swear to me that Maxine Pike is dead, that Mr. Weir never made it this far and that Nick and Olivia's bodies are being bashed against Alyssum's rocks as we speak."

Max closed her eyes and tilted her head back against the wall. Forcing even breaths in and out of her chest, she told herself that if they were wrong about her being dead and about Grey, then they were wrong about Olivia and Nick. She had to believe that.

"I called Jonah," Murdoch said. "He's checking for me."

"Where's Jillian?"

"In the garden looking for Arthur."

"He's been conspicuously absent for some time now."

"He's probably dead."

"Yes, that might have been a bit premature." After a moment he added, "It doesn't make sense to kill the only person who knows were the sword is. Does it? We nearly didn't get the stone because Pike died too soon."

"We'll find the sword."

"I wish I shared your confidence." The floor creaked as he turned. "The stone might as well be a piece of granite without the sword."

"Like I said, we'll find it."

What followed was ten or fifteen seconds of silence containing so much tension Max could practically feel it seeping under the folds of the tablecloth.

Max was a little surprised that Rhys was the one to break the silence. "Where did you put my luggage?"

Murdoch hesitated only a moment before saying, "In one of the bedrooms upstairs."

"Show me where it is." He paused. "I think I'll take a shower."

If Murdoch thought it odd timing for a shower, he didn't let on, sounding almost enthusiastic as he said, "Sounds like a good idea, sir. Nothing you can do right now. I mean—"

"Show me this room."

Max waited until Murdoch came back downstairs before crawling out from under the table. He'd walked toward the back of the castle—perhaps heading toward the kitchen or the rear exit, so Max headed toward the front stairs and up to the second floor. Arthur had told her most of the bedrooms were on this floor with a few more, including hers, on the third. She crept down the hall, putting her ear to each door, listening for sounds of occupancy. Once she figured out the room, she'd have some serious decisions to make. She was guessing that Murdoch would give Rhys the stone, but getting it from him was going to be sticky. Even if he was in the shower.

As she pressed her ear to the next door, hearing only her own breathing, noisy plumbing clanged on across the hall.

A shower? She crossed the hall, cracked the door and listened. What she heard was running water and then something else. She stuck her head in the room. Unbelievable. Rhys was alternately humming and singing a medley of Andrew Lloyd Weber tunes. As he slipped from "Music of the Night" into "Memory," a surge of laughter rose from her gut. Once she identified it as nerves-induced, it dissipated and she stepped into the room, closing the door behind her. A cloud of steam wafted into the bedroom from the open bathroom door.

The tub was behind the door, so unless Rhys saw her reflection in the mirror across from the tub, he wouldn't spot her.

His clothing was laid out on the bed. Max worried it was too easy, then reminded herself that if the stone wasn't among Rhys's belongings, it wouldn't be easy at all.

She worked quickly, patting down the pockets of his slacks and jacket, then going through the valise on the floor of the wardrobe. Nothing. Damn. She glanced at the bathroom door. He was singing the theme from *Phantom*. Max supposed no one had ever had the nerve to tell him that he couldn't carry a tune. Puffs of steam hovered around the door which was open against the tub.

Approaching the door from the hinge side, she could see the vanity and mirror. And there it was. The stone lay beside Rhys's leather shaving kit, on the far side of the basin. Max hesitated. The green gem on white marble looked like bait.

You can do this, Max. Snatch the stone and run. She wiped her damp palms on her jeans and dropped down on her hands and knees to avoid a reflection in the mirror. Then she crawled in.

Beyond the vanity was the toilet and bidet and behind the door was a claw-footed tub with a white, wrap-around shower curtain. She inched her way past the door, leaving its relative shelter. Now all she had to do was reach up and grab the stone.

With a bang, the door slammed shut behind her and metal screeched against metal as the shower curtain swung open. "Well, hello, Maxine."

Her spine turned to jelly and she slumped against the vanity. The water still ran and, as the room clouded with steam, she saw Rhys Lewis standing in the shower.

"I was beginning to think you weren't going to make it." He turned away from her to twist the shower knob and Max told herself to go for it. But she couldn't. Her body refused to follow her brain's command. She could not reach up and take the stone.

Rhys shook his head like a huge, pink retriever and slicked back his hair. Then he used his fingers to wipe water from his eyes and face.

"Be a dear and grab me a towel, would you?"

She didn't know whether it was fear or something else that rendered her motionless, but she was frozen to the spot.

"Never mind. I'll get it." As he stepped out of the tub, a spray of water hit her cheek. He plucked a thick, white towel off the heated rack and began to briskly rub his matted hair.

Pressing her back into the vanity, Max concentrated on sensations—the floor's hardness, the steam dampening her face and the cuff of her sweater brushing against her knuckles. She managed to shift her legs, folding them beneath her so she could rise quickly.

Rhys propped one foot on the toilet as he dried his leg. "Arthur's dead, you know."

She found her voice. "No, he's not."

"You're in denial, Maxine."

Rhys didn't appear to be watching her, but Max knew he followed her movements. While he was much larger and stronger than she, he might not be quicker. She rested her hand against the side of the vanity and began to edge it up toward the counter. The stone was only inches away.

That was when Rhys threw the towel beside the basin, covering the stone. He stepped toward her, so that less than a foot separated them, and rested one hand on the edge of the vanity. Max didn't know where to look. If she looked up at him, all she saw was his penis hanging there just above her. If she looked away, he'd know why.

"So, tell me," he said. "Do you still want to be the one?" He paused. "Now that you know what the prize is."

She tried to focus on his eyes, which were warm and brown. "I'm not impressed," she said, hearing and feeling the tightness in her voice. While she stayed fixed on his eyes, it was impossible not to notice the erection forming above her. A flush of heat rose from her groin to her chest and face; her mouth filled with saliva that tasted of salt. She shuddered, twisted her neck and spat on the black and white tiled floor.

"Rhys?" The woman's voice came from the bedroom.

Max went weak with relief. The tiles blurred together.

"I'm in here, Jillian," Rhys said.

The door flew open at the same time Jillian announced, "They found one of Simon's men. He's been sh—" Gaping at Rhys, down at Max, then up at Rhys again, Jillian looked as though she'd just caught her lover with the maid.

"He's been shot?" Rhys said, casually picking up the towel and patting his chest with it.

Jillian nodded.

"Where was he found?"

"In the garden." She was still staring at Max.

"Have you found the sword yet?"

Jillian worked her jaw a couple of times before saying, "We're still looking."

He nodded at Max as he dried his crotch. "By the way, this is Maxine Pike."

Then he turned toward the mirror and took a brush from his shaving kit. "I wonder if she can tell us where it is."

Chapter 53

"I've got to call the pub." Nick had to restrain himself from lifting the receiver, had to tell himself that whoever picked up the phone could still be on the line. He grabbed his cell phone, pressed a couple of buttons and confirmed his assumption that it was not waterproof. Fortunately, his watch was, and it told him they had maybe five hours.

"We have to get out of here first, Nick." Olivia sounded calm as she spoke. "We need to look for Max. You aren't going to do them any good if you get yourself killed before you can warn them. You've got time—the bomb isn't going off for—I don't know . . ." She glanced at her watch, flicked it with her fingernail.

"Five hours. Tops." Nick said.

"Five hours." She nodded as though that were reasonable. Then, in a harsh whisper she added, poking her thumb at the desk phone, "Don't even think about picking that up."

She was right. The only way he could warn the pub was to get out of here first. Pushing his splayed hand through his hair, he forced himself to concentrate. Their only option was to walk out that door into who knew what. "I'll have a look outside. See what we're into."

He cracked the door an inch and saw nothing but dim light and more cave. Opening it wider, he was relieved to see no one waiting for them, but dismayed to find their direction anything but apparent.

"Which way do we go?" Olivia had come up behind him and pushed past him into the cave.

The mirrored room was, basically, a large box in the middle of the cave and there were a number of tunnels to choose from. Where were they in relation to the castle?

"I've got no sense of where I am," Olivia said.

Nick wasn't so sure anymore either. Using the direction they'd come from the sea, he determined what he believed to be the most southern route. "Let's try this way." They started down one of the tunnels. The walls had crude light fixtures attached to them, illuminating the passage just enough so they could see where to put their feet. But after about twenty feet, the series of lights ended. Within a few steps, the corridor angled slightly to the right and they were in the dark again. Resigned to the probability that he'd chosen the wrong path, Nick struck Olivia's lighter to get some sense of their surroundings. The flame didn't catch, but in the half second it existed, there'd been something in front of them.

Olivia sucked in her breath. "A ghost."

Her hand closed on his arm as he frantically thumbed the lighter, producing only sparks. Then there was a click and a bright light blinded him. Shielding his eyes with his hand, Nick was barely able to make out the figure who stood only a few feet in front of them, thrusting a flashlight in their faces.

"Don't you move." The order was issued by a deep, male voice. The figure backed off a couple of steps.

When he was able to squint into the light, Nick saw the man had his right arm extended and in that hand was a small caliber gun which he seemed to have trouble holding still. While the figure had more substance than a ghost, Olivia's mistake had been understandable. In that flash of light, he would have looked like a disembodied head. The young man's skin was the color of watered-down milk, and his black hair thin and closely cut so that his scalp shone through. Pale eyes bulged behind his thick-lensed glasses. He wore a dark plaid flannel shirt buttoned at the collar and cuffs.

"Simon said you might find your way down here. You're trying to stop us." He wet his thick lips and closed his left eye as though taking aim. "I'm not going to let that happen."

"Who are you?" Nick asked, thinking the man's deep voice seemed out of line with the scrawny body—almost as though a ventriloquist were working him.

The man opened his eye and regarded Nick with disgust. "I'm Jonah. This is my place. And I run it. All of it."

Olivia stepped toward Jonah, but he didn't take his eyes from Nick.

"Turn around and head back to the big room." He wagged the flashlight in the direction they'd come from and its beam careened off the walls. "And you better not have touched anything."

Nick glanced at Olivia who gave him a slight nod. "You mean those computers?" he asked.

Olivia added, "The ones with all those organized pranks?"

Jonah pointed the gun at Olivia.

"What does 'system error' mean?" Nick said, stepping to his right.

As Jonah swung the gun toward Nick, Olivia moved to her

left. Now they were far enough apart to make it impossible for Jonah to hold the gun on both of them. From the way he jerked his head back and forth a couple of times, he had worked that out for himself.

"What'd you do to it?" Jonah demanded.

Nick shrugged. "The screen went blank."

"You *moron*." Jonah slipped his finger in front of the trigger.

"At least I didn't drop one on the floor." Nick jerked his head toward Olivia.

Still frozen in place, Jonah shifted his eyes toward Olivia, who shrugged.

"You dropped my computer?"

"Oops."

"You bitch." He swung the gun toward Olivia, squared his shoulders and just stared at her, his body so taut he shook. When he spoke again, his voice was strained, as though it took effort to control. "You had better tell your friend to start moving back to the computer room."

When neither moved, he barked, "Now." Then he twisted his mouth into what might have been a smile. "Or I will kill her."

Nick had no reason to doubt him. "Okay, okay. I'm going." He waited while Jonah continued to hold the gun on Olivia, moving only when he saw Jonah's smile dissipate.

As he started back toward the big room, Olivia and Jonah following, he tried to come up with a plan. First he needed to keep Jonah from calling Murdoch. He figured he had two options: take out the phone or take out Jonah. Even then, Murdoch was likely expecting to hear from Jonah. At best, Nick would be buying them some time.

When they got to the room, Jonah grabbed a handful of Olivia's collar, put the gun to the base of her head and told

Nick to open the door. "Walk in and straight ahead, so I can see you. Try anything weird and the bitch dies."

"Don't you think your boss would be a little annoyed if you killed us before he could talk to us?" Olivia said. "We know things—"

Jonah snorted. "I don't think he cares."

As Olivia argued their fate, Nick pushed open the door, stepped into the room and froze. To his right, standing near the copier in the corner, were three men—one quite tall with reddish hair and a beard, another slender with dark hair, and the third stocky and wearing a cap. He had never seen any of them before. In the fraction of a second he had to make a judgment, he determined he had nothing to lose in assuming they were an improvement over Jonah, who would not be able to see them until he was in the room.

"Quit arguing with him, Olivia." Nick called over his shoulder, keeping his eyes on the three men. "Where am I supposed to go, Jonah?" The dark-haired man motioned for the others to get down, which they did, effectively hiding behind the drawing table.

"Walk straight ahead to the desk and sit in the chair."

He did. Behind him he could hear Jonah and Olivia following. When he reached the chair, he turned and saw that the dark-haired man had crept up behind Jonah, but he made no move as Jonah released Olivia, giving her a little shove. "You sit in that other chair." Then, as Jonah lowered the gun slightly, the man behind him grabbed his wrist, forcing it down toward the floor with a twisting action. Jonah cried out and the gun hit the plywood with a thunk.

The man had scooped up the gun before Jonah recovered and pushed him down into the chair Nick had been assigned. Then he turned toward Nick and Olivia and said, "Would you be Nick Llewellyn and Olivia Pike?"

"We are," Nick said, glancing at Olivia, who shook her head to indicate she didn't know him either. "Who are you?"

"Greyson Weir. Grey."

The other two men had come up behind Grey. The taller one introduced himself as Arthur Penn and the other man as Earl Jessup.

"How do you know us?" Nick asked.

"Max has told me about you."

"Is she okay?" Olivia blurted.

"She's fine."

"You're sure? Because Murdoch said she was dead."

"I saw her this morning."

Olivia closed her eyes, sighing deeply.

Grey nodded toward Nick's head. "You all right?"

The blood had caked and the skin felt tight on his forehead. "Not as bad as it looks." He'd almost forgotten about it.

"Where'd you come from?" Nick asked.

"One of these tunnels leads to the castle. About halfway down, there's an exit to the garden. An elaborate manhole cover. If you go all the way to the castle, it comes out at an elevator shaft."

Nick wondered what he and Olivia had been heading for, decided it didn't matter right now and said to Grey, "Murdoch instructed our friend here to look for us." He nodded toward Jonah. "If Jonah doesn't call, we may have company."

Grey handed the gun to Nick, then crouched in front of Jonah. "What's your full name?"

Jonah sat with his face in his hands; his shoulders twitched. Without lifting his head, he answered, "Sewell. Jonah Sewell."

"All right, Mr. Sewell. No one has to get hurt here. Not if you follow our directions."

Jonah's shoulders jerked with a raw-sounding laugh. "Yeah, right."

"Look at me, Mr. Sewell."

When Jonah finally lifted his head, Nick saw that he'd mustered up some contempt. "Who the hell are you anyway?"

"Right now I'm the person who may let you live." Grey stood and reached across the desk, dragging the phone towards them. Then he pulled Jonah out of the chair and handed him the receiver. "What's Murdoch's number? And don't try anything clever, I know your boss's voice."

After a few moments, Jonah recited a phone number. As Grey punched it in, he said, "I want you to tell him you've inspected the area and there's no one down here." He held the phone between them so Jonah could talk into the receiver, but Grey could still hear what was being said.

"Uh, yeah, Mr. Murdoch," Jonah said. "I, uh, looked. Nobody down here. . . . Yeah. . . . Sure. . . . Okay."

Grey hung up the phone. "Nicely done." He smiled slightly and while it seemed genuine enough, his eyes were a bit distant. Weir was also older than Nick had first assumed. His hair was graying and some of the lines etched into his face looked like what Nick's mother called "worry lines."

While the business with the phone call was being handled, Arthur Penn had been walking around the room, inspecting every inch of it. He had the look of someone who was witnessing the aftermath of a terrible storm. He came to a stop by the computer with the graphic images. Nick tapped one of the keys to bring up the "Downward Spiral" logo and the barbed wire twisted into a tornado, which spun lazily back and forth across the screen. Arthur scrolled down and, as his eyes tracked down the screen, his mouth tightened into a thin line and he began to shake his head. "This is ugly." He turned away from the computer, and when he saw Jonah slouching, arms crossed over his narrow chest, he said, "You may revel in this ugliness to your heart's content. But you're not going to do it on Alyssum, and I will liquidate every pound I possess and use it to stoke the castle's fires before Simon Murdoch or Rhys Lewis get their hands on it."

Jonah smirked, shaking his head at Arthur's naiveté. "Simon says—"

Olivia kicked one of the wheeled desk chairs toward him. "Simon says sit down and shut up." The chair bounced off his leg and spun around once.

Nick felt himself smiling. God, she had her moments.

"Sit!" Olivia pointed, and he dropped down into the chair. "Why don't we tie and gag this asshole?"

"I'll find something to use," Earl said. It was the first time Nick heard his voice, and he was a little surprised to hear the American accent. He wondered how the strange trio came to be.

"Here, take this," Penn said, tossing Earl a flashlight.

Grey sat in the other chair and wheeled it up to Jonah's, studied him for a moment or two, then said, "What are you concocting down here?" The question conveyed only curiosity.

Jonah rolled his eyes, apparently amused that Grey thought he'd share this information, and shifted his focus to the floor. Grey rested his elbow on the edge of the desk and watched the violent scenes on display. "This is quite a montage." He paused while a few more scenes passed. "Ode to carnage."

Jonah didn't respond.

Grey picked up the manual on computer viruses that Nick

had seen earlier, and also found the notepad. He exchanged the manual for it and stared at the blocky letters for several moments, then looked up as though trying to focus on something only he could see.

" 'Jonah's Life,' " he said, turning toward Jonah with narrowed eyes. "I doubt you're talking about your own life." He glanced around the room. "Since you apparently have none."

Jonah kept his gaze on the floor.

Grey continued, "And since you've got an impressive collection of literature on computer viruses, I don't think it would be unreasonable for us to assume you've created your very own." He paused. "Your very own life."

Jonah lifted his gaze to meet Grey's.

"I'm right, aren't I?"

Jonah didn't look away.

Nick glanced at the others, who were all watching Grey draw the young man out. He reminded Nick of a teacher he'd had—the one who kept him in school that last year when he decided there were too many other things pulling at his life.

"A computer virus." Grey's brows drew together and he began to nod. "It is life. It meets the minimum requirement for life," he continued. "It has the ability to replicate itself."

Jonah was nodding, a smile pulling one corner of his mouth up. "It's also smart enough to recognize an environment as hostile or friendly."

Leaning toward Jonah, Grey clasped his hands under his chin and said, "Tell me about your life, Jonah."

When Jonah didn't respond, Grey said, "You wouldn't waste your time with some hoax virus that clutters people's mailboxes. Would you?" He appeared to be concentrating, thinking it over. "No, you're down here creating something . . . elegant. Aren't you?" He was almost whispering. "What does it do?"

Jonah shook his head but didn't speak or take his eyes off of Grey.

"It's not as if I can tell anyone."

Jonah glanced at the computer screen which was displaying an image from a computer game—a muscular hero slicing a masked thug in two. "That's right," he said, nodding. "You guys aren't getting off this island anyway."

"So why not tell us?"

He smiled. "Why not?" He swiveled his chair so he faced his computer display. "It's simple. My life injects one of these images into every twenty-fifth frame of a visual display."

They all crowded around the computer as Jonah brought up the barbed-wire tornado, and watched as he typed some commands into the computer that slowed the display to a crawl. Viewed as such, they could see how the images were embedded.

"Brilliant," Grey said, sounding genuinely impressed. "Subliminally-suggested violence." He pulled at his lower lip. "And a person wouldn't know their computer was infected."

Jonah was nodding and smiling, caught up in a mixture of pride and enthusiasm. "That's right."

Nick looked at the others and saw varying degrees of disbelief, edging toward alarm.

Olivia, who was standing right behind Jonah, muttered something about a "sick bastard."

"But does it work?" Grey persisted. "I don't know that anyone ever showed that subliminal advertising had the desired effect."

"It does," Jonah said, eager now. "It's been tested. Just one person so far, but the results are encouraging."

"To what end?" Arthur demanded and Jonah started, as though just realizing there were others in the room. "Why would anyone want to make people more aggressive? More violent?"

Jonah turned in his chair so he faced Arthur, and spoke as if he were tired of explaining such a simple concept. "Because it's what people want."

"I'm not having this discussion," Arthur said. "Not with a sociopath."

He moved away from them and stepped into the center of the room, hands sunk into his pockets, and turned to take in the entire area. "I can't believe this place exists."

That was when Nick realized this was the man who owned the island.

"No reason you should," Grey responded.

"Of course there is! I live here. How could all of this have been done without my knowledge?"

"You spend a few weeks a year off the island," Grey offered. Then he said, "Who hires the people who work here?"

Arthur nodded to himself. "Everyone but the cook and the stable manager was hired by Simon."

"That would mean the gardeners and the staff in the house."

Still nodding, Arthur bowed his head. "I've been oblivious."

"Alyssum can have that effect on people."

"But why?" Nick said. "Why build this installation in a cave on a remote island?"

"Because this isn't just any island." Grey looked up at him.

Before Nick could ask him to elaborate, Earl returned with a handful of rope and some tape. "There's a whole room full of supplies down that way. And an office." Nick took the tape from him. "Weapons too."

"Did you see any explosives?" Grey asked.

"Yeah." Earl eyed him as he unwound the rope.

Nick handed the gun to Olivia and peeled off a length of duct tape.

Still standing in the center of the room, Arthur did a one-hundred-eighty-degree turn. "I want this—all this—destroyed."

"You can't do that!" With this outburst, Jonah launched himself from the chair, catching Olivia off-balance. He grabbed her as she started to fall backwards and tore the gun from her hand. A second later a shot went off, freezing the group into a bizarre tableau. Then Jonah dropped to the floor, jerked once and was still. His eyes remained wide open as the dark stain on his chest expanded.

Earl looked at the gun he'd just fired and jammed it into his pocket. He picked up the pile of rope and tossed it on top of the dead man.

Olivia, rubbing the small of her back as she collected herself, said, "Thanks, Earl." She picked up the gun from the floor beside Jonah and gave it back to Nick.

"Getting back to this cave," Grey said, studying Earl.

But before he could continue, Nick interrupted. "I need to contact the police and my pub." He nodded toward the laptop. "While nosing about on their site, we learned they're planning to set off a bomb there tonight."

"Is the name of your pub the Fife and Firkin?" Grey asked.

"It is," he answered, fearing the worst and believing he wouldn't be able to go forward from here. "God, please don't tell—"

"It's all right," Grey said. "It's been reported. The police have dismantled it, and no one came to any harm. Your pub is safe."

"How did you—"

"That's for later, Nick." He must have read the questions

in Nick's eyes. "Please trust me."

Nick gave him a nod, thinking he was placing an awful lot of trust in a man he'd met ten minutes ago.

"Speaking of explosions," Grey said, adding a grim smile. "The only way I can think to destroy this cave is to blast it out of existence." When Earl looked up at him, he added, "Unless I'm mistaken, you were a demolitions expert in the Army."

"Uh, yeah," Earl admitted, glancing at Nick before focusing on Grey.

Nick studied the short, unremarkable man who had turned out to be surprising on several levels.

"This cave has infested the island," Arthur said. "The surface above it is dead. I won't have it." He turned toward Earl. "I'd appreciate anything you can do to blow this place out of existence."

"What about the castle?" Nick said. "If the tunnel goes directly to the castle, isn't an underground explosion going to bring the whole thing down?"

"I think we only need to destroy the caves and tunnels on the north end of the island," Grey said. "Once they're gone, I think the connecting tunnels will atrophy."

"Okay," Earl said. "I could use some help."

"Nick, can you assist him?" Grey asked.

"Sure," Nick said, thinking he had a question or two for Earl. "There's a lot to this cave. We'll need to spend some time checking it out first."

"Yeah, that's right," Earl agreed.

Grey consulted his watch. "Can you do it so the charges go off in three hours? You shouldn't have to map every inch of the cave; destroy the main part and whatever else you can."

Earl nodded and said, "I'll go see what we've got."

"We need to have the information on these computers. I'd

say take them out of here, but if one of them should come down here, I don't want him to see they're missing." Arthur glanced at his watch, then said to Olivia, "Can you download these files?"

"Um, sure," she said.

"Nick," Grey said, turning to him, "your uncle believes this is all his." He took Nick aside and began telling him things about his uncle that hadn't been passed down through family lore—the way in which Rhys spread his vision, using Alyssum, and his potential for the future. Oddly, the possibility that Nick had been wrestling with—his uncle really had been fathered by a demon—didn't matter much to him in the end. Rhys was what he was. And either he would kill his uncle or his uncle would kill him.

Finally, Grey said, "You're going to have to face your uncle, you know."

He had no argument. "I know." He felt woefully overmatched.

Grey's dark eyes didn't waver. "Keep Rhys out of your head. That is where he does battle. Control your anger. He feeds off it. He wants the sword—"

"I haven't got the sword."

"He wants the sword," he repeated and tapped the side of Nick's head. "He has to go through here to get it. Destroy him before he destroys you. The last thing you can afford to be is merciful."

Chapter 54

"Where's the sword, Maxine?"

Simon Murdoch sat on the coffee table, elbows on his knees, as he leaned toward Max. She fought the impulse to pull back into the chair. Murdoch liked to intimidate with proximity. "I don't know," she said, trying not to sound too convincing. As long as they believed she knew where Caliburn was, they had reason not to kill her.

"I think you do."

Behind him, Jillian stood, watching. Her jaw was too square—it gave the impression she was constantly gritting her teeth.

"You got no reason not to tell us," he said. "Arthur's dead."

"I don't believe you."

"We'll find it. With or without you."

She didn't respond.

He regarded her for another minute, perhaps hoping she would cave under his scrutiny. Then, abruptly, he stood and walked over to a desk in the corner of the room. From one of its drawers he removed a syringe.

He's going to kill me, she thought. *It can't end like this.* She looked around for a way out, an option. Maybe if she could keep him talking. Murdoch liked to hear himself talk.

"What's that?" she asked.

He took his time answering. When he did, his voice matched his movements—calculated and smooth. "The only reason I need you alive is to tell me where the sword is. You won't do that, so I might as well kill you." He removed the cork from its tip and slipped his thumb onto the plunger. "Heroin. Pure. Very painful, I hear."

Max crossed her arms over her chest. Jillian was watching Simon, an expectant look drawing up the corners of her mouth. Murdoch returned to the glass-topped coffee table, pulling it a few inches closer to Max. He sat on it and extended his left hand, as though expecting her to give him hers. Maybe she didn't have a lot of choices left, but she had a few.

"All right, Simon, you've made your point," Rhys said as he strode into the room. "Put that down." His hair was still damp and slicked back from his forehead.

Simon looked up at him, confused and maybe a little disappointed. "What do we need her for?"

Before Rhys could tell him, Max heard movement by the door. When she looked, she saw Arthur standing there, Caliburn in hand. The way he gripped it—assured but relaxed—indicated to her that he knew how to use it.

"There you are, Simon," he said, sounding like a host greeting guests. Only the hardness in his eyes suggested there was more going on. "Sorry to keep you all waiting."

Murdoch rose from the table slowly, and Max wondered

how much effort it required to maintain his casual air. "Arthur," he said. "I've been looking for you."

"Yes. I'm sure you have." Arthur had a good six inches on Murdoch and, when he stood next to his half-brother, looking down at the syringe, Max could see the shine on Murdoch's forehead.

Murdoch held up the syringe. "Truth serum. Trying to get our little thief here to talk." He walked around the chairs and tossed the needle into the desk drawer and slammed it shut. "Looks like we won't be needing this. Where'd you find it?"

"Ask her," Jillian said, moving away from the windows so she could stand above Max and look down on her. Her pale brows were drawn together, reducing her eyes to slits. "Like father, like daughter."

Max's foot shot out and smacked Jillian in the knee. It was almost a reflex. She hadn't much momentum going, but it must have been a solid hit because Jillian yelped and nearly folded onto the floor. She managed to stay upright by bracing one hand against the coffee table while the other cradled her battered knee. "You little bitch!"

Max was out of her chair. "My father was not a thief." She glanced at Rhys, who was smiling down at the floor. "And I'm not going to let the bastard daughter of a murderer call him one."

His head came up and he let his warm, brown eyes bore into Max for a moment before they softened and he held his arms out in an encompassing gesture. "Please, ladies, let's not spoil this occasion. All our emotions are at the surface, but we don't have to give into them."

Stuff it, Max thought. From the sideways glance Jillian gave her father, she might have had the same suggestion.

"She didn't steal it," Arthur said, "it was moved. That's all."

He placed the sword on the coffee table. Caliburn's edges reflected in the beveled sheet of glass and the blade shimmered in the sun, giving the impression that the sword was floating on water. He stepped back and took in each person in the room. "Let's see what the stone has to say."

Jillian managed to stand on both legs. Rhys crouched before the sword, examining the two gems. He glanced up at Arthur, then removed the heartstone from his pocket.

Max wiped her damp palms on her jeans. She was so aware of her own breathing she was afraid it might stop. But she managed to sit back in the chair and cross her legs so she might appear calm. Then she gave Jillian a little smile. It was an Olivia smile—the one that said: "I haven't even started yet."

It must have worked because Jillian was so busy watching Max that she didn't realize Rhys was trying to hand her the stone. It took every ounce of control for Max not to turn away. Finally, Rhys touched his daughter's arm. She started, but then was immediately drawn in by her father, holding the stone out to her. By the time she took it from his hand, she was practically quivering. She knelt beside Caliburn.

This could not happen. Max grabbed the edges of the seat and slid forward a couple of inches. She looked up at Arthur and was struck by his composure. Then he turned his eyes on her and in their depth she saw no fear, no doubt, only faith in the endurance of his vision. This woman would not destroy it. Max eased back into the chair.

Jillian had the stone poised over the hilt. Then, with her thumb and forefinger, she set the heartstone in the cavity. It went in crooked and she had to push it down on one side to straighten it. When she stood, Rhys stepped over to her, put his arm around her shoulder and kissed her cheek.

"Nicely done," he said.

Max waited, and a sense of calm filled her lungs, her heart and her head. She looked up at Arthur and his expression hadn't changed. *It's not over.* Max wasn't sure where that little voice inside her came from, but it was adamant. She looked at the sword again, at the three stones in the hilt: red, green and green again. Something about the center stone was different. Did it bulge slightly? She moved up in the chair an inch. Yes. The stone wasn't in all the way. She glanced at Jillian and was dismayed to find her smile fading as she was examining the hilt. Had she seen it, or was she simply disappointed nothing had happened? Jillian looked over at Max, who dropped her gaze to the floor, afraid Jillian might read something in her eyes.

Jillian leaned over the table. "It's not quite right." With her forefinger, she pressed down on the stone. It sank a hair's breadth, there was a loud pop and then the glass table shattered, swallowing Caliburn in a cascade of glass that glittered like a thousand stars. Jillian screamed, covering her face as she fell back against Rhys. The sword crashed to the floor, throwing glass as it landed. The heartstone flew out and landed inches from Max's toes. She dropped to the floor, crunching glass beneath her knees, and plucked the stone from the shards. Her hand stung and a thread of blood appeared across its heel. She reached toward the hilt and lowered the stone into the cavity, which sucked it up like a powerful magnet. With a loud crack, a spark of red exploded within the stone. She sank back onto her heels. "Damn." *I made that happen.*

When Max looked up, Arthur was beside her, bending to retrieve the sword. He took it in his right hand and offered Max his left. They rose together.

"Not so fast, brother." Murdoch had drawn a gun. "Put the sword down."

Arthur moved in front of Max, shielding her from Murdoch.

"How d'you want to do this, Rhys?" Murdoch asked.

Rhys stepped around his daughter, who was still sprawled on the floor. Glass popped beneath his shoes as he made his way toward Max and Arthur, approaching from the side so Arthur couldn't protect her from both men at the same time.

Max tried not to look at Rhys, told herself that as long as Arthur was here, Rhys couldn't touch her.

"That's far enough, Mr. Lewis," Arthur said.

Rhys slowed, but kept coming. Max focused on Arthur's hand, wrapped around Caliburn's hilt.

"Congratulations, Miss Pike," Rhys said. "Your father—"

"Move away from her." The voice came from the doorway.

Although Arthur blocked Max's view, she recognized the voice. Peering around him, she saw Grey had come up behind Simon and put a gun to the back of his head.

"Give me the gun, Simon."

Murdoch turned his head far enough to see the gun, then a little farther to see who held it. His mouth contracted into a tight line and his throat reddened. He kept the gun pointed toward Arthur and Max, and as his eyes darted back and forth, Max wondered if he thought he might be able to shoot Arthur before Grey killed him.

With an impatient scowl, Grey cocked his wrist and slammed the pistol's butt into the back of Murdoch's head. Murdoch's eyes widened, as if he had a moment to recognize what had happened, and then his knees buckled and he dropped to the floor. Grey stooped to retrieve Murdoch's gun, then stood and swung his own gun around and took aim at Rhys.

"Don't, Grey!" It was Arthur. "A gunshot could bring others."

Grey didn't move. His arm was rigid and his eyes dispassionate.

Rhys just stared at Grey, almost as though he were daring him to pull the trigger. Max wondered if perhaps Grey was right—Rhys did consider himself immortal.

"Grey," Arthur warned.

Outside the window, a bird chattered and wind rustled the leaves.

Finally, Grey said, "I told you to move away from her, Rhys."

Rhys's pale brown eyes examined Max from behind half-closed lids. He could see right through her. A flush of heat rose from her chest.

Grey came at Rhys, crossing the room in three long strides. Rhys lifted both hands, palms out.

"Back up," Grey said.

Rhys retreated two steps.

"Max, Arthur, go," Grey said. "Get as far away from here as you can."

When Arthur hesitated, Grey said, "Reinforcements will be along any minute."

Arthur took Max's hand and led her across the room, nodding at Grey as they slipped through the arched doorway and into the hall.

Chapter 55

The cave was more extensive than Nick had realized, with enough cubbies for a rabbit warren. Numerous offshoots from the main room, most of which led nowhere or ended in spaces too small to be of use, lent credence to Grey's explanation of how the cave was created. He felt Rhys's presence and half-expected each turn into another narrow, twisted passage to bring them face-to-face.

Earl had suggested concentrating the explosives in the larger areas, targeting the support walls. Knowing next to nothing about blowing things up, Nick went along.

As he watched the other man's stubby fingers deftly twining wires together and handling the explosives with a combination of facility and deference, he couldn't stop himself from asking the question: "How did Grey know about the bomb at the Fife and Firkin?"

At first he thought Earl was so intent on his job that he

hadn't heard him. And Nick figured he ought not to push it—if Earl needed to make himself oblivious to the rest of the world in order to do this, then so be it.

He went back to the map he'd been sketching as they explored the cave, preparing it for its destruction. While he wasn't sure how much use it would be, at least it was a task he could do. He added a few labels while waiting for Earl: here was the food storage area, the late Jonah's room—

"I told him." Earl pushed himself up from the floor and turned to face Nick, who was at least a head taller so he had to look up at him.

"How did you know?" Nick asked, thinking he already knew. He just wanted to hear this man tell him that he'd created a bomb that was intended to rip apart the lives and the place that was, at least until recently, Nick's universe.

Earl wore his baseball cap so the visor covered his neck and Nick could see the sweat on his brow through the half-circle created by the plastic adjustment strap. Now he turned the cap around again, tugging the visor down over his eyes. "They asked me to do it," he said.

" 'They'?"

"Your uncle and his kid."

"Did you?"

"No." He shook his head, then bent down to collect his supplies.

"You told my uncle no?" He didn't think many people got away with saying "no" to Rhys.

"Not exactly. I just got off the plane from Chicago and couldn't see straight." He shrugged. "I guess they figured I'd screw it up."

Nick hesitated, thinking there ought to be more to say, and finally realizing that were it not for a remarkable set of co-incidences, no one would have known about the bomb until it was too late. But he had one more question and waited until Earl was standing to ask it. "Why are you helping us now?"

Tipping his head back so he could look past the beak of his cap and into Nick's eyes, Earl said, "Because Arthur asked me to."

"I see," Nick said after a moment, a little surprised to find that he did understand. Then he waved his hand toward the darkened end of the tunnel. "Let's keep moving."

They came to an odd chapel sort of place, which wasn't more than a large closet with a woven mat on the floor and a flat rock in one corner. When Nick stepped into the alcove, the temperature dropped at least ten degrees. A faint metallic odor tinged the air, and Nick imagined he could hear the surrounding stone walls heave and crack with the earth's movements. He crouched beside the rock, directing the flashlight's beam on its surface, which was black with gray striations and appeared smooth, as if it had been polished, but a powderlike substance dulled parts of the surface. He dabbed his finger in the substance, rubbing it between his thumb and forefinger before smelling it. Blood.

"Nick?" It was Earl, who had stayed out in the corridor. "We gotta go."

"Sure," Nick said, wiping his fingers on the leg of his jeans as he rose. He left the room feeling jittery, as though his nerves had been struck with a giant tuning fork. He tried to suppress the sensation by concentrating on their task and found that watching Earl at work actually did calm him.

The bombs were being set to detonate in 115 minutes. Nick couldn't rid himself of the nagging concern that destroying the cave meant destroying Alyssum. While he tried to tell himself these thoughts were prompted by whatever Rhys had instilled in him, Nick had a difficult time moving past the image of the entire island imploding and all of them being sucked into a hole at the bottom of the sea.

"Only one to go after this." Earl lowered himself to the stone floor, turned his cap around and got to work.

"We're almost there." It was taking longer than Nick had imagined, but Earl didn't need to hear that.

Chapter 56

Jillian picked herself up from the floor, brushing chips of glass from her skirt. Her knee hurt and her face stung.

"Do you know what you've done?" Rhys exploded.

She shrank back a step, then realized Rhys had directed this toward Greyson Weir.

"Yes," Weir replied, calm.

He swung his hand toward the south door, from which Arthur and Maxine had exited. "That can't be the future!"

Weir reminded Jillian of a hawk—watchful, potentially deadly. When he didn't respond, Rhys pounded a fist against his chest. "I am the future."

"Not in my book."

Beads of blood dotted the backs of her hands and she picked a sliver of glass off her chin. While thinking if she'd had a gun, she'd have shot the little bitch, Jillian warned herself not to lose sight of what she needed to do. If she got through this, there'd be time to deal with Maxine Pike.

Murdoch lay in a heap on the floor in front of the south door. She hoped he was dead. The more people Rhys lost, the more he needed her. Unless she proved to her father she was useful, she was dead. She didn't have much time.

"What are your plans, Weir?" Rhys was asking him. He didn't sound as shrill, but Jillian sensed he was making an effort in the face of Weir's apparent composure.

"To keep you from accomplishing yours," he replied.

"You can't beat us."

"I'm here, aren't I?" Weir gestured with the gun toward the couch. "Sit down."

Rhys didn't move.

"Sit!" Weir sounded like he was commanding a dog.

When Rhys made no move to comply, Weir leveled the gun at Rhys's head.

After a moment, Rhys glanced over his shoulder, found the couch, then lowered himself into it. *He must be crazy with rage,* Jillian thought—for Jillian's failure and then for letting the little bitch get away. But Rhys's anger only showed if you knew where to look.

"And you," Weir wagged the gun at Jillian. "Sit here." He kicked one of the chairs.

Jillian did not want to sit across from her father, where there would be no avoiding his eyes. But she complied, because she didn't see a choice.

"What now?" Rhys said, carefully placing his palms on his knees.

"We wait." Weir had moved so he faced the door with his back to the wall of windows.

Rhys was watching her. She tried to hold his gaze, but her eyes burned.

When she thought of Maxine Pike, Jillian nearly went

blind with spite. She had been so close to having it all—the kid, Alyssum, her father's approval and maybe, eventually, his love. Thanks to that little bitch, she'd be lucky to make it out of this room alive.

Weir paced back and forth in front of the window. As Jillian watched him, she noticed a man standing outside next to an oval bush, looking into the room. It was one of the men who had flown over here with her and Murdoch. The large one with the round head. He ducked out of sight after a moment.

"We should have seen to it that you went to prison for embezzling all that money," Rhys was saying. "We'd have made sure you didn't survive your term."

"That's where you recruit your best and brightest, isn't it, Rhys?"

Jillian glanced around the room. She had to do something. Murdoch's thug wouldn't be able to take Weir unless there was a distraction.

When Rhys didn't respond, Weir added, "Men like Barney Waldrop."

"Who?" Rhys frowned, leaning forward slightly.

"Barney Waldrop," Weir repeated.

At the mention of Rhys's hired assassin, Murdoch groaned. Jillian stood and, without hesitation, walked between the chairs.

"Sit down!" Weir said.

She kept walking. "I'm going to see if he's all right. You nearly killed him."

As she crouched beside Murdoch, she touched the back of his head where a gash bled heavily. She understood that head wounds tended to be bloody and that didn't necessarily mean they were serious.

Weir stood over her now. In order to watch both Jillian

and her father, his back was to the south door. She had to keep him right there.

Looking up at him, she said, "Have you got a handkerchief? He's bleeding badly."

Weir hesitated. Just then Murdoch groaned again and opened his eyes. When they focused on Jillian, she saw Murdoch's confusion. Weir glanced over at Rhys who was watching from the couch, then he reached into his back pocket, pulled out a limp, rumpled handkerchief and tossed it to her. She applied it to the base of Murdoch's skull and he winced. Jillian placed her hand on his arm and squeezed as hard as she could.

"What the—" Murdoch was reviving fast. He tried to pull away and when he couldn't, he reached out to swat her away.

Weir backstepped and a moment later a huge bulk rammed him, slamming him back into a window. The impact shattered one of the panes. Before Weir could recover, his attacker delivered three hard punches to his stomach, doubling Weir over, then laced his beefy hands together and brought the fist down on the back of Weir's head. Weir dropped to the floor and didn't move.

"Nice going, Tommy," Murdoch grunted as he pushed himself up from the floor. With some effort, he collected Weir's gun and then his own, which lay beside Weir. Groggy as he appeared, Murdoch managed to point his own gun at the base of the man's skull.

"Wait," Rhys stopped him.

Murdoch lowered the gun and looked up at Rhys.

"I've got plans for him." Rhys paused, twisting his jaw the way he did when he was thinking.

Murdoch's eyes met Jillian's and she shrugged her eyebrows.

"All right," Rhys finally said. "Tommy, get some rope and

tie him up. Let's get him down to the cave. I don't want anyone assisting him." Rhys gave Weir's leg a not-too-gentle kick. Then he said to Murdoch, who seemed a little woozy, but otherwise all right, "Take care of Arthur and bring me the girl."

After Murdoch and Tommy left, Jillian felt the silence closing in on her. She couldn't look at Rhys, but just kept staring down at Weir, and told herself that none of this was her fault.

"Well executed diversion, Jillian."

She nodded, not trusting her voice.

Rhys placed his hand on her head and stroked her hair. Once, twice. Then he wrapped his fist around a clump and twisted, snapping her head back, and she was looking into the eyes of a rabid dog.

"Nice going, dear."

Chapter 57

"You'll be safe here until the situation is under control," Arthur told Max as he ushered her into the near-empty room. "That shouldn't be long."

Max nodded, taking a moment to catch her breath. Arthur had hustled her up to this small room on the third floor in the section of the castle that had been closed off. The room contained only two pieces of furniture: a wardrobe painted a faded green and a child's rocking chair with a blue-and-white quilt folded across its arms. The room, located halfway down a long hallway, appeared to be a random choice. Or was it?

Arthur walked past her to one of two windows that looked out onto a portion of the rear lawn and the stables. He lay Caliburn on the floor next to the wall, then opened the window and gazed out as though he were seeing it for the first time.

Max thought she understood—sometimes a moment changed everything.

She came up beside him. "Was this your room?"

He appeared almost startled, either by her question or from finding her standing right there. But then he smiled and said, "Yes, in fact it was."

Outside, a horse's whinny carried in the still air and a bird with a splash of red on its tail winged past the window.

With the three stones setting off Caliburn's hilt, the sword appeared to have shed years. The blade shone as though it had just been wrought. "Did you think I'd stolen it at first?"

"I'm afraid that was my initial reaction." He bowed his head, maybe a little contrite, stroking his beard with his thumb and forefinger. "And I must admit the thought of your betrayal upset me almost as much as Caliburn's disappearance."

His eyes found hers then and he lowered his hand to the windowsill. "Maybe more." He swallowed. His cotton shirt was open at the collar, which brushed against the hollow of his throat.

She looked down at the sword again and the enormity of what she'd done engulfed her, stripping all the doubt, confusion and indecision from her and leaving only a small, hard nugget of faith, so that when he said, "I'll be back as soon as I can," she grabbed his arm.

"Where are you going?"

"To see if Grey needs help." He touched her hand. "Nick, Olivia should be coming—"

"They're here?"

"Yes, they've a part in this as well."

"Where are they?"

"Nick is helping to destroy the caves and Olivia is moving some computer equipment."

Before Max could ask some obvious questions, Arthur went on, "But, in case they haven't gotten to the castle yet, Grey may need some help."

"He doesn't." She said this, knowing Grey would want her here with Arthur.

"Probably not, but it's best to be certain." He bent over to pick up the sword.

"I don't think you should leave."

"Why?" He looked up at her.

"Because . . ." She waited until he stood again. "Up until a few minutes ago, I wasn't sure what I was doing here. First I wanted to find Ben; then when it got harder to deny the fact of his death, I wanted to see where this stone that Ben gave me took me. But now I know it's not about Ben anymore. I placed that stone and I'm the only one who could do it."

"I know." He seemed pleased that she'd come to this.

She fisted her hand, trying to wring the right words out. "And I knew it would happen. When I picked that stone up, I was as sure that the sword would accept it as I am of your faith." She paused to read his eyes. "That's an incredible feeling."

"Go on."

"This is where it starts," she said. "I can do this with you."

This moment . . . this beginning of everything else that will ever matter . . . needed to be affirmed. Ignoring it would be just plain wrong. He had to see that. She raised up on her toes and kissed him.

He wrapped her in his arms, responding with equal intensity. He tasted cool and sweet. When it ended, he drew her to his chest, tucking her head beneath his chin.

After several moments, he said, "Max." She felt his lips brush her hair.

She released him, went over to the rocking chair and took

the quilt from its arms, then spread it like a picnic blanket over the bare, dark wood floor. Then she reached out to Arthur.

Without hesitation, he came to her, and this time he initiated the kiss. It was gentle, but deliberate. He pushed a strand of hair from her cheek and traced the curve of her jaw with his finger. He kissed her nose, her cheek, touched her hair. Just before he kissed her on the mouth, she saw how his eyes glistened.

Max had made love to a man because she wanted him to love her back; she'd made love because her body demanded it; because she wanted to be as close as two people can be. But she'd never made love to make life. That made it sacred. She didn't know what this life promised, where it would take her or how long she would be allowed to be a part of it, but it began here.

Her fingers went to work on Arthur's buttons, fumbling as she hurried. He took her hands with his, kissing her fingertips, then he released them and took her face in his hands. He kissed her on the mouth. Trembling, she unbuttoned one button, then another, watching his chest rise and fall, matching her breath with his.

Chapter 58

Tommy did a thorough job tying Weir's hands behind his back, binding his ankles and then tying together his wrists and ankles so he resembled a strung bow.

Jillian didn't understand why Rhys wanted her to accompany them down into the cave, and at first she feared he planned to kill both her and Weir in this grimy, damp place. But there was no point tying up someone you were going to shoot.

As far as she knew, her father had never been here before, yet, despite the labyrinth of tunnels, he'd taken them directly to this small room without a wrong turn or even a hesitation. A woven mat covered the floor in front of a large, flat stone approximately three feet square, which appeared to be a sort of altar. Weir had been deposited directly on this stone.

Despite the coolness, the back of her neck was sweaty and she could taste salt above her lip. She had many questions for her father right now, but feared that any one of them might set him off. She cautioned herself that it was best to wait until this was over. Oddly the first answer she wanted was: Did he still want her? He should, shouldn't he? She had placed the stone; Maxine Pike had merely replaced it. She was the one who counted. But judging from her father's predatory posturing toward the Pike woman, he didn't quite see it her way. She would have to convince him.

"Jillian," Rhys said, and it took all she had to look up at him. "I want you stay down here with our guest. I can't afford to have him surfacing at an awkward moment."

"Of course," she said.

He nodded at Tommy. "This gentleman will be busy tying up loose ends."

Knowing how her father was used to everything going according to his plan, and how he detested loose ends, Jillian realized that this must be hell for him.

"You didn't see Jonah, did you Tommy?"

Tommy grunted something that sounded like "no."

"Look for him first. He could have fallen asleep under a computer."

After Tommy left, Rhys took a moment to survey the room. He touched the walls, which had some kind of glittery mineral in them, breathed in a lungful of the stale, damp air and nodded as though he had the place built to his specification and was pleased with the results. Then he removed an automatic pistol from the pocket of his jacket and handed it to Jillian. "If he causes any trouble, feel free to shoot him; just be sure you don't inflict a fatal wound."

Jillian turned the gun over; the cool, harsh metal warmed quickly in her hands.

"I know you may be tempted," Rhys said, and she looked up at him, surprised that he'd seen into her mind.

"I am," she said, more curious than shocked at the blood-spattered images skittering through her mind. "How did you know?" Weir had caused them trouble, but she'd never seen him before today.

He reached out and put his hand on her shoulder, squeezing it. "The world is full of violent images, Jillian. Some of us are more sensitive to them than others."

"Lately I dream them," she confided, staring at a deep cleft in one of the sparkling walls.

"I know." He placed his other hand on her shoulder and she looked up at him again. "But this time I want you to control those urges. That's what strength is about, isn't it?"

She nodded, not at all sure she agreed with him.

He released her and crouched beside Weir, resting his forearms on his knees. "Because when this is all over, I'm going to make a gift of Greyson Weir." He touched the smooth, flat stone on which the man lay. "I'm going to give him to my father. Right here." He patted the stone. "I will honor him."

He stood. "You'll make sure he's alive."

"Yes."

"Of course you will." He brushed off his hands. "Because if I don't have Greyson Weir to give him, you know who I will have to offer him?"

She forced herself to nod, at the same time praying to whatever dark god was listening that he wouldn't make her say it.

"That's my girl."

Chapter 59

Max traced the line of Arthur's collarbone. They lay together on the quilt, damp where their bodies touched. Her head rested on his chest and his arm encircled her shoulders.

She'd dozed for a few minutes, feeling both safe and exhausted, and dreamt of a tiny fish swimming inside her in an ocean of warmth. A magpie cawing outside the window woke her.

He kissed her forehead. "I would love nothing more than to stay here for the afternoon. Just like this." Beneath her, he sighed.

"But we can't," Max finished for him. She kissed him and pushed herself up from the floor, then started sorting through their pile of clothing, pulling Arthur's pants leg out of itself. When she went to toss them to him, the way he was looking at her made her stop. "What?"

"Would you consider living here?"

"Seriously," she said, smiling. He caught the pants without taking his eyes from her.

Just as he started to return the smile, his eyes widened and he spun to face the door. Max heard a faint creak. It could have been one of the noises a castle makes. But it could also have been the sound of old door hinges or someone trying to walk quietly over old wood.

They dressed quickly, without speaking. The air felt cold now and the floor gritty beneath her bare feet. It was not supposed to happen this way.

She heard another creak that sounded louder. They both glanced warily at the door. Arthur fastened two buttons on his shirt and left the rest. He pitched his vest onto the tiny rocking chair and retrieved Caliburn from beneath the window.

When Max had her jeans and sweater on, she gathered the quilt and her shoes. Arthur motioned her toward the wall on the hinge side of the door. She backed up against the wall, clutching the quilt to her chest. It smelled like the two of them. Together. Arthur stood on the other side of the door, Caliburn poised above his shoulder.

They waited one minute. Then another. Just as Max began to think maybe the creaks had been old house sounds, the doorknob turned. To the left and then the right. Arthur nodded; his long fingers moved, adjusting his grip on the sword. Max locked onto his gaze as she waited for the door to burst open.

Instead, there came a soft knock and a familiar voice said, "Max?" Another tap.

"Olivia." Relief made her knees weak.

Arthur unlocked the door and Olivia poked her head into the room. Her hair was damp and straggly and her eyes smudged with mascara. When she saw Max, she threw her arms around her. It was probably the first spontaneous embrace Max had ever received from Olivia, made more bizarre by the fact that she smelled like seawater instead of *J'adore*.

Then Olivia seemed to remember herself, and she stiffened slightly and released Max, giving her shoulder a little pat before letting go.

Despite her bedraggled state, Olivia still managed to be beautiful. She smoothed down a corner of her jacket, but when she released it the wrinkles popped right back into the beige fabric.

"When are you gonna learn, O? Linen just doesn't travel well."

Olivia raised her chin and Max could see some snappy retort in her eyes, but then her brows drew together, creating a furrow between them. She seemed to be on the verge of saying something serious or asking Max a question when Arthur came back into the room from checking out the hall.

As he closed the door behind him, Olivia said, "There's trouble." She tucked a strand of hair behind her ear, and pulled her gaze from Max. "Nick and Earl are still in the cave, I think. I'd finished downloading files," she patted the stiff, curling leather of her shoulder bag, "and I was waiting for them in the garden—like Grey told me to do—and I saw Grey. That big thug of Murdoch's had him over his shoulder and was taking him down into the cave. I couldn't do anything. I mean, the guy looks like a Humvee. Rhys and his daughter were with him."

Then she said to Arthur, "I remembered you told Grey something about using your old room as a place to hide if necessary and he asked what floor it was on. I was pretty sure you said the third floor." She held out her right hand as though admiring a ring. "I've worn my knuckles out knocking on doors. This is a very large house."

"Did you see Simon?" Arthur asked.

"No."

Without hesitation, Arthur said, "I'm going to get you two off the island." He opened the door, checking the hall again. "I'll take you to St. Helen's. I know some people there. You'll be safe."

"What about Grey?" Max slipped her feet into her shoes.

"I'll stay here and find Nick and Earl," Olivia said.

Arthur regarded Olivia for a moment, then sighed. "I wish I could urge you to come with us, but you're right. No one else can tell them where Grey is."

"We'll get him out." Olivia frowned. "I wish I were packing something other than manicure scissors."

"There's a gun on the boat I can give you," Arthur said.

He herded them into the hall, then maneuvered so he led the way down the stairs and out the door. Olivia took hold of Max's arm, as though she thought Max might lose her way on her own. Amused by her sister's behavior, but also scared enough to recognize they needed to be cautious, Max allowed herself to be led from the castle. For the first time since she'd arrived, its silence seemed ominous and she was glad to be leaving.

She had never been to the landing quay, but given Alyssum's size, she figured it couldn't be far from the castle. Nothing was. They skirted the gardens and took the path around the lake, heading northwest. This was the way Max had come when she'd first washed up on Alyssum. She must have passed the dock without realizing it.

"What about this guy, Earl, who's helping?" Max asked Olivia. "Is he kind of short, stocky? Wears a Cubs cap?"

"That's him."

Now Max grabbed Olivia's arm. "He's the guy who broke into my apartment. He's with them."

451

"Not any more." Olivia dismissed her concern by barely addressing it. "Now he's with us." They had to trot to keep up with Arthur's loping pace, and they were both a bit winded. "He's okay."

Max could see the boat now, tied up to the dock that protruded into the small bay. It reminded her of how she'd been ready to board a boat piloted by a drunk in order to get to Alyssum. Instead, she'd wound up in a helicopter flown by the man who had murdered Ben. As misguided as that plan had turned out, would she have even gotten here if she'd gone with the drunk?

Once they reached the dock, Arthur became more tense, watchful. He waited, looking back toward the island as Olivia and Max boarded the boat, *Nimuë*, it was called, then climbed on after them. Max estimated the cabin cruiser, which had a polished wood deck, was about twenty-five feet.

Knowing her sister's eye for luxury, Max was watching Olivia, anticipating her reaction to the vessel, so she knew something was wrong when Olivia's eyes widened and she mouthed the word "shit." Max followed her gaze and saw the hatch had opened and Simon Murdoch was climbing out of the cabin, his gun drawn.

The boat dipped slightly and Max heard Arthur behind her. Before she could warn him, he had wrapped his arm around her waist and flung her aside and out of the way. Time froze for a moment, and she seemed to have all kinds of time to imagine the outcome of a match between a man armed with a sword and one armed with a gun.

But she'd underestimated Arthur, who had regained his stance, and now gripped Caliburn's hilt with both hands. His moves were smooth and without apparent effort. When he swung it, striking out at Murdoch, he used his wrists to control its descent. Max didn't see how it was possible for a weapon the size of Caliburn to possess such grace.

Murdoch got a shot off, but not before Caliburn had found its mark. The shot went wild and Murdoch cried out, dropped the gun and grabbed his wrist. Arthur picked up the gun and threw it over the side. Then he crossed the deck and stood over his half-brother, the sword poised over his shoulder. As blood seeped down Murdoch's wrist, staining his khaki jacket, he wiggled the fingers of his wounded hand, apparently amazed to find they still worked. By the time he got to his feet, he'd lost the bewildered look, and now his face was curdled with anger.

Arthur spoke first. "Why?"

"You're a fool," Murdoch spat the word out. "You piss away the foundation's money on crap—save a fucking panda. You don't get it! You're no philanthropist. You're a fucking, do-gooder loon."

Max saw it first in Arthur's shoulders. They sagged slightly, as though the air had been released from his chest. His eyes looked weary and he stared at Murdoch as though he were some sad, new creature that he didn't want to live long enough to understand.

Murdoch bent at the waist, pulling his wounded hand closer to his body. Something about the gesture spun Max back to the airstrip at Helston. Arthur must have caught it too, because she saw his struggle. Killing Murdoch would be the same as abandoning him. But then he adjusted his grip on the sword's hilt, preparing to strike. Murdoch and the foundation could not co-exist.

Arthur swung Caliburn at the same time Murdoch fired the gun he'd drawn. For a moment there was only the sound of water lapping against the boat's hull. Then Murdoch made a gurgling sound, looked down at his bisected chest, shook his head and fell to the deck. Blood flowed from his mouth.

Arthur staggered and dropped to his knees, a dark red stain blossoming on his white shirt.

Max reached him as he pitched over, taking him in her arms. Warm blood soaked the back of his shirt. Her chest tightened. Caliburn thumped to the deck. She eased Arthur down, cradling his head in her lap. As she wrapped her hand around his, he blinked and found her with his eyes.

"This didn't quite go according to plan," Arthur said.

"We're not finished."

"Will I be in your future?"

"Always." She squeezed his hand, willing her strength into him. "Trust me, Arthur."

"I do." He managed a slight smile. "I really do."

He held onto her gaze until his eyes went vacant. Max bowed her head, touching her forehead to his. A sob welled up and exploded in her chest. "No!" she wailed, burying her face in the curve of his neck.

A hand touched her shoulder. When she looked up, she saw Olivia, her face drawn and pale. "I know, Max," Olivia said. She slipped her hand around Max's arm. "Nick's here. We've still got things to do."

Nick had dropped down beside them, and now he pressed his middle three fingers against Arthur's throat, feeling for a pulse. "I'm sorry," he murmured, drawing his hand away.

As they looked on each other for the first time, here over Arthur's body, Max had a sensation of having lived the moment many times, of having shared the same losses and the same loves. The past flowed around her and through her, and she and Arthur and Nick—all of them—had been touched by the blood of kings and swept along in this incredible current toward a future where it would all be played out. Did their choices even matter anymore? Did they ever?

Max lowered Arthur to the deck and passed her hand over

his face, closing his eyes. Her own arm was soaked with blood. She wiped her hand on the seat of her jeans.

Arthur's sword lay on the deck. Kneeling beside it, she wrapped one hand around the hilt and slipped her other hand beneath its blade. Then she stood and faced Nick. He looked nothing like she'd imagined and yet he couldn't have looked like anyone else. She held the sword out to him. "Caliburn is yours now." He didn't move and she saw his doubt in the way he eyed the sword. "Arthur chose you." She wasn't sure if she meant King Arthur choosing Bedwyr, Arthur Penn choosing Nick or some future allegiance yet to be known, but believed that in all ways that mattered, it was the same choice.

Nick glanced down at Murdoch, his chest split open and the blood pooling around him. Then he took the sword from Max, turning toward the boat's stern as he raised it, wielded it, learning its heft.

"Where's Earl?" Olivia asked.

"We split up after leaving the cave. He's looking for the others." He stopped and took a breath. "Does anyone know where the others are?"

"Jillian was with Rhys and that big guy who tried to shoot us," Olivia said. "They took Grey down to the cave."

"We've got to get him out," Max said.

Nick glanced at his watch. "We haven't much time. Those explosives are set to blow in forty minutes." He swallowed and continued, "Here's what we'll do. Olivia, you go find Grey, Jillian and the big guy. See if you can find Earl first." He paused. "Is that—?"

"That's fine, Nick," Olivia said.

"I'll bet Rhys isn't down there anymore. He's looking for me and, as far as he knows, I don't know the caves exist." He glanced down at the sword. "I suppose it's time we found each other."

"Olivia, do you know your way around that cave?" Max asked.

"I can find my way out of the French Quarter at three a.m. after four mint juleps," she said. "I'll find him."

"Here." Nick dug a folded piece of paper out of his shirt pocket and handed it to Olivia. "I drew up a map while Earl and I were down there. Once you're in the tunnel, it'll take you ten minutes to get to the cave. You'll need ten to get out. That gives you fifteen minutes to find him and get back to the tunnel. Allow an extra five minutes in case the timers are off, and let's hope they're not off any more than that."

"Give her your watch," Max said to Nick.

Without a word, he removed his watch, which had some elaborate dials and buttons, and handed it to Olivia, then returned to the map, pointing to a few of the squares drawn off the passageways. "Here's an office. This is a storage room. But I'm betting if Grey is down there, this is where Rhys put him. He's fashioned himself an altar of sorts. That's just a guess." He looked at Olivia. "Promise me this: If you can't find him, you'll give yourself time to get out of there."

"*We* will," Max said.

"You can't go," Nick said, as though it had been discussed at length and rejected. "It's too dangerous."

"Olivia needs my help."

"No she doesn't," Olivia said, bending down to pick up Murdoch's gun that lay beside his outstretched hand.

"Max," Nick said, "at the risk of making the rest of us sound expendable . . ." He glanced at Olivia. "Well, we are." Then he looked down at Arthur's body and said, "And he wouldn't have wanted you to go."

When she didn't protest, Nick continued. "Could you take the boat to one of the other islands?"

"I don't know how to drive one of these things."

He squinted out at the water, then nodded. "How about taking it a hundred yards out?"

She shook her head. "For all we know, they've got a boat. I'd be a sitting duck out there." She allowed a half-second for rebuttal, then said, "I'll go with Olivia to the gardens. It's probably the best place to hide on the island."

Olivia gave her a wary look, but didn't comment.

The three of them made their way to the lake, where Nick took the path toward the castle. Max and Olivia moved quickly past a row of tall yews and entered the garden from the south end.

"You think you're going down there with me, don't you?" Olivia said, swatting a low-hanging branch out of the way.

"I am."

"No, you're not."

"I have to try. Ben's dead, Antony's dead and now Arthur. I can't do this without Grey."

"You don't think I can get him out by myself?"

"You might need help."

Olivia stopped and grabbed Max's arm, pulling her around so they faced each other. "You can't go, Max." She wasn't arguing anymore, just stating a fact.

"Why not?"

"You're pregnant." Max was too stunned to respond. "Don't ask me how I know, but I do. I knew it the minute I saw you with Arthur." She glanced down at the map in her hand. "Your energy is dispersed."

"That's impossible."

"That you're pregnant?" She seemed confused.

"That you know." At the same time, she knew it wasn't impossible. She'd accepted enough on faith in the past few days to know that. The fact that the pronouncement came from Olivia, the most pragmatic person she'd ever known, made it, in an odd way, more credible.

"I knew you weren't dead, either, but I wouldn't let me believe myself." She sighed. "I've got to stop ignoring myself."

Max saw the fierce resolve in her sister's eyes and it nearly choked her up. "It's going to be fine, Olivia. We're going to go down there, get Grey and come back up here to live the rest of our lives. I know that. I'm especially sure of it now." Olivia's expression didn't soften. "Now, either we go down together or I'll follow you down."

"Bitch," Olivia said, but it was more an utterance of resignation than contempt.

Chapter 60

The castle's front stairs rose, twin curves of marble, from either side of the foyer. Nick climbed the steps on the right. Across from him, a large oil painting of a knight on horseback dominated the wall. *Ironic,* thought Nick, feeling more like a knave than a knight. What had possessed him to take this sword, and now that he had it, what made him think he could use it? Doubts pummeled him. The more he thought about it, the more he believed that Max had no intention of waiting it out. Both she and Olivia had probably gone after Grey. Now, with every step he feared the rumble of premature explosions.

As he neared the top, he tightened his grip on Caliburn and his stomach churned. Who was he fooling? He could no more kill a man with this sword than he could burn one alive. He'd seen Simon Murdoch lying there with his chest split open. The sword's weight pulled at his arms, and the stones in the hilt seemed lifeless. Why didn't he just lay the sword down on the step and leave the castle? Leave Alyssum. He could manage that boat. Go back to St. Mary's and then to the mainland. Never return.

Just as he realized he was having some of the same fears he'd experienced at his uncle's house, he reached the top of the stairs and found Rhys standing in the hall facing him, waiting for him, his hands folded calmly on the hilt of a weapon at least the size of Caliburn.

On instinct, Nick backed up, placing his foot on the top step. He'd do better outside. He retreated another step. And another.

Rhys started down the staircase, holding the sword out in front of him, waving its tip at Nick. "You don't have your girl-friend here to protect you." His eyes danced with cold mirth as he looked down on his nephew.

Re-establishing his grip on Caliburn, Nick questioned his own sanity. He'd never held a sword before, much less fought with one. Rhys appeared at ease as he came at Nick with his, raising it above his shoulder to strike.

Nick lifted Caliburn to deflect the blow, but when it came he was not prepared for its impact. The weapons clanged as steel met steel, and Nick's foot slipped off the edge of the step. He had to release Caliburn as he groped for a baluster, found more empty air and tumbled down the steps, landing face down on the floor. Pain sliced through his ribcage. At first he thought he'd impaled himself on his own sword, but then he saw it lying a few feet from him across the large black and white marble squares. Ignoring the stab of pain in his side, Nick lunged for the hilt. Before he could reach it, Rhys intercepted him and seized Caliburn.

Chapter 61

The pounding of Max's heart reminded her of the seconds ticking away. Olivia led, shining the flashlight on the craggy floor, and they moved as quickly as they could, checking out each corner and passage in the cave. Max refused to even think about leaving without Grey, without finding him.

Olivia shone the flashlight on Nick's watch and cursed. "We're almost out of time," she whispered, but neither stopped moving. Max was willing to hedge on Olivia's promise to Nick. Assume the timers were in sync with the watch. Pray that the tunnel back to the garden held while the cave disintegrated.

They'd already checked out the office and storerooms, which had turned up nothing. Now there was Rhys's altar.

"According to our mapmaker, this passage ought to branch off right around here." Olivia swung the flashlight's beam over the dark walls.

"There," Max said. "Back a couple of feet on the right."

The light settled on the narrow opening. Before entering, they checked the map again. Maybe ten feet in, it hooked to the right and opened into a small chamber.

"Kill the light," Max whispered.

They proceeded in the dark. Max walked with her left hand against a wall to keep from getting disoriented. When she saw a faint light coming from around the corner, she raised the gun and pushed her way past Olivia. Peering around the corner, she saw Jillian standing over Grey, pointing a gun at his head. He lay on his side, his eyes closed, and his cheek resting on a flat stone.

Max raised her gun and fired.

Jillian yelped, dropped the gun and grabbed her upper right arm. As she spun around to face them, her foot smacked the gun and it spun out into the dark corridor. Then she looked down at the blood on her arm and began screaming, her face red and fierce. "What are you doing? I wasn't going to touch him. I wasn't! I just—why did you do this?"

Max handed her gun to Olivia and dropped to her knees beside Grey. God, don't let him be dead. She didn't see a mark on him. She touched his face. He was warm. She gave his shoulder a shake. "Grey? Grey!" His eyes fluttered open and when they found her, he groaned and blinked hard a few times.

He said something, but his voice was weak and she couldn't hear him over Jillian, who was warning Max, in a shrill voice, not to touch Grey.

"We're getting you out of here." Max pulled him toward her so she could get to his bindings. Then it hit her. God, how stupid could she be? Of course he'd be tied up. What was her plan? Gnaw through the rope with her teeth? The knots were tight and when Max tried one, she couldn't get it to budge.

"Olivia, please tell me you've got a knife, or something to cut this rope?"

"Here." Olivia dug into her purse and tossed Max her manicure scissors. "It's all I've got."

"Shit." Max went to work, snipping away at the twine like a mouse gnawing its way to freedom. The rope tying Grey's hands to his feet arched his back into an awkward, painful-looking position, but the tension helped. She had to cut through only half the twine before it gave. Grey rolled onto his stomach with a groan. "There isn't time, Max," he said. "You've got to get yourself out of here."

She started on the knot tying his feet together.

"Max," he hissed.

The rope gave and she rubbed his ankles, urging the circulation.

Behind her, Jillian continued her protests. "I am bleeding. I need a bandage."

"Would you shut up," Olivia snapped. "You're lucky it was my sister with the gun. If it'd been me, you'd be bitching about the hole in your head instead of the scratch on your arm." Then she said, "We're out of time, Max."

"Go!" Grey said. "I can barely feel my feet. You've got to get yourself out of here."

"None of you are going anywhere," Jillian said. "My father will be down here any minute now."

"Good," Olivia said. "He'll be here in time to blow up with the rest of it."

Max crawled behind Grey and started on the rope binding his hands.

"What are you talking about?" Jillian said.

"This place is blowing up in a few minutes."

"You're crazy," she said, and her disbelief seemed genuine. "You can't blow this place up. It's not possible."

"That's right, Jillian. You just sit here and wait," Olivia countered. "You'll be the first to find out you're wrong." Then, "Max, would you hurry?"

Her hands shook as she snipped. Grey was protesting, but he was also pulling his wrists apart as much as he could, so when it started to give, the final threads tore apart.

As soon as his hands were free, he twisted around on the floor, so he faced her. He looked tired but angry as he rubbed at the indentation circling one wrist. "You've no right to endanger yourself, Max. It isn't just you anymore."

"Shut up and move." She took Grey's arm and tried to pull him up, but his ankles gave out and he dropped to his knees.

"Go," he said. "Get out of here. I can barely walk. You haven't the time."

She grabbed two fistfuls of his sweatshirt and pulled him up. "You are coming with me."

This time he let her help him up. "I am going to slow you down."

"Not with me hauling your ass," Olivia said, handing the gun to Max. She hooked his arm over her shoulders and held it there with one hand, and clutched him around the waist with her other arm.

"You lead the way," Olivia said to Max as she maneuvered Grey out of the chamber.

When they turned the corner into the tunnel, Max glanced back. Jillian stood by the stone altar, looking like the loneliest person on the planet.

As Max led them through the tunnels, she prayed her sense of direction didn't fail her, relying on her memory and quick glimpses at the map to navigate the cave. If they were lucky, they had one chance of making it out of here.

But when she made the turn that she thought would have

gotten them to the central area by the big room, and found they'd entered another tunnel instead, she was afraid their luck had run out.

"Are you sure that last turn wasn't supposed to be to the left?" Olivia said.

"I hope you're right," Max said as they doubled back. "Why didn't you say something?"

"Let's not start."

"You're not down here without a map," Grey said, his energy returning.

"Shut up," Olivia snapped.

The retraced their steps and corrected the turn. Max couldn't tell one tunnel wall from another, but it didn't seem right.

"Wait," Olivia said. She raised her head and called out: "Earl! Help! Earl!"

Two seconds later came the response: "Here! Over here!"

"Straight ahead," Grey said, managing on his own now. "Move."

"Keep talking," Olivia called.

A long three seconds followed before Earl answered. "I'm here. By that room. The big one."

His voice was getting closer and, after making one more turn, they spilled out of a tunnel, nearly colliding with one of the mirrored walls of the computer room. Max's heart was racing. Earl ran up to them. "What the hell—"

"I know," Olivia said.

The area they were moving through was probably packed with explosives. Max imagined she could hear the timers ticking louder as they neared detonation. As she started down the castle tunnel, she glanced behind her to see if she the rest of them were keeping up. "Let's—"

"Max!" It was Olivia.

Max spun around just in time to avoid colliding with a man whose large bulk filled the passageway. Their eyes met and his narrowed in recognition. She thought she saw a gun in his hand, but couldn't be certain. All she knew was that they didn't have time to negotiate their way past him.

She raised her gun and fired. He fell, and they kept going.

Chapter 62

Slowly, Nick pushed himself up from the cool floor, the pain in his side sharp but not disabling. He stood and retreated a few steps, keeping out of Caliburn's range. His head throbbed and he had to squint to see his uncle, backlit against the open door, a sword in either hand.

Rhys admired Caliburn at arm's length, then took three steps out the door and hurled the other sword toward the lawn. He came back in, turning Caliburn over in his hand, and stood over Nick. "That one's yours, nephew." His features were pinched with contempt. "See if you can hold onto it." He stepped aside, as though to let Nick pass.

Telling himself he had no room left for pride, Nick started for the door. Rhys lunged at him. As the sword descended, Nick dove past Rhys, sliding across the slick floor. Rhys whirled around and charged. Nick rolled out of the way as Caliburn struck a black marble square, cracking it.

Scrambling to his feet, he feinted to the right and then to the right again, countering his uncle's moves. He read both arrogance and fervor in Rhys's expression as he approached, the sun glinting off Caliburn's blade.

Nick backed up toward the door; he didn't stand a chance without a weapon. "I'm unarmed Rhys; is that the only way you can fight?"

"Life isn't fair, Nick."

"That's right. You can't win unless you've got the advantage. Going up against a crippled old man."

Rhys kept advancing, taunting Nick with the sword. "Don't try to shame me, Nick. People who have to be eliminated are. Whether they died in a so-called fair fight hardly matters."

If he turned and fled out the door, could he reach the other sword before being skewered? He hadn't seen where it had landed. He glanced over his shoulder; he was nearly to the door.

"Look at me."

Nick couldn't find the strength to disobey. Rhys took one step toward him, then another. Frozen to the floor, he watched his uncle approach. He thought of Max. If he were to die here, who would be there for her?

"Maxine's protector." The words resounded in Nick's head. "What a comfort you must be to her. First there was your father. How different things might have been if you'd gone with him. And your mother." His words taunted, summoning images to the edges of Nick's mind. "You think she's all safe and tucked away? That little pub of yours and your friends who work there." He made a tsking sound. "You've fatally disappointed them all."

An image of the Fife and Firkin burst into his mind. Flames raged from broken windows and he saw charred bodies behind the remains of a wall that had been blown out.

With his next step, Rhys drew Caliburn over his shoulder. If Nick didn't move, he would die here. He curled his hands into fists and his father's ring dug into the flesh of his palm. The ice encasing his feet began to melt.

"You're the last in a long line of self-important fools." Rhys closed in on Nick.

Nick moved into the foyer. How long did he have before the charges went off? It had to be soon. But not before they got out of there.

He stepped out onto the granite slab, the sun warm on his neck. Rhys followed him into the light. "It's an island, Nick," Rhys said. "You can retreat only so far before your feet get wet."

He still couldn't see the other sword. It was a heavy weapon; Rhys couldn't have thrown it far. Nick glanced behind him toward the courtyard. He saw only the curved stone walk, the ancient oak shading it and a peacock by the gate. Just as he spotted a narrow slice of silver in the green beside the walk, a blow to the chest sent him flying backwards into the courtyard, knocking the wind from him. Blinking, he looked up into the dark branches of the oak.

Then Rhys was on him, planting one foot on Nick's chest and settling the point of Caliburn's blade at his throat.

Nick hadn't gotten his breath back yet.

"Tell me where Maxine is."

Rhys must have read Nick's response in his eyes, because he nodded and said, "A Llewellyn to the end."

He tilted the sword so the sun filtering through the oak leaves caught the gems in its hilt. "Where is she?"

"You go back to hell."

Rhys's jaw tightened as he wrapped both hands around Caliburn's hilt.

Nick recalled telling Olivia that believing was hard and faith difficult to come by. As his uncle raised Caliburn's blade above Nick's heart, Nick understood just how difficult it was. A corner of his soul believed his family hadn't been the guardian of the heartstone for centuries, only to be done in by its instrument. The rest of his body sought a more practical solution.

As Rhys drew back the sword, Nick grabbed his ankle and pulled, attempting to jerk him off balance. Just then the earth rocked with the first explosion. Staggering from the concussion, Rhys's swing went wild, and he buried the sword's blade in the trunk of the oak at the same time Nick yanked his leg out from under him. Rhys fell backwards, arms flailing. Nick jumped up, seized Caliburn by the hilt and drew it from the tree.

Rhys stood and the second blast went off. Nick saw the anger building in his uncle's eyes. His rage increased with each subsequent blast, as though it were feeding off them.

"All you've succeeded in doing is killing your friend," Rhys said. "Let go of it, Nick."

Nick swung the sword. Rhys sidestepped the blade, but not before it slashed the sleeve of his pale sweater. Nick saw no blood, but his uncle's face darkened and his eyes bore into Nick's. "You face me armed with that sword and your faith. It's not enough, Nick. The sword is too much for you. And faith," he snorted, "faith destroys its own."

A landscape of scorched grass and naked trees filled Nick's vision. The air blew hot and smelled of death, and he knelt before a young man with red hair wearing a tattered black cape. The young man raised Caliburn above his head and plunged the blade through Nick's chest.

Nick swung at the picture, embedding the blade in the ground.

"You will tire, Nick. Your arms will weaken. Each attempt to lift Caliburn will be more painful than the last. Your heart will burst with the effort. You will die, Nick, and all I have to do is wait."

Even as he rejected the words, his shoulders seemed to be ripping from their sockets as he tried to draw the sword from the earth. Rhys fixed his eyes on Nick's and Nick saw his rage turning to complacency.

Not so easy. Nick adjusted his grip on the hilt. "You've lost, uncle. Look at what's left. What good is Alyssum to you now?" The sword moved: maybe only a centimeter, but it moved.

"You can't do it."

"Watch me." Nick pulled. "Your father gave you life so you could destroy his enemy." The sword drew up a few more centimeters. "We blew up his bloody house." A few more. "The one it took him more than a millennium to construct."

"Die. Here."

As his arms began to cramp, Nick sought his uncle's anger. And found it. "You couldn't stop us."

Rhys came at Nick, eyes blazing. He took Nick's throat in his hands, his grip like a hot vise. Nick imagined his brain was turning to molten lava.

Nick squeezed Caliburn's hilt and felt the heartstone pulse against his hand. With one final heave, he yanked the sword from the ground. The momentum drove its hilt into Rhys's chest. Stunned, Rhys staggered backwards, clutching his chest and screaming as though mortally wounded. Nick reversed his grip and raised the sword as Rhys charged him.

Caliburn ran clean through his uncle's heart.

Chapter 63

They were still in the tunnel when the first blast went off. The air filled with dust and debris, but the tunnel held. It became difficult to breathe and almost impossible to see, even with the flashlight. The four of them linked arms, so no one got turned around as they felt their way along the wall. Finally they came to a crude rope ladder.

Max climbed out first, then Earl. He helped Olivia and Grey. She squinted into the sun, welcoming its light and warmth. It felt as though she'd been down there for months. She shook some of the dirt from her hair and wiped her face on the arm of her sweater.

"We found Jillian," Olivia said to Earl, and pointed down the shaft.

Earl nodded. "Yeah, I couldn't find her up here." He pushed up the sleeve of his jacket to check his watch. "I got worried the stuff wasn't going off. Thought maybe the timers were bad."

"Just slow," Olivia said. "Thank God." Then she said, "Where's Nick?"

Earl shook his head. "Haven't seen him."

Grey crouched on the grass, ashen and exhausted. "We find Rhys, we'll find Nick."

Then he looked up at Max.

She shook her head. "Arthur didn't make it."

He closed his eyes and bowed his head as he nodded. Then, bracing his hands against his thighs, he pushed himself up.

Max took his arm. As they began walking, she looked over her shoulder at the dust rising from the hole. Some of it glittered. "I guess Jillian stayed down there," she said.

"Good riddance," Olivia muttered.

Earl grunted.

As they made their way toward the castle, they remained alert. The island seemed so quiet; all Max could hear was the wind nudging the leaves and the sound of their footsteps in the thick grass.

When they came to the courtyard, they found Nick standing over Rhys's body, the sword Caliburn in his hand. Rhys's chest was covered with blood and his eyes stared up at the bright, cloudless sky. The sight both horrified and elated Max. Judging from the way Nick's chest heaved with each breath, the encounter had just occurred. He watched as they converged. "I was about to go looking for you. I—"

Max heard movement behind her, and then Jillian's voice. "You can't kill my father." Her pitch intensified with each word. "No one can kill my father."

She approached Rhys's body like a cat edging around a broken urn. She was covered in a fine layer of dirt and dust; a small piece of wood clung to a strand of her hair. At her side, she held a gun, which she must have recovered from the cave.

Jillian looked down at Rhys and then up at Nick. Her face had lost what little color it had, and she seemed quite small. "You did this?"

"I did."

She knelt beside Rhys and when Nick took a step closer to her, she threatened him with the gun. He stopped. They all waited. Jillian leaned over her father and placed her hands over his wound, pressing down. She pulled her hair back and put her ear to Rhys's mouth. Although her expression didn't change, she appeared to be listening or maybe she sought the warmth of his breath. Then she kissed her father on the forehead and stood, sighing deeply. Her chin tightened as she swallowed. She turned toward Max and raised the gun. Grey, Olivia and Earl moved as one to shield Max from her. Jillian stood without moving for almost a minute. Then she turned her head to look at Nick and down at Rhys again, placed the muzzle of the gun to her temple and pulled the trigger.

The gunshot startled a small flock of birds from an olive tree bordering the courtyard gate. Aside from the blurred brown wings, nothing moved. No one spoke. It felt like either the beginning or the end of time. Maybe both.

Jillian fell so that her head rested on Rhys's chest and her fingers touched his chin.

Finally, Nick walked over to the bodies, kicking the pistol away as he looked down at Rhys. Max counted fifteen heartbeats before Nick said, "He's gone."

"You're sure?" It was Olivia.

He nodded. "Quite."

"Did he tell her to do that?" Olivia asked, wrapping her arms across her chest as though she were cold.

"I suppose we'll never know," Grey said.

Nick regarded the four of them and said, "There's something I've got to do." Resting the sword's blade against his shoulder, he walked through the gate and down the path toward the lake.

Chapter 64

As Nick stood at the lake's edge, feeling the cool afternoon air on his face, the swan emerged from the reeds and slowly glided across the still surface. Thin clouds, which turned shades of rose and coral as they overtook the sun, were making their way toward Alyssum, and the breeze rustled the branches of the willow.

He lowered Caliburn from his shoulder and held it out before him so it touched the blades of grass. At first he believed he'd come here to complete a cycle. But it was more than that. It was paying homage to a dead man and pledging himself to the future.

Lifting the sword, he turned it over, holding his palm beneath its hilt. The stones stayed fixed in their setting. More than anything, this convinced Nick that the heartstone did exactly what it wanted to do, absolving Bedwyr of any transgression.

Bracing his feet in the grass, Nick raised Caliburn and drew the sword back over his head as far as he could bend, then swung it forward, releasing it at the highest point, and propelling it up and over the pool. He watched it turn end over end, its stones glinting in the setting sun, knowing it wasn't the sheer strength in his arms that made it cartwheel like that. Its tip broke the surface at the pool's center; then the blade sliced into the water. The last thing to disappear was the hilt.

Nick stood there, expecting more and ashamed that he was disappointed. He shouldn't need a miracle to believe anymore.

He glanced over his shoulder and when he saw that the others had followed him, he slowly made his way up the incline.

Max grabbed his arm. "Look!"

He turned, half expecting to see an arm in white samite brandishing the sword, and when he saw only the pool's calm surface he was confused. Then he saw the slash of red where the sun's final rays hit the water. Caliburn floated beneath the surface, as though suspended, for several long seconds. The heartstone faded as the sword drifted to the bottom.

Chapter 65

The swan cut a v-shaped wake through the lake's flawless, green surface. Nick's shoulders sagged and he bowed his head. Max thought she understood what that cost him.

After a few moments, he turned to her and said, "It wasn't mine to keep."

She looked down at her hands, which were caked with blood and dirt. Pushing up the sleeves of her sweater, she walked down the slope and knelt by the edge of the water, where she rinsed Arthur's blood from her hands and arms. Then she crossed one leg in front of the other and sank to the grass. She looked out over Alyssum. A cloud of dust hung over its northern tip where the cave had been destroyed. Max imagined the particles contained the evil that rose from below the ground to dissolve in the crisp, April air.

Nick, who had been gazing in that direction, turned toward Earl and said, "Nice work."

Grey thanked him as well, and Earl colored slightly and nodded, then fell gratefully to the grass and dug his hands into the green.

Olivia settled near Max, resting her arms on her bent knees. She glanced at her sister. "How are you doing?"

Max plucked a blade of grass and folded it. "Overwhelmed." When she looked up, Nick and Olivia were watching her. "Look at all the people who died for this—Ben, Antony, Arthur." The swan blurred and her eyes stung. "Arthur. God, what an extraordinary man."

"He was," Grey said. "And what he has begun here will not end."

She ached for all of them. Felt like they'd given her an incredible gift and it would be a long time, a lifetime, before she could look back and see if she'd been worthy. Then she remembered how Ben had trusted her, believed in her. He was dead, but his faith in her wasn't.

She looked up at the sky, fading blue in the late afternoon. As she listened to the murmur of Nick and Grey talking a few feet from her, she felt the grass blades tickle her bare ankles and drank in the elements—the rich, earthy smell, the sound of a small creature splashing in the water, the mix of the warm sun and cool breeze against her damp arms and face. She had the odd but pleasant sensation of being drawn into the island, could feel her heart slowing as her body adjusted to Alyssum's rhythms.

Beside her, Olivia whispered, "I'll make a great aunt, you know."

Max turned to her and saw that Grey was watching them. "You just might," she said.

Olivia flicked a small, brown spider off her sleeve and quickly brushed off her other extremities. Then she tucked a strand of hair behind her ear and regarded Max for a moment before asking, "Are you going to stay here?"

"Yes," she answered, thinking of only one thing she needed to retrieve from Chicago. "And I'm bringing Fiona over here, too."

"Fiona?"

"You'll have to meet her."

They talked for a while longer, until the beating of helicopter blades could be heard above the wind in the trees.

Max sat up and found the dark speck in the eastern sky. As she watched it grow larger, she thought how that must have been the last sound Ben heard before he died.

Then Olivia was standing, brushing grass off her butt. "We're going to have one helluva time explaining all this."

"We have help," Grey said. "Arthur made some phone calls, sent some communications earlier today . . . after he realized what was happening. A couple of his friends are on their way. This should be them now."

"I hope he was convincing," Olivia muttered as she moved ahead with Nick and Earl.

Max wasn't ready to leave the lake. She stood by its edge, watching the helicopter approach Alyssum. The wind had picked up and brought with it the evening chill. She pulled the sleeves of her sweater down to her fingertips and hugged her chest. Grey stood behind her; she could feel him there. Then she heard him draw in his breath.

"What you did was foolish, Max." Anger resonated in his words. "You could have died in that cave."

She spun around, prepared to defend herself, but then she saw how his eyes smarted. He looked away.

"I guess it was foolish." She watched him as he squinted at the horizon. A fine layer of dust coated his hair. "But I'll tell you what else is foolish. The idea of doing this without you around. Ben and Arthur trusted you. I trust you. I also need you."

"I'm not going anywhere, Max," he said, shaking his head. Then he turned toward her and added, in almost a whisper, "Where else would I be?"

She wanted more. "You'll be here for the child?"

"For the child, and for you."

"You and I started something," she said, and saw that he was waiting for more. "I don't know what it's to become, but I do know it's not over yet."

He studied her for several moments, nodded once and then they headed up the path toward the castle.

About the Author

Deborah C. Brod has written fiction most of her life, but didn't think she had a novel in her until after she graduated from Northern Illinois University with an M.A. in journalism. It was then that she decided if she could spend 120 pages discussing postal oppression of the radical press, she could write a novel. She was right. Her first novel, *Murder In Store*, featuring private detective Quint McCauley, appeared two years later in 1989. Four more novels in the series followed. The fifth one, *Paid in Full*, was published by Five Star Publishing. Her short stories have appeared in *Alfred Hitchcock Mystery Magazine* and several anthologies.

She veered off the mystery path when her love of Celtic mythology, the British Isles, and a really impressive gemstone (she also likes things that sparkle) got her imagination cooking. She has an undergraduate degree in English from

Western Illinois University and has worked as a technical/marketing writer, and as a fiction editor. She lives in St. Charles, Illinois, with her husband, Donald, and a cat, Travis McGee. When she's not reading or writing, she enjoys watercolor painting, travel, theater and baseball.